THE NEXT TO DIE

Vicki was baffled by the note someone had typed on her computer. Why were they pretending to be her? It didn't make any sense.

The stove light flickered on in the kitchen. It was an old stove and the light always blinked a few times whenever she first turned it on. Vicki swiveled around and noticed a plastic tarp covering her kitchen floor. "Honey, is that you? What are you doing there?"

Warily, she moved toward the kitchen, where she saw a shadow sweep across the wall. "Did you write that note on my computer?"

"Uh-huh," he replied.

"Why? What's going on?"

He didn't answer.

Heading into the kitchen, Vicki stepped onto the tarp. It was slippery and she glanced down at the floor for a second. When she looked up again, she saw a figure coming toward her. She reeled back, but the plastic sheet slid beneath her feet and she started to lose her balance.

The last thing she saw was the garden sickle coming down at her. . . .

Books by Kevin O'Brien

ONLY SON

THE NEXT TO DIE

MAKE THEM CRY

WATCH THEM DIE

LEFT FOR DEAD

THE LAST VICTIM

KILLING SPREE

ONE LAST SCREAM

FINAL BREATH

VICIOUS

DISTURBED

TERRIFIED

Published by Kensington Publishing Corporation

KILLING SPREE

KEVIN O'BRIEN

PINNACLE BOOKS
Kensington Publishing Corp.
www.kensingtonbooks.com

PINNACLE BOOKS are published by

Kensington Publishing Corp.
119 West 40th Street
New York, NY 10018

All Kensington titles, imprints, and distributed lines are available at special quantity discounts for bulk purchases for sales promotions, premiums, fund-raising, educational, or institutional use. Special book excerpts or customized printings can also be created to fit specific needs. For details, write or phone the office of the Kensington special sales manager: Kensington Publishing Corp., 119 West 40th Street, New York, NY 10018, attn: Special Sales Department; phone: 1-800-221-2647.

ISBN-13: 978-0-7860-2987-7
ISBN-10: 0-7860-2987-0

First printing: January 2007
Fourth printing: March 2012

10 9 8 7 6 5 4

Printed in the United States of America

This book is for Lolita Annear and her family,
Judy, Sue, Jeff, Tammy, and my wonderful friend, Dan . . .

And for a terrific guy, Rich "Slip" Annear (1929–2005)

ACKNOWLEDGMENTS

My dear pal, Cate Goethals, once told me that a good friend is someone who brings out the best in you. I think the same can be said of a good editor. John Scognamiglio is tops in both categories. Many thanks to John, and my other friends at Kensington Books, especially the marvelous Mr. Doug Mendini, whose generosity never ceases to amaze me; and Janice Rossi, who designed the deliciously creepy book cover.

A huge thank-you goes to my literary guardian angels, Meg Ruley and Christina Hogrebe, and the rest of the gang at the Jane Rotrosen Agency.

Thanks to my friends and fellow writers who read parts of this book and helped me so much with their feedback. Cate Goethals, Dan Monda, David Massengill, Soyon Im, and Garth Stein all poured hours of work into this book. I'm very grateful for their generosity, talent, and friendship.

I'd also like to thank my friends and the many booksellers who have gone out of their way to push my books and give me their encouragement, support, and friendship: Lloyd Adalist, Dan Annear & Chuck Rank, Marlys Bourm, Terry & Judine Brooks, Tiffany Caruso, Jim & Barbara Church, Anna Cottle & Mary Alice Kier, Ruthanne Devlin, Paul Dwoskin, Tom Goodwin, Cathy Johnson, Ed & Sue Kelly, Tina Kim, David Korabik, Jim Munchel, Tony Myers, Sheila Rosen, John Saul & Michael Sack, Chad Schlund; Bill, JB, Tammy, and the gang at Seattle Mystery Book Store; Dan, Doug & Ann Stutesman; George & Sheila Stydahar; Marc Von Borstel, Michael Wells & the gang at Bailey/Coy Books.

Thanks also to The Friends of Mystery in Portland, Oregon, for giving their Spotted Owl Award to my last book. What an honor!

A very special thank-you to Tommy Dreiling.

Finally, all my love and gratitude to my family.

Chapter 1

All the crazies were out tonight.

What did he expect? It was Halloween, and the streets of Greenwich Village overflowed with people—drunk, laughing, screaming people, all in their stupid costumes. Tonight he'd seen a husky, bearded man in a nurse's dress and cap; an attractive couple (and boy, didn't they know it) as Adam and Eve, wearing strategically placed fig leaves and nothing else; and innumerable gay guys dressed up as characters out of *The Wizard of Oz.*

Amid the partyers, one person stood out to him. Wearing thick glasses and a rather nerdish cardigan sweater, the young man walked down the street alone, his hands shoved in his pants pockets. He seemed timid and detached. Strapped around his stomach was what looked like six sticks of dynamite and an alarm clock. Only a few people seemed to notice him, and when they did, they laughed. But it was nervous laughter.

Greg felt a bit like that lonely nerd, like a human time bomb about to go off. If he didn't get out of the Village soon, he was going to explode.

Driving a cab in New York on Halloween night was pure torture.

Greg prayed that his next fare would take him to another part of town, far away from this crazy place. He planned to put one more hour on the meter before going home to his dumpy studio apartment so he could memorize an audition piece for tomorrow. It was a commercial for allergy medication, and he desperately wanted the job. Greg was living a cliché: the struggling thirtysomething actor by day and cabdriver by night. He'd convinced himself two years ago that driving a taxi would give him a chance to study people and better develop his craft. Huh, what a crock. After a few months, the only thing he'd learned was that there were some real jerks in the world.

And a lot of them had come out tonight.

Greg spotted the couple, waving at him from the corner of Hudson and Charles. The guy was dressed up as Zorro—with the cape, hat, mask, and the sword. The girl had gotten dolled up in a Spanish dancer outfit—a yellow dress with black lace, an elaborate headdress, and castanets. Approaching them, he heard her clicking those castanets and giggling. He saw her pretty face light up as he pulled toward the curb. She smiled.

Greg let out a grateful sigh. She looked like an angel.

She had long, light brown hair and a creamy complexion. The sexy-slutty señorita outfit looked so absurd on such a fresh-faced, sweet woman. He guessed she was in her late twenties. The way she weaved a bit, he could tell she was slightly drunk.

"Oh, thanks so much for stopping!" she gushed, climbing into the backseat with her masked boyfriend. "The last two taxis just sailed by—"

"1017 West Thirty-seventh," barked Zorro, interrupting her.

Greg set the meter, then glanced at them in the rearview mirror.

The girl's eyes met his as she settled back in the seat and buckled her seat belt. She grinned and clicked her castanets once more. "Hola! And Happy Halloween. How come you're not wearing a costume?" She worked the castanets again.

"Cut that shit out," Zorro grumbled.

"Huh, grouch," she muttered, slipping the castanets into her little black purse. She gave Zorro a playful pout, then cleared her throat and called to Greg. "I'm having the best time! This is my third night in New York, and I love it! I don't ever want to go back to Portland." She raised her voice as if making a declaration. "I want to live in New York City and write best-sellers!" She laughed, then tapped Greg on the shoulder. "I'm getting a book published next month— my first. I'm an author."

"Congratulations," Greg said. "What kind of book is it? Will it—"

"You don't need to make friends with the driver, dopey," the man interrupted. He pulled her toward him. "Come here." He kissed her neck and cupped a black-gloved hand over her breast.

She squirmed a bit. Greg noticed her looking at him in the mirror. She seemed embarrassed at the way her boyfriend was pawing her. "Quit," she whispered.

"You fucking love it," the masked man replied, pulling away from her for only a moment. He shut the Plexiglas divider between the front and backseat. Then he started fondling her again.

From what Greg could see, she didn't seem to *fucking love it*. She tried to laugh and push the man away, but his hands and mouth were all over her. Greg saw her wincing. Her eyes connected with his. She seemed to plead for some kind of intervention. The man started to climb on top of her.

Greg had put up with couples fornicating in the back of his taxi before. But in all those cases, the women had seemed pretty damn willing. He could tell this woman wasn't the type. No, not at all. This guy was humiliating her.

Greg thought about stopping the cab, opening the back door, and throwing Zorro out on his ass.

A car horn blared, and Greg suddenly realized he'd drifted into oncoming traffic. He swerved the taxi back into his lane.

He felt someone kick the back of his seat, and heard a muffled cry. Greg checked the mirror again. "Shit," he muttered under his breath.

She wasn't resisting anymore. Zorro was on top of her, and one of her legs had wrapped around him. She clutched at the back of his cape. She had her eyes closed, but her mouth was open and her lips slid along his neck.

Greg was so disappointed in her. For a crazy moment, he'd felt a connection with this sweet, fresh-faced young woman from Portland. He'd even thought he could *rescue* her. But now, she was letting this asshole screw her in the back of his taxi. And she seemed to be having a swell time of it.

Frowning, Greg stared at the road ahead. Through the Plexiglas divider, he could hear muffled moaning back there. But thank God, the traffic and street noise mostly drowned her out. He didn't want to listen to her in the throes of ecstasy. He just wanted to get them the hell out of his cab. Jerks.

Greg turned onto West Thirty-seventh Street, a block full of little specialty stores with apartments above them. He pulled up in front of the address the guy had given him. It was a travel agency, closed for the night. Was this the right address?

He heard the Plexiglas divider whoosh open behind him. Greg glanced over his shoulder. The pretty brunette numbly stared at him, catching her breath. Zorro had finished with her. "I'm in a hurry," the guy said. "She's paying."

Before Greg could respond, Zorro ducked out of the cab. His black cape billowed as he ran down an alley beside the travel agency. He disappeared into the darkness.

Greg shifted forward in his seat. "That's eleven-fifty, ma'am," he grunted. He checked the rearview mirror.

He couldn't quite read the look in her eyes. She still seemed to be catching her breath. She muttered something back to him, but it was like a whimper. He couldn't hear her past the rumbling motor.

Then he saw the dark red smudges on the handle to the Plexiglas divider. Zorro had opened it with his gloved hand.

Greg saw that she had tears in her eyes, and she was trembling.

"I'm stabbed," she whispered. "Dear God . . ."

He swiveled around. Her hands clutched at the front of her yellow dress with the fancy black lace. The material was slashed across her belly—and drenched with blood.

"Police in Manhattan are searching tonight for a man dressed as Zorro," the pretty, Asian anchorwoman announced. She wore a tailored black suit, and behind her was a red, bloody *Z*, a grisly take on the Mark of Zorro. "He's wanted in connection with the stabbing of a twenty-eight-year-old Portland, Oregon, woman. The victim, whose identity is being withheld pending—"

"Her name was Jennifer Gilderhoff," the man said to the TV. "And she *'wanted to live in New York City and write best-sellers!'* Huh, poor, sorry bitch."

"The victim was stabbed in the backseat of a taxicab, during a Halloween celebration in Greenwich Village," the news anchor continued. "She was rushed to Roosevelt Hospital, where her condition is listed as critical."

The man stared at the TV screen. "She's not dead?"

The TV anchor paused for a somber beat. "In Queens tonight, a Halloween prank turned into a four-alarm fire when a group of teenagers—"

He grabbed the remote and switched off the TV. He couldn't

believe Jennifer was still alive. Of course, she wouldn't be for long. He'd studied surgical procedures recently, and knew those stab wounds he'd made were fatal. She was probably in a coma.

Half-dressed and with his hair still wet from a shower, he wandered over to the honor bar, and poured himself a Scotch.

On the bed, with its hunter-green and maroon paisley spread, his suitcase was open and almost completely packed.

He chilled his drink with a few cubes from the ice bucket. Beside the plastic bucket on the desk was a paperback thriller, *The Mark of Death* by Gillian McBride. He'd been reading a passage from it earlier, and used a postcard to keep his place. He'd received the postcard in the mail several weeks ago. It announced the publication of a book by another author, Jennifer Gilderhoff, *Burning Old Bridesmaids' Dresses and Other Survival Stories*. The postcard showed the predominantly pink book cover, with a cartoon woman brandishing a cigarette lighter wand.

Considering what he'd done to Jennifer tonight, he figured her lighthearted collection of "chick-lit" stories wouldn't fare so well commercially. It certainly had to put a damper on a reader's enjoyment when the author of such cutesy fluff got stabbed to death—or *almost* to death. He didn't think she'd last out the night.

He sipped his Scotch, and flipped to the page he'd marked with Jennifer's postcard. He tossed the card aside. Moving toward the bathroom, he read the passage in Gillian McBride's *The Mark of Death*. He was very, very familiar with it:

Her blood was still warm and wet on his hands as he raced toward the alley beside the beautiful estate. His Zorro cape billowed behind him. He listened to the material flapping in the wind. The masked man felt such a rush of adrenaline. He felt like a superhero. . . .

He stopped in the bathroom doorway, and closed Gillian McBride's book. He gazed at the bathtub. The water in it had turned pink. His Zorro costume was soaking. After another rinse or two, all the blood would be gone.

He glanced at the book in his hand. "I did it better," he whispered. "I did it better than you, Gillian."

Chapter 2

MEET THE AUTHOR! read the sign by the desk at the front of the Barnes & Noble store in Woodinville, Washington. *GILLIAN McBRIDE signs copies of her new thriller, BLACK RIBBONS: A MAGGIE DARE MYSTERY!*

The author photo on the sign showed a beautiful, haughty-looking woman who could have passed for twenty-five. Gillian hated the photo, but her agent and editor were crazy about it. "The picture says, 'I'm savvy, I'm smart, and I have a best-seller-in-the-making here,'" her agent, Eve, had told her.

"I think it says, 'I'm smug, I'm arrogant, and I have absolutely no interests beyond myself, my hair, and what I'm wearing,'" Gillian had countered.

To the photographer's credit, he had taken about ten years off Gillian's age (she was thirty-seven), and he'd erased scores of freckles from her face (they came with being a redhead). But he'd failed to capture Gillian's warmth and vulnerability. The woman seated at the desk, behind a stack of books, looked like the nice, down-to-earth, slightly older sister to that smug ice princess in the author photo.

Gillian wore a lavender silk blouse and black pants. Her

shoulder-length, tawny hair was pulled back in a ponytail, and she kept a smile fixed on her face.

Some authors had throngs of rabid fans at their signings, roped-off lines of people around the store impatiently waiting for a brief moment with their favorite scribe. Gillian wasn't one of those authors. She'd been sitting at the desk for over ninety minutes and had sold eight books so far. She'd had one fan show up—a very nice, middle-aged woman named Stella who had read all five of Gillian's previous thrillers and e-mailed her once in a while. Stella had chatted with her for about ten minutes, but had to rush off to meet a friend. Then Gillian was by herself again. "I'm sorry, I've never heard of you," was what people usually said when they stopped by her table to check out one of her books. But most people didn't stop at all. They passed by her table and avoided eye contact—as if she were some panhandler on the street.

So Gillian sat there, forcing a smile, and wondering if anybody saw the desperation on her face. It was like eating alone at a fancy restaurant. She felt onstage—and very pathetic. She'd done these author signings dozens of times before, and knew the score. *Just keep smiling.*

That was what Gillian told herself as she dealt with this new potential customer, a woman in her early twenties with a ratty, brown pullover sweater, blond hair, and heavy eye makeup. She was on her cell phone as she approached Gillian's desk. She glanced at *Black Ribbons,* then quickly put it down again. "No way, not if you're gonna get fucking drunk again tonight," she said into the phone. She picked up another one of Gillian's books, and scowled at the back cover. "You do so," the young woman continued on her cell phone. "Why the fuck should I even plan on doing anything, if you're gonna be drunk most of the time? I mean it, you have a problem. I'm fucking serious. . . ."

The blonde went through all six of Gillian's books, barely looking at them. Gillian wondered how many times this cell phone woman said *fuck* during a given day. She felt like The

Invisible Author. Finally, she started drumming her fingers on the desktop and stared up at the girl.

"Well, maybe I need to rethink our relationship," the blonde was saying into her phone. She suddenly glared at Gillian. "Would you mind your own fucking business? Jesus!" She wandered away from the table. "No, I wasn't talking to you," she grumbled into her cell phone. "There's this stupid woman in the bookstore. . . ."

If I was in a relationship with you, sister, I'd be getting drunk every night too! Gillian wanted to yell at the woman. But she said nothing, and kept smiling.

She saw someone else approaching.

"Are you the author?" asked a middle-aged woman with a stiff-looking helmet of black hair. She adjusted her glasses and picked up a copy of *Black Ribbons*. "I read three books a week. I haven't heard of you."

"Well, I'm Gillian, and—readers like you are my favorite kind of people." She held out her hand, but the woman was studying the back of Gillian's book. Gillian slipped her hand back under the table.

"Black Ribbons: A Maggie Dare Mystery," the woman muttered. "What's this about anyway?"

"Well, Maggie Dare is a seventy-year-old retired police detective," Gillian explained. "She's a 'very tough old broad.' This is my second mystery-thriller with Maggie. This time, Maggie's investigating a series of murders in Western Washington." The woman said nothing, so Gillian continued. "Um, each time this particular killer abducts a new victim, he ties a black ribbon around a nearby tree, post, or landmark. And the body is always found twenty-four hours later—with a ribbon around the neck, in a pretty bow. It's not quite as grisly as it sounds. It's more suspenseful than gory."

The woman frowned. She put the book down on the table as if it were someone else's used Kleenex. "I don't think I care for that at all."

Gillian kept smiling.

"What about this one?" the woman asked, picking up another book.

"That's *Killing Legend,* my first. It came out two years ago."

"What's the plot?" she asked, scrutinizing the back cover. "I don't understand the title."

"Well, instead of a living legend, this man is a *Killing Legend*. I was inspired by the rumors after James Dean's death. People claimed he was still alive, but so horribly disfigured by the auto accident that he'd faked his demise. Anyway, in my book, this *legend* is a sexy leading man, an overnight sensation in movies. And everyone thinks he's dead after a car accident. So now, he's preying on all the people who made his life hell on his way to the top of the Hollywood heap. There's show business mixed with murder, plus a little—"

Gillian stopped as she noticed the woman shaking her head again. She had that same sour look on her face as she plopped the book down. "I hate stories set in Hollywood."

Gillian nodded. "Yes, well, it's not everyone's taste," she said lamely.

"What about this one?" the woman asked, picking up another book.

Are you for real? Did you come here to torture me?

Gillian kept smiling and explained the plot of her second thriller, *Highway Hypnosis*. It was a very creepy tale of a former surgeon who turned killing hitchhikers into big business. He sold the victims' identities on the black market—as well as their internal organs.

That wasn't Old Sourpuss's cup of tea either, Gillian could tell. The woman shook her head and clicked her tongue against her teeth. But before Gillian could thank her for stopping by, the lady sighed and picked up another one of her books. "What's *this* about?" she pressed, waving a copy of *The Mark of Death*.

Now it was Gillian making a face and shaking her head.

"Oh, I don't think you'd like it. My books aren't for everyone. But thanks for stopping by." She felt as if she were trying to *break up* with her and let her down gently: *This isn't working out. It's not you, it's me and my books. We're not a good fit. Move on—please . . .*

The woman scowled at the back cover of *The Mark of Death* for another moment, then she set the book back down on the desk. "You're right," she said. "This one doesn't look very interesting either. So—where's the Travel section?"

Fifteen minutes later, Gillian was walking across the mini-mall's parking lot. The events coordinator and a clerk had bought copies of *Black Ribbons*, and she'd signed them. Pity purchases, most likely. But she was grateful just the same. They'd asked her to come back when the next book was released, God bless them.

She'd signed at this particular store twice before—on Saturday afternoons. This was her first night signing here, and she hadn't realized until now that the rest of the mini-mall shut down early. All the other storefronts were dark.

Gillian hiked up the collar to her trench coat as she made her way toward an opening in a row of trees at the far end of the lot. The bus stop was on the other side of those trees.

She still had a few minutes to catch the 8:40 bus to Seattle. At one time, Gillian had owned a car, but not anymore. She'd been forced to sell her Saturn two years ago. Immediately afterward, the man who had made her sell it beat her so severely she'd had bruises on her face, back, and arms for over two weeks.

But Gillian didn't want to think about that right now. Even though the problem hadn't quite gone away, she didn't want to dwell on it. Not tonight.

She had a bus to catch—then a transfer and another forty-minute ride back to Seattle. It was a hell of a long trip merely to sell eleven books, but that came with being a *medium-selling* author. She glanced back at the bookstore.

Maybe for the next book signing she would drive herself here, and find a line of people actually waiting for her. *Oh, dream on, Gillian.*

The wind howled. Leaves and debris scattered across the parking lot pavement. It was a cold, damp November night, and Gillian could see her breath. There were fewer cars around the farther she moved away from the bookstore. It was also darker at this end of the lot. The opening in the line of trees was just ahead.

Gillian thought she heard something behind her—a clicking noise or footsteps. She looked over her shoulder, and didn't see anyone. One of the floodlights above was sputtering. Maybe that was what made the strange noise.

As she turned around again, Gillian saw a minivan slowly pull into the lot. Its headlights swept across her, blinding her for a moment. The vehicle headed toward the bookstore, but then it pulled a U-turn. Once again, those headlights were in her eyes.

Then they went off.

The minivan pulled up alongside her. Gillian veered away from it, and picked up her pace. But she didn't break into a run. She didn't want them to think she was scared. There was no one else around. She couldn't see the driver—or anyone inside the car. But the way the minivan inched alongside her, she could tell the driver was looking at her.

Gillian carried a little canister of pepper spray in her purse, but it always took forever to find *anything* in that satchel. With a shaky hand, she frantically dug into the bag and groped around for the pepper spray. She kept walking toward that opening in the trees, and pretended to ignore the minivan just a few feet away from her. She could hear traffic noise on the other side of the trees up ahead. But would anyone hear her if she screamed?

The minivan picked up speed, then stopped between her and the trees at the edge of the lot.

Gillian stopped too. Suddenly, she couldn't move. Her feet froze up and became rooted to the pavement. She stared at the driver's door as it opened.

A tall, gangly man climbed out of the front. The baseball cap he wore cast a shadow over most of his face, so all she could see was his unshaven jaw and a crooked smile. His denim jacket was slightly askew; he had his right arm in the sleeve and the other in a cast. The left side of the jacket was draped over his shoulder, half-covering the bandaged arm.

Gillian thought about Ted Bundy. That was one of his ploys. He sometimes approached his victims with one arm in a cast—and a friendly smile.

Gillian kept searching for the pepper spray in her purse. It was too dark to see anything in the bag, and when she looked up, he was coming toward her. She backed away.

"Pardon me," the man called. "Mind if I talk to you for a minute?"

Staring at the man, Gillian took another step back. She thought she felt the pepper spray canister at the bottom of her bag.

"Aren't you Gillian McBride, the author?"

She said nothing.

"I recognized you. Is it too late for an autograph?" He hoisted his bandaged arm. "Think you might sign my cast?"

Gillian hesitated. She heard another door click open, and she glanced over at the minivan. A young girl—about twelve, with a ski jacket and her hair in pigtails—jumped out of the passenger side. "Is it her, Dad?"

Gillian let out a little sigh. As the girl came up to her father's side, Gillian noticed a well-worn copy of *Black Ribbons* in her hand.

"The wife is a big fan of yours," the man explained. "She's home with the flu, otherwise she'd be here. You really scared her with this new book."

A hand over her heart, Gillian cracked a smile. "Well, tell your wife you got even with me tonight."

Gillian autographed the book for the man's wife, and signed his cast too. Rolling up her coat sleeve, the daughter asked Gillian to autograph her arm. Gillian complied. She talked with them for a few minutes. The man asked if she needed a ride someplace. Gillian lied and said she was fine. As the man and his daughter pulled away in the minivan, Gillian waved. And when she was sure they could no longer see her, she started to cry.

Those few moments with that man and his daughter had made her feel important. Maybe the long bus trip here was worth it after all. So why was she crying?

She'd been doing that a lot lately—when she was sure no one was around to see her.

Gillian found the pepper spray in her purse while fishing out some Kleenex. She dried her eyes at the bus stop.

There was something else in Gillian's purse—her mail. They'd been late delivering it today, and she'd grabbed it out of her mailbox on her way to catch the bus to Woodinville. Now, on the near-empty 409 back to Seattle, Gillian glanced over her mail—and tried to ignore the unabashed gaze from a creepy, bearded man with a bad toupee, seated in one of the Handicapped Only spots.

Most of the letters were bills, some past due. But she'd also received a postcard from her best friend, Dianne Garrity, vacationing in Palm Springs. She and Dianne had grown up together. As a kid, Dianne had been considered a weirdo because she'd had scoliosis and wore a back-brace through tenth grade. But that didn't bother Gillian, who was never very athletic or popular anyway. They read each other's diaries, and Dianne was the first person to tell Gillian that she should be a writer. "I mean it," Dianne had said back in high school. "You're going to be a famous author someday." She was saying the same thing when Gillian was trying to sell her first thriller to scores of uninterested agents and publishers.

Saw "Black Ribbons" in a Walgreens here in Palm Springs,

Dianne mentioned in the postcard. *You were at eye level, right next to Stephen King—well, okay, NOW you're there. I moved it.*

There was also a letter from her agent. It was a Xerox of the first few paragraphs of a *New York Daily News* article. Her agent had attached a Post-it. *Doesn't this seem familiar?* it said.

The bus went over a few potholes, but Gillian barely noticed. She was studying the headline: POLICE HUNT FOR 'ZORRO' KILLER. The article told of a stabbing on Halloween night in New York. A man dressed as Zorro had sliced up a woman in the back of a taxi. The clipping was only a portion of the story, and the victim's last name had been cut off: . . . *visiting from Portland, 28-year-old Jennifer—*

Biting her lip, Gillian set down the news clipping.

The story was familiar, all right. She had written a scene like that in one of her books.

He noticed the curtain move in the front window. For the last hour, he hadn't seen any activity in Gillian McBride's half of the quaint, cedar-shaked duplex, but he knew the kid was home. Gillian and her son, Ethan, occupied the first floor of the duplex. The woman who lived in the small unit above them hadn't been home for several days.

The duplex had a certain unkempt charm. Fallen leaves covered the sidewalk in front of the place. Gray with dirty white shutters, the converted house had a park bench on the front porch—between the doorways to the units. The basement had a separate entrance on the side. The light outside the cellar door was activated by a motion detector. There was no garage, which couldn't have mattered much to Gillian McBride because she had no car. The yard was tiny, but the duplex sat on the edge of a ravine. Through some of the bare trees, he could see St. Mark's Cathedral, a brick and mortar monstrosity, looming on the other side of the ravine.

He felt as if he knew every inch of Gillian's place. He'd been watching it—off and on—for the last few days.

Mostly he sat in his parked car across the street, listening to his iPod and playing his Game Boy to relieve the tedium. Every once in a while, he walked around the block to stretch his legs and peek into the windows.

He was halfway down the block when he saw the curtain move in the front window. Then he heard her door open. Ducking behind a wide evergreen, he watched the kid step outside. Gillian's son, Ethan, would turn fourteen in a few days. He was skinny with wavy brown hair he must have recently cut himself, because the bangs were all askew. Despite a trace of adolescent acne, he was a handsome kid.

Ethan stepped out on the front porch, then looked left and right. He wore a sweatshirt and jeans, and clutched a small, black, plastic bag against his stomach—almost as if he were trying to conceal it. Padding down the porch steps, he crept around the side of the house. The kid seemed to shrink as the light above the basement door automatically went on. He hurried to the garbage cans, opened the lid to one, and dug out a loaded Hefty bag. He dropped the little plastic bag into the receptacle, then loaded the Hefty bag on top of it. After another furtive glance around, he replaced the garbage can lid.

From behind the evergreen, the man watched Ethan hurry back inside the duplex. The curtain in the front window moved again. Obviously, the kid wanted to make sure no one had seen him. If he was concerned about anyone finding what he'd thrown out, Ethan was a bit early. The trash collection at Gillian's place was every Thursday morning. That gave him two more days to go through that garbage and unearth whatever the kid was hiding.

He saw someone coming up the sidewalk.

It was Gillian, back from her book signing in Woodinville. He'd seen the announcement in the newspapers. He wondered if it was successful.

Clutching the collar of her trench coat, she headed toward her duplex. Even though she was at least half a block away and couldn't see him, he blew her a kiss.

Gillian stopped in her tracks. She stared at the duplex in the distance. The automatic light to the cellar entrance just went off. It was operated by motion detection. What was moving around the basement door?

She quickly reached inside her purse, and found the pepper spray without any trouble this time. As she continued toward the house, Gillian told herself it could have been anything—maybe a raccoon. That was one of the disadvantages of living so close to a ravine. Ethan was home, but it couldn't have been him. The only things in the cellar were the washer and dryer, and he didn't even know how to operate them. He couldn't have been taking out the garbage—not on his own, not without her asking him at least three times to do it.

Approaching the house, she saw no sign of anyone, no raccoons scurrying about. The trees swayed in the autumn breeze and leaves flew up from the sidewalk. Maybe the wind had set off the automatic light.

Gillian took another cautious look around before she ascended the porch steps. She quickly dug her keys out of her purse. As she opened the door, a waft of stale smoke hit her. "Ethan?" she called. "Ethan, are you home?"

He came around from the kitchen. "Hey, what's up?"

"Were you burning something in here?" she asked, closing the door behind her.

"Oh, um, I—yeah, I tried to start a fire in the fireplace, but I screwed it up," he said, shrugging. "Sorry. I didn't know it stunk so much."

She waved a hand in front of her face. "Well, from now on, maybe you shouldn't try to have a fire when I'm not here. Okay?" She put her keys and the pepper spray back in her purse, then moved over to the front window and opened it a bit. "Were you outside just a minute ago?"

Ethan quickly shook his head. "No. Why do you ask?"

"Well, something just activated the light by the basement door." Gillian slipped out of her trench coat. "It gave me a little scare for a minute."

"Oh, well, I—I think I saw a raccoon out there earlier. How did your book signing go?"

Gillian hung up her coat. "There was a line of five hundred people around the store, and a riot broke out when they ran out of my books. They had to call the cops in."

"Did you sell *ten* books at least?" he asked.

On her way into the kitchen, she kissed him on the cheek. "A whopping eleven. Did you get any dinner?"

"I had a DiGiorno."

"But you had frozen pizza last night." Gillian peeked into the refrigerator. "There's a perfectly delicious casserole in here. I told you all you had to do is heat it up. And there's salad—"

"I just felt like pizza again," Ethan replied, plopping down at her computer. It was in an alcove just off the kitchen. Gillian's husband had converted the pantry into a writer's nook. There was a tiny window with a view of the ravine, a bookshelf full of her books along with tomes about true crimes and serial killers, and framed family photos of Gillian, her husband, and Ethan.

Ethan often used her computer to play video games. She didn't object. The poor guy had to entertain himself somehow. It was bad enough she left him alone every Thursday night so she could teach her creative writing class at the community college. But now, with the recent release of *Black Ribbons,* she'd been gone more evenings than she'd been home the last three weeks. She felt as if she'd been neglecting her son for book signings, book club dates, and interviews with newspapers and tiny fifty-watt radio stations all over western Washington State.

Gillian figured she probably wasn't in line for The Worst Mother Alive Award, but she certainly had a dishonorable mention coming to her. Plus they were practically broke. It was a long wait between royalty checks, and the money she made teaching that creative writing class wasn't much. Gillian wondered how she would pay those bills in her purse.

She took the casserole out of the refrigerator, peeled back the aluminum-foil cover, and picked at the cold chicken and noodles. She studied Ethan's profile. The computer screen lit up his handsome, chiseled face. He was getting over his gawky-adolescent phase, and starting to look like his father. Gillian felt a little pang in her stomach.

She hadn't seen her husband for two years. Neither had Ethan. They didn't know if he was alive or dead. They rarely talked about him—except in the past tense. But that didn't mean they never worried or wondered about him.

Gillian put the casserole back in the refrigerator. "So—is your homework done, honey?"

"Almost," he replied, eyes riveted to the computer screen.

"Did you practice your violin?" He'd been playing for three years now, and was quite accomplished at it.

"Yeah, Mom," he said, preoccupied. "You got another book signing tomorrow night?"

Gillian sighed. "Yes, over in Redmond. I'm going to the market in the morning. I'll buy some microwave dinners so you don't starve."

"Pick up another couple of DiGiornos while you're at it, okay?"

"Sure," she muttered, cracking open the window above the sink. The kitchen smelled of stale smoke too.

Gillian gazed out the window. For a moment, she thought she saw someone in the side yard ducking behind a tree. Was that why the outside light had gone on and off earlier? She kept staring, and finally told herself it was nothing. She was just on edge tonight for some reason. Hell, in the mini-mall's parking lot, she'd almost pepper-sprayed that poor man in the cast—the husband of a fan, for God's sakes.

Her thriller-writer's imagination was working overtime tonight.

Gillian took one last look out the window, and then started fixing a salad for her dinner.

Chapter 3

Dear Ms. McBride,

I just finished your new book, BLACK RIBBONS, and I liked it a lot. Very scary! Detective Maggie Dare rocks! I love how she doesn't take crap from anybody. Did you know there's a spelling error on page 219? Didn't you mean 'alarmed' instead of 'alarms'? Thought you should know. Otherwise, it's a kick-ass book. Keep up the good work.

Sincerely,
Karen Linde

"Well, thank you, Karen," Gillian said under her breath.

It was 11:15. Wearing a sweatshirt and flannel pajama bottoms, Gillian sat at her computer with a cup of Earl Grey. The apartment still smelled a bit smoky—especially in the bathroom. She'd noticed it while in there washing her face twenty minutes ago. Ethan had gone to bed, but a telltale strip of light still shone under his closed door.

She had an oldies station playing softly. Janis Ian was singing something depressing. *Music to Slit Your Wrist By.*

Gillian typed out a cordial reply to the e-mail, which had come through her Web site. It was the only fan letter today. She made sure to apologize for the spelling error.

She checked her regular e-mail, and found a note from her agent:

Hey Gill,

How are you doing on the new outline? I promised your editor we'd have it in his lap by the end of next week. Should I start cracking the whip? We'll talk soon.

Eve

Gillian e-mailed her agent back, and said the outline was going well. This was a total lie. She didn't even have an idea yet. "And thanks for sending along that news clipping about the 'Zorro' Killer," she added. "That's very bizarre & a bit unsettling. I hope they catch him."

After sending the e-mail, Gillian stared at the computer screen for a minute. She couldn't stop thinking about that stabbing in New York. She'd been at this very spot when she'd created her own "Zorro" killer.

Now someone had made him real.

Shifting in her chair, Gillian logged onto Amazon.com, selected Books, and typed in *The Mark of Death, Gillian McBride*. The sales rank was unspectacular, but there were two new reviews. The most recent reviewer, *Imalegend2,* gave her book two stars, calling it trite and clumsy. But *Imalegend2* added: "The masked-man, 'Zorro' murder, however, is a shining, inspired moment, an oasis in this otherwise barren piece of pulp literature."

"Oh, screw you, *I-Male-Gender-Two,* or whatever your name is," Gillian muttered. She checked out the other new review. *Wanderemik3* gave the book four stars, and summed it up nicely:

Gillian McBride delivers a scary story of a creepy serial
killer who believes he's some kind of superhero. In one
scene, he even carves an S on his chest with a razor
blade. In another, he disguises himself as Zorro, and
crashes a masquerade party. There, he seduces the
host's daughter in the back of a guest's parked car, and
then he stabs her to death. . . .

Digging through her purse, Gillian fished out the partial
news clipping her agent had sent. She reread the truncated
last line with half of the victim's name cut off: ". . . visiting
from Portland, 28-year-old Jennifer—"

Frowning, Gillian set the clipping aside. She pulled up
the *New York Daily News* on the Web, then tapped into their
archives for November 1st. She found the complete article,
and stopped reading when she came to the identity of that
twenty-eight-year-old woman who had been stabbed. "Jennifer
Gilderhoff," she whispered. "My God . . ."

Gillian knew her.

She reached across the desk to her "pending" box, and
dug through the unpaid bills, announcements, and mail that
needed her response. She found the postcard, heralding the
publication of *Burning Old Bridesmaids' Dresses & Other
Survival Stories* by Jennifer Gilderhoff. On one side of the
card was the book cover, with a cartoon of a woman who
looked a bit like Jane Jetson. She wore a cocktail dress, and
held a lighter wand. The flip side of the card had Gillian's
address and a blurb for the book. Along the margin, Jennifer
had scribbled a note: *"To my terrific writing teacher—Thanx
for all your encouragement! Hi to my old Seattle pals!"*

Gillian hadn't seen Jennifer Gilderhoff in two years. But
she remembered her. Jennifer was pretty with blue eyes and
light brown hair. She had a certain dippy, kittenish quality
that a lot of men found attractive and many women found irritating. But she was a pretty good writer. Jennifer had been

one of Gillian's students the first year she'd taught the night class at Seattle City Experimental College.

Gillian read the rest of the *Daily News* coverage, and kept shaking her head over and over again. She couldn't believe this had happened to someone she knew. She checked the *Daily News* archives for a follow-up story, and found only one brief article—dated three days ago—mentioning Jennifer Gilderhoff was still comatose in Roosevelt Hospital in New York. The man who had stabbed her was still at large.

Getting up from her chair, Gillian moved into the living room and started pacing. If her agent hadn't sent her the news clipping, she might never have known about this. But now Gillian felt involved, maybe even *responsible* in some way for what had happened. She knew the victim. She'd invented the killer, and drawn the blueprint for the murder.

If she called the police in New York, would they think she was crazy? She couldn't offer them much—except that she knew Jennifer, and there was a possibility that "Zorro" might have read one of her books. Did she know "Zorro" too?

This was one of those times when she really missed her husband. If Barry were here, she could talk with him and figure out what to do.

Her fictional heroine, Detective Maggie Dare, would know the best course of action. Fortunately, Maggie hadn't sprouted solely from Gillian's imagination. The *tough old broad* sleuth had been patterned after her friend, Ruth Langford, a sixty-eight-year-old widow and retired detective. Gillian used Ruth as a technical consultant on all her thrillers. Ruth was also one of her writing students, and she'd been in that same class with Jennifer Gilderhoff.

Ruth, no doubt, was asleep right now. Gillian returned to her desk and fired off an e-mail to her. She sent an attachment of the *Daily News* article. "This is the same Jennifer Gilderhoff from our night class two years ago," she wrote to her friend. "Do you have any contacts with the NYPD? I want to know more about this case."

Gillian clicked on the Send icon, and she suddenly felt better. She'd discuss the case with Ruth in the morning. She wasn't so alone in this.

Getting to her feet, she crept toward the back hallway and checked Ethan's bedroom door. The slice of light at his threshold had gone out. He was sleeping.

It still smelled a bit like smoke in the apartment. "Phew," Gillian muttered, waving a hand in front of her face as she wandered back toward the living room. Small wonder the smoke detector hadn't gone off. But she couldn't be mad at Ethan for his attempt at building a fire in the hearth. He was probably just trying to make the half-of-a-duplex—minus a father, mother, and home cooking—seem more like a home.

Gillian glanced at the fireplace to see the mess he'd made.

It was clean—with two fresh, pristine logs supported by the andirons, not a trace of soot or smoke beneath the mantel. "I tried to start a fire in the fireplace," he'd told her. "But I screwed it up." Gillian frowned. It didn't make sense.

She heard a tonal *ping* from her computer: an e-mail coming in. She thought perhaps it was Ruth getting back to her already. Maybe her friend wasn't sleeping right now after all.

Gillian sat down at the desk again and retrieved the e-mail. It wasn't from Ruth. She didn't recognize the sender's address. And there was no subject. Gillian opened the e-mail.

"Oh, my God," she whispered, staring at the unsigned message:

> Gillian, I found your husband.

He thought Gillian McBride looked cute in her sweatshirt and flannel pajama bottoms, her red hair haphazardly clipped back with a barrette. She could have passed for a teenager, and he liked teenage girls—very much, maybe too much.

From the edge of the ravine, he watched her most of the night, pacing around the kitchen and living room. The garbage cans were just outside the kitchen window, so he still hadn't gotten a chance to hunt for whatever the kid had thrown away earlier.

He took a break, and drove to a late-night Taco Bell on Broadway. He bought two burritos to go. He didn't dawdle. Last night, he'd seen her peel down to her black panties and a tank top before slipping into bed. He didn't want to miss the show tonight.

He returned to his same spot, this time carrying his midnight snack. As he wolfed down his food, he stared at her, hunched over the computer in her little writing nook.

Licking red sauce off his fingers, he watched her get up and turn off the lights. Then she reappeared through the thin, gauzelike drapes of her bedroom. The big, aluminum-clad picture window had tall, thin panes on each side, the kind that push out with the handles. There was a shade too, but Gillian didn't use it much. With the ravine in her backyard, she probably figured no one could see her. But he could. He took another bite out of his Taco Bell delicacy and stared. She pulled the sweatshirt over her head, and the T-shirt underneath started to ride up. But she tugged it down before he got a peek at anything. As she shucked off her sweatpants, he saw she was wearing white panties tonight. He kept hoping she'd peel them off. He even imagined breaking in there and removing them for her. He figured she might just like that.

After all, it had been two years since her husband, Barry Tanner, vanished. As far as the man knew, Gillian hadn't gotten herself a boyfriend in all that time. It was just the kid, her books, and the night class. That was it. He imagined Gillian McBride wouldn't mind a night visitor, someone ready to take care of her needs.

He watched her crawl into bed and switch off the night-stand lamp.

Her room was dark, and he couldn't see anything.

But he stayed anyway.

Gillian couldn't sleep worth a damn. She kept thinking about Jennifer Gilderhoff, now lying in a coma with multiple stab wounds in a New York hospital. Was it just an eerie coincidence she'd created a "Zorro" killer in her book *The Mark of Death*? Gillian kept telling herself that she would figure it out with Ruth in the morning. Ruth would have some answers.

But who could explain that cryptic e-mail about Barry? Gillian had tried to respond to the unnerving message, but her reply had bounced back at her: "MAILER-DAEMON . . . Returned Mail: User Unknown."

Curled up in bed, Gillian hugged Barry's old pillow to her chest. She remembered a night about two years ago, when she'd been lying in this very spot, hugging *him,* and he'd suddenly started shaking. He'd let out a low rasp, almost like a death rattle. For a moment, Gillian had thought her husband was having a heart attack. Then she realized Barry was crying. She kept asking him what was wrong, but he just went on sobbing. Finally, he threw back the covers, jumped out of bed, and started pacing around the darkened bedroom.

Gillian sat up in bed. "Honey, for God's sakes, what is it?"

She stared at his lean silhouette against the gauzelike drapes. Clad in his boxer shorts, he marched back and forth at the foot of their bed. "It's nothing—I can't—" He stopped, and ran a hand through his wavy brown hair. "It's just—I'm such a fuckup. You would have been better off if you'd never met me."

They'd met in college at the University of Illinois, where Gillian studied journalism. Barry majored in business administration. Everyone adored Barry Tanner, and he'd picked *her*. He swept Gillian's mother off her feet too. "Oh, honey, you hold onto that one," she'd whispered to Gillian after first meeting her future son-in-law. "So handsome, so charming . . ." Perhaps if Gillian's father had been alive to meet Barry, things might have been different. Perhaps her dad wouldn't have been so captivated by Barry's charm.

Mr. and Mrs. Barry Tanner moved into a cozy apartment in Evanston. Barry nabbed an advertising job with Leo Burnett Company, and Gillian wrote features for a small suburban press. Some of her pieces even won awards—and circulated in other newspapers around the country. Some of the credit had to go to Barry. He'd proofread and even edited several of those pieces. Gillian was grateful for his input—and for the extra money those articles brought in.

For some reason, they were always in a financial pinch. But Gillian didn't complain. A lot of people were much worse off than they were. She longed for a bigger place after Ethan was born, but they couldn't afford it. So for the first four years of his life, Ethan slept in a crib, and his bedroom was a converted walk-in closet. Gillian painted a window with a lovely seaside view on his wall to make up for the fact that her son was sleeping in this claustrophobic little space. When he was five, they got him a bigger bed—on stilts, with a ladder. Beneath the bed, Barry had arranged a small dresser, lamp, and an old bean-bag chair. Ethan loved it, because it looked like something in a submarine. But Gillian felt frustrated. After all these years, they were still in their "starter" one-bedroom apartment. Their son deserved his own room with a window, for God's sake. Where was all their money going?

It got so every time Barry bought her an expensive present, Gillian nagged him about spending beyond their budget. Then afterward, she'd feel horribly guilty and ungrateful.

One Saturday morning, Barry went off to work for "a couple of hours," and by 11:15 that night, he still hadn't returned home. Gillian hadn't been able to get ahold of him. She was going out of her mind, and kept busy doing laundry all evening. On a trip up from the building's basement with a load from the dryer, she saw him sneaking into the apartment. His back was to her, and his suit looked dirty and disheveled. He had his key in the door.

"Where in the world have you been?" she whispered.

Barry swiveled around. Gillian gasped and dropped the laundry basket. His beautiful face had been savagely beaten. His right eye was swollen shut, and dried blood was caked around his nose and mouth. "I got mugged," he replied, talking out of one side of his mouth. His lip was split. "These two guys jumped me."

In the bathroom, she helped him clean up his face. They spoke in whispers, so as not to wake Ethan. Barry didn't want their son seeing him like this. "It'll give him nightmares."

The more Gillian asked exactly how it had happened, the less Barry wanted to talk about it. Finally, he admitted he hadn't gone to the police yet. "Two teenage boys made me fork over all the money out of my wallet—along with my watch and my wedding ring," he said. "Then they kicked the shit out of me. Please don't humiliate me any further by making me tell this all to the cops."

Gillian called the police anyway.

"I really wish you wouldn't have done that," Barry grumbled, changing his clothes to go to the station.

They had a neighbor sit with Ethan, and drove to the station house together. Barry was friendly, but not terribly helpful to the detective questioning him. He had a tough time recalling what his assailants had looked like, and was vague about the exact time and location of the incident. The police didn't think he'd get back the wedding ring or the watch.

Two days later, Barry told Gillian of a fantastic job offer with a new ad agency in Seattle. Apparently, a former superior from Leo Burnett had recently defected there, and he'd asked for Barry. The job meant more money. The only catch was they needed him right away. So Gillian packed up and they moved—all very hastily, almost stealthily. She should have known something was wrong. But the mugging had soured them both on their neighborhood. And she imagined a fresh start with a chance for a real home.

Gillian found the duplex within days. Eight-year-old Ethan finally had a genuine bedroom—with a window, and a view of the ravine.

They hadn't even finished unpacking when Barry gave her the bad news. The ad agency had gone belly-up. He scurried around looking for a job, any job. That was how the former ad executive ended up driving a delivery truck. As for Gillian, even with her file full of prize-winning syndicated stories, all she found was part-time grunt work at a Seattle weekly newspaper.

Barry had to be up at 3:30 in the morning to make his route, so he was usually in bed and asleep by 8:30—unless one of his union meetings went late into the night. They often interfered with weekends too. Gillian filled the nights alone by writing her first thriller—in notebooks and on an old laptop at the kitchen table. Later, Barry converted the pantry into her writing alcove. He was always doing things like that.

In three years, Gillian had written two thrillers, *Killing Legend* and *Highway Hypnosis,* and she'd started *The Mark of Death*. The two completed manuscripts collected a total of seventy-two rejections from literary agencies and publishers. Barry was always sneaking into the local union headquarters after hours and using their Xerox to make extra copies for her. With her husband's encouragement, Gillian took all the literary rejection in her stride. She kept revising, rewriting, and resubmitting her manuscripts.

Then something happened that gave them hope. A coworker told her about a literary agent in San Francisco. Her name was Marcia Tokata, and she was accepting new clients. Gillian e-mailed her with a brief synopsis of *Killing Legend*.

The next day, Marcia telephoned Gillian and told her that the plot of *Killing Legend* had best-seller potential. She was eager to read the manuscript. And yes, she wanted to read Gillian's other book too. Could she send them both over-night mail? In the meantime, she wanted Gillian to make a list of hot leading men they could approach to play her sexy-star-turned-psycho-slayer in the movie version. She had a partner at one of the big entertainment agencies in Los Angeles. What did Gillian think about Colin Farrell?

In all the months and months she'd been trying to land an agent, this was the first time Gillian felt a connection with someone. Never had she met an agent this enthusiastic about her work—and Marcia hadn't even read her manuscripts yet.

Three months later, Marcia still hadn't read her manuscripts—and she wasn't answering Gillian's calls or e-mails. Gillian had long since abandoned the notion of Clive Owen starring in the film version of *Killing Legend*. She wrote Marcia a polite note, hinting that after three months of nothing, she wanted to pursue another agent to represent her.

The manuscripts came back the next week—along with a letter:

Dear Gillian,

Have read your manuscript, KILLING LEGEND, and it's not what I expected. I had a hard time believing any of the characters, and at times, felt the dialogue was—well, just silly. I think it was written in a hurry by someone who doesn't understand anything about plotting or pace. I didn't even try to read HIGHWAY HYPNOSIS. I seriously think you should give serious thought to giving up writing. You will save yourself and others a lot of tedious hours and heartbreak. This may sound harsh, but in the long run, I believe I'm helping you.

Best regards,
Marcia Tokata, MXM Literary Agency

"She's a moron," Barry concluded. "And look at this sentence, 'I *seriously think* you should *give serious thought* to *giving* up writing.' Huh, got the word repetition or what?"

Ethan had the brilliant suggestion that his mother name a nasty character in one of her books *Marcia Tokata,* then kill her off—painfully.

Gillian didn't give up writing. Barry wouldn't let her. She sent *Killing Legend* to five more agents. One of them was Eve Kohner in New York. Eve thought she should revise her first chapter, and Gillian obliged her. Two months later, Eve sold the manuscript to Shalimar Books.

In celebration, Gillian, Barry, and Ethan went out for an expensive dinner, and she didn't nag Barry about overspending when he ordered champagne. The five-thousand-dollar advance for the book went to buy a new sofa and pay off their Visa bill. The release of *Killing Legend* didn't exactly make Gillian a household name. It didn't make them rich either. But Gillian was thrilled. She was a *published author*. Readers actually wrote fan letters to her publisher—okay, only a handful of people wrote to her, but it was still a very heady experience. The local supermarket didn't carry her book. But Barry always told her—and anyone who would listen—whenever he noticed *his wife's book* in one of the stores on his delivery route.

Gillian received another twelve grand to fulfill a two-book contract with the already completed *Highway Hypnosis* and *The Mark of Death*. Eve explained that the pressure was on for her to deliver two thrillers a year. Gillian was up for it. And the money came in the nick of time, because she'd been laid off at the weekly. Just as well. The jerks there didn't even review or promote her book. The contract money went to pay bills too. Gillian had been hoping they could buy a house, but realized that wouldn't happen any time soon. What did happen was their landlord came to the door one morning after Barry had gone to work and announced that they had thirty days to evacuate the premises or he'd call the police on them. Their last two rent checks had bounced.

Barry, the former business major, always paid the bills and balanced their checkbook. Gillian had written enough checks to keep track of how they were doing, and it didn't make sense that they'd been bouncing checks. In a panic, she called the bank, and they confirmed that the savings and checking accounts were overdrawn. Their credit cards had been maxed out as well. Barry's tabulations in the checkbook didn't reflect any of this.

Gillian put in a distress call to her mother in Florida. Mrs. McBride cashed in some bonds and wired them five thousand dollars. Gillian paid their landlord everything they owed—plus two more months in advance. "I really didn't want to evict you folks," the landlord explained, almost apologetic. "Until the checks bounced, you've been swell tenants, Mrs. Tanner. And your husband is such a nice guy."

Barry was so ashamed. He was like a little kid, caught in a lie. He confessed he'd made a bad investment a few months before—a real estate venture in Nevada that was supposed to be a *sure thing*. He didn't want to tell her about the ensuing catastrophe until things looked less bleak. He hadn't been very honest with her about a series of recent "union meetings" either. He'd been taking on extra shifts in an effort to recoup their losses.

Gillian kept thinking she should have known. If something like this had happened to the heroine in one of her books, the woman would have realized early on her husband was lying to her. How could her heroines be so smart when she was so stupid?

They got some unexpected help from Sweden and the Czech Republic, when the foreign rights for *Killing Legend* were sold to publishers in both countries for a combined eight thousand dollars. It didn't completely abolish their debt.

But it undid some of the financial and psychological damage from Barry's bad investment. Gillian was in a better position to forgive him, and forgive him she did. "Just don't ever lie to me again, okay?" she asked.

From then on, Gillian paid the bills and balanced the checkbook. She'd sent a resume to the Seattle City Experimental College, along with a proposal to teach a creative writing class on Thursday nights. They hired her. The job was good for grocery money—at least. Gillian figured if she watched their budget, they could be out of debt by the end of the year.

That was why it seemed so odd—months after their *almost* eviction—Barry was crying in the middle of the night, calling himself a "fuckup," and saying Gillian would have been better off if she'd never met him.

"Barry, stop pacing around and tell me what happened," she said, raising her voice a bit. "I'm going to find out eventually. So you might as well tell me now. Did you—make another bad investment? Is that it?"

With a sigh, he plopped down at the foot of the bed. He sat there for a moment, shoulders hunched forward. Gillian ran her hand up and down his back. "What is it?" she whispered. "Tell me."

He shook his head. "It's nothing. I just started thinking about what a bum deal you got when you married me. You thought you were getting an advertising executive, and maybe some nice house in Winnetka or Lake Forest. Instead, you ended up with a truck driver in a dump of a duplex in Seattle. If it weren't for your mother and your books bailing us out, I would have sunk this family. Me and my stupid schemes . . ."

"Oh, Barry, that's old business," she said, hugging him. "It's forgotten. We're doing okay now. You have a wife and son who both worship you."

They tumbled back on the bed and held onto each other. Barry kissed her deeply. Gillian sensed he still harbored some awful secret. But she didn't dare ask. She had a feeling the twelve years they'd spent building a life together and raising a son would all go down the drain if he told her what was really troubling him. So she didn't ask. She just clung to him.

There was suddenly something inside her too—a feeling of dread in the pit of her stomach. That awful foreboding sensation didn't go away, not even after they'd made love that night. Gillian remembered it was only two weeks before Barry disappeared. All that time, the knots in her stomach hadn't gone away. It was as if her body had known what was going to happen.

Barry took two suitcases with him. But he'd left so much behind. Most of his clothes still hung in their closet. His favorite coffee mug was still on the kitchen shelf. She and Ethan still waited for him to come back.

Gillian hugged his pillow, and wondered about that mysterious e-mail: "Gillian, I found your husband." Did it mean she was closer to seeing Barry again? Or was it an indication that she and Ethan had lost him forever?

She heard rain pattering against the bedroom window. Gillian opened her eyes to see the dawn's gray light seeping through the thin drapes. Then a shadow passed across the very edge of the window. It made her sit up.

The wind howled, and rain continued to tap against the glass. That thing fluttered along the window's edge again. It looked like a bird or something. Maybe it was caught in the rosebush beside the window.

Climbing out of bed, Gillian threw on her robe, and crept to the window. She parted the drapes and peered outside. Past the rain-beaded glass, she studied the ravine: nothing, just a slight rustling amid the forest of trees and bushes. She didn't see anything in the backyard.

Then it appeared again. Someone's trash—a food wrapper—had become momentarily entangled in the rosebush by her window. Gillian caught a glimpse of the Taco Bell wrapper before the wind carried it away.

She shucked off the robe, and crawled back into bed. Hugging Barry's old pillow to her chest, Gillian closed her eyes and prayed for a little sleep. It wouldn't come easy, she knew, because that awful feeling in the pit of her stomach was back.

Chapter 4

This book is dedicated to my oldest and dearest friend,
Dianne Garrity.
Di, you told me I should be a writer, and taught me
to pursue my dreams.
Everyone should have a friend like you.

The man on the Chicago El train was reading the dedication in Gillian McBride's *Killing Legend*. Just five days ago, he had been in New York City, where the woman he'd stabbed was still in a coma.

He'd dog-eared another page in Gillian's book. It was a passage describing how the killer, a former Hollywood hunk now disfigured from a car accident, snuck into his latest victim's house to poison some milk in her refrigerator. Afterward, the killer typed a suicide note on the victim's computer so people would think she'd killed herself.

The man got off at the Belmont El stop, and a cool, damp blast of wind hit him—courtesy of Lake Michigan. With Gillian's book tucked under his arm, he walked three blocks to an old brownstone apartment building.

He'd arrived in Chicago yesterday, and had immediately gone to work, tracking down this address. He'd found *Garrity, D* on one of the four mailboxes by the front door. Walking around to the back of the building, he'd snuck up the back stairs to the third floor. There, he'd peered into the kitchen window, and spotted one of Gillian's paperback book covers taped to the refrigerator door.

He'd found the right Dianne Garrity.

Pulling a small, unmarked vial from his coat pocket, he studied the liquid inside it—clear, colorless. It was supposed to be almost undetectable, except for a slightly bitter aftertaste.

The woman stepped into her kitchen. He quickly ducked away from the window, almost knocking over a garbage can by the back door. He prayed she didn't see him. He didn't want to have to kill her right there. It would have ruined everything. He held his breath and waited. After a moment, he peeked into her window again.

She was glancing at a Pottery Barn catalogue. She wore a pink terry-cloth robe, and had a coffee mug in her hand. He guessed she was in her mid-thirties. She was pretty with long dark blond hair and bangs. He watched her move to the refrigerator and pour some cream into her coffee.

He looked at the vial of poison again and smiled.

He hung around the apartment building for almost two hours, freezing his ass off. He watched her step out the front door and start down the block. She was all bundled up in her ski jacket and cap. He went around back again, and up the stairs. He used a skeleton key on the kitchen door. Breaking into the unit, he went directly to the refrigerator and took out the container of cream.

He'd told himself that by the time she noticed her coffee had a funny aftertaste, the poison would already be in her system, killing her.

Now, almost twenty-four hours later, he'd returned to the

brownstone, hoping to view the fruits of his labor. There weren't any police cars or ambulances in front of the building. That stuff was fast-acting. She probably didn't even have time to call 911.

He walked around to the back of the brownstone. Someone was doing laundry; gray clouds of sweet-smelling vapor billowed from a vent in the basement window. He crept up the back stairs to the third floor. Approaching Dianne Garrity's kitchen window, he noticed her coffee mug on the breakfast table. He half expected to see her corpse—in that pink terry-cloth robe—sprawled on the tiled floor.

Instead, he saw her stroll into the kitchen, talking on a cordless phone. She wore jeans and a pullover sweater. He darted to one side of the window, but continued to watch her. Cradling the phone with her shoulder, she kept up her conversation while she retrieved her coffee mug and refilled it. Then she went to the refrigerator and added a dash of cream to the brew. It wasn't the same container.

"Shit," he muttered under his breath.

He waited until she headed out of the kitchen; then he lifted the lid from the garbage can by the back door. He saw the carton of cream he'd poisoned the day before. There was enough cream there for a few days. She couldn't have tasted it, or she'd be dead right now. Why had she thrown it out? Maybe she'd thought it smelled funny. Or maybe she was just a careless, wasteful bitch.

He was livid. He wanted Gillian's friend dead today. He had a schedule to keep.

An hour later, when she left the building, he followed her. Even half a block away at a crowded street corner, she was easy to spot. Her lavender ski jacket gave her away. At one point, she glanced over her shoulder, and he quickly ducked into a storefront alcove. She continued on, walking under the El tracks and turning down an alley. He trailed after her, and picked up his pace, narrowing the gap between them. There was no one else in the alleyway; just a few parked cars and some Dumpsters. On both sides of them were the backs of apartment buildings, the tallest one about four stories. The rear stairways and fire escapes were empty. He didn't see anyone looking out their back window. He was only twenty feet behind her now.

He heard the El approaching. The sound of steel wheels on the elevated rails became louder and louder. With all that noise, he imagined no one would hear her scream.

At the end of the alley, she paused and looked over her shoulder again.

He quickly ducked behind a phone pole. He stood perfectly still.

Just a block away, the El train clamored by. The load roar started to fade.

His heart was racing, and he realized that excitement had replaced his anger. He liked this challenge.

She gazed into the alley, and listened to the El go by. The cold wind seemed to whip through her, and she shuddered.

Funny. A couple of blocks after leaving the apartment building, she'd thought somebody might have been following her. He'd been very elusive. She never got a look at him—just glimpses of a shadowy figure lurking behind a Dumpster, and then in a building doorway. She'd thought she lost him.

But a moment ago, she'd noticed her own reflection in the windshield of a parked car as she passed by it. And she'd seen someone—or something—behind her. Was it that man from before?

She told herself it must have been her imagination, because she was staring at an empty alley. But then she noticed something behind a phone pole—a little swirling vapor cloud almost six feet from the ground.

It was his breath in the cold.

"Oh, my God," she whispered. Swiveling around, she hurried up the side street toward Belmont, where she hoped to lose him in the crowd. She stopped to catch her breath at a traffic light in the busy shopping area. She was surrounded by people, waiting for the WALK sign. Glancing back, she didn't see anyone.

She still didn't feel safe. After crossing the street, she ducked into a women's clothing store called Attitude, just down the block from Urban Outfitters. It was warm inside the store. But she couldn't stop trembling.

Hanging back, he kept his eye on her lavender ski jacket as she merged into the crowd of pedestrians. He watched her hurry inside a clothing store. He waited a few minutes before going in after her—and the wait was excruciating. He couldn't jump the gun. If Gillian's friend had gone in there to escape from him, she needed time to feel reassured, time to be distracted by all the merchandise.

The tactic worked. Once he stepped into the store, he had to chuckle. Typical woman. She couldn't resist the sale rack— even after she thought someone had been following her a few minutes ago. She'd already gathered several items on hangers, and was now talking with a saleswoman, who pointed her toward a curtained-off area.

He remembered a scene from another Gillian McBride mystery, where a woman was strangled to death in a department store changing room. He hadn't planned to kill Dianne Garrity this way. He'd wanted to poison her—just like that scene in *Killing Legend*. But this might work out better. He remembered the changing room murder very well. It was one of Gillian's better killings. The murderer had studied his victim's face as he choked the life out of her.

After secretly spying on Dianne Garrity all morning and

part of yesterday, he imagined being face-to-face with her. No more dodging behind phone poles or ducking beneath windowsills. He would stare into her eyes while he killed her.

All he had to do was sneak into the curtained-off area and do it. The saleswoman wasn't paying attention. No one was looking. The plans had changed, but he could still make this work.

He just had to take a page from another book.

The postcard from Dianne Garrity fell to the floor.

Gillian had accidentally brushed it off the desktop while reaching for the partial news clipping about "Zorro."

"My agent sent me this piece from *The New York Daily News*," she said into the phone. "That's how I found out about it."

Gillian was at her desk, with the computer on. She hadn't been able to uncover any more details or updates about the stabbing on Halloween night.

"Let me make some calls to New York," said her friend, Ruth Langford, on the other end of the line. "I'll dig around and get back to you, hon. In fact, I might hit you up for lunch or coffee—unless you have an autograph session in Timbuktu or some other place."

"Not until later tonight. Lunch would be terrific. My treat. Thanks, Ruth." Gillian leaned over and retrieved Dianne's Palm Springs postcard. She set it back on her desktop.

After she hung up the phone, Gillian retreated to the bathroom for a quick shower. Maybe it would revive her a bit. Going on two hours of sleep, she'd dragged herself out of bed this morning to fix Ethan a hot breakfast. The poor kid had just wanted a bowl of Captain Crunch. Instead, he got French toast with heated maple syrup—all because she felt guilty about the dinners he'd had to fix for himself this week while she was out pushing her book. She invited him to tonight's signing in Redmond. The bookstore had a café attached. He could eat dinner there. "How long is the bus ride?" he asked warily.

"We'd have to transfer, so about an hour each way."

He cut into his French toast. "Sounds like a drag. Would you be pee-o'd if I passed?"

"No, that's fine, honey."

Gillian watched him head for the school bus stop, half-way down the block. She hadn't mentioned anything to Ethan about the cryptic e-mail from someone claiming to have found Barry.

She hadn't said a word about it to Ruth either. Maybe she'd tell her at lunch. For now, Ruth was doing enough detective work for her with this "Zorro" stabbing. Ruth had remembered Jennifer Gilderhoff from Gillian's creative writing class two years ago. "Wasn't she the pretty one with big eyes and brown hair? Kind of irritating and ditzy?"

Nothing got past Ruth. She didn't pull any punches either. It didn't matter if Jennifer Gilderhoff was lying in a coma with multiple stab wounds. Ruth still recalled her as *"kind of irritating and ditzy,"* and she was right, of course.

"You'll have to add a dash of charm and sweetness to this Detective Maggie Dare character you're patterning after me; otherwise, people will hate her guts," Ruth had advised. "I'm so damned tactless."

But Gillian's fictional Maggie Dare did fine without the sugarcoating. The Ruth-inspired character was introduced in Gillian's third thriller, *For Everyone to See*. It was about a serial killer who liked to murder—the same way some people liked to make love—in public places. Detective Maggie Dare was hunting down a maniac who strangled women in elevators, restrooms, movie theaters, and department store changing rooms. *For Everyone to See* was Gillian's best-selling book to date. Her agent, Eve, had suggested she bring back Maggie Dare for her most recent thriller. And so *Black Ribbons: A Maggie Dare Mystery* came about.

While Gillian showered, she took solace in knowing that right now, the woman who had inspired Maggie Dare was on the phone with her contacts in New York, finding out everything she could about this stabbing on Halloween night.

The pipes squeaked as Gillian turned off the water in the shower. She could hear someone who sounded like her agent saying good-bye on the answering machine. Then a *beep* signaled the end of the message. Grabbing a towel, Gillian quickly dried off, threw on her robe, and hurried into the living room to check the answering machine.

"Hi, Gill, it's Eve. Maybe you're working too hard on that outline. I didn't send you any news story on a 'Zorro Killer.' Are you talking about that poor woman who was stabbed in a taxi on Halloween night? I read about it in the newspaper a few days ago, but didn't send you anything. Did you want me to?"

Eve mentioned the new outline, but Gillian wasn't listening. She wandered over to her desk and glanced at the partial news clipping: POLICE HUNT FOR 'ZORRO' KILLER. It had come in an envelope from the Eve Kohner Agency.

"I'm headed out to a sales conference right now, an overnighter in Atlantic City," Eve was saying on the machine. *"Give Becky a call if you want her to dig up that old article and send it to you. Talk to you later, Gill. Bye."*

Beep.

Gillian studied the handwriting on the Post-it attached to the news story, and realized there wasn't much resemblance to her agent's penmanship.

"Doesn't this seem familiar?" it said.

Before stepping into the fitting room area, she glanced back at the store. She didn't see anyone suspicious. Most of the customers in Attitude were women.

If someone had been following her, he must have given
up, because she didn't see him now. Maybe she was just
imagining things when she'd been outside earlier. She'd gotten the feeling that someone had been in the apartment while
she was out yesterday too.

You're paranoid, she told herself, shaking her head.

She'd been on her way to another clothing store, and hadn't
planned on stepping inside this place. But actually, it was a
pretty nice boutique. A few sale items had caught her eye.
She took them into the changing area—a curtained-off alcove with a full-length mirror at one end, and four little
booths, each also curtained off. The stalls looked empty. She
ducked inside one, hung a batch of items on the hook, then
closed the drape behind her.

The saleswoman wasn't looking at him. He stood by a
display of scarves, near a tall mirror. He could see his own
reflection, and behind him, the entrance to the fitting room
area. He took a sheer, pale pink scarf off the rack, discreetly
rolled it up, and stuffed it inside his coat pocket. Then he
picked out another scarf. This one was dark blue and very
pretty. The material was silky, but strong—strong enough to
choke the life out of someone.

He stashed the blue scarf in his other pocket, then wandered toward the changing room area.

Peeling off her ski jacket and sweater, she paused for a
moment. The curtain hooks clinked in the booth next to hers.
She had company. With a sigh, she stripped down to her bra
and panties, then tried on a short, blue cocktail dress.
Stepping out of the booth, she checked herself in the mirror
at the end of the alcove. The curtain fluttered on the occupied booth beside her. She didn't pay much attention. She

was scowling at her reflection. The blue dress made her look dumpy.

Retreating back into her stall, she started to climb out of the ugly dress. She heard the curtain next door whoosh open.

She tried on a form-fitting, pale green sweater. Pulling it over her head, she was blinded for a moment. She heard a curtain move again, and it sounded like *her* curtain. Something tickled her bare back, and it sent a wave of panic through her. Shuddering, she yanked the sweater over her head. She bumped against the wall and gaped at the curtain—still closed. Then she noticed the tag on the sweater— dangling from a long string. She let out a little laugh and brushed her hair out of her eyes. It had been the stupid clothes tag tickling her back. Good God, why was she so jumpy? What was her problem?

She tried on the sweater again, along with a pair of slacks. As she stepped into the pants, a sheer scarf drifted over the top of the curtain and gently landed on her head. Startled, she swiped it away and almost tripped. A shadow moved on the other side of the drape. "Hey!" she said, annoyed. "What—"

She didn't get another word out. The curtain ripped open, and she saw him. He had another scarf in his hands, this one all knotted up.

Before she knew what was happening, before she could scream, the scarf was around her throat.

God, no . . . please . . . wait . . . no . . .

The man was staring into her eyes. He had a determined look on his face, almost passionless—except for a tiny little smile on one side of his mouth.

She frantically clawed at his hands, and struggled. She fought as hard as she could.

The scarf tightened. She couldn't even wedge her fingers between the silky material and her throat. *This isn't happening . . . God . . . please . . .*

Her mouth open, she tried to breathe, but couldn't. It was too late.

She had already taken her last breath.

Lateasha, the twenty-four-year-old saleswoman in Attitude, was wearing a new dress today. It was a long-sleeve, off-the-shoulder, form-hugging red outfit. And it looked pretty damn good with her trim figure, the gold hoop earrings, and her hair pulled back in a bun. She was admiring herself in one of the store's full-length mirrors when she saw someone dart out of the changing area. Lateasha only caught a glimpse of him; then he ducked behind the tall jewelry display case, and threaded around some clothes racks to the front door. She'd busted enough shoplifters during her two years in retail. But this guy was different. He seemed like a phantom. He moved quickly, but no one else seemed to notice him.

He didn't set off the alarm. Lateasha wondered if she'd find a bunch of the store's antitheft tags cut off in one of the changing rooms.

Frowning, she parted the curtain to the back alcove and peeked down the little corridor. A sheer, pink scarf was on the floor—a few feet in front of the mirror.

Lateasha had pointed a customer—some dishwater blonde in a ski jacket—toward the changing rooms about ten minutes before. Was the woman still here? "Hello?" she called softly. "Is anyone back here?"

The curtains were halfway open, exposing three empty stalls. Only one drape was closed. "Hello? Anyone in here?" Lateasha pulled aside the curtain.

The blond woman stared back at her. It was a dead stare—from a purple, contorted face. The long, blue scarf was so tightly wound around her neck, some of her flesh folded over the material. It was like a hangman's noose, with another

loop in the scarf tied around the clothes hook. She wore a
pale green sweater from the store, and the slacks she'd been
trying on were bunched down around her knees. Her feet
didn't touch the ground.

She was suspended from the hook on the wall.

She hadn't uttered a sound.

Strutting down the street, he wiped the cold sweat from
his forehead and let out a chuckle. It had been amazing. As
he'd strangled Gillian's friend, she hadn't gasped or even
whimpered. Still she'd put up a damn good fight, struggling
and clawing at him. He glanced at the red marks on his
hands. The bitch had even drawn a little blood. But she hadn't
made a peep.

He remembered how in *For Everyone to See,* Gillian
McBride had referred to the changing-room murder as a
"silent strangulation." He was amazed at the dead-on accu-
racy of that description.

He breathed on his hands to warm them up a bit. The new
scratches made them extra-sensitive to the cold. Chicago's
Finest would probably discover some of his skin under Dianne
Garrity's fingernails, but so what? They would have a hard
time finding him after today.

He was still sweating, but felt exhilarated. Ducking into an
alley off Belmont, he pulled her wallet from his coat pocket.
He had fished it out of her purse after hanging her up on that
hook. The police would probably think robbery was a motive.

He opened the wallet, and saw her identification. "What
the fuck?" he whispered. "What is this?"

The woman had a Wisconsin driver's license. She was
from Milwaukee, and her name was Joyce Millikan.

Minutes later, he was barreling down the sidewalk, practically pushing people out of his way. He kept one hand in
his coat pocket. The woman's wallet was in his fist—almost

crushed to a pulp. He was outraged. That woman was *not* Dianne Garrity. It didn't make any sense. What the hell was she doing in that apartment?

Making his way to the brownstone apartment building, he headed around back again. He was so angry, he had to remind himself not to stomp up the back stairs. After taking a few calming breaths, he made a quiet ascent up to the third floor. He used a skeleton key on the kitchen door, as he had the previous morning.

When he'd poisoned the container of cream, he hadn't gone beyond the kitchen. Between the name on the front entrance buzzer and Gillian's *Black Ribbons* cover taped on the refrigerator door, he'd figured he had found the home of Gillian's friend, Dianne Garrity. But now he wasn't so sure.

He didn't have to go far to figure it out. In the front hallway, he studied a batch of framed photographs on the wall. One was of two teenage girls—both rather gawky and borderline homely. Still, the picture was cute. They wore party hats, and were laughing. One wore a back-brace. He wasn't sure if that was part of a joke or what. The other girl was unmistakably Gillian—before she started to get pretty. Gillian's friend was in most of the other snapshots—minus the back-brace. The brown-haired, slightly husky woman in the photos was obviously Dianne Garrity. There were other photos of Dianne with Gillian—both grown up and far more attractive. But the photo that caught his eye was of Dianne with a pretty, long-haired blonde in front of the Jefferson Memorial. It was Dianne's friend from Milwaukee, Joyce Millikan.

On the other side of the front door was a table—with a note on it. He read it, and had to chuckle. "Dear Joyce," it started; and then there were instructions about watering plants, operating the TV and DVD player, and a phone number in Palm Springs where she could be reached. "Have fun!" it concluded. "XXXXXXX—Dianne."

He hadn't killed Gillian McBride's "oldest and dearest friend." He'd strangled a woman who was house-sitting for

Gillian's "oldest and dearest friend" while she was in Palm Springs. He wondered if Gillian even knew Joyce Millikan. It could be days—or weeks—before Gillian even found out about the murder. And how much would that really matter to her?

If Gillian didn't know about this "silent strangulation" in the changing room, his work here in Chicago would be in vain.

He thought about the tree falling in the forest with no one hearing it. Gillian McBride needed to hear about this Joyce woman's murder—and soon.

He would see to it that she did.

Chapter 5

"Oh, that's just disgusting!" grumbled Ruth.

She got up from their window table at The Joe Bar Café, and hurried to the door. Ruth was a plump, black woman with a big voice and a big, shiny helmet of auburn hair. Everyone within a block must have heard her as she stepped out of the café and yelled: "Hey, you—with the baseball cap on backwards! Get your sorry ass back here and pick up your trash!"

Grimacing, Gillian now sat alone at the table and watched the scene outside. Three young men, who looked like gang members, had strutted past the café a few moments before. One of them had been sipping from a twenty-four-ounce soda container with a Burger King logo on it. He'd unceremoniously tossed the container on the sidewalk, never breaking stride with his buddies.

Ruth didn't like litterbugs—as this young man, and nearly everyone on the block, was now discovering.

"Did you hear me? Get back here!"

He swiveled around and flipped her the finger. "Yo, fuck off, bitch!" he called.

"Come here and say that to my face. Don't run away when I'm talking to you! What, are you afraid of me, you weasel? Afraid of an old lady? Get your skinny ass back here, and pick this up!"

Watching from inside the café, Gillian rolled her eyes and took another sip of coffee.

"Is she going to be okay out there?" The emaciated young woman who had taken their order was now standing beside Gillian and gaping out the window. She had piercings in her nostril and eyebrow. "Think I should call the police?"

"She *is* the police," Gillian replied. "Or at least, she *was*. She's retired now. Give it another minute, and let's just see what happens."

Gillian had been through this before with Ruth. Whenever Ruth Langford saw a wrong, she had to right it. Litterbugs, illegal parkers, people who didn't clean up their dog's poop—they were all gambling with the wrath of Ruth when they committed their petty transgressions in her presence.

The young man—with his baseball cap on backwards, and the waist of his jeans down below his butt—was goaded by his two buddies to go face-to-face with the old lady who had been screaming at him. One hand holding onto his jeans to keep them from falling down, the boy stood, slouch-shouldered in front of Ruth, apparently half-listening as she talked with him. Ruth even poked him in the chest with her finger a few times. He nodded tiredly, almost ashamedly. He shuffled back to where he'd discarded the twenty-four-ounce drink container, swiped it off the sidewalk, then marched to a nearby trash can and threw it in there.

A few people who were watching from in front of the movie theater across the street applauded. Ruth patted the young man's shoulder. He waved her away, then ambled back to his friends, who were laughing—and applauding with the other spectators.

"I think we're all right," Gillian told the barista.

Ruth strode back into the café, and sat down at the table.

"Did you catch the pants on that kid? The zipper was down at his knees, for God's sakes. I've seen some stupid fashion fads come and go, but that one takes the cake. Cops in all the major cities keep finding these slain gang members with their pants down around their ankles. These idiots can't run away from rival gangs with their pants riding down so low. Morons!"

Gillian grinned at her. "Feel better now? Did you blow off some steam?"

"I do, and I did. And that kid will think twice before he tosses his trash on the sidewalk again." Ruth sipped her Coke. "Now, where was I?"

"You were talking to a friend with the NYPD about the Jennifer Gilderhoff case. And by the way, thanks again for doing this, Ruth."

"No thanks necessary, hon. I live for this kind of shit." She leaned forward, and her voice dropped to a whisper. "So Jennifer flew from Portland to New York two days before Halloween. She was traveling alone, and registered at the Best Western Hospitality House in Manhattan. Jennifer met with her publisher for dinner the night after her arrival. Halloween night, she was seen leaving the Best Western in a saucy flamenco-dancer getup, complete with castanets. She took a cab to a Greenwich Village bar, where later she was spotted with someone dressed as Zorro. No one could come up with a decent description of the guy, except to say he was white, about thirty, and looked like—Zorro. Duh! Anyway, Jennifer and her 'Z-Man' caught a cab outside the bar. The address Zorro gave the driver was for a travel agency that has been closed for two months. The driver said this character flew out of the taxi and ran into an alley, and only then did he realize the girl in back had been stabbed."

The barista arrived with their lunch orders. Ruth started digging into her crepes. But Gillian didn't touch her salad.

"So Jennifer must have been dating this guy who stabbed her," she said.

"Not necessarily," Ruth replied, her mouth full. "According to Jennifer's friends and her family, she hadn't been seeing anybody recently. And she didn't know a soul in New York—except her editor."

"But their Halloween costumes complemented each other. They must have planned it ahead of time together. It's too much of a coincidence—"

"It was *Halloween*, Gill," Ruth interrupted. "Jennifer bought the dress at a little thrift shop in St. Mark's Place that very afternoon. The receipt was in her purse. The salesperson said she came in there alone."

"Well, maybe this 'Zorro' killer sent her there to buy the outfit," Gillian argued.

"The cops think the coincidence of the costumes is probably what brought them together at the bar that night. The taxi driver and several witnesses in the bar said it looked like a pickup situation." Ruth glanced across the table at Gillian's plate. "You're not eating. Huh, rabbit food. Lord, they have the best crepes in the world here, and you order salad. No wonder you're so skinny."

Gillian obligingly took a bite of her salad, then put down her fork. "Then it's just a coincidence that I knew Jennifer— and that this 'Zorro' stabbing is straight out of *The Mark of Death*? You don't think this guy was at all influenced by the stabbing scene in my novel?"

Ruth shifted in her chair. "I don't mean to put you down, hon, but no. Sales-wise, that book didn't exactly make Stephen King nervous. A thriller, whether it's a book or a movie, has to be a hit before it spawns any real-life imitators. And a 'hit' *The Mark of Death* was not. I had to explain to my cop friend who you were and what the book was about, and he still didn't see a connection. Sorry, hon."

Gillian didn't say anything. She just picked at her salad.

"This happened on the other side of the country. You barely knew Jennifer Whatever-her-last-name-is. She took a class from you, one lousy semester—what—two years ago?

Her being in a coma right now has nothing to do with you or your books."

"Still, isn't it a bit bizarre someone pretending to be my agent would send me that clipping?"

Her mouth twisting to one side, Ruth seemed to mull over the question for a moment. "When your agent left this voice message today, had she asked around at the agency to see if anyone else there might have sent you the article?"

"She didn't say," Gillian muttered.

"Well, check with her. I bet somebody at the agency sent it to you—an assistant, or a sub-rights person. You get notes and memos from other people at that agency, don't you?"

Sighing, Gillian nodded. "Maybe you're right." She turned to stare out the window of the café. A couple of raindrops hit the pane.

Ruth shoved her plate aside. "Lord, you should see yourself. You asked for my connections and my expertise on this. So I'm telling you, you're not in any way responsible for that stabbing in New York. You should be relieved. Instead, you look like your pet squirrel just died."

"There's something else," Gillian admitted. "I got a very unsettling, anonymous e-mail last night from someone claiming to have located Barry."

Ruth frowned. "Exactly what did it say?"

"It said, 'Gillian, I found your husband.' When I tried to respond, it bounced back to me marked 'invalid address.'"

Ruth sipped her Coke. "Could be a crank."

Gillian shrugged. "When I read that message, I didn't know whether to be scared or happy or sad—or what."

"You already know how I feel about the Barry situation," Ruth said. "You should divorce him on grounds of desertion and have a long-overdue fling or two—or seven. But you don't want to hear that. You still care about him, even though the rat ran out on you and your son. Honey, you've been in a holding pattern for two years. Move on already."

Gillian rubbed the back of her neck. "You're right, Ruth.

I don't want to hear it. Let's not talk about this anymore, okay?"

"Tactless Ruth strikes again," her friend muttered. "Listen, if you get another one of those e-mails, let me know. Maybe I can dig up somebody over at the East Precinct who's a computer expert. It's worth a shot."

"Thanks, Ruth," she replied quietly.

As she stepped outside with her friend, Gillian thought about how everything happening now seemed reminiscent of two years ago, when Barry had disappeared. She'd been teaching that class, and Jennifer Gilderhoff had been one of her students. It had been such an awful time to find herself suddenly alone. A series of homicides had plagued the campus where she'd taught her night class. The victims had been students at the college, and their age didn't matter to the killer—as long as they were women. The predator had made the campus his hunting grounds—as well as his dumping site. He'd left their bodies in various locations in and around the college. It baffled police, and spread terror throughout the area. He'd dressed his victims—grown women, all of them—in Catholic schoolgirl uniforms: a white blouse, madras kilt, knee socks, and saddle shoes. By the second murder, people were already calling him The Schoolgirl Killer. For several weeks, every woman at that community college had feared for her life.

"You look like your mind is about a million miles away," she heard Ruth remark.

Suddenly, Gillian was aware of her friend standing beside her—in front of the café. She felt the light, misty rain on her face. "I was thinking back to two years ago—and everything that happened, including the Schoolgirl Murders. I remember before Barry left, I thought I was getting an ulcer. I had this constant feeling of dread in the pit of my stomach. And it wouldn't go away, not for a few months. It was like—evil all around me." She shrugged. "I know it sounds crazy."

"You were going through a lot back then, hon," Ruth

replied, patting her shoulder. "But you've survived. And they caught the Schoolgirl Killer. That case is closed. Maybe it's time to make a decision about your AWOL husband and close the book on that too. Screw the past and all the stuff that happened two years ago. Get on with your life, Gill." Ruth nudged her. "Y'know, we're standing here in the rain. Do you want a lift home?"

"No, thanks, I'm fine," Gillian said. "I can walk home. It's only a few blocks. Thanks, Ruth."

The two women hugged good-bye on the street corner. Gillian watched Ruth start toward her car. She hadn't told her friend about something else that had happened last night. She hadn't told her that the knots in the pit of her stomach had come back.

The automatic light over the cellar door went on as he crept around the back of Gillian's duplex. At one o'clock in the afternoon, it shouldn't have been noticeable, but the skies had turned dark within the last few minutes. A silent, gentle rain came down. The ravine behind the gray cedar-shaked house remained oddly still.

Gillian wasn't home. He'd watched her step out an hour ago.

He skulked past the kitchen window toward the garbage cans and the recycling bin. He wanted to know what her kid had thrown away last night—and why he'd been so secretive about it.

The two large aluminum garbage cans stood between the kitchen window and Gillian's rosebushes. He opened the lid to the first, and dug out a couple of lawn bags full of yard waste. This wasn't it. He tried the next can—and found a big, garbage-filled Hefty bag. It stank. But beneath it lay a small, black plastic bag—resting on top of some loose debris. The kid had taped shut the bag's opening.

He pulled at the plastic until the bag ripped. It felt like

some loose papers. He reached inside, but then quickly pulled out his hand. His fingertips were smudged with black soot. The kid had burned something—and obviously gone to a lot of trouble hiding what was left of it.

Reaching inside the bag again, he pulled out a half-burnt scrap of paper. It looked like part of a magazine article.

Suddenly, he heard footsteps—someone climbing the steps to the front porch. "Shit," he murmured. Tucking the plastic bag under his arm, he crept around toward the front of the duplex. He hovered near the side of the house, and peeked around the corner. He couldn't see Gillian, but he recognized the back of her trench coat as she stopped to check the mailbox. Though less than twenty feet away, he wanted a better look at her. He took another step forward.

The automatic light over the cellar door went on.

Gillian must have seen it too, because she glanced over her shoulder.

He turned and ran into her backyard—and along the ravine's edge. Then he zigzagged through some bushes into the neighbor's yard. All the while, he clutched the plastic bag under his arm.

And all the while, he was grinning.

Gillian slammed the door shut behind her. Fumbling for the dead-bolt lock, she accidentally dropped her purse and keys. The contents of her bag spilled across the living room floor. Gillian almost tripped over the mess as she ran for the phone in the kitchen. Snatching the cordless off its cradle, she switched it on and anxiously listened for a dial tone. At least he hadn't cut the phone lines.

She glanced out the kitchen window, and spotted a figure darting through the bushes into the neighbor's yard. Gillian didn't get a look at his face or what he was wearing. *Dark clothes, Caucasian, medium build, dark hair*—that was all she could tell the police. Even when she'd spotted him from the front porch moments before, she'd merely caught a glimpse of some man hovering near the cellar steps. If the automatic light hadn't gone on, she might not have noticed him at all. His face and everything else about him had been a blur. All she'd thought about was getting away, ducking into the apartment and locking him out.

Now she watched him scurry across the neighbor's lawn. Then he disappeared behind a clump of trees at the ravine's edge. Staring out the kitchen window, Gillian noticed one of the garbage can lids on the lawn. She leaned closer to the glass, and stood on the tips of her toes. Right below the window, a Hefty bag full of trash was leaning against the garbage can.

In her hand, the cordless phone's dial tone continued to hum. Gillian plopped down at the breakfast table. Numbly, she stared at the phone. She'd been through this before. For a few weeks following Barry's disappearance, she'd often come home to find somebody had gone through her garbage. They'd leave the trash cans tipped over, with torn bags and debris strewn across the back lawn. Gillian sometimes dug into her mailbox to discover personal letters that had been ripped open. The notes would be out of their envelopes, some even crumpled up and discarded on the porch floor.

The people looking for Barry weren't very subtle about it.

Gillian remembered one spring afternoon, driving home from the supermarket. She still had the Saturn back then. She was chiding herself for having just bought a six-pack of Heineken, Barry's beer of choice. He'd been missing for two weeks, and hadn't contacted her. Buying his favorite beer wouldn't bring him home any quicker.

Gillian stepped inside the apartment with two grocery bags. She started toward the kitchen, then stopped abruptly. In the mirror over the living room sofa, she saw someone's reflection. A stranger stood in her kitchen, studying the photographs on her refrigerator door. Gillian's heart seemed to stop for a moment. She backed toward the front door, which was still slightly ajar. All the while, her eyes stayed riveted on the mirror—and the short, black-haired man with a goatee reflected in it. Suddenly, he turned and his dark eyes locked with hers. Gillian dropped the grocery bags, and reached for the door.

The image in the mirror vanished. All at once, he was on her.

Gillian started to scream, but he slapped his hand over her mouth. She felt the door slam against her back. "Where is he, Mrs. Tanner?" he asked, his face an inch away from hers. She could smell cigarettes on his breath. "Where's your husband?"

He kept her pinned against the door. Gillian felt the weight of his body crushing her. He slowly moved his hand down from her mouth to her neck. He started to squeeze her throat.

"I don't know where he is," Gillian managed to say. She couldn't catch her breath. "I swear, I don't."

He let out a curtailed grunt, a sort of insolent laugh.

Gillian stared into his dark eyes, and suddenly her fear turned to anger. She was mad at these creeps for harassing her and invading her home. And she was furious at Barry for deserting her.

"I'm telling you the truth!" she growled. "You and your low-life friends can keep going through my garbage and reading my mail. And if you discover something—like where my husband is or when he's coming back—you can tell me. Okay? Because I haven't heard from the son of a bitch since he ran away two weeks ago."

The man let go of her throat. Stepping back, he glanced down at the groceries spilled on the floor. He nudged one of the bags with his foot. A couple of the Heineken bottles had broken, and beer leaked onto the carpet. "So you don't know where Barry is or when he's coming back, huh?" he said. "Then what's this? You don't drink this stuff. You drink wine. I know, because I've been through your garbage."

"Yes, you and the other rats," Gillian muttered, glaring at him.

He kicked one of the broken beer bottles. Shards of glass flew across the living room carpet. "Why did you buy the beer, Mrs. Tanner?"

"Because I'm stupid," she said evenly. "And maybe too sentimental for my own good. I bought it, hoping he'd surprise me and come home. But that's not going to happen, not any time soon. I realize that now. Maybe you and your friends should come to the same realization."

He gazed at her for a moment. Finally, he pulled a pack of cigarettes from his shirt pocket. "You know something, Mrs. Tanner?" he said finally. "I believe you. I really do. We might have to try another tactic. Maybe your kid knows where his old man is."

"You stay away from my son," she whispered.

He lit his cigarette and tossed the match amid the spilt groceries on the carpet. The flame hadn't gone out yet, and it started licking the edge of the grocery bag. "Or you'll do what?" he retorted.

"I'll have the police on you so goddamn fast, you won't know what hit you."

"You wouldn't do that," he replied with a cocky smile. He stepped toward Gillian and blew some smoke in her face. "Barry's in as much trouble with the cops as he is with me and my buddies. Step aside, Mrs. Tanner." He glanced down at the mess of groceries on the floor. One of the bags was catching on fire. "You might want to put some water on that."

Gillian recoiled as he caressed her neck with the back of his hand. He smirked at her, then opened the door and stepped outside.

Hearing the door shut behind her, Gillian hurried into the kitchen and grabbed a saucepan from the drying rack. She filled it with water, rushed back into the living room, and doused the fire before it spread any further. Still, the smoke alarm went off. The detector was on the ceiling outside Ethan's bedroom door, but the loud, obnoxious beeping echoed though the entire apartment. Gillian ran to the hallway. With the saucepan, she swiped at the alarm and knocked off the plastic cover. She hit it again. The battery flew out, ricocheted off the wall, and landed on the floor.

Silence.

The man was gone, the fire was out, and she'd stifled the smoke alarm. But Gillian was still shaking horribly. She made her way back to the kitchen, set the pan in the sink, and reached for the cordless phone. She sat down at the breakfast table with the phone in her trembling hand. She knew about Barry's *trouble* with the police. But Barry was gone, and this man had invaded their home and he'd threatened to go after her son.

She dialed 911, and as calmly as she could, Gillian explained to the operator who she was and what just happened.

Ten minutes later, a young, husky, baby-faced cop with a strawberry-blond crew cut showed up at her door. He walked around outside the house to make sure Gillian's intruder had indeed left. He even helped her clean up some of the mess on the living room floor—the broken beer bottles and half-burnt, soggy bags. Since Barry's disappearance, the police had been harassing Gillian almost as much as these hoods. She'd become very wary of Seattle's Finest. But this polite, young cop, who kept calling her "ma'am," restored her faith in local law enforcement. She told him about the intruder threatening to go after Ethan.

"Well, ma'am, it's almost three o'clock," the officer said. "If you want to go pick up your son at his school, I can follow you in the patrol car and make sure this guy doesn't show up again. Would that help?"

Gillian wanted to hug him. "Yes, thank you very much."

They arrived at Ethan's school a bit early. Gillian pulled

up about half a block behind the school buses. In the rearview mirror, she watched the squad car park behind her. The young policeman got out of his vehicle. He came around to the passenger side of her Saturn and opened the door. "Do you see this guy who threatened you anywhere on the premises, ma'am?"

Gillian took a careful look around. "No, thank God."

To her surprise, the policeman climbed into her passenger seat and closed the door. "I doubt he'll show," the cop said, glancing toward the school. "But if he does, I'll grab him."

Gillian saw the school's main doors open. The children began to pour out. She recognized a couple of Ethan's classmates. Biting her lip, she watched for her son.

"There's Ethan now," the cop said. "I see him."

Gillian spotted him too—wandering out the door alone after a group of taller boys. She hated to see him by himself. He had one good friend, Craig Merchant, who was quite athletic and popular. Ethan was so skinny and uncoordinated. They made an odd couple, but they'd been best friends since the fourth grade.

As Gillian watched Ethan emerge from the school alone, she almost wanted to explain to the cop that her son wasn't totally friendless. But then she noticed the young officer staring intently at Ethan. Something didn't seem right. "How did you recognize my son?" she murmured, squinting at the cop. "Out of the kids there, you were able to point him out."

The young cop turned to her with an icy stare. A tiny smile flickered across his face. "Oh, we know him, ma'am," he said quietly. "And if you don't start cooperating with my buddies, you'll never see Ethan again. Now, where the fuck is your husband?"

"I—I don't know where he is, I swear. You have to believe me." Gillian helplessly shook her head and started to cry. "I'm at the point right now where I'd turn in Barry just to get you people off my back and have a little peace and quiet."

This wasn't exactly true. But now her son's life was in jeopardy, and nothing else mattered. She would have said anything they wanted to hear.

His head down, Ethan headed toward his school bus.

The young officer was staring at him. He pulled his gun out of his holster. "Honk your horn and wave at him," he said.

"What?" Gillian asked, bewildered.

"Do it," he grunted.

She tapped her horn twice. Several children glanced in her direction—including Ethan. Gillian rolled down her window and waved at him. All the while, every muscle in her body was rigid, and she felt a knot in her stomach. She hoped against hope that for some reason Ethan would decide to run away. Maybe some sixth sense would warn him of the danger.

For a moment, Ethan seemed confused. Cocking his head to one side, he stared at the Saturn, but didn't move.

"Keep waving at him, Mrs. Tanner," the cop said. "Now, here's the deal. Before your son gets here, I'll step out of the vehicle. I'll look after your boy. You'll drive to 811 Olive Way, where my friend is waiting. '811 Olive Way'—say it."

"811 Olive Way," Gillian repeated, still waving at Ethan. Tears stung her eyes.

"My friend will tell you what to do, and you'll do it. Otherwise, this is the last you'll see of your son. Do you understand, Mrs. Tanner?"

She stopped waving to Ethan and turned to the cop. "What can I do? I don't know anything! For God's sakes, please—"

"I can shoot him right here in front of you, Mrs. Tanner. And then I'll shoot you. I'll say you grabbed my gun and went crazy."

"No, no, please—"

"You were acting irrational after your 911 call, and I followed you here. Your husband is a criminal, wanted by the police. They'll believe me. Is that what you want?" The

young policeman opened the car door. "You have exactly fifteen minutes to get to 811 Olive Way. If you're not there in
fifteen, my friend's going to call me, and I'll cut Ethan's
throat." He stepped out of the car. "And don't try to call the
police again, because you'll get somebody else just like me.
Now, move." He shut the car door.

Through the windshield, Gillian saw Ethan—halfway to
the car—stopping in his tracks. He seemed baffled at the site
of a cop climbing out of his mother's Saturn.

The young officer tapped on the hood of her car, then
waved her forward.

"Oh, God, please," Gillian whispered. She pulled away
from the curb, and watched Ethan gaping back at her.

"Mom?" he called.

Biting her lip, she passed him. Then she passed the
school bus and glanced in the rearview mirror. The young
cop was approaching Ethan.

"HEY! Watch it!"

Someone let out a high-pitched shriek.

Gillian suddenly noticed a woman with two schoolchildren
right in front of her. The woman was trying to pull the kids
out of the way. One child was screaming. Gillian slammed
on the brakes. Her tires made a loud screech.

"Stupid!" the woman yelled at her. "What's wrong with
you? You're in a school zone!"

"I'm sorry!" Gillian called back, tears in her eyes. Shaking,
she glanced in the rearview mirror again. She couldn't see
Ethan or the cop anymore. She checked her wristwatch: 3:18.
Fifteen minutes, the cop said. She had to get moving. She
had no choice. Gillian felt her stomach lurch as she stepped
on the accelerator.

She knew 811 Olive Way. It was close to downtown,
about five miles from Ethan's school. If she didn't get held
up by traffic or too many stoplights, she could make it in
time. Gillian turned down one of the side streets to get away

from the school, where so many parents had double-parked their SUV's and children milled around. As soon as the road opened up, Gillian pressed harder on the gas. All the while, she kept a lookout for patrol cars. She couldn't afford to wait around for an officer to write her a speeding ticket. And if she arrived at 811 Olive Way with a patrol car on her tail, Ethan was as good as dead.

She drove on a bridge over the freeway. I-5 was jammed, not a good sign. It could affect traffic on the side streets. Gillian hit her first stoplight, and impatiently drummed her fingertips on the steering wheel while waiting it out. "C'mon, c'mon," she murmured. "Turn green, damn it."

She glanced at the digital clock on the dashboard: 3:23. *About ten minutes.* She sat there, trying to remember to breathe. But she kept thinking about Ethan—and the confused, forlorn look on his face as she drove past him. She'd left him there with that crooked cop. What was he doing to Ethan right now?

The light switched to green. Gillian turned onto Lakeview, which ran alongside the congested freeway. The car in front of her took a right, and the road became clear ahead. Gillian sailed through a yellow light, and followed the street as it curved under the freeway and zigzagged up a hill. The speed limit was thirty; but her speedometer hovered just above forty-five. Her knuckles turned white as she clutched the wheel. Someone at the freeway exit started to turn in front of her, but Gillian didn't slow down. She swerved around them. She ignored the car horn blaring at her.

But she couldn't ignore the awful feeling in her gut. She kept thinking about Ethan. She shouldn't have left him back there with that cop. But what else could she have done? Called the cop's bluff? She'd seen the gun in his hand; she'd seen his eyes. He wasn't bluffing. She had no choice—except to do what he said.

The dashboard clock read 3:28. She had five minutes to

cover two more miles. But there were several traffic lights along the way.

Gillian barely hesitated for a stop sign on Belmont Avenue. She turned left and floored it up another hill. Her tires squealed as she took a sharp right onto Bellevue—a long residential stretch without any stop signs.

811 Olive Way. She wondered who—and what—was waiting for her there. The area had some car dealerships. Gillian didn't remember any apartment buildings or bars along that block. She wondered where this rendezvous was supposed to take place. The sleazy cop said they wanted her to *do* something for them. She'd already made it clear she didn't know Barry's whereabouts. What exactly did they want her to *do*?

Three blocks from Olive Way, she had to slow down for a traffic light. One car, an SUV, was waiting in front of her at the intersection.

The light changed. The SUV didn't move. Gillian tapped her horn. She could see the driver was a woman—on her cell phone. Finally, the SUV moved, but at a slow crawl. "Get off the phone and drive!" Gillian yelled—to no one, since her window was closed.

She saw a break in oncoming traffic, and quickly cut into the other lane and passed the idiot in the SUV. Gillian sped into the next intersection, Olive Way. She swerved to the right, and then sailed through another yellow light. She glanced at the clock. She should have been there two minutes ago.

"You have exactly fifteen minutes to get to 811 Olive Way. If you're not there in fifteen, my friend's going to call me, and I'll cut Ethan's throat."

Gillian was crying. She was in the eight-hundred block, with car dealerships on both sides of the street. But she couldn't find the address. She passed 805, then 819. No 811. She was like a crazy woman. "Oh, God, please . . . please . . . where is it?" she screamed.

She was three minutes late. Ethan could already be dead.

Finally, she turned down an alley between two car lots. Someone emerged from a little alcove off the alleyway, and Gillian slammed on her brakes. He was talking on a cell phone—and smirking at her. Hunched over the wheel, Gillian caught her breath and stared back at the short, dark-haired man who had invaded her home less than an hour before.

With a flick of the wrist, he closed his cell phone. He strolled over toward the car. Gillian wiped the tears from her eyes, took a deep breath, and then rolled down her window. "Before we go any further," she said steadily. "I want some reassurance that my son is all right. I need to talk with him—"

"Shut your hole," the squat man growled. "You're in no position to make demands, Mrs. Tanner. You'll talk to your son when I say you can." He took a step back and glanced along the length of her Saturn. "Where are the papers for this heap—at home or in the glove compartment?"

Gillian didn't understand. "They're here—in the glove compartment. Why?"

"You're going to sell this car, and give me the money. Consider it your down payment to pay off a debt, Mrs. Tanner. Now, I had a chance to check the odometer a few days ago. The Blue Book value for a two-year-old Saturn with forty-nine thousand miles is about seven grand." He nodded toward the used-car dealership next door. "So—you go get me some money, Mrs. Tanner. And if you come back here with anything less than sixty-one hundred, I'll call my buddy and have him slice your little brat a brand-new smile—right across his throat."

Two minutes later, as Gillian pulled into the used-car lot's customer parking area, a thin, sporty-handsome woman with short-cropped brown hair stepped out of the building to greet her. She introduced herself as Roseann, and invited Gillian into the office for some coffee. Gillian glanced back across the lot—with the wires overhead, displaying little triangle-shaped, plastic flags that flapped in the wind. She didn't see the man in the alley across the way. "Um, no, thank you," Gillian answered distractedly. "I'm in kind of a hurry. The truth is, I—well, I need some money, and I don't really use my car much. It's in excellent shape. I think I have all the paperwork you'll need."

Roseann gave her a pleasant smile and nodded. "Well, then, I'll just have our mechanic give your Saturn the once-over. And meanwhile, we'll step into my office and take a look at all the legal stuff. You sure I can't get you some coffee?"

Roseann had a tiny office with framed certificates and awards on the wall—along with photos of her Dalmatians. Sitting in front of Roseann's desk, Gillian didn't touch her coffee. She couldn't stop thinking about Ethan. Where were they keeping him?

"Are you feeling all right, Gillian?" the car dealer asked, glancing up from the documents.

Gillian worked up a smile and nodded. But she kept a tight grip on the armrests of the chair. It felt as if the walls of the tiny office were closing in on her. Even when Roseann stepped out to consult with the mechanic, Gillian still couldn't breathe right. She just needed to get out of there—and see Ethan again.

Roseann breezed back into the office. "I can offer you fifty-four hundred, Gillian. It's slightly below the Blue Book price, but I feel—"

"I need sixty-one hundred dollars," Gillian interrupted, her voice cracking. "I'm in a horrible bind here. I have to come up with that amount, no less. And I need it today—before the banks close. I know the Blue Book value is around seven thousand. If I can't get sixty-one hundred here, I'll go somewhere else. And I really don't want to. There isn't enough time. Please—Roseann, I'm begging you, help me . . ."

Frowning, the woman leaned back in her desk chair and tapped the eraser end of a pencil on her desktop. She locked

eyes with Gillian, and after a moment, her expression soft-
ened. Roseann let out a sigh.

Walking away from the dealership's lot, Gillian didn't
look back at her old car. She was thinking about Ethan,
whose stocking cap and gloves were in a bag along with several other personal items that had been emptied out of the
Saturn. Gillian clutched the bag to her chest and headed toward the alleyway. She peeked into the little alcove, where
the creepy man with the goatee was leaning against a
Dumpster and smoking a cigarette.

Gillian opened her purse. She pulled out the check from
the dealership, and handed it to him. "I had them make it out
to cash," she said. "Sixty-one hundred. Now, will you take
me to my son?"

The man tossed aside his cigarette. He studied the check,
folded it, and slipped it inside his shirt pocket. "Screw you,"
he said, finally. "Take yourself to him—if you can find where
we dumped the little brat."

Gillian glared at the short, smarmy man. The bag and her
purse dropped out of her hands. All at once, she lunged at
him and started hitting him in the face. In a blind rage, she
kept swinging her fists. Her knuckles stung, and she felt
warm, wet blood on them. Whether it was her blood or his
didn't matter. She just kept pummeling his face and chest.

Suddenly, he grabbed her by the shoulders and slammed
her against the Dumpster. It knocked the wind out of her.
Gillian stared at him and blinked. Only then did she notice
the blood streaming out of his nose, coating his teeth, and
mingling with his goatee.

"You sorry bitch," he growled. He drew back and punched
her in the face—again and again. Gillian felt the hammerlike
blows. But she couldn't see; everything was just bright,
blinding flashes against a murky black. She couldn't hear beyond the ringing in her ears. After the first couple of punches,
she felt nothing—except her mouth filling with blood.

She would have fallen down if he hadn't pinned her against the Dumpster. He paused for a moment. Gillian coughed, and sprayed blood. Her head throbbed, and she tried to get her vision back. That was when he delivered a sucker punch to her stomach. She lurched forward and fell to her knees. She couldn't get a breath. She thought she was going to die.

She was vaguely aware of him shaking out her purse and taking money from her wallet. "Seventeen bucks?" he said, disgusted. "Shit . . ."

She couldn't hear any more; just fragments past the high-pitched ringing in her ears. He said something about this down payment buying her a little time. Then he started to walk away.

Gillian was still on her hands and knees—on the cold, filthy pavement. She finally got a breath, and managed to call to him: "Where's . . . my . . . son?"

He ignored her, and kept walking.

"WHERE'S . . . MY . . . SON?" she shrieked. But the man was gone.

A loose piece of paper from her purse fluttered past her. Gillian grabbed it, and tried to focus on the printing. Blood from her hand smeared on the white paper. It was a listing of the night class she taught at the community college. Ruth Langford was on that list—along with her address, e-mail, and phone number. She'd already had Ruth over to the apartment once—a few weeks back. She'd asked the retired police detective for some technical advice on her new book. Gillian needed Ruth's help again.

The creep with the goatee had taken all her bills, but he'd left behind some change. Gillian gathered the coins from the pavement. She managed to pull herself up.

At a phone station a half block away, Gillian called Ruth. Passing motorists gaped at her from inside their cars. Gillian knew she was a sight, beaten and bloody, leaning against the Plexiglas shell of the phone station. The bagful of personal effects from the Saturn was at her feet. She heard a click on the other end of the line. "Yes, hello?"

"Ruth? This is Gillian McBride. I—I need you to do me a favor—"

"Gillian, you sound awful. What's wrong?"

She started to cry. "Ruth, I need you to help me find my son."

Ruth eventually found him. He was at home.

The stocky, blond cop had approached Ethan, saying his mother was needed to answer some questions at police head-quarters, questions about his dad. The cop had instructed Ethan to take the bus home, and wait for his mother there. Ethan had done what the policeman had told him to do.

Ethan was very mindful of Ruth too. He rode in the car with his mother's friend to the used-car dealership on Olive Way.

Roseann had wanted to call an ambulance. But Gillian said she was all right. She used the bathroom at the dealer-ship to clean herself up. She tossed several bloodstained paper towels in the garbage. Gillian found herself telling the same lie Barry had used on her shortly before they'd left Chicago. She convinced the saleswoman that she'd been mugged, but assured her there was no need to worry about the check from the dealership because she'd hidden it in her bra.

The lie about a random mugging was passed on to Ethan as well. But Gillian told Ruth the truth.

"The sooner you dump this in the lap of the law, the bet-ter off you'll be," Ruth whispered. They sat at the kitchen table. Ruth nursed one of the surviving Heinekens from the six-pack that was dropped. Gillian held a bag of frozen peas to her face—to lessen the swelling. They spoke in hushed tones, because Ethan was in the living room watching TV.

"I'll be with you when you report it," Ruth continued. "I'll make sure they do right by you, hon. We'll see to it that Internal Affairs pounces all over this crooked patrolman's ass. And then we'll go after these *Sopranos*-wannabes who've been hounding you—"

"We can't," Gillian argued, shaking her sore head. "Obviously, these people have police connections. Going to the cops right now could only make matters worse."

"Hon, these are small-timers. They spent all afternoon putting the screws on you for a measly six grand and some change. Hell, any self-respecting mobster wouldn't waste his time and manpower. They probably have one or two crummy loser-cops on their payroll, and made one of them request patrol duty in this neighborhood after Barry pulled his disappearing act. We have a good shot at getting these guys—*if* you'd go to the police." She sighed. "If you don't report this, it'll just happen again."

Gillian took the bag of frozen peas away from her face for a moment. "The guy in the alley told me that the sixty-one hundred dollars bought me some time. I don't think they're going to—"

"Oh, come on, Gill!" Ruth interrupted. She glanced in the direction of the living room, where Ethan was still glued to *The Simpsons* on TV. She leaned closer to Gillian and lowered her voice. "Did you really believe him? I mean, he's not exactly a reliable source, is he? This is the same guy who had you speeding through rush hour traffic so you could meet him in some alley within exactly fifteen minutes or they'd *cut your son's throat*. They were jerking you around, honey, putting you through the paces for their own amusement."

Gillian started to cry, and it made her head throb even worse. "They're threatening Ethan." She pointed to her battered face. "*This* is what happened when I called the police today. But I feel lucky, because Ethan's all right. I'm not pushing my luck, Ruth."

In fact, the short, dark-haired creep who had beaten her up was actually true to his word. While Gillian felt a constant police presence around the duplex, the mobsters—or whatever they were—had more or less disappeared, for a while anyway.

As she sat at the kitchen table with the phone in her hand, Gillian thought back to that discussion with Ruth in this same spot nearly two years ago. Not much had really changed. She'd published a few more books. She still hadn't heard a word from Barry. And these hoodlums were back.

Gillian knew why, too. Someone had called the house one night several weeks after the Saturn-selling episode. Ethan had picked up the line. They'd convinced the ten-year-old that his family had been entered in a radio contest. From Ethan, they'd gotten the dates of his birthday, his parents' birthdays, and their wedding anniversary. Later, as each of these landmark dates approached, Gillian would catch little telltale signs that she and Ethan were being watched again: more mail tampered with; garbage can lids askew and debris scattered in the backyard; a sudden rash of phone calls asking for Barry and hang-ups.

These unsettling events—along with carols on the radio— came at Christmastime, too. Obviously, they figured Barry might get sentimental and want to come home for one of these special occasions. Or maybe they thought he'd send a card—with a postmark on the envelope or a PO box where he could be reached.

A special occasion was coming up. Ethan's fourteenth birthday was only a week away.

Gillian shouldn't have been so surprised to find someone lurking near her front porch a few minutes ago. She should have expected it—along with someone rummaging through her mail and garbage again. They counted on Barry contacting his family for his son's birthday.

Despite everything, Gillian secretly hoped against hope for the same thing.

"If you'd like to make a call, please hang up and try again. If you need help, hang up and then dial your operator . . ."

The cordless phone started to make a loud, pulsating

alarm sound. Gillian switched it off, then got up from the breakfast table.

She wasn't going to call the police, not if there was even a small chance of Barry coming back soon.

As she replaced the receiver on the cradle, she noticed there were four new calls on the Caller ID box. All of them were from her friend, Dianne Garrity in Chicago.

Gillian had thought Dianne was still vacationing in Palm Springs. She checked the answering machine: no messages. The four calls from Dianne's home phone in Chicago were all made within minutes of each other. All of them were hang-ups.

Gillian switched on the phone again, then dialed area code 773, and Dianne's number. She got her friend's answering machine: *"Hi, this is Dianne, and due to personal and technical difficulties, I'm unable to come to the phone right now. So leave me a message after this slightly irritating beep. Thanks a bunch."*

Beep.

"Hi, Di. It's Gill. Looks like you tried to call me this morning. I thought you were still in Palm Springs. By the way, thanks for the postcard. Anyway, give a call and *leave a message* if I'm not in. Take care and we'll talk later."

After hanging up the phone, Gillian stepped outside and headed around to the backyard. She quickly cleaned up the mess by the garbage cans. She put the lid back on the second receptacle, and then took a long look around the backyard. Biting her lip, she studied the ravine as well. She didn't see anybody.

"Hey Ethan!" she heard someone shout. *"How's it fagging, Ethan?"*

"Look at the fairy sail by!"

Gillian came around toward the front of the duplex.

His head down, Ethan approached the front porch with his knapsack full of books strapped to his back. Three boys, all on bikes, had stopped on the street to yell at him.

"Hey faggot! Want to blow me?"

Gillian hurried to the front yard. She glared at them. One of the boys let out a howl, and the other two burst out laughing. They rode away on their bikes.

Ethan slipped inside the house, and Gillian started in after him. Her heart was breaking for him. "Are you okay, honey?" she asked.

"Fine," he answered, heading toward his room.

"Those boys—" she started to say.

"They're just being jerks, Mom. Forget about it." He ducked into his room and shut the door.

Gillian went to his door, and was about to knock. But she hesitated. She felt so useless—and helpless. Ethan obviously didn't want to talk about what had just happened. Gillian wasn't eager to broach the topic herself. She and Barry used to discuss the possibility that Ethan might be gay. Even as far back as kindergarten, Ethan's teacher had mentioned during their private parent-night conference, "Ethan is a very nice boy—sensitive. During playtime, he—um, seems more interested in the girls' activities than the boys' activities. Most of his friends are girls. But he gets along well with everyone. . . ."

Later, on their way home in the car, Barry took his eyes off the road for a moment to throw her a crooked smile. "Gosh, I think Ethan's teacher was trying to tell us back there that he's different from all the other little boys."

"Well, you couldn't expect we'd be the only ones to notice," Gillian replied. "She also said he was very nice."

Now that he was an adolescent, Ethan seemed to be struggling with the issue, and unwilling to acknowledge it.

Barry used to be so good with him. If he'd felt any shame or disappointment in his son's questionable masculinity, Barry had never shown it at all. Gillian wished he were there right now, so he could tell Ethan that he was a great kid and they both loved him. At this moment, Ethan needed his father.

* * *

Sitting in his parked car, a block away from Gillian's duplex, he sorted through the half-burnt contents of the black plastic bag. Ethan Tanner had ripped a magazine into several small pieces, set some of it on fire, taped it up in a bag, and buried it in the garbage.

Until he saw it was a magazine, he'd thought the kid had stashed some letters from his long-lost papa in that bag. He didn't understand why the brat had gone to such lengths to destroy and hide a stupid magazine. Then he discovered what kind of magazine it was. A few pictures in the magazine had survived the torch job.

He chuckled.

He took out his cell phone and made a call. "Hey, yeah, it's me," he said after his cohort answered. "You were saying the other day that the kid might know where his dad is. Well, if that's true, I think I figured out a way we can get to him."

Chapter 6

Two hours later, and twelve hundred miles away, along an on-ramp to Interstate 90 in Rapid City, South Dakota, a black Honda Accord slowed down for a hitchhiker. The driver told the hitchhiker, named Sean, to throw his hiking pack in the backseat and sit up front with him. "Maybe you can find us a decent station on the radio," he suggested, pulling back onto the highway. "None of this country-western shit."

Sean was twenty-eight. He'd been backpacking throughout the country for the last few months, sort of a spiritual journey. He'd worked hard as a graphic designer for this big computer company for seven years. "Then one day, I just said, 'Screw this, I'm out of here,'" Sean explained. He was very much on his own. He'd broken up with his longtime girlfriend last year, and was estranged from his family, who had become a bunch of Holy Rollers.

The man behind the wheel said he'd just flown in from Chicago. He was driving the rest of the way to Seattle so he could see the country, "maybe meet a few interesting people along the way." He was a writer, though so far, every attempt at publishing his work had failed. He was going to see a woman in Seattle. "She's an author too," the man explained. "Have you read any Gillian McBride thrillers?"

Sean wasn't familiar with her work.

"She wrote one called *Highway Hypnosis*. Ever hear of that?"

Over cheeseburgers at a truck stop, the driver told Sean the plot of Gillian McBride's *Highway Hypnosis*. "I guess it's not something you should talk about while you're eating," he joked. He went into detail about the book and how its scheming maniac villain murdered a number of hitchhikers in order to sell their identities and their internal organs.

Sean chuckled. "Huh, should I be nervous? Are *you* a maniac?"

Smiling, the driver nodded. "Oh, I'm certifiable, a regular menace to society."

"Well, when you sell my liver, don't take any less than five grand. It's in terrific shape. I gave up drinking years ago."

They were still laughing and joking under the stars—on their way back to the Accord in the parking lot. Sean volunteered to spell him at the wheel for a while.

"No, thanks, I got it," the driver replied. "Besides, you're going to be tired pretty soon."

Sean buckled his seat belt. He squinted at him. "What do you mean, I'll be tired?"

The driver started up the engine. "Oh, you know, sometimes a person can get sleepy after a big dinner."

Sean stared at him in the glow of the dashboard lights. The guy had the strangest little smile on his face.

About ten minutes after they pulled onto the Interstate once again, Sean read a sign: SHERIDAN—49 MILES. But it was a little blurred. Maybe he was tired after all. There was nothing wrong with his eyesight. His old girlfriend, who always wore glasses, used to say she wanted to inherit his beautiful blue, twenty-twenty-vision eyes.

He suddenly thought about that book the driver liked, the one with somebody selling people's organs.

Sean reached for the button to lower the car window, and he couldn't find it in the darkness. Everything seemed fuzzy. "I think I'm a little carsick," he said, surprised to hear himself slurring his words.

"That's just some initial nausea," the driver said, studying the road ahead. "It'll pass. You'll be sleepy soon."

Numbly, Sean stared at him. But he couldn't get the guy into focus. "Wh—what do you mean? What are you talking about?"

The driver switched off the car radio. He kept his eyes on the road. "Just relax," he said.

The constant humming of the car tires was almost hypnotic. Ahead, headlights swam in the darkness. Sean tried to reach for his seat belt, but he could barely move. "What—what's going on here?" he asked.

"I did a lot of research on pharmaceuticals. This one works pretty damn fast . . ."

Numbly, Sean stared over at the driver. For a moment, his vision was right, and he saw the headlights sweep across the man's face. Hands on the wheel, he was watching the road ahead.

Then everything went out of focus again. He heard the man talking, but it seemed to come from someplace far away, and he only caught snippets: *"It'll just knock you out, Sean . . . when you got up to go to the bathroom at the restaurant . . . why your Coke tasted funny . . . right about now . . . a sort of paralysis . . . know exactly what you're experiencing, Sean. I read up on it when I was studying surgical procedures."*

Sean couldn't move. The headlights' glare had now become muted spots swirling in front of him. The driver's voice, so calm and steady, was fading out. Sean felt himself surrendering to unconsciousness. Minutes seemed to pass, or perhaps it was just a few seconds, but he heard the driver say something else.

   "See, this was Gillian's idea," he said. *"It's all for her . . ."*
Sean didn't hear anything else after that.

The clever killer in Gillian's *Highway Hypnosis* was a former surgeon. He conducted his operations in a remote, hidden bunker in the desert outside Las Vegas. His private little OR featured sterilized, state-of-the-art equipment. His patients received first-class treatment—right up until he had surgically removed what he needed from them. The unfortunate hitchhikers were expendable, but their organs were making him money.

He had it pretty nice, the lucky son of a bitch. Gillian's demented doctor didn't have to look for an isolated spot in the middle of the night and set up a makeshift operating area. He was never expected to improvise. He didn't have to buy all his surgical accoutrements on the same day he was picking up his victim. Yet only an hour before stopping to give Sean a lift, he'd been at a medical supply store that served Rapid City Regional Hospital. And before that he'd bought some camping and gardening equipment at a hardware store.

The mad genius surgeon in *Highway Hypnosis* wasn't nearly as resourceful as he was. Hell, he was always doing Gillian's fictional killers one better. In *The Mark of Death*, the girl had been stabbed by "Zorro" in the back of an empty car. But he'd pulled off the same thing with a taxi driver in the front seat. The department store dressing room strangulation in Gillian's *For Everyone to See* ended with the victim in a heap on the floor. But he'd left his victim hanging on the wall like a hunter's trophy. And now, working from what he'd learned on the Internet and in books, he was about to perform surgery—in the most primitive of locations.

While driving along Interstate 90, he'd noticed dozens of road signs for campgrounds, but he only started paying attention to them after Sean had passed out. His hitchhiker "patient" was slumped in the front seat with his head resting against the window. The shoulder strap and seat belt seemed to be holding him in place—like a piece of lifeless cargo.

When they pulled off the highway and stopped at the closed gates to a campground twenty-three miles south of Billings, Montana, Sean didn't even stir. The campsite was closed for the winter. No one was around to hear him shoot the chain lock off the gate.

Driving down the unlit, gravel road, he couldn't see anything beyond his headlights. The tall trees surrounding him seemed to form a dark, endless tunnel. It was scary and exciting. He felt his heart racing. By the dashboard light, he glanced at Sean, still asleep in the passenger seat. He smiled.

Moonlight peeked through the trees and helped him find a clearing off to one side of the road. He spotted several picnic tables and a restroom facility that was boarded up. He pulled over by one of the picnic tables, climbed out of the car, and immediately went to work.

Dragging Sean out of the vehicle and laying him on top of the picnic table was the hardest part. Though still breathing, the hitchhiker was just dead weight. He covered his patient with a rain slicker—to keep him warm. Then he dug two battery-operated lamps from the trunk—as well as two suitcases full of medical equipment.

He kept his gun in his coat pocket. He wasn't worried about Sean waking up. No, the gun was for uninvited guests. Bears and other forest creatures were likely to smell the blood—and there would be a lot of it. He didn't want any of them interrupting his work.

Sean might not be his only kill tonight.

He set up the lights, and then opened one of the cases. It

was full of surgical tools, mostly clamps and scalpels, along with a suction device that looked like a turkey-baster.

"Sean?" he said, removing the rain slicker from him. "Sean, can you hear me?"

His patient didn't move. His closed eyelids didn't even flutter.

He unbuttoned the man's shirt, and pulled it off. He stared at Sean's slightly hairy chest, watched it move up and down with each breath. Then he glanced at the scalpel in the open case, the same tool that would be slicing through Sean's skin within a few minutes.

He donned the rain slicker. Even with all the clamps he had, there would still be an awful lot of blood. He didn't want to ruin his clothes.

He opened the other case and gazed at the stainless-steel retractor that would fit over Sean's chest. It would open up his rib cage. The sight of that shiny, new contraption excited him. He couldn't wait to use it. He felt like a kid, trying out a new toy.

He heard some noise in the woods, trees rustling, but something else too. The four-legged inhabitants of this forest sensed something was about to happen. Perhaps they could already smell the blood.

He could too.

Ethan's mother's book signing was a minor success. A book club, made up of a dozen women around his mother's age, had shown up to hear her talk. Plus a few stragglers came by and sat down. Ethan watched from the bookstore's café. He finished some trigonometry homework while eating a grilled-cheese sandwich. They had these lousy, all-natural "vegetable chips," instead of fries or regular potato chips—and no Coke, only lemonade, but it wasn't so awful.

Watching his mother "at work" was nothing special for Ethan. But he remembered what it was like two years ago, when she'd just been starting out. He recalled a trip with his parents to the Northgate shopping mall, where they'd found his mother's debut thriller, *Killing Legend,* on the shelf at Waldenbooks. It was the first time he'd seen his mom's book in a store. Ethan wanted his mother to know he was impressed *("Oh, wow, that's SO cool!"),* and maybe he milked it just a bit. A few people in the store turned their heads to see what all the fuss was about. Most of them smiled when they realized an author was there with her husband and son. But Ethan noticed a skinny, twentysomething blonde with her boyfriend in the Self-Help aisle, and she was imitating him in a mincing, effeminate way. She flailed her limp wrist and whispered, *"Wow, that's SOOO cool!"* in a lisp-inflected falsetto. At that moment, Ethan's heart sank, and he prayed his parents didn't see the woman's little pantomime.

He immediately shut up, and retreated over to the Sports section, where he tried to look interested in a basketball book. All the while, he fantasized about that skanky blonde getting mowed down by a truck in the parking lot.

Instead, something happened to his dad when they stepped out to the lot. A short man with dark hair and a goatee approached his dad outside the mall's south doors. "Barry, old pal," he said, grabbing his father's hand and pumping. "Good to see you. I'd like a word."

His dad seemed a little put off. With a tight smile, he told Ethan and his mom to go wait in the car. He'd only be a couple of minutes.

The Saturn wasn't parked far away. Ethan sat in the backseat and through the rain-beaded windshield, he watched the man talking with his father. He kept punching his father's arm—like they were old friends or something. Finally, his dad pulled out his wallet and gave the dark-haired man some money. Then he headed back to the car.

Ethan remembered his mother asking about the man. "Oh, that's Leo, from my union meetings," his father answered, starting up the car. "He was hitting me up for a few bucks. I would have introduced you, honey, but I think he was embarrassed."

"He didn't seem embarrassed to me," Ethan's mother replied. "In fact, he seemed pretty pushy. There was something about his manner, I—"

"Honey, relax, he's not such a bad guy. Like I say, he's a friend of mine."

For some reason, the memory of that dark-haired man talking to his dad stuck in Ethan's head. Three months later, after his father had disappeared, he saw that *not-such-a-bad-guy* leaning against a parked car about a half block from the duplex. Ethan was on his way to the bus stop for school. He recognized the guy, but couldn't remember from where. The man with the goatee was drinking from a Starbucks carry-out container and staring at him.

Around that time, someone had been periodically picking through their garbage and their mail. His mother had explained that certain people were looking for his father. She'd cautioned Ethan about strangers who might approach him, perhaps someone claiming to be a policeman or a friend of his dad's. He had to be extra careful.

Ethan avoided eye contact with the goatee man. It wasn't until he'd gotten on the bus that he remembered where he'd seen him before.

Later that afternoon, his mother drove to school, honked the horn, and waved at him—only to speed away. A uniformed cop told him to go home and wait for this mother there. When Ethan finally saw his mom again, her face was horribly bruised and swollen. She said she'd been mugged. Ethan kept wondering if it was that creepy man with the dark hair and goatee who had beaten her so severely.

His mom had sold the Saturn the very same day. Had the goatee guy stolen the car too?

That night, he asked his mother for the truth. She kept telling him to calm down. Getting angry wouldn't do any good. It had happened just as she'd told him. She'd already reported the mugging to the police. As for the Saturn, she'd been thinking about selling it for a while now.

He was skeptical, but couldn't challenge her story—not when she was almost pleading with him and her face was all battered. He knew she was just trying to protect him. Ethan's heart broke just looking at her.

The more Ethan thought about that creep using his mom for a punching bag, the more enraged he became. He didn't care how much older and stronger the man was. If he ever saw that son of a bitch again, he'd kill him. He'd take a rock and bash his head in.

But Ethan never saw the man again, and that had been almost two years ago.

From across the store, Ethan watched his mother spinning stories for the book club ladies. They were just starting the Q & A session. Ethan put away his trigonometry homework, and then carried his tray—with half a plateful of uneaten "vegetable chips"—to the bus area.

With time to kill, he decided to wander around the store. Ethan paused near the Gay & Lesbian Studies section. He noticed an oversized "art" book, *Loving Men,* with two naked men embracing on the cover. Ethan felt a pang in his stomach—a strange mix of excitement and repulsion. He stood there for a moment, pretending to be interested in the Nutrition & Wellness Studies section on the other side of the aisle. But his eyes kept roaming back to that book cover. His mother was around the corner; he could hear her talking to the group.

He wanted so much to look inside *Loving Men,* but too many people were around. Besides, hadn't he vowed yesterday that he would change? He didn't stand much chance of becoming normal if he kept giving into temptation with these gay books and magazines.

Three weeks before, he'd felt sorry for this homeless woman and bought a *Real Change* newspaper from her. A few blocks later, he'd decided to toss it away in a recycling bin next to an apartment building. Opening the bin, he discovered a magazine amid the piles of old newspapers and crushed cardboard boxes. Ethan felt his heart racing. He glanced around to make sure no one could see. He snatched up the magazine, stuck it in the middle of the homeless newspaper, then stuffed it in his jacket.

His mother had been at a book signing earlier, but just his luck, she was home when he came through the front door. He felt like a drug smuggler as he stole past his mom in her writing nook, giving her a quick "How's it goin'?" before ducking into his bedroom. He immediately hid the magazine under a loose flap of carpeting under his bed. He didn't even look at it until later—at one o'clock in the morning, when he knew his mother was asleep.

The magazine was called *Stallion,* and it was full of pictures of naked men. Ethan had never been so disgusted with himself—and so turned on at the same time. It was crazy. A while back, his best friend, Craig, had given him an old *Playboy* he'd inherited from his older brother. Page after page of beautiful naked women in erotic poses, and it didn't do a thing for Ethan. But this sleazy magazine with pictures of guys who weren't even that good-looking had him foaming at the mouth. He felt like a total pervert.

That skanky blond woman who had made fun of him at the bookstore two years ago had had his number. She'd seen what Ethan had been trying so hard to keep secret. He was gay, but he didn't want to be.

He wished his father were around, because he could have talked to him about this. At least, he imagined he could have. The truth was, he hoped to cure himself—or grow out of it—before anyone ever discovered his secret. He couldn't tell his mother—even though she had a lot of gay and lesbian acquaintances. Hell, he didn't even want his mother to know he had sexual feelings—no less *homosexual* feelings. He couldn't say anything to Craig either.

His best friend was a mega-jock, and a bit homophobic. Ethan was terrified that Craig already suspected something.

During his last sleepover at Craig's house, they'd been sitting in their underwear on the twin beds talking and listening to music late at night. Craig had a great body, lean and muscular. During one of his many trips across the room to change the CD or tinker with the volume, Craig suddenly swiveled around. "Are you checking out my ass?" he whispered, eyes narrowed at him. "Shit, you were eyeballing me just now, weren't you? I saw your reflection in the window."

Ethan tried to laugh. "What are you, nuts?"

Of course he'd been checking him out. He had a tiny crush on his best friend, but had always done his best to cover it up. Now he'd been found out. That night, Craig dug a robe from the back of his closet and put it on. Before then, Ethan hadn't known Craig even *owned* a robe.

Maybe Craig had always suspected something, because he'd often said things like, "Don't fag out on me, Ethan," or "You know, you're acting like a faggot."

Ethan couldn't help it. Then again, maybe he could. Last night, he'd decided to get rid of the *Stallion* magazine he'd been hiding for three weeks. Ethan figured it was like alcoholism. If he just didn't give in to it, he'd be all right. Someone seriously going off the sauce wouldn't keep a bottle of Scotch under his bed. Besides, he'd been taking a big risk going off to school every morning with that thing in the house. His mom could have found it—somehow. He'd already pushed his luck to the limit.

So last night, while his mother was at her other book signing, Ethan had one last "fling" with the magazine. Then he tore it up. Still, that wasn't good enough, so he burned it in the bathtub. Thick smoke started to fill the bathroom, and the detector alarm went off. Ethan quickly doused the flames, switched off the alarm, and opened some windows. His mother was due home at any minute. Frantic, he cleaned up the mess in the tub, then stuffed what was left of the half-burnt, torn magazine into a black plastic bag. He taped up the bag and buried it in the garbage can outside.

He would have taken the damn thing down the block and thrown it into someone else's garbage, but there wasn't enough time. In fact, his mother came home just a few minutes after he'd thrown away the dirty magazine.

Talk about a close call.

With the "evidence" of his perversion destroyed, Ethan had figured he could skate by for a while without his sexuality coming into question. Of course, he was wrong.

He barely even knew those guys who had been taunting him after school this afternoon. They were sophomores. Last week, one of them, Tate Barringer, had passed him in the hallway between classes. "Hey, fag," he'd said, slapping his arm. Ethan's stomach had tightened into a knot, and he'd frozen in his tracks. Continuing down the crowded corridor, Tate had smirked over his shoulder at him. Ethan had been left to wonder what he'd done to warrant being called a "fag." Maybe it was the violin case he was carrying around half the time. Or maybe it was just him.

There were two more brushes with Tate, and in each encounter, the sophomore had taunted him for being "queer." Now Tate had recruited some friends to torment him too. How soon before the whole school was in on it? Ethan had imagined Tate talking to Craig: *"Hey, Merchant, why are you hanging around with that homo Ethan Tanner?"*

But he'd never imagined Tate and his pals calling him a fag in front of *his mother*.

Ethan had holed up in his bedroom all afternoon. He couldn't face his mom. Part of him just wanted to die. He thought about killing himself. They wouldn't find anything sexually incriminating in his room—except that old *Playboy*, which had belonged to Craig's big brother. Hell, Tate and his buddies would be forced to admit they were wrong about him.

Ethan had figured he'd have the evening alone. But then his mother knocked on his door and asked him to come with her to this book signing. He tried to get out of it, saying he had a ton of homework. But his mother insisted. He could bring his books with him, she said, and he could eat dinner in the bookstore's café. It was a long bus trip back and forth, with transfers, and she wanted some company.

He couldn't have been much *company* for his mom, sitting next to her on the bus with his nose in *A History of Western Civilization* the whole damn time. He'd been terrified she might try to talk to him about what had happened in front of the duplex this afternoon.

She hadn't brought it up on the bus—thank God. She'd let him study without interruption.

Ethan heard a smattering of applause coming from the bookstore's lecture area around the corner. Two or three at a time, the book club women started to emerge from the alcove. Ethan took one last look at the cover of *Loving Men*, and then he skulked away from the Gay & Lesbian Studies section. Rounding the corner, he found his mother autographing her paperbacks for a few stragglers.

After the last fan left, his mother slung her arm around the shoulder of a stout, thirtysomething woman with a scar from her ear to her cheek. She introduced her as Gayle, from the bookstore. "Oh, you're so handsome," Gayle said, shaking Ethan's hand. "You must have the girls following you home from school and scratching at the front door every afternoon."

His mom laughed, and Ethan forced a smile. He didn't want his mother reminded about what had happened this afternoon outside their front door.

As they headed out of the bookstore, his mother took a swig from her bottled water. "Lord, I'm so tired," she announced. "I'm all talked out."

He hoped she meant it. On the bus, he feigned interest in his history book again. Ethan figured his mother wasn't about to ask him if he was gay while within earshot of other passengers.

At the bus transfer station, Ethan sat next to his mother

and kept his eyes riveted to *A History of Western Civiliza-tion*. They were alone on the little concrete island, under a steel and Plexiglas shelter. The transfer station was along Route 520, just on the other side of the floating bridge over Lake Washington. Cars zoomed by with their blinding head-lights. Ethan and his mom shivered in the damp, chilly wind off the lake.

"Honey, we need to talk about something."

The words Ethan had dreaded.

"Can it wait, Mom?" he replied, not looking up from his book. "I'm right in the middle of this."

"No, honey, this is important. The homework can wait for a minute."

Reluctantly, Ethan closed the book, and looked at her. His stomach was in knots. "So—what's going on?"

"Those men who were looking for your dad a couple of years ago," she said. "They're back for a return engagement, and up to their same old tricks. This afternoon, I spotted a man hanging around outside the house. He'd been through our mail—and our garbage."

Ethan stared at her. "He was looking in our *garbage*?"

His mother nodded glumly. "Remember how they pulled this same thing around Christmastime last year? My guess is they're thinking that with your birthday coming up, your fa-ther might want to contact us. Anyway, that's why I pres-sured you into coming to the signing tonight. I didn't want to leave you home alone, not if these people are prowling around. . . ."

His mother went on about how he had to be cautious and not go off on his own if he could help it. She even mentioned buying him a cell phone tomorrow, so he'd have it for emer-gencies.

But Ethan was hardly listening. All he could think about was that someone had gone through their garbage today.

When they arrived home, his mother threw some left-overs in the oven. She asked if he'd had enough to eat at the bookstore café. Ethan couldn't have eaten anything—even if he was starving. His stomach was doing flip-flops.

While her dinner cooked, his mom went into the bathroom to take a shower. Ethan seized the opportunity. Ducking outside, he crept around to the backyard and pried the lid off the garbage can he'd used last night. He hadn't bothered putting on a coat, and he was shivering. He pulled the big Hefty bag out of the receptacle. He didn't see the small, black, plastic bag. Was there a chance it had slipped a little lower inside the garbage can?

Ethan pulled out the bottom trash bag. Nothing. The black, plastic bag was gone—and with it, the evidence of his sexual secret: that torn, half-burnt, dirty magazine.

Someone had taken it.

The sign on the front door of Rudy's Golden Oldies Café in Billings, Montana, said OPEN NITELY 'TIL 1 A.M.! Penny, the waitress on closing shift, glanced at the Coke clock on the wall: 12:58. The last remaining customer, the guy at table six, didn't look like he was going to budge. Penny had just poured his third coffee refill. He was in his thirties, and handsome in a slick, cocky way. At first, Penny had thought he was cute, but he'd been flirting with her for the last hour and a half, and she'd grown wary of him. From cute to creepy in ninety minutes. Penny had a feeling he was hanging around so he could make a move on her after closing. Or maybe he planned to follow her home.

That was one of the many drawbacks to working the late shift at Rudy's Golden Oldies Café. The place was trying to pass itself off as a fifties diner with a jukebox and red vinyl upholstery for the booths and bar stools. But the posters of Marilyn Monroe, James Dean, and Elvis were cheesy artists' renderings from the late eighties, and except for two Buddy Holly recordings, the jukebox featured such fifties favorites as Puff Daddy, Britney Spears, and Eminem. Located about halfway between Montana State University and I-90, Rudy's was on a rather sketchy block—next to a vacant lot with patches of overgrown grass and trash scattered about. The clientele were mostly highway travelers and people from Deaconess Hospital nearby. Penny didn't get many fellow students from the university in there.

She was a sophomore, and pretty with blue eyes and straight, shoulder-length black hair. She had a voluptuous figure that turned heads despite her ugly, orange polyester uniform. Penny was used to getting hit on at work. The only time it really bothered her was when the restaurant was ready to close and the aggressive customer wouldn't leave— like Mr. Slick at table six right now. He still hadn't pulled out his money to pay the check.

He grinned at Penny as she approached his table by the window. "Sorry, but we're closing," she said. "I need you to pay up."

He reached for his wallet. "You mean it's all over between us?"

She nodded. "Afraid so."

"Well, it was fun while it lasted, eh, Penny?"

She just nodded again. Sometimes she hated having to wear the stupid name tag.

"You know what else might be kind of fun?" he continued. "What do you say you and I get together after you finish here? We could go someplace—"

"After I finish here," Penny interrupted, "my boyfriend is coming to pick me up, and I have to study all night for a philosophy exam in the morning." It was a total lie: she had neither a boyfriend nor a philosophy test. But the fabrication usually discouraged customers like Mr. Slick.

"Oh, that's too bad." He put his money on the table. "Because I thought you and I kind of had a connection here. I mean, it's a shame we can't explore the possibilities—"

"Yeah, it's tragic," Penny muttered, swiping up his money.

"I'll be back with your change." She started toward the register counter.

"Huh, keep it," she heard him grunt. "Put the extra dough toward an operation to remove that bug up your ass."

He got to his feet, grabbed his coat—an ugly beige, rubbery-looking rain slicker—and stomped out of the diner.

A half hour later, Penny was putting on her own coat. The cook and the bus boy had already left. So it was just her and the old, near-deaf custodian, Fernando. Only a few lights were on—including a pink neon FINE FOOD sign in the window. Penny stepped out the door, and waved to Fernando, who locked up after her. She started toward her car, but suddenly stopped dead.

Huddled in his ugly beige raincoat, Mr. Slick leaned against the hood of his old Volkswagen, parked next to her own car. He'd been waiting out there for her all this time. His face was in the shadows, but she could tell he was staring at her. "Penny?" he said, almost a whisper.

"You need to leave me alone," she announced.

But he took a couple of steps toward her. Penny swiveled around and hurried back toward the restaurant. Through the window, she saw Fernando slip into the restroom. She banged on the glass door, and frantically pulled at the handle. Obviously, Fernando couldn't hear.

Penny glanced over her shoulder. The man in the rubbery raincoat was approaching. "Penny?" he called softly. "Hey, I just want to talk to you. . . ."

She ran around back to the diner's service entrance—by the Dumpsters. She tugged at the back door, but that was locked too. She pounded on it, but to no avail.

The man came around the corner, his hands shoved in the pockets of his raincoat. He let out a strange chuckle. "Penny? What's wrong with you? I just wanted to tell you—"

"Leave me alone!" she screamed. "Get the hell out of here!" She reached for the little canister of Mace in her purse.

"Jesus, you're crazy!" he shot back. "I just wanted to apologize for earlier—"

"I said, leave me alone!" she yelled.

"Oh, screw you," he muttered, waving her away.

Catching her breath, Penny watched him retreat toward his VW. She heard him gun the motor. With apprehension, she came around toward the front of the diner. Something in the vacant lot next door caught her eye. There, amid the patches of overgrown grass and debris, she spotted a car with its headlights off. In the darkness, she couldn't quite see what was going on. It looked like a man was pulling something out of the backseat of his car.

Mr. Slick gunned his engine again, then switched on the lights of his VW. As he peeled out of the lot, his headlights swept across the abandoned lot. The lone figure ducked back into his car. But he'd left something on the ground. It looked like a dead, skinned animal. Penny wasn't sure. It happened so fast, she didn't get a good look at the driver—or the make of his car. He drove away with his headlights off.

The customer in his VW sped away in the opposite direction.

Penny knocked on the restaurant's front door again. Fernando still hadn't emerged from the restroom. Penny took out her cell phone. She was about to call the police, but hesitated. What would she tell them? *I saw someone dump something in this vacant lot, but I don't know what it is.* She'd already overreacted with Mr. Slick. She didn't want to make a fool out of herself with the police too.

Climbing into her car, Penny pulled out of Rudy's lot, then drove half a block to what was once a driveway—at least there was a break in the curb. Turning into the deserted lot, she rode over the gravel, debris, and clumps of tall grass until she saw a fleshy, white thing lying on the ground. Penny slammed on the brakes.

She took out the cell phone again, and edged closer to the cadaver. It was dead, she knew that much. She dialed 911.

Her headlights illuminated the half-naked corpse. "Oh, my God," Penny murmured.

"Police Emergency," the operator answered.

Penny didn't say anything.

"Police emergency. Is anyone there?"

Penny still couldn't respond. She was staring at a dead man—with his eyes open, and the bottom half of his face torn off. All his fingers were missing. And in his chest, there was a bloody, gaping hole where his heart used to be.

Chapter 7

"Hi, you've reached The Merchants. No one can come to the phone right now. If you'd like to leave a message for Tom, Stephanie, Ted, Amanda, or Craig, please—"

"Hello?" A voice came on the line to interrupt the recording.

"Hello, Steph?" Gillian sat in her writing nook with a cup of coffee on the desk. She'd sent Ethan off to school an hour before. She was surprised Stephanie Merchant had picked up. She'd been trying to get ahold of Craig's mother all week.

"Stephanie, it's Gill McBride. How are you?"

"Oh, hello, Gill. I'm fine, thanks, just—busy."

"Well, I'm glad we finally connected," Gillian said with a little laugh.

"Um, yes, I've been meaning to call you back. It's been crazy here lately."

"Oh, then now is probably a lousy time to ask if Ethan could spend a couple of hours at your place tonight." Gillian had to teach her writing class, and she didn't want to leave Ethan home alone.

"I'm sorry, Gillian," Stephanie said. "I'd like to help you out, but I can't. In fact, I'm afraid I can't help with that party next week either."

Gillian had been trying to organize a small surprise party for Ethan's birthday. She'd discussed it with Stephanie last month, and Craig's mother had been all gung ho to pitch in. Gillian had already booked the bowling alley and restaurant. All she needed was Craig's help with the guest list. She didn't understand Stephanie's abrupt turnabout here.

"What happened?" she asked.

"As I said, I'm extremely busy. I just can't spare the time right now."

"Oh. Well, then maybe I can meet with Craig. All I need are the names and phone numbers of a few of Craig's and Ethan's friends—"

"Craig can't attend the party, Gillian. He has another commitment. I'm sorry—"

"What are you talking about? You've known about this for a month, Stephanie."

There was silence on the other end of the line.

"Did Craig and Ethan have a fight or something?" Gillian asked.

"Maybe you should talk to your own son," Stephanie replied coolly. "I'm sorry, Gill, but I—I really need to dash. Good luck with the party. I'm sure it will be very nice."

"Stephanie—"

"Good-bye."

Gillian heard a click on the other end of the line. "What the hell?" she said to no one. She hung up the phone.

Stephanie Merchant was one of those married girlfriends who'd gone from close to distantly cordial once Barry had disappeared. But at least her fondness for Ethan hadn't seemed to diminish. Gillian didn't know what had warranted this sudden cold-shoulder treatment.

And what was she supposed to *talk to her own son* about?

She hated the idea of leaving Ethan home alone tonight when these hoods were lurking around the duplex.

She also hated the idea that he'd have a crummy fourteenth birthday. Without Craig attending, no one else would show up. Ethan's last two birthdays—along with their Christmases—had been so lousy. They just weren't the same without Barry. On each special occasion, they couldn't help hoping he might somehow return. And each time, it was a horrible disappointment.

Ethan's birthday two years ago had been the turning point. Only a week before, Barry had woken her up in the middle of the night, sobbing about how he'd failed her. She should have been paying attention to these early warning signs.

They had 6:30 dinner reservations at the Space Needle restaurant. It was going to be just the family and Craig. But at 6:50, Barry still hadn't come home from work. Gillian couldn't get ahold of him. By 7:15, she ordered pizza, made up some excuse to the boys about Barry, then had Ethan open his presents. The call from the police station came at 8:20, just after Ethan had blown out the candles on his cake.

"My truck got hijacked," Barry explained. Gillian had switched to the bedroom connection. She could hear Ethan and Craig playing a video game on TV in the living room. The game was one of his birthday presents, and it had all sorts of bells, whistles, and buzzers.

"I was hauling a load of cigarettes," Barry continued. "These guys worked me over too. The cops took me to the hospital. I've got a few stitches in my left eyebrow."

"Oh, my God, Barry—"

"I'm all right, honey. Honest. I'll probably be here at the police station for at least another hour. I have to fill out a ton of paperwork."

"How did it happen?" she asked.

"Tell you later. How's Ethan?"

"He's fine. But honey—"

"They're telling me to wrap it up. See you in an hour. Hug Ethan for me, okay?"

Barry came home about an hour after Stephanie Merchant had picked up Craig. For Ethan, he spun this *Indiana Jones*–like account of the hijacking, stressing how he'd gotten a few good punches in. "I guess the lesson here is," he said with a grin on his swollen, battered face, "when a couple of guys with guns try to steal your car or truck, don't put up a fight!"

Barry laughed at his own remark, but Ethan barely cracked a smile. He sat at the kitchen table surrounded by birthday cake, the empty pizza box, and dirty plates. As he listened to his father, he had this pained, wondering look on his young face. Gillian knew how he felt. It hurt to look at Barry, and his version of what had happened seemed like a shoddy fabrication.

After Ethan went to bed, Gillian poured Barry and herself a drink. She threw on a sweater, and asked to talk to him on the front porch. It was the furthest they could go from Ethan's bedroom without leaving the duplex.

She set her drink on the porch railing. "So what *really* happened?" she asked.

Barry shrugged. "Basically, it's just what I told Ethan—without the frosting. I wasn't trying to be a hero. I lipped off to one of these guys and he let me have it." Barry sipped his bourbon on the rocks, then held the glass on his swollen cheek. "They ambushed me near the base in Tukwila, timed it perfectly. No one was around. This old Cadillac suddenly came out of nowhere and pulled in front of me. I slammed on the brakes. These two thugs—Neanderthals—got out of the back. They were pointing these sawed-off shotguns at me—"

Eyes narrowed at him, Gillian slowly shook her head.

"What?" he asked. "What is it, honey?"

"You're lying to me," she said.

His mouth open, Barry stared back at her.

Gillian was thinking about the time he was "mugged" in Chicago, and their hasty move to Seattle. She was thinking of the money he'd lost, and how they'd never been able to put away any savings. She was thinking of that little man in Northgate Mall's parking lot, and Barry sobbing in the middle of the night last week, saying he'd failed her.

"Tell me the truth, Barry. I can't listen to your lies anymore. I've done that for too many years—"

"I don't know what you're talking about—"

"Yes, you do," she said, clutching the sweater around her shoulders. "What kind of trouble are you in?"

He rubbed his forehead. "They gave me a painkiller at the hospital. I think it's wearing off. God, I feel like crap." He turned toward the door. "I need an aspirin."

Gillian stepped in front of the door. "It can wait. Now answer me."

Barry swallowed the rest of his drink, then looked down at his feet.

"What have you been keeping from me?" she asked, a tremor in her voice. "Please, Barry. Do you know how hard it is for me to ask this? Something's been wrong for years— I've known that much. I've tried to ignore it. But we can't pretend anymore. Even Ethan can see you're lying."

Barry looked at her. Tears filled his eyes. "I'm an addict, honey," he whispered. He wrung his hands nervously. "I—I gamble. It's a sickness. I've always hoped I could stop before you ever found out. But I got into a hole. I owed these guys. So—I arranged to let them hijack the truck. They beat me up to make it look real. Only—because I was so late with my payments, they didn't pull their punches. I'm still into them for fifty grand."

Numbly, she gazed at him. "Who are these people?"

"Creditors, shylocks," he muttered, eyes downcast. "And I'm in real trouble, honey. Something went wrong, something really bad." He started to cry.

She wanted to reach out and comfort him, but she was afraid of what he hadn't told her yet. So Gillian stood immobile, her hands in fists as she clutched at her sweater. "What is it?" she asked.

"The guys who took the cigarette truck, they ran over a homeless man, killed him. There were witnesses. Now the police are leaning on me. They don't know I arranged it all, but I can tell they suspect something. If it comes out, I'll go to jail—if these thugs don't kill me first."

Gillian shrugged helplessly. "Well, maybe—maybe the police would go easy on you if you just told them everything."

"You mean, make a deal with them?" Barry asked. Frowning, he shook his head. "Honey, these guys will cut my throat before I get one word out to the police. I'm a dead man either way."

The next evening, two police detectives came by the house and talked to Barry for an hour. Apparently, there were some holes in his account of the hijacking, facts that didn't gel with the accounts of the truck dispatchers. They also had questions about certain "associates" of his—and his activities in the past few weeks.

The following morning, Barry disappeared. He left Gillian a note, begging her forgiveness and telling her to forget about him.

But how could she forget that she was married to a hunted man when these hoods were still harassing her and Ethan? Not only did Barry Tanner owe them money; he could also implicate them in a truck hijacking, a hit-and-run, manslaughter, and a number of other crimes. They wanted him dead, and the police wanted him in jail.

Gillian figured the only reason she and Ethan hadn't been unceremoniously "whacked" was because Barry might be lured back to them. Live bait always worked best to catch a fish.

Gillian leaned back in her desk chair, and sipped her coffee. It was cold. She thought about Ethan's birthday party, and figured the only people attending would be a couple of hoods, waiting for Barry to show up. She wondered why Stephanie and Craig Merchant had bailed out on her. It didn't make sense.

Gillian stood up and started across the kitchen to refill her coffee cup. She heard someone on the porch steps. Turning toward the living room, she saw a shadow move on the other side of the window curtains. She started to set down the coffee cup on her desk, and just then, the door bell rang. The cup tipped over. Coffee spilled across the desk and dripped down onto the linoleum floor.

"Shit," Gillian muttered. Glancing back at the mess, she headed toward the front window. She moved the curtain aside on one end and peeked out at the porch.

It was her upstairs neighbor, Vicki, a perky blonde in her early forties. She was a flight attendant. Barry used to call her The Centerfold, because she had a terrific body that she showed off in tight-fitting clothes. Vicki admitted she rarely set foot outside her unit upstairs without first "putting my face on," and the result was a perpetual fake-prettiness. But Gillian liked her—in small doses, which worked out fine, because she was away so often. She'd been gone all last week. Now she was back.

Vicki rang the bell again.

Gillian hurried to the door and opened it. "Well, hi, Vicki—"

"Do you believe in love at first sight?"

Gillian shrugged. "Only when I need it to work for the plot of one of my books."

Vicki leaned against the door frame. She had a trench coat over her flight attendant's uniform, and a small tote-suitcase at her side. She smiled dreamily. "I met the most gorgeous man this morning. You won't believe how, Gill. I called home to get my messages last night, and there was one from this guy who says I don't know him, but he was on my Seattle-to-Minneapolis flight last week. He says he took one look at me and he was smitten. He actually used that word, *smitten*. He has a friend with the airline, and that's how he got my phone number. And he says, please don't be mad, but could he meet me? So—okay, I'm thinking—total stalker here. But I figure, what the hell, he has my number already, I might as well call him back and find out who this jerk is who gave him my phone number. So I called him. Gill, we talked on the phone for *two hours*!"

Gillian glanced back toward the mess she'd left in the kitchen. "Um, that's terrific. . . ."

"Oh, but wait, there's more," Vicki said. "He's a charter airline pilot out of Montana, and he says, 'Let's meet for breakfast when you get into Sea-Tac tomorrow. I can fly in.' Gill, he's six-two, brown hair, blue eyes, a total hunk. We *made out* for an hour in the parking lot stairwell at Sea-Tac. I feel like I'm in high school again. It was so hot, I mean it. Am I still flushed?"

"A little," Gillian said. "Listen, Vicki, I—"

"I know what you're going to say," her neighbor interrupted. "I hardly know the guy. But c'mon, if he was a serial killer, he could have strangled me in the stairwell when no one was around. Right? Anyway, he's coming over late tonight. We're going to pick up where we left off."

"That's great, Vicki," Gillian said, working up a smile. "Listen, what I was going to say is that I have to clean up this mess I made in the kitchen. So I should scoot—"

"Well, I won't keep you. I was wondering if some packages arrived for me. I went on this shopping spree while I was away."

Gillian nodded. "Yes, a couple of big packages. I put them inside your door with the mail. And I watered the plants two days ago."

"Thanks, Gill, you're a lifesaver." Vicki reached for her tote-suitcase. "I'm going to see if Jason has a friend for you. We'll put you back in circulation. The only time you ever go out is to teach your class or sign your books at stores." She pulled her suitcase toward the far side of the porch and started to unlock her door.

"Vicki?" Gillian called. "You just reminded me, I have my class tonight. What time is—um, Jason coming over?"

"Not until after ten. Why?"

"Well, if you're not going out before then, could you do me a favor? I don't want to leave Ethan by himself. I'd feel better if I knew you were home upstairs."

"No sweat. I'll be around if Ethan needs me."

"Thanks, Vicki." Gillian watched her neighbor step inside her unit. After Vicki's door shut, Gillian glanced out at the street, and then toward the side yard. She didn't see anyone.

Retreating back inside, Gillian went to clean up the spilt coffee.

"I'll take . . . um, Bozeman."

"Um, okay, we'll go with Eberhart."

Dressed in his gym sweats, Ethan stood shivering near the bleachers with three classmates: fat, bespectacled Alex Sloane; tiny anemic-looking Dylan Gubner; and gay-as-a-goose Mark Phair.

Pick me, pick me, pick me, was the mantra going through his head. He didn't want to be chosen last. Mark Phair could be picked last; he never seemed to mind. In fact, he acted proud of it.

Craig Merchant was one of the captains picking soccer teams for the PE session. Craig wasn't the best-looking guy in the freshman class, but his passing resemblance to Ewan McGregor definitely put him in the upper ranks. He and Ethan had been best friends since fourth grade. Craig had always been more athletic and more popular than Ethan, but that had never mattered until recently.

Ethan was still kicking himself for gawking at his best friend in his underwear during the last sleepover at Craig's house. If only he could take that moment back. But it was too late, he'd been caught looking.

Craig was spending most of his time with other friends now. When they weren't playing or watching football, they were getting drunk. It was the new thing now that they were in high school. Craig had even smoked marijuana a few times. Ethan was afraid that if he got stoned, he'd say or do something he'd really regret. His buddy was far more adventurous than him. Ethan's idea of a great time was going out for a movie and pizza, or just staying at home and watching TV. He had his violin and a different TV lineup to keep him company nearly every night of the week.

Maybe Craig's new buddies had said something to him about his *queer* friend. Or maybe Craig was just figuring it out for himself. Whatever, things were suddenly different.

Craig wouldn't look at him. It was his turn to pick, and his eyes kept darting back and forth from fat Alex to anemic Dylan. "Um, I guess we'll take Gubner."

Ethan tried like crazy to keep the same blank, waiting-for-a-bus expression on his face. He didn't want anyone to know that he was dying because his best friend had just betrayed him. When choosing teams, Craig had never before let him stand there among the final three bottom-of-the barrel rejects. Ethan felt as if he were drowning in quick-sand, and his best friend wouldn't even budge an inch to help him.

"Tanner," the other captain grunted. The son of a bitch even rolled his eyes a little.

But Ethan nodded and ran toward his team. He shot a look at Craig, who continued to ignore him.

During the soccer game, Ethan just ran alongside the pack like an ineffectual sheepdog. He tried to make eye contact with Craig a few times, but to no avail. After a while, he knew damn well no one would kick the ball to him, so he let his attention wander. That was when he noticed the old black Mustang, parked on the other side of the chain-link fence around the playfield. He didn't know how long it had been there. But he'd seen the car before.

This morning, at his bus stop, the black, vintage Mustang had driven around the block no less than three times, slowing down in front of him on each round. Ethan had noticed two people in the front seat. He hadn't gotten a look at their faces.

His mother had warned him about these guys who were looking for his dad. Were they following him around now?

"Hey Tanner!" someone yelled.

He turned and saw the ball bouncing toward him. *Jesus, please, don't let me screw up,* he thought. Every nerve in his body stiffened for a second. But somehow, he was able to react. He stopped the ball with his foot, and nudged it forward for a few strides until he saw a teammate who was open. Then Ethan kicked the ball in his direction. And it reached the guy—thank Christ.

By the end of the game, his team lost to Craig's team, but at least no one could blame him.

The losing team had to run a lap around the field. Ethan and his teammates had to merge with the sophomore gym class, who were already on the track. Just when he thought he might get through the gym class without any further humiliation, Ethan spotted Tate Barringer among the sweating, panting sophomores.

He'd managed to avoid his tormentor for the last couple of days. Seeing Tate strut down the school corridor, Ethan would head the other way or duck into a stairwell. Until a few weeks ago, he hadn't even known Tate's name. In fact, he used to think the sophomore with the blue eyes and messy black hair was kind of handsome—despite his ruddy complexion. Now Ethan was constantly on the lookout for the ugly, pock-faced creep.

For a moment on the track, Ethan and his nemesis were almost neck and neck with each other. Tate didn't seem to notice him. So Ethan poured on the speed, putting as much distance as he could between Tate and himself.

Ethan was winded as he finished his lap. Along with a handful of teammates, he staggered toward the pathway between the sets of bleachers that led to the school's athletic wing. He glanced over his shoulder, and didn't see Tate among the sophomores on the track. Ethan smiled inside. He must have lost him.

The boys' locker room was huge, with two separate shower areas. Ethan hadn't even known until today that he and Tate Barringer had the same gym period. Ethan figured if he quickly ducked in and out of the shower, he could leave without running into Tate at all.

He hurried across the street to the school. There was a little annex between the outside double doors and the entrance to the boys' locker room. Ethan was just about to enter the locker room when he heard it: *"Hey, Tanner! You can't go in there! No fags allowed!"*

Ethan hesitated. He recognized Tate Barringer's voice. Should he just keep walking or should he turn around? Several guys brushed past him into the locker room.

"Somebody stop him! He shouldn't be in there. He's gay!"

Ethan turned, and saw Tate barreling toward him. He tried to laugh. "Would you give me a break?"

Tate shook his head. "I'm not letting you in there. That place is full of naked guys. It's not for faggots. Somebody drops the soap in the shower, and you'll be all over them."

One of Tate's dumb-ass friends was behind him, chuckling. And behind the two of them was Craig. He stared at Ethan. It was the first time he'd made eye contact with him in the last ninety minutes.

"Craig?" Ethan whispered.

His friend looked away, then swept past him into the locker room.

"Get the fuck out of here, Tanner," Tate was growling. "I'm serious." He turned to his friend. "Better guard the door. Make sure this fag doesn't get in. I don't want him eyeballing me." Tate headed through the doors with his friend.

But Tate's pal didn't go very far. His arms crossed, he stood on the other side of the threshold. Every time the door swung open, Ethan caught the guy glaring at him. Ethan couldn't believe it, the guy was actually standing guard.

The little annex began to fill up with guys pouring through to the locker room. Someone shoved Ethan to one side. His stomach was all cramped up, and he was shaking. He started to tear up, but didn't want Tate's dumb-ass pal to see him. He retreated back outside.

Ethan walked back toward the bleachers. The field was empty now. He'd wait until the next gym class started. By that time, Tate and his buddy would be gone. Ethan would be late for his American Literature class, but tough. It didn't matter. Nothing mattered.

As he stood under the bleachers, fighting back the tears, Ethan just wanted to die.

Then he saw it again. The black vintage Mustang came

cruising up the block. It slowed nearly to a stop as it approached him. The sun glared across the windshield, and Ethan couldn't see who was inside.

The Mustang crawled past him, then continued down the block until it turned and disappeared around a corner.

Chapter 8

"Honey, I think I'm gonna have to eat crow. You might have been onto something with your theories about that 'Zorro' stabbing in New York. Maybe it's not just a coincidence."

Sitting in the passenger seat of Ruth's Toyota Camry, Gillian squinted at her friend. Headlights swept across Ruth's face. She was watching the road ahead, and nervously drumming her fingers on the steering wheel.

Ruth always gave her a ride to and from class at the Seattle City College. They often stopped for coffee someplace afterward. Though only five minutes away from Interstate 5 in North Seattle, the community college was at the edge of a forest, and seemed in the middle of nowhere. The large parking lot, with its humming halogen spotlights, was stark and creepy. Gillian was glad for Ruth's company on these trips.

"What made you change your mind?" Gillian murmured apprehensively.

"Late this afternoon, I got this e-mail from a friend on the Internet. Her name's Hester. She's also a fan of yours, Gill. She read the interview you gave with that online *Mystery*

Maniacs Magazine a while back, the one in which you mention *moi*. She wanted to get in touch with the *real* Maggie Dare, she said. Anyway, we've e-mailed back and forth. Hester lives in Great Falls, Montana. She sent me a news story about a bizarre discovery in Billings early this morning. A waitress found the body of a young drifter in an abandoned lot. According to this news article, the police couldn't identify the corpse, because he was missing his teeth. In fact, his whole lower jaw had been torn off. His fingers were missing too."

"My God," Gillian murmured. "But I—I don't understand what this has to do with Jennifer Gilderhoff."

"This dead man's heart had been surgically removed." Ruth took her eyes off the road to glance at Gillian for a moment. " 'Isn't this just like *Highway Hypnosis*?' my friend asked in the e-mail."

Gillian numbly stared back at Ruth and shook her head.

"Gill, I think you have a copycat."

Biting her lip, Gillian turned toward her window. "Do you—" She took a deep breath. "Do you suppose this unidentified drifter is someone I might have known?"

"If you're thinking of Barry and that e-mail you got—"

"That's exactly what I'm thinking."

"It's not him, Gill. The article my friend sent said the dead man was in his late twenties. It's not Barry."

Gillian let out a little sigh.

"But you're right, hon. This *Highway Hypnosis* victim in Montana might be someone you know. Jennifer Gilderhoff was from that class you taught a couple of years ago. I'm wondering if this poor son of a bitch who's missing a heart was in that same class."

Gillian could barely concentrate on her class for the first hour. While students read their stories, she couldn't follow along. She kept thinking about this new murder in Montana.

Had the victim been sitting in this classroom two years ago—alongside Jennifer Gilderhoff?

During the ten-minute break, Gillian headed down to the administration office. She called Ethan on her cell phone. The reception was poor in the gloomy, cinder-block stairwell. But she got through to him.

"So—are you okay?" she asked. "Is Vicki still home?"

"Yeah, I'm fine, Mom," he replied through the static. "Vicki's upstairs. I can hear her stomping around. Everything's cool."

"Are you feeling better? You seemed so moody this afternoon."

"I'm fine," he answered, a little edge to his voice. "I gotta go. I have a DiGiorno in the oven."

"You're having pizza *again*? I bought you all sorts of perfectly good microwave dinners—"

"Mom, I wanted pizza! God! I gotta go take it out of the oven before it burns."

"All right. Well, call me or call Vicki if you get worried or anything."

"I will. Bye." There was a click on the other end of the line.

Sighing, Gillian switched off the cell phone. She stepped out to the first-floor hallway, where some students were milling about. The administration office was on the other side of a counter with a sliding glass window. Gillian peeked into the drab, little room, crammed with file cabinets, four metal desks, and four bulky old computers. In one corner was a huge, hanging, half-dead philodendron plant with its vines drooping down to the floor. In the other corner there was a water cooler—and Rick, the only person on night duty, filling a paper cup for himself. He glanced toward the window-counter and gave Gillian his trademark cocky grin. "Well, if it isn't the famous mystery author. . . ."

"Hi, Rick," she said, working up a smile. "I need to ask you for a favor."

She loathed asking Rick for anything, because she was always turning him down whenever he asked her out—which was often. Rick was in his early thirties, and some might say handsome with his blue eyes, receding wavy black hair, and a permanent five o'clock shadow. He was also extremely hairy. A bicycle fanatic, he often wore his biking attire—T-shirt, spandex shorts, bike shoes—to work. With all the hair on his arms and legs, he looked like a gorilla. A lot of women probably found him sexy. Gillian wasn't among them.

"A favor?" he asked. Sipping his water, he strolled up to the window. He was wearing jeans, with a tight, red, V-neck T-shirt that said, BIKERS DO IT BETTER, and showed off a tuft of chest hair. "Do you need my connections to get you on *Oprah*?"

She worked up a lame chuckle. "Actually—"

"Did I tell you that someone left one of your books in the laundry room of my apartment building with all these other reject paperbacks and magazines?"

She nodded quickly. "Yes, you told me that a couple of weeks ago, Rick. Anyway, I was hoping you could go into the archives for me, and print up my class list from September two years ago."

Rick's mouth twisted to one side. "Hmmm, if I do this, what will the famous and beautiful mystery author do for me?"

"I could personally autograph that book you found in the basement of your apartment building."

He leaned against the other side of the counter and casually scratched the tuft of hair above his T-shirt collar. "Actually, I was thinking maybe you and I—"

"Rick, I'm not going out with you," Gillian cut in. "Now could you just do this for me, please? My class reconvenes in two minutes. I don't have a lot of time."

Rick frowned, and then he shuffled back to his desk and plopped down in the chair. He glanced up at her. "Course title?"

"It's my class for the Experimental College. The course title is Fiction Writing: Preparing to Publish."

He started typing. "And you want the class list from September two years ago?"

"That's right," Gillian said. "I appreciate this, Rick."

"Two years ago," he repeated, eyes on his computer screen. "Huh, that's when those women were killed. Were any of them in your class?"

"No," Gillian answered soberly. "I didn't know any of the women who were murdered."

"Want to hear something weird? Every time one of them got it, the cops questioned me. For a while there, I figured they were going to pin the killings on me. Did you ever meet Boyd Farrow?"

Gillian shook her head. "No, I didn't know him." She didn't want to talk about this right now.

"Seemed like a nice enough guy, not at all the serial-killer type. It never made sense to me that he taught here for six years and nothing. Then suddenly, boom, he's abducting women, dressing them up like Catholic schoolgirls, and shooting them. Something in him must have snapped." He glanced up from the computer screen. "Hey, how come you've never written a mystery based on that? *The Schoolgirl Murders,* it would make a good one."

"I just haven't, that's all."

"Shame," Rick said. As he pulled away from his desk, he hit one last key, which started up the printer. He got to his feet, retrieved the listing, and handed it to her.

Gillian glanced at the printout, and saw Jennifer Gilderhoff's name on the list of a dozen students. She knew she had the right class. "Thanks, Rick," she said. "Sorry I got snippy earlier."

He grinned. "That's okay. I'll see you make it up to me."

Gillian tucked the list into her purse, and hurried for the stairwell. She ran back up to the second floor, where she found Ruth waiting for her outside the classroom. Ruth had her coat on.

"Oh, hon, I hate to leave you high and dry for a ride," she said anxiously. "But I just called home for messages, and my grandson, Darnell, fell and hit his head against the coffee table. My daughter's freaking out. There's blood everywhere. She had to pile all three kids into the car and drive to the hospital. I got through to her on her cell. She wants me up in Everett—*pronto*. I need to take off. Can you get a ride home from someone else?"

"Oh my God, of course," Gillian murmured. "Don't worry about me—"

"Well, I don't want to leave you alone tonight, not when this copycat-nut is on the loose. Promise you'll take a cab home if you can't get a ride from someone in class."

"I promise," Gillian said. "Now, get going. Call and let me know once you find out how Darnell's doing. Be careful."

"*You* be careful, hon. I mean it," Ruth said grimly. Then she turned and hurried toward the stairwell.

"Sarah Lee was surprised when her roommate, Connie, stepped into the shower with her. 'I'm in a hurry,' said Connie. 'And you'll hog all the hot water. Scrub my back, Sarah Lee! Use that peach-scented soap. My boyfriend likes the smell!' Sarah scrubbed her roommate's strong, supple back. Connie's skin was silky to the touch. . . ."

Burt was one of Gillian's older students, a grandfatherly type with gray hair, glasses, and a penchant for flannel shirts. He was writing a novel about a sixtysomething college professor's affair with a beautiful young student. It was short on characterization, and long on the sex scenes—especially between his heroine Sarah Lee and other beautiful, nubile women. The rest of the class tolerated Burt's fantasies, because it was the only time his writing came alive. Besides, he didn't take criticism well. He refused to change the title of his novel in progress, despite everyone telling him that *In Pursuit of Sarah Lee* sounded like it was about a dessert fiend.

Though things were getting hot and steamy in the shower with Sarah Lee and her roommate, Gillian wasn't paying attention. The words Burt read aloud seemed to blend together, just so much background noise.

Gillian was at her desk, gazing at the class without really focusing on any one of the fourteen students seated in front of her. It was an eclectic group varying in age, race, sexual orientation, and writing ability. Sometimes it was a chore dealing with the diverse, often conflicting personalities in the class. There was a lot of pride, ego, and temperament in one small classroom. All these people expected her to help them get published, and she barely eked out a living at it herself.

Gillian had the same second-floor classroom from two years ago. The windows looked out on an asphalt roof and across to another wing of the school. There had always been something wrong with the heat. In the winter months, everyone stayed bundled up in their sweaters or jackets throughout the class.

She remembered Jennifer Gilderhoff had usually occupied the chair-desk right next to where Burt sat now. People always seemed to take the same seat session after session. Ruth had become a fixture in the first row. It was strange to see her chair now vacant. She'd hardly missed a class. In fact, the last time that front-row seat had gone unoccupied had been two years ago, right after Gillian had been forced to give up her car. The bruises from the beating she'd endured were still painfully vivid on her face. Ruth had offered to drive her to class, but she'd gotten sick at the last minute.

Now that Gillian thought back on that November evening two years ago, she saw how much it was like tonight—the same cold weather, and the same strange feeling in the pit of her stomach that something bad was about to happen. Ruth had insisted Gillian take a cab to and from the college on that night too. Even back then, Ruth had been wary of the bus—and not without a good reason.

A twenty-two-year-old night student named Kelly Zinnemann had been missing for three days, and the last place she'd been seen was the bus stop by the school. Her purse—with money and credit cards still in it—had been found in a clump of bushes nearby.

Bulletins were posted around the small campus with the word MISSING under the pretty blonde's photo, and a description underneath. Warnings to female students and faculty members were posted alongside the bulletin. Different incidents prior to Kelly's disappearance were cited, everything from a purse-snatching to a flasher to an attempted rape. The dark forest bordering the parking lot seemed like a haven for criminals and sex offenders. At that time, the halogen spotlights and campus security phones hadn't yet been installed.

Heeding Ruth's advice, Gillian had taken a taxi to class that night. She explained her battered appearance to her students by saying she'd gotten into a car wreck. The fabrication also helped explain why she was suddenly without a car.

After class, Jennifer Gilderhoff approached her in the corridor. She seemed nervous. "Gillian, it might be none of my business, but I wanted to tell you something." She spoke in a whisper, and glanced around to make sure no one in the hallway could hear her. "I know someone who counsels abused wives, and if you need any help—"

"Oh, no, thank you," Gillian said, with a little laugh. "That's not how this happened. I really did smash up my car. But thank you for your concern, Jennifer."

"Um, is your husband coming to pick you up?" she asked.

"No, that was the family car. I'm taking a cab home."

"Oh, let me drive you," Jennifer offered. "You shouldn't be waiting around for a cab, not when they've posted those warnings all over the school. Plus, I could use the company. You know what they say—safety in numbers and all."

Gillian accepted Jennifer's offer. But she couldn't help feeling there was something phony about her concern, something slightly condescending.

"God, it's scary to think there might be someone around here abducting women," Jennifer said as they stepped outside together.

Gillian felt a chill, and turned up the collar to her trench coat. In the dark, wet parking lot, it was hard to miss the red flashing police lights. Two patrol cars had pulled into the corner of the lot, near the forest. An old, beat-up Monte Carlo was parked between them.

"Do you think they caught somebody?" Jennifer asked. She started toward the squad cars. But Gillian hesitated.

"Don't you want to see what's going on?" Jennifer asked.

Gillian still had that feeling of dread in the pit of her stomach. Nevertheless, she followed Jennifer toward the police investigation site. They were about twenty feet away when one of the cops started shaking his head at them. "Ladies, please," he called. "Go back. You don't want to see this. . . ."

"Oh, my God," Jennifer whispered.

Gillian saw the rain-beaded windshield of the Monte Carlo. Then she realized some of those drops were red—and they came from inside the car. Slumped in the passenger seat was a young woman with blood matting down her blond hair and caked along the side of her neck.

They'd found Kelly Zinnemann.

Later, the details emerged. The Monte Carlo had been reported stolen five nights before. The coroner estimated that Kelly had been dead approximately eighteen hours before the police discovered her in the abandoned car. She'd been shot in the head execution-style. The clothes she wore weren't from her wardrobe. Twenty-two-year-old Kelly had been dressed in a schoolgirl's uniform—a blue blazer, madras skirt, and knee socks. Gillian found out from Ruth that the dead woman was also wearing saddle shoes, her size. Ruth's police connections were pretty certain the killer had bought the shoes some time before abducting Kelly. He must have been watching her—and planning her death—for quite a while.

Kelly had been the first.

Gillian remembered that scary, lonely time from two years ago—with her husband deserting her, no car, and a serial killer roaming around the campus where she taught her night class. Two more women were killed, both of them shot execution-style, both of them dressed in Catholic schoolgirl uniforms. Attendance among female night students dropped by nearly a third as the college was held in the grip of fear for seven weeks. Women came to their classes with knives, Mace, or pepper spray in their purses.

They eventually caught the "Schoolgirl Killer." But Gillian suspected they had the wrong guy when they arrested Boyd Farrow. He insisted he was innocent, and so did several people who knew him. But Boyd Farrow was never tried or convicted for the Schoolgirl Murders. He was found dead in his jail cell a month after his arrest.

Still, the killings stopped after his incarceration.

Now it seemed another set of killings had begun. Jennifer Gilderhoff lay in a coma in a New York hospital after being stabbed repeatedly. And in Montana, the body of a hitchhiker had been discovered with his heart surgically removed. Had he also been a student in her night class two years ago? Gillian wondered if there was a connection between this "copycat" and the Schoolgirl Murders.

Burt finished reading his latest entry from *In Pursuit of Sarah Lee,* and his classmates valiantly struggled to come up with some helpful positive criticism. After class, Gillian stepped out to the corridor and called for a taxi. They kept her on hold for ten minutes. Meanwhile, the school emptied out. The hallway got quieter and quieter—until the only sound she heard was the hold-music on her cell phone.

The taxi dispatcher finally came on the other end of the line. They couldn't get a cab to her for another twenty-five minutes. "Never mind, thank you," Gillian said into the phone. She switched off her cell, folded it up, and shoved it into her purse.

There was no one in the cold, gloomy stairwell, and she hurried down the steps to the first floor. Gillian passed the administration office window, and saw the darkened office beyond the glass. The hallway lights started to dim just as Gillian stepped out a side door.

The humming halogen spotlights gave the parking lot an eerie, otherworldly glow that was almost more sinister than the darkness. Gillian spotted a group of students headed toward the bus stop, and she followed them for a while—until they all piled into an SUV. Gillian kept walking at a brisk clip as the SUV pulled out of the lot. She didn't see anyone else around—and very few cars. She glanced toward the forest—and the corner of the lot where they'd found Kelly Zinnemann in the abandoned car two years ago. No cars were there now.

And no one was waiting at the bus stop by the parking lot entrance. Gillian checked her wristwatch: 9:20. Then she consulted the bus schedule posted on the side of the shelter. She had another twenty-five minutes until the next bus came along. Hell, she could have waited for the damn taxi and arrived home sooner.

She sat down on the little bench in the shelter. The area was well lit by one of those humming halogen lights overhead. Across the street from the stop was an abandoned lot. About half a block down was a 7-Eleven, and beside that, a dump called Wok Like a Man Teriyaki Hut. Both places were just far enough away that she couldn't expect a response if she screamed for help.

Gillian looked over her shoulder at the clump of bushes where they'd found Kelly Zinnemann's purse two years ago. She shifted restlessly on the bench, then reached into her purse and pulled out her class list from two years ago. Looking at the first few names, she drew a blank. But she remembered some of them besides Jennifer. There were two older women writing romance novels; and Chase Scott, a somewhat pretentious, but talented young man whose real name was Scott Chase; and a sweet, chubby girl, Shauna Hendricks, writing a mystery. There was Glenn Turlinger, an old man with a three-pronged cane; his dry Civil War military saga bored everyone stiff. She remembered Todd Sorenson, a young, "tortured" artist-poet whose writing was a rambling, incoherent mess. He hadn't gotten along with anyone in the class, and quit before the end of the semester. And of course, there was Ruth, working on her true-crime thriller.

She would have to ask Ruth if she remembered the others. The "drifter" murdered in Montana could have been Chase Scott or Todd Sorenson, or one of the two other men whose names were on the class list.

Perhaps one of them was the murderer. This copycat killer had gone after Jennifer Gilderhoff for a reason. Only someone connected to that class—or the school—would know that Jennifer had been one of her students.

Past the constant hum from the halogen lights, Gillian heard a rustling noise. She swiveled around and studied the bushes. She didn't see anything.

She wished there was more traffic on the street. In all this time waiting at the stop, only about a dozen cars had driven by. Gillian took out her cell phone. She was about to call the taxi company again. But she hesitated and glanced at the phone numbers on the class list. They were two years old, but it was worth a try.

She tried the number to one of the men she couldn't remember: Vincent G. Connelly.

A woman answered on the other end. "Hello?"

"Yes, hello," Gillian said. "Is Vincent Connelly there, please?"

"*Vincent?* Is this a telemarketer?"

"No, I was his creative writing teacher at Seattle City Experimental College two years ago."

"Oh, well, okay, just a second." Then Gillian heard her call out: "Gary, telephone! It's someone from that writing class you took. . . ."

Gillian suddenly remembered. *Gary* Connelly was a stocky man in his late forties, with glasses, a dark cocoa complexion, and graying hair. He'd been working on a detective novel. Or was it a sports novel?

"Hello?"

"Gary, this is Gillian McBride," she said. "I don't know if you remember me—"

"Of course, I do! How the heck are you, Gillian?"

She now recalled Gary's jovial disposition and his big, booming voice. "I'm fine," she said, peeking down the street for a sign of the bus. "Um, I just wanted to touch base with a few of my old students. Are you still writing?"

"Oh, I take it out and dabble with it once in a while. I came up with a new title. *The Ballpark Murders.* What do you think?"

"Well, it—it's got potential. Keep at it, Gary. Listen, I was wondering if you've heard from anyone else in the class recently."

"Yeah, I got an e-mail from Jennifer What's-her-name. It was one of those mass e-mails, announcing she'd gotten a book published. I fired off a quick congratulations, and didn't hear back from her. That was about a month ago."

"No one else?" she asked. "Chase Scott maybe?"

"Wasn't he the pompous one who was writing some kind of thriller? I remember the pages of endless description. It took place down in Jamaica or someplace—with scuba diving and sex on the beach."

"That's right. You haven't heard from him?"

"Oh, God, no. I think he said about two words to me the

whole semester. He was kind of a squirrelly dude, almost as bad as that psycho-case Ted."

"You mean Todd?" Gillian asked. "The one who left before the end of the semester?"

"That's right, Todd," Gary said. "Talk about strange. I think he was on drugs half the time. And how about the way he was stalking you?"

"Stalking me?" Gillian repeated, watching a car whoosh by.

"Yeah, didn't you know? When I'd wait for my wife to come pick me up after class, I used to see him hanging around. He'd follow you and your friend out to the parking lot—and just watch you."

"I had no idea," Gillian murmured. Her cell beeped.

"What is that, another call?" Gary asked.

"No, my battery's going," Gillian said. "Um, are you sure Todd was stalking me?"

"Well, I remember once, one of the old ladies was wondering where you lived, and Todd piped up. He knew. He said, 'She lives on Capitol Hill—in a duplex.' Isn't that right? Did you live in a duplex? I think he even mentioned that you had a front porch."

Gillian felt a shiver pass through her. "That's right."

"I'm sorry, what did you say? You're breaking up."

"This battery's going on me. Do you remember anything else about Todd?"

"Wasn't he"—the line broke for a moment—"novel about a rock band in Tacoma or Fort Lewis—" The connection went out again. "I couldn't make heads or tails of it. No one could."

"Yes, it was a difficult story to follow. Listen, Gary, I better hang up. We're losing the connection. I'll call you later this week."

He must have said something that didn't go through, because all Gillian heard was an aborted "—from you too, Gillian. Bye." Then the line went dead.

She clicked off the cell phone, and tucked it into her purse with the class listing. Gillian checked her wristwatch again. The bus should have come five minutes ago. She peered down the empty street, and sighed.

She remembered Todd Sorenson as crudely handsome with cold blue eyes and messy brown hair. He was lean, and dangerous-looking. He always wore the same torn black sweater to class. The chapters he turned in were usually on dirty, crinkled paper—with dozens of typos, scratch-outs, and notes in the margins. He used an old manual typewriter too. She recalled the slightly raised "e."

His writing was more like stream-of-consciousness rambling, something he'd produced while under the influence. She remembered him looking a bit stoned during some of the classes, slouched in his chair, blue eyes at half-mast.

She couldn't believe Todd had been stalking her. He must have been casing the place during those weeks following Barry's disappearance. Todd, the cops, those hoods, and God only knows who else were all hanging around. Hell, with all the people out there watching from the shadows, she should have set up a concession stand and made a few bucks.

Gillian let out a stunned little laugh.

She heard the bushes rustling behind her again, and she stopped laughing. She stood up. Turning, she caught her reflection in the shelter's Plexiglas wall. Merging with her own image, she saw some movement in those bushes. Her hand automatically reached inside her purse for the pepper spray. But her feet couldn't move. They seemed rooted to the pavement.

"Who's there?" she called nervously.

Twigs snapped.

Shadows swept across the Plexiglas and steel shelter. The bushes' branches and leaves seemed to move again. It took a moment for Gillian to realize another vehicle was coming up the street. It was the bus.

The number 502 pulled up to the curb, and the door

whooshed open. Gillian glanced over her shoulder at the bus stop shelter. She didn't see anyone.

Still, even as she took her seat and the bus pulled away, she had to look back again at the bus stop—the last place Kelly Zinnemann had been seen alive.

Gillian noticed something moving in the bushes, a strange silhouette. She wasn't sure if it was a human or an animal or just another clump of bushes. The bus was going too fast. Considering the spot was sort of a morbid landmark, Gillian couldn't help wondering if she'd just encountered a ghost.

She really couldn't be certain about anything—except the awful feeling of dread in the pit of her stomach. It just wouldn't go away.

Chapter 9

"Tie a Yellow Ribbon on the Old Oak Tree" played over the din of people screaming, slot machines churning, and roulette wheels spinning in the Grand Room of the Midas Mountain Casino in Missoula, Montana. The handsome, dark-haired, forty-one-year-old, whose luck and money were running out on the dollar slot machine, didn't even hear the other man addressing him.

"I said, *'Hey!'*" the other guy yelled. He had just hit the jackpot on the next slot machine over. He handed the man a silver dollar. "Here, Jack, take this for luck!"

"My name's not Jack," the first man said with a half smile.

"In this place it is. *What happens in Missoula stays in Missoula!* Isn't that what they say about Vegas? So—you're Jack and I'm Mike, okay? Let me buy you a drink, Jack."

"The drinks here are free," "Jack" reminded him.

"Yeah, but I'm a generous tipper," "Mike" replied. "And this has led to a very intimate rapport with a very hot-looking waitress. But some of these babes, they're like cuff links, beautiful baubles traveling in pairs. She has this friend, who I hear is quite the looker, and she doesn't want to leave her alone tonight. This is where you come in, Jack."

Jack threw him a wary look, then slipped the silver dollar into the slot and pulled the lever. It came up cherry, lemon, and a dollar sign. "I didn't score with your lucky dollar, *Mike*. Sorry. Try your luck with someone else, okay?"

Mike waved down a tall, thin waitress with wavy brown hair and dimples. Her skimpy, midnight-blue uniform showed off a gorgeous pair of long, tapered legs. She balanced a tray full of dirty glasses against her hip. "How are you doing over here, Mike?" she asked. "Want another?"

"Yeah, Fran, thanks," he said. "And my buddy, Jack, here could use something."

Fran turned toward Jack and gave him a big smile. "Well, Jack, what will it be?"

He couldn't help smiling back. She was so cute. "How about a Scotch on the rocks?"

One Scotch on the rocks became five.

Mike convinced Jack he was the perfect escort for Fran's friend. He'd been watching Jack earlier at the roulette table, and there was something smooth, polite, and polished about him. "Class, that's what you got," Mike told him over a steak dinner in the restaurant attached to the casino. "I trust you with Fran's friend, and Fran's going to trust you. It's a good deal for everybody. Now, they get off work at one-thirty in the morning. . . ."

Jack had yet to meet Fran's friend, but Mike stepped away from the diner booth a couple of times to firm up their rendezvous plans. "They're going to freshen up and come by your motel at two," Mike said.

"How do they know where I'm staying?" Jack asked, his thinking a little fuzzy.

"The Aces High Motor Inn, Room 220," Mike said.

"How did you know that?" Jack squinted at him. "I didn't tell you."

"Yes, you did. C'mon, let's get you outside for some fresh air. We'll go for a drive. I don't want you too drunk for the girls. They'll change their minds about us."

As they headed out to the parking lot, Jack told Mike he didn't need any help walking, thanks. But Mike kept grabbing onto his arm, and Jack realized he was indeed almost ready to topple over. He'd had too much to drink. "Jesus, don't let me do anything stupid, okay?" Jack whispered to his new friend.

"No sweat, buddy," Mike replied. He led Jack to a black Honda Accord, parked near the corner of the lot. He unlocked the passenger door and opened it.

Hesitating, Jack glanced at a single sneaker left on the floor of the passenger side. "Huh, somebody lost a shoe," he muttered.

"Oh, that." Mike snatched up the tennis shoe, and then helped Jack into the front seat. "I picked up this hitchhiker in Rapid City last night. He kept coming on to me. Some people don't get it when you're just being friendly. I finally had to dump his queer ass in Billings."

He tossed the shoe on the backseat. "This must have fallen out of his knapsack. You all in and buckled up, buddy? Ready to take a little drive?"

Jack nodded. "Yeah, thanks. Like I say, just don't let me do anything stupid."

"I won't," Mike said, then he shut the car door.

"Of course Todd Sorenson was stalking you. I'd be a pretty crappy detective if I hadn't caught on to that."

The phone had rung just as Gillian was heating up some soup for dinner. It was 10:25, and Ruth was home from her daughter's house in Everett. Her nine-year-old grandson, Darnell, had received six stitches in his forehead. She'd cleaned up the blood in her daughter's living room, washed the dinner dishes, and helped put the kids to bed. "Anyway, we have damage control," Ruth had cracked. "So did I miss anything tonight?"

Gillian had told her about her phone conversation with Gary Connelly. Ruth hadn't been at all surprised about Todd's Sorenson's after-school activities.

"Todd wasn't exactly a *subtle* stalker either," she said. "He'd follow us out to the parking lot after every class—up to a point. Then he'd just stand there and watch us get into the car. I was tempted to run him over a couple of times. I pointed it out to you, Gillian."

"Well, I don't remember," Gillian said into the cordless phone. She stirred the pan of Progresso Cream of Chicken and Wild Rice Soup on the stove.

"I probably mentioned it around the time Barry disappeared," Ruth surmised. "Communicating with you was like talking to a fire hydrant for a few weeks there. You were so out of it. Anyway, he seemed harmless enough—until he went nuts on us and quit the class."

"Refresh my memory about that incident. Wasn't he upset at the way everyone reacted to his latest chapter or something? I keep thinking it was my fault for not moderating the critique session better."

"Oh, please, he was challenging everyone, *'You don't like it because you know nothing about poetry or art.'* And then in the hallway during the break, we were hanging around the vending machine. You weren't there. But he called all of us *'fucking ignorant assholes.'* That includes sweet old Edna. Her jaw dropped so low, I thought her dentures were going to pop out. And him, I thought the crazy son of a bitch was going to kill somebody."

"Do you think he has?" Gillian asked soberly. "Killed someone—I mean."

Her friend didn't answer for a moment. "No, Todd wouldn't wait almost two years to release his wrath on the class—one by one. I could see him coming back to class the following week with an assault weapon and doing us in with a few rounds. But no, Todd wouldn't have the patience and the smarts for something as methodical as these copycat killings."

Ruth paused on the other end of the line. "Listen, I used my daughter's computer and went online. I dug up a couple of stories about the Montana murder, but they're sketchy. The article my Internet pal, Hester, sent has the most details so far."

"Well, thanks for checking, Ruth." Gillian looked at her soup again, and then switched off the stove.

"Did you talk with anyone else from the old class besides Gary?"

"Well, my cell phone went out on me on the bus. But I made some calls when I got home. I didn't have any luck reaching Todd, Chase Scott, or Shauna Hendricks. The phone numbers aren't good anymore. I didn't find any listings for them in the Seattle phone book either. But I got through to Edna."

"Well, how is the old girl?"

"Still dabbling with her bodice-ripper romance novel," Gillian said. "But she mentioned something that might be worth checking out. She ran into Jennifer Gilderhoff near the ferry terminal downtown last month. She went on and on about how sweet and pretty Jennifer was. I didn't have the heart to tell her what happened. Anyway, according to Edna, they talked briefly, and Jennifer was with a friend named April. End of story. But—well, maybe this friend knows something useful. I figure—"

"Hon, the police already talked with Jennifer's friends, and came up with bupkis. What makes you think this April character would tell you something she didn't spill to the cops?"

"Because they're the police and I'm a woman. Anyway, it might be worth pursuing."

"Maybe," Ruth allowed. "I don't know why I'm even talking to you. I'm really ticked off you went ahead and took a bus home after I warned you not to. How was the rest of the class session after the break? Did I miss anything?"

"Burt read another chapter from his story."

"*Searching for Little Debbie?*"

"Close. *In Pursuit of Sarah Lee,*" Gillian said. "You didn't miss much."

"Are you going to be okay tonight?" Ruth asked.

"I think so," Gillian replied. She poured the steaming soup into a bowl. "My upstairs neighbor is back. So it's not like we're totally alone here. In fact, she has a *gentleman-friend* coming over tonight. The joint is jumping. We'll be fine."

After she hung up with Ruth, Gillian carried her bowl of soup to the kitchen table. She noticed the strip of light under the door to Ethan's bedroom. She went to the door and knocked.

"Yeah?"

Gillian poked her head in. Ethan was lying on top of his bed, reading a history book. "I'm having soup for dinner," Gillian said. "Do you want some? Or would your body go into shock if you fed it something besides pizza?"

He glanced up from his book. "No, thanks."

Gillian came in and sat down on the edge of his bed. "How are you doing?"

Ethan sat up. "I'm fine."

Gillian frowned. She thought about those boys taunting Ethan in front of the duplex yesterday afternoon. She wondered if it was a regular thing Ethan had to endure. "Well, you don't seem fine," she said. "Did something happen at school today?"

He shrugged evasively. "Nothing happened. I'm fine."

"I haven't seen Craig in a while. Did you two have a falling-out?"

Ethan rolled his eyes. "No. I just—he's busy, Mom. That's all." He nodded at the book in his hands. "I really gotta study."

Gillian got up from the bed. "Well, think about what you'd like to do for your birthday next week. Okay?"

"Okay," he answered. He glanced toward the door. "Thanks, Mom."

She leaned over and kissed the top of his head. Then she left him alone and closed the door to his room.

Gillian retreated to the kitchen, sat down at the table, and tried to eat her soup. It was cold.

At one in the morning, Jack still felt a bit wobbly as he got out of Mike's Honda Accord. They'd parked in back of the Aces High Motor Inn, where Jack had a room with a kitchen. He'd told Mike the unit was kind of cheesy, but it was clean and had a view of the pool. The plan, as Jack understood it, was that once Fran and her pal came by, they'd all have a drink in his room, and eventually, Mike and Fran would go off by themselves. "But I have to be honest with you, buddy," Mike pointed out. "Fran has made no bones about the fact that she sure likes you. You may end up with her tonight. But I hear her friend is a knockout too. So we're both doing all right. I mean, we're farting in silk underwear either way."

"That's a charming expression," Jack chuckled, fumbling with his keys to the motel's side entrance.

"Hey, you don't recognize me at all, do you?" Mike asked.

Jack squinted at him. "Huh?"

"Never mind." Mike was still holding onto his arm. His new friend somehow seemed to know the way as they headed down the corridor to the pool area. Jack bumped into a patio recliner chair and it scraped against the cement deck. "My room's right over there," Jack announced, pointing to one of several sliding glass doors on the other side of the large, kidney-shaped swimming pool.

Mike shushed him. Most of the units were darkened with

the drapes shut. All the patio lights were off, but the pool light was still on.

Suddenly, Mike stopped and peered down at something in the shallow end of the pool. "Wait a second," he whispered. "Is that a dollar bill?"

Squatting, he rolled up his sleeve and reached into the iridescent blue water. "Holy shit, look. We're recouping your losses tonight, Jack. There are three twenty-dollar bills here—if I can reach these suckers. Help me out, buddy."

Jack got down on all fours beside him and gazed down into the pool. "I don't see anything," he murmured.

"You need to look closer," Mike said, moving behind him. "See them down there? Lean toward the edge. See them now?"

"No, I—"

All at once, Mike grabbed him by the scalp and slammed his head against the edge of the pool. There was a loud snap, the sound of the man's skull cracking. He slumped forward. Mike grabbed him under his arms, the same way he'd been keeping Jack from falling down most of the night. He just held him for a moment, and then gently lowered him into the pool.

The blood began to bloom red in the shallow end of the chlorine-blue water. *"Like a scarlet cloud sweeping across a blue horizon,"* Mike murmured to himself. That was how Gillian had described the blood in the water after her poolside murder in *Killing Legend*.

He glanced at the sliding glass doors around the pool area—still darkened, the drapes still closed. Smiling, he turned to gaze at the dead body floating in the water. He wiped his wet hand on the side of his pants, and then rolled down his sleeve.

He kept glancing back at his handiwork as he headed toward Room 220. There would be no time to linger while he went through the guy's room for personal items. He had a plane to catch. He needed to be in Seattle by morning.

Chapter 10

"I'm looking for a book called *Burning Old Bridesmaids' Dresses and Other Survival Stories*. The author is Jennifer Gilderhoff. It's brand-new, might not even be released yet."

Brian, the bearded, nerdy-cute, young clerk behind the counter at Broadway Books, consulted his computer, and then checked a microfiche file. "Hmm, looks like that'll be available next week, Gillian. We have five on order. Want me to reserve you a copy?"

She leaned on the counter. "Those five books haven't come in yet, have they? I know you sometimes get them before the pub date. I just want to take a look at it."

"You know, that title sounds really familiar," Brian said. "Let me go back and peek at the inventory list."

"Thanks, Brian."

While he retreated to the back room, Gillian checked for her book in their Mystery section. Broadway Books was her neighborhood bookstore and had always been very supportive. They threw Gillian a book-signing party every time she had a new thriller published, and stocked all her books. They still had several autographed copies of *Black Ribbons* and the others. The books weren't exactly flying off the shelf. It was discouraging to see—and typical of her day so far.

She'd started the morning bawling her eyes out after watching Ethan trudge off to his bus stop. She wondered if they were teasing him at school. Was he on his way to endure the same type of cruelty she'd witnessed in front of the house the other afternoon? She felt as if she were watching him go off to his doom.

Eventually, she dried her eyes and called the bowling alley. She got an answering machine, and left a message canceling her reservations for Ethan's birthday party next Saturday afternoon. If Craig wasn't helping her with the guest list—or even attending the party—no one would be coming. She had to figure out something else to do for Ethan's birthday.

It was after eleven in New York when she called her agent's office. Eve was still at a sales conference in Atlantic City. Gillian asked Eve's assistant, Becky, if she had sent the *Daily News* article about the "Zorro" stabbing. Becky didn't know what she was talking about. Gillian couldn't think of anyone else at the agency who might have sent her the article. She wondered if somebody had gone into the agency and stolen some of their envelopes. Whoever had sent her that clipping about Jennifer had gone to a lot of trouble to stay anonymous.

She also phoned the college to see if they had more current contact information for Todd Sorenson, Chase Scott, and Shauna Hendricks. The woman she spoke with in the administration office seemed annoyed with her. "I happen to be very busy," she said curtly. "I don't exactly have a lot of time to look this up for you right now. Just—just—give me your e-mail address. I'll send you the information when I can get around to it, okay?"

"Thank you, it's—"

"No, don't delete that," the woman was saying to someone else in the office. "I'm going to buy that . . . no, the pink one. It's on sale. . . . No, it's only available online." She cleared her throat. "Okay, what's your e-mail address?"

Through her teeth, Gillian gave the woman her e-mail address and hung up.

She'd decided not to hold her breath waiting for the e-mail response. So Gillian had thrown on her coat and taken a walk on this gray morning to her local bookstore.

"Hey, Gillian, I have something for you," Brian said, emerging from the back room. He was holding a copy of *Burning Old Bridesmaids' Dresses*. "I remembered—the author sent us an advance reader's copy. It was in the to-be-recycled stack. You're welcome to keep it."

"Oh, thank you, Brian." She took the book and opened it to the Acknowledgments page. No new author could resist including an Acknowledgments page. Going without it would be like winning an Oscar and not thanking anyone. Gillian started scanning down the list of people Jennifer thanked, which included two other creative writing teachers, her agent, a bunch of people connected with the publisher, her parents and family, her cat, and finally: "Thanks also to my friend, April Tomlinson, for sharing with me her crazy stories and her wild sense of humor."

"Brian, could I hit you up for the phone book?" Gillian asked.

Five minutes later, she was standing outside the bookstore and dialing the number for *Tomlinson, April J.* A woman picked up after the third ring. Gillian could hear a radio in the background. "Hello. Is April there, please?" Gillian asked.

"No, she isn't. Can I take a message?"

"Do you know where I can get ahold of her? I was hoping to talk with her this morning."

There was a long pause on the other end of the line.

"Um, I was in this writing class two years ago with this friend of hers named Jennifer," Gillian said. "I understand she might be able to tell me something about Jennifer's condition."

"Oh. Well, you might try April at her job. She works at the Seattle Aquarium."

Gillian took the bus downtown, and then walked another mile to Seattle's waterfront area. She crossed under the Highway 99 viaduct, and waited for a streetcar to pass. On the other side of Alaskan Way, she saw the Seattle Aquarium, a huge warehouse structure on the edge of Puget Sound's Elliott Bay. The area was crowded with tourists—as well as people trying to catch the ferry at the pier terminal next door.

It was dark inside the Aquarium, but the walls were bathed in rippled blue-green shadows from all the illuminated fish tanks. Gillian asked the ticket-taker—a thin Asian man in a navy blue SEATTLE AQUARIUM shirt—if he knew where she could find April Tomlinson.

"She's working in the souvenir shop," he said. "It's just to your right. Enjoy your visit."

Passing a display on the wall that mapped out the different attractions at the Aquarium, Gillian noticed the souvenir stand, a long counter linking two totem poles. Books, snow globes, T-shirts, and hats filled the shelves, but there weren't any customers. The two women working the cash registers looked bored. One was a short, round black woman with a diamond stud in her nostril. The other was pale and waiflike. She looked about thirty—and anorexic. She wore black-cherry lipstick, and her hair was arranged in a short, stiff pageboy that was more a maroon color than red. Gillian wondered if this was the woman with the *"crazy stories"* and *"wild sense of humor."*

She approached the counter. "Excuse me. April?"

The thin woman squinted at her. "Are you the one my roommate just called me about? Jennifer's friend?"

Gillian nodded. "Yes, hi—"

April turned to her coworker, who was suddenly busy with a customer. "Hey Sonya, I'm going to take a Marlboro break, okay?" Not waiting for an answer, she grabbed a rain slicker and purse from under the counter. "I didn't get your name," she said to Gillian.

"I'm Gillian McBride. Jennifer was one of my students in a writing class two years ago."

April had started out from behind the counter, but now she hesitated. "You were her teacher?"

Gillian nodded. "What's wrong?"

"Nothing. I just—I pictured someone older, that's all. Listen, I'm sorry, but I won't have a lot of time to talk with you. I really shouldn't leave my coworker alone here."

"No, it's okay, go," the other woman piped up as she worked the register. She shooed away her friend with a wave of her hand. "Go on. You told me ten minutes ago you were dying for a cig. Go."

April gave Gillian a pinched smile, and threw her jacket over her shoulders. "I need to watch my back here," she said, starting toward the front doors. "My boss is a real stickler about us taking too many breaks." She stepped outside and paused just outside the doorway. "So—you wanted to find out how Jennifer was? Then I guess you heard about it—the stabbing, I mean."

Gillian nodded. "Last I heard she was in a coma."

"She still is," April muttered, looking down at the sidewalk.

"Aren't you going to have your cigarette?" Gillian asked.

"No. Like I said, I don't have time." April glanced over her shoulder at the Aquarium doorway. "Anyway, I talked to Jennifer's mother this morning. No change. They're thinking about taking her off the machines." Her voice cracked a little. "I wish I were there."

"And the police still have no idea who stabbed her?"

April shook her head. "No idea," she echoed.

"Do you know if she was seeing anyone in New York?"

"The cops already asked me that. She was meeting her editor. That's it. She didn't know anyone else in New York."

"Do you think a boyfriend or someone might have followed her out there?"

"Jennifer has had a lot of boyfriends. But as far as I know, for the last few weeks, she hasn't been seeing anybody in particular." April's eyes narrowed at her. "You sound just like the police. Why are you asking me these questions?"

"I'm just in shock. I'm trying to figure out what happened. You've been friends with Jennifer for a long time, haven't you?"

A sad look passed across April's face. "Eight years now. I'm practically her best friend."

Gillian pulled the advance reader's copy of *Burning Old Bridesmaids' Dresses* out of her purse and showed it to April. "I figured as much. I saw what she said about you here in the acknowledgments." Gillian sighed. "You sure you don't want a cigarette? I could use one."

Gillian hadn't smoked since college, but she wanted this woman to bond with her and open up to her a little—even if it meant having to get nauseous on a cigarette.

"No, thanks," April said with a smile. "I'm trying to cut back."

"I hate to keep asking you these stupid questions. But do you know if Jennifer kept in touch with anyone from that class I taught?"

April shook her head. "No, I don't think so. No." She glanced back over her shoulder again. "Listen, I need to get back to work—"

"Does the name Todd Sorenson ring a bell? Or Chase Scott? Did Jennifer ever say anything to you—"

"No. I'm not good with names anyway." She shrugged. "I'm sorry, but I better scoot or I'll get in trouble with my boss. It was nice to meet you, Gillian. Jennifer thought you were a very good teacher."

Gillian reached into her purse and fished out a card promoting her new book, *Black Ribbons*. "My phone number and e-mail address are on there," she said, handing the card to April. "Could you please let me know if you hear anything about Jennifer?"

Nodding, April tucked the card inside her pocket. "I sure will. Bye." She ducked into the entrance.

Gillian stood by the Aquarium doors for a moment. Jennifer's best friend hadn't been much help at all. Gillian could tell she was holding something back.

A streetcar passed behind her. Gillian turned, crossed Alaskan Way, and got in line for the streetcar bound for Pioneer Square. She could catch a bus home from there. She was the last passenger to board the streetcar. The bell rang, and they started moving. Gillian plopped down on a seat. Frowning, she gazed out the window at the Seattle Aquarium as they passed it.

On the pier beside the Aquarium, she saw a woman standing by herself, huddled in a rain slicker. She seemed to be watching the seagulls swoop down toward the water. Even in the distance, April Tomlinson looked a little sad.

She leaned against the pier railing and lit up a cigarette.

Biting his lip, Ethan watched chubby Alex Sloane waddle toward his new teammates.

"Shit," he heard someone mutter from Craig's team. "All that's left are a pair of fags."

Standing beside Ethan in his too-tight gym sweats was Mark Phair. He was slender and almost "pretty" with his perfect, British-schoolboy-cut, bleached blond hair.

Ethan pretended he didn't hear the "fag" comment. Like an epidemic, Tate Barringer's taunting had spread. And now, he was lumped in the same category as Mark—The Fairy—Phair. Mark was in-your-face *out,* and he totally embraced all the gay stereotypes. He got teased and picked on, but always seemed to shrug it off. Sometimes he'd shoot back a real humdinger of a sarcastic comment to his tormentor.

Still, people gave him shit every day. Ethan felt sorry for him, but kept thinking, *He only has himself to blame*. Maybe if Mark Phair didn't act so gay all the time, people would leave him alone.

Ethan didn't think he acted gay. So why were people picking on him? How could people tell? Was it really so obvious?

It wasn't such a big deal for upperclassmen to be gay. A bunch of juniors and seniors were gay and "out," and no one seemed to care. There were always exceptions, and little antigay incidents, but mostly from outsiders. It was extremely uncool for upperclassmen to be homophobic.

But for the freshmen and most sophomores, all bets were off. It wasn't smart to be different. There were a few theater types who were "suspect." They banded together for protection. They took dance class, which excused them from gym, the lucky sons of bitches. Ethan thought they were kind of stuck up. He didn't want to be like them. He didn't want to be like Mark Phair either.

And God help him, he didn't want to be picked last.

"It's just you and me, honey," Mark said.

"Please don't call me honey," Ethan growled. He'd never noticed Mark in the locker room, and wondered where he changed his clothes. Maybe a nearby restroom? Mark probably didn't need to take a shower. He rarely broke into a sweat during gym class. Considering what had happened yesterday, Ethan wondered if he'd be relegated to dressing for gym in some nearby bathroom with Mark Phair.

He hadn't seen Tate Barringer yet today. The sophomores were playing touch football at the other end of the field.

He'd worry about Tate later. One godawful hurdle at a time. That was how he'd managed his days at school lately— like running an obstacle course. He navigated the hallways between classes, avoiding Tate and his buddies; he endured lunch periods alone; and prayed he'd survive gym class with some of his dignity intact. Afterward, in the locker room, he always kept his eyes downcast, and wouldn't look at anyone in the showers (at least, he wouldn't be caught looking). And every day it was a crapshoot whether or not he'd make it home on the bus without someone trying to steal his violin case. Until recently, he'd always had Craig to remind him that he wasn't totally friendless and pathetic. Not anymore.

Craig wasn't looking at him. But a couple of Craig's teammates were staring—and smirking. They whispered to each other and cackled.

Ethan wondered if Craig had told them all about the last sleepover, when Craig had caught him checking out his butt. Craig probably had a bunch of other stories about him acting like a "fag."

"Okay, we'll take Phair," Craig grumbled.

Mark nudged Ethan. "Better luck next time, honey." He sauntered toward Scott's team.

His head down, Ethan slinked toward the opposing squad. That was the extra twist of the knife in being picked last—most of the time, they didn't even bother calling your name.

He played miserably. He was trying too hard, and every time the soccer ball bounced his way, Ethan got all clutched and kicked it wrong. Twice Craig's team intercepted his kicks. Ethan even tripped over the ball once.

There was no excuse for his poor performance. He had nothing to distract him today. The vintage black Mustang was nowhere in sight. He'd half-expected to see it while waiting for his bus this morning, but he hadn't noticed any cars cruising the area. He figured it must have been a fluke. He was glad he hadn't told his mother about the black Mustang. She couldn't have done anything about it anyway—except worry even more.

Suddenly, he noticed the ball rolling toward him again. But Craig intercepted it. Ethan stayed on his friend, trying to guard him. He ran alongside him for a quarter-length of the field before Craig kicked the ball toward a teammate. But it was a wild kick, and the ball sailed over the field's boundary line.

Craig suddenly turned and slammed into Ethan with his elbow. It hurt like hell. Ethan went crashing to the ground. He fell on his back, and got the wind knocked out of him. Just then, he heard the coach blow the whistle.

Craig stood over him for a minute, looking off toward the coach. Ethan couldn't believe the stupid coach was ignoring what Craig had just done. Hell, it was a foul. But the coach was making a call about the stinking ball flying out of bounds.

Ethan caught his breath and managed to get to his feet. "Why'd you do that?" he whispered to his friend. He brushed himself off. "Craig? What's going on? I don't get this. Why didn't you pick me for your team?"

His buddy frowned at him. "Can I help it if you aren't any good?"

"That didn't matter before," Ethan said in a quiet voice. "What happened? Why haven't you talked to me? Don't you—" He was about to ask, "Don't you want to be friends anymore?" But that sounded so pathetic. He really didn't want Craig to bring up the sleepover incident when he'd been *caught looking*. But he had to know. He swallowed hard. "Why are you being this way?"

"Fuck off," Craig muttered, not looking at him. He trotted toward a bunch of his teammates on the other side of the field.

Craig's team lost, and they had to run a lap. The sophomores were still at the other end of the playfield. Ethan hoped to get in and out of the locker room as quickly as possible, maybe even go without a shower. Otherwise, he might bump into Tate. He dreaded a replay of yesterday's episode, and imagined how it could be even worse this time. What if Tate started picking on him in the showers—while he was naked?

Ethan beat a path toward the school's athletic wing. He

was hurrying through the break in the playfield's bleachers when he heard someone call his name: "Hey, Tanner! Tanner, wait up!"

Keep walking, keep walking, keep walking, he told himself. His heart pounded furiously.

"Hold it a minute!" Someone patted him on the shoulder.

Ethan swiveled around. He was looking at Larry Blades, his team captain. Larry had wavy, light brown hair, perfect teeth, and an almost-too-muscular body. He slapped Ethan on the arm. "Hey, that was great the way you stuck with Craig Merchant out there. You were on him like stink on a monkey. It really threw off his game. I thought for sure he had a goal coming, but you snatched that away."

Ethan felt himself blushing. "Oh, well . . . thanks."

"I'm really glad you ended up on my team, Tanner." Larry patted his shoulder again, then ran ahead of him and started talking to someone else.

Ethan stood and just watched him walk away for a moment. He thanked God for Larry Blades. A few classmates brushed past Ethan, and he continued toward the locker room door. He hadn't totally sucked after all. He'd redeemed himself. Maybe he wouldn't get picked last tomorrow.

"Hey, Tanner!"

Ethan still had a dazed smile on his face as he stopped in front of the entrance. He turned to see a horde of sweaty, exhausted boys coming at him. Ethan stepped aside as they poured into the locker room. "Hey, Tanner! Hold it right there!"

Ethan saw who was calling his name, and the smile fell away from his face.

Tate Barringer emerged from the crowd. Tate's dumb-ass friend, the one who had stood "guard" at the locker room door yesterday, was now behind him. He was grinning. "I told you, the men's locker room is not for faggots," Tate said.

Ethan felt this awful vise-like grip in his stomach. He started shaking. "Listen, why don't you just leave me alone, okay?" he said, a tremor in his voice. He tried to get a breath, but it wouldn't come. "I've never done anything to you. Why are you picking on me? I hardly even *know* you."

Tate and his friend snickered. "But I know *you*, Tanner," Tate replied, grabbing the collar of Ethan's sweatshirt and tugging the material up to his chin. "I know you, and you're a homo. And I don't like homos watching me get undressed. So—you aren't going inside that locker room. Do you understand me, queer?"

A few stragglers were still brushing past them. Tate dragged him by the collar and pushed him against the wall—right by the locker room door. "Understand?" he repeated. With a flick of his finger, he snapped at Ethan's ear. "Did you hear me?"

It hurt. Ethan winced and felt tears stinging his eyes. But he wasn't going to cry in front of Tate Barringer, goddamn it. His hands clenched into fists.

Tate gave his ear another flick. "Did you hear me, faggot?"

"Hey, you guys are blocking the door. Would you mind getting the hell out of my way?"

The voice belonged to a good-looking older guy, probably a senior. He wasn't in gym clothes. He wore jeans, a black T-shirt, a brown leather jacket, and boots. He was about six feet tall, with black hair, light green eyes, and full lips.

Tate glanced over his shoulder at the guy. "Go around us," he muttered with a little chuckle. "I'm just trying to keep the faggots out of the locker room."

"Nasty job, but somebody's got to do it," Tate's lamebrain buddy said with a snicker.

The young man didn't laugh. He scowled at Tate. "Say that to me again."

Ethan felt Tate's grip on his sweatshirt slacken. "Say what?"

"Say you're not going to let faggots in there. Say it to *me*."

Tate let go of Ethan and turned toward the other young man. He cackled. "What the fuck is your problem?"

His back pressed against the wall, Ethan saw a look pass between Tate and his buddy—as if they figured the two of them together could beat the crap out of this pest.

"Assholes like you are my problem," the young man whispered.

Approaching him, Tate's friend laughed. "Hey, you can suck my—"

He didn't finish. Before Tate's friend got another word out, the young man kicked him in the groin—very hard. There was only a gasp, and then Tate's pal crumpled to the ground. Clutching his lower stomach, he started to curl up into a ball.

"What the . . ." Tate started to say.

The young man punched him in the nose, a direct hit. Ethan thought he heard something snap. Blood seemed to explode from Tate's face. Ethan blinked, and felt the warm, wet spray on his cheeks.

Tate let out a howl. A hand went up to his crimson-soaked face. It left the rest of him vulnerable. The young man swung at the side of Tate's neck with his elbow.

Ethan dodged Tate's body as it came crashing toward him. "Jesus!" he heard someone say. A couple of stragglers from gym class had stopped to witness the assault. Tate collapsed beside his buddy, who was still curled up on the ground, gasping for air.

The young man gave Tate a savage kick in the stomach. "What are you gonna say now, hotshot?" he growled. "Want to call somebody a fag?"

In response, Tate could only sob. He rocked back and forth on the cement. His face and hands were covered with blood. "If you harass this kid again, I'll rip your fucking head off," the young man said. Then he turned toward the two stragglers from gym class. "What are you guys looking at?"

"Nothing . . . nothing!" one of them answered nervously. They quickly retreated into the locker room.

His back against the brick wall, Ethan gaped at the crazy young man who had just come to his rescue. His heart was racing.

"Well?" the handsome guy said to him. He cracked a tiny smile. "What are you standing there for, dude? Go get cleaned up. You'll be late for your next class."

His mouth open, Ethan wordlessly nodded.

Then he did what the young man said, and hurried into the locker room.

No one was stopping him.

Chapter 11

"Hi, Gill, it's Dianne. I—I'm sorry I've been a couple of days getting back to you. . . ."

Gillian ran across the living room and snatched up the phone. "Dianne?" she said, switching off the answering machine. "Hi. I just got in the door. How are you?"

"Um, not too good, Gill. The last forty-eight hours have been—awful." Gillian heard a muffled little sob on the other end of the line. "My friend, Joyce . . . you've heard me talk about her. . . ."

"You mean Joyce from Milwaukee?" Gillian set her purse on the desk, and kept the phone against her ear while she took off her trench coat. "What happened? Was she in an accident?"

"She—she's dead. She was house-sitting for me while I was in Palm Springs. She went out shopping the other morning. They found her in the changing room of this clothing store. She'd been strangled."

Gillian blindly felt around for her chair, then she sank down on it. "Oh, my God," she murmured. "Di, I'm so sorry. Do the police know who did it? Did they get the guy?"

"No. It looked like a robbery, they said. Joyce's empty wallet was found about two blocks from this clothing store. I can't imagine she had much money on her." Dianne started to cry. "It's just so senseless."

"When did this happen?" Gillian asked.

"Day before yesterday."

"Oh, my God, Dianne, I—I think Joyce tried to call me around one o'clock that day. Did you get my message about the hang-ups?"

"Yeah, but it couldn't have been Joyce. She was killed at around ten-thirty in the morning."

"But the hang-ups were from your home phone, Di. There were four of them, all just a few minutes after one o'clock. Even with the time difference, that's still a little after eleven in Chicago."

"Gillian, I'm telling you, Joyce was already dead by eleven o'clock. She was in the changing room in a clothing store several blocks from here. She couldn't have made those calls."

"Well, *somebody* called from your place. Did Joyce have someone else over that day?"

"How would I know?" Dianne answered testily. "I was in Palm Springs, for God's sakes. Gill, you sound just like the police."

"I'm just trying to make sense of this."

"You can't make sense of something that's senseless. And you can't expect to solve a murder here in Chicago when you're in Seattle and you just found out about it." Dianne's voice was cracking. "This isn't one of your books, Gill. This is real. Joyce was my friend, and she was murdered."

"I'm sorry," Gillian muttered. But it was something from one of her books; she realized that now. *A woman strangled . . . a department store changing room*—it was right out of her book, *For Everyone to See*. And *somebody* had repeatedly called her from Dianne's place shortly after the murder.

Dianne let out a sigh. "I didn't mean to bite your head off, Gill. I'm tired. The police have been questioning me for the last day and a half, and I've been helping Joyce's family with the funeral arrangements." She started crying again. "I just keep thinking, *Why Joyce? Why her?*"

Gillian felt awful for her friend. And the same question haunted her: *Why Joyce?* She wondered if this copycat killer had originally gone after Dianne, and found the wrong woman at Dianne's place. But how did he even know Dianne was good friends with his *favorite author?* Gillian hadn't talked about Dianne in any of her interviews. She might have mentioned "my friend, Dianne from Chicago" to her night class on occasion, but she'd never used Dianne's last name.

"Gillian, can you hold on for a second?" Dianne asked. "My other line just beeped. It's been like this all day. Be right back."

Gillian kept the phone to her ear. She glanced over at her desk, where the advance reader's copy of Jennifer Gilderhoff's *Burning Old Bridesmaids' Dresses and Other Survival Stories* was sticking out of her purse. She stared at the book.

That was how the killer knew about Dianne. He read about her in a book. Dianne's name was at the beginning of Gillian's first thriller: *"This book is dedicated to my oldest and dearest friend, Dianne Garrity."*

The blurb under Gillian's author photo on the inside back cover of *Killing Legend* said she was born and raised in Chicago. It couldn't have been too tough to put it together that Dianne Garrity still lived there. All he had to do was check a Chicago phone book for Dianne's address.

She'd done exactly the same thing to track down Jennifer's friend, April Tomlinson.

It was horrible realizing that she and this killer had the same way of thinking.

"Gillian, are you still there?"

"Um, yes, hi."

"That was my mom. I'm calling her back later. She says hello. She's reading *Black Ribbons,* by the way. But I think she'll be putting it down for a while. This thing with Joyce has really shaken her up. Huh, I'm not doing too well either. The police were here last night, going through Joyce's things . . ." There was a tiny break on the connection. "Oh, damn, another call. I'm sorry, Gill."

"Go ahead," she said. "I'll hold. If you need to get rid of me, I understand."

"Be right back," Dianne said.

Gillian heard a little click on the line. While she waited, she scrolled down the numbers on her Caller ID box. She looked at the four calls from yesterday afternoon:

WED 11/06—1:04 PM—773-555-0948—GARRITY, D
WED 11/06—1:06 PM—773-555-0948—GARRITY, D
WED 11/06—1:06 PM—773-555-0948—GARRITY, D
WED 11/06—1:07 PM—773-555-0948—GARRITY, D

After he'd followed Dianne's friend, Joyce, to that clothing store and re-created the changing-room strangulation from *For Everyone to See,* the killer must have returned to Dianne's apartment. It was only a few minutes past eleven Chicago time. Joyce had been killed around ten-thirty. From Dianne's phone, he made those four aborted calls to his favorite author in Seattle.

He must have figured out she had Caller ID, or maybe he'd just taken a chance that she had it. He'd counted on her responding to those hang-ups. And she'd fallen right into his hands. She'd tried calling Dianne back yesterday. She'd planned to try again tonight. He must have known she'd keep trying until she got ahold of her friend.

He'd wanted her to be one of the first people to talk to Dianne Garrity after the murder of her friend, Joyce. He'd wanted her to know what he'd done.

She'd created a fictional murder, and this was his twisted, horrible homage.

"God, I'm a wreck," Dianne said, getting back on the line. "Gillian, are you still there?"

"Yes. Do you need to take that?"

"No, I'll call them back later. Where was I?"

"The police were going through Joyce's belongings."

"Yeah, anyway . . . God, I keep thinking . . . poor Joyce . . ." She paused. Her voice was choked with emotion. "You know, this might not have happened if I hadn't asked her to come here and house-sit for me."

"It's not your fault, Di," Gillian said. "It's not your fault at all."

No, she thought, *it's mine.*

REDI-RENTAL! NATIONWIDE SERVICE! said the large magnet on the side of Gillian's refrigerator. She'd used Redi-Rental a few times when she couldn't take a bus or a cab to a book signing. There was an 800 number on the magnet—and a crude little map of the United States with stars signifying cities where you could rent a Redi-Rental car.

Gillian peeled the magnet off the refrigerator, and sat down at her desk. She hadn't told Dianne her theory about why Joyce Millikan had been murdered. Poor Dianne didn't need to hear it right now. Gillian needed to uncover something more substantial to back her theory about this copycat killer. In the meantime, she figured Dianne was safe in Chicago. One look at the little map on that Rent-a-Car magnet assured Gillian that Joyce's killer had already left Chicago.

With the magnet in front of her, she jotted notes:

NYC—Halloween—10/31: Mark of Death—J. Gilderhoff (knew killer?)
Chicago—11/6: For Everyone to See—Joyce M. (supposed to be Dianne?)

Billings, MT—11/7: Highway Hypnosis—Unknown (some-one from class?)

Gillian glanced at the little map again. Her killer was making his way across the United States.

And he was headed toward Seattle.

"Cool it, Eustace!" Ruth hissed at her Jack Russell terrier. The dog kept barking and jumping at Gillian anyway. Eustace was just about the only living thing Ruth couldn't intimidate. "Eustace, did you hear me?"

Gillian had phoned Ruth, asking if she could come by and borrow her car. She needed something else from Ruth, but wanted to talk to her about it in person.

Ruth lived on Sixteenth Avenue, near Group Health Hospital. It was only about a mile from Gillian's place. Threatening gray rain clouds filled the November sky. Walking to Ruth's place, Gillian had repeatedly looked over her shoulder. She hadn't been able to shake the sensation that someone was watching her.

Ruth's house was a quaint saltbox from the forties, prettied up with some window flower boxes and a recent paint job—yellow with white trim. Standing in Ruth's doorway, Gillian scratched Eustace behind the ears, and he calmed down. Ruth dragged him away by the collar. "C'mon, killer," she muttered. "Get off the company. Save your strength. You have a busy night ahead, eating and napping."

Gillian closed the door behind her and stepped into Ruth's living room, which was more like an office. There was a big, old wooden desk with a computer on it, and a gray metal file cabinet. African art and tapestries covered the walls, and newspaper sections were strewn across the maroon sofa. The fire in the hearth gave the room a cozy feeling. And as usual, the house smelled of coffee brewing.

Ruth led Eustace into the kitchen, and then emerged, carrying two cups of coffee. "I'm sorry about Dianne's friend in Chicago," she said soberly. "You mentioned on the phone that this copycat might be on a cross-country killing spree."

Nodding, Gillian pulled the list she'd made—showing the dates, the cities, the books that inspired the killings, and the victims. She set it on Ruth's desk. "Three cities so far. The first victim—at least, the first *known* victim—was my former student, Jennifer, in New York. Then in Chicago, I think his original target might have been my friend, Dianne. But he settled for her house-sitter."

"And we don't have an identity yet for this dead drifter in Montana," Ruth said, over her coffee cup. "But the poor guy might have been in the same night class as Jennifer. But not necessarily. His targeting your friend in Chicago—or your friend's friend—shows he's not just limiting his—*prey* to people from that particular class. So—New York, Chicago, Billings, Montana. The next logical stop is here in Seattle, where he'll probably go after someone else you know."

Gillian nodded glumly. "Ruth, I dedicated my first book to Dianne. I think that's why he might have gone after her. My fourth book is dedicated to you. You're mentioned in all my acknowledgments since the third book. I've talked about you in several interviews. And you were in that night class with Jennifer."

"Is this your sweet way of telling me that I should get my will in order and wear clean underwear for the next few days?" She put her coffee cup down on the desk. "Do me a favor and stop publicly thanking me, okay?"

"I'm sorry," Gillian muttered.

"Lighten up, honey. I can look after myself." She patted Gillian's back. "Sit down, take a load off."

"In a minute," Gillian said, still looking at her list. "Do you have a phone number or address for your Internet friend, the one who e-mailed that article to you about the murder in Montana?"

"You mean Hester?" Ruth shrugged. "I know she lives in

Great Falls, but no, I don't have a phone number or an address for her. Why?"

"E-mail her."

"Now?"

Gillian nodded. "Please."

Ruth plopped down in her chair and her fingers started working the keyboard. Her AOL e-mail account came up. She scrolled down her recently read correspondence, and clicked on one.

Standing behind her friend, Gillian read over Ruth's shoulder:

Dear Ruth,

About the newspaper article, you're very welcome. I love reading thrillers (especially Maggie Dare Mysteries!), but true stories like that one in Billings are very disturbing indeed. My husband thinks I'm crazy, but after reading that news story, I made him check & recheck the locks on all our windows & doors. Oh, well! I have to rush off to the vets' to give my cat a shot. . . .

Gillian skimmed over a few more lines of idle chatter before the signoff: "Affectionately, Hester."

Ruth hit the Reply key. "So—what do you want me to say to her?"

"Anything. Thank her for sending the article."

"I already thanked her. Didn't you read her note?"

"Thank her again. Just a line, then send it."

"Okay," Ruth sighed. Her fingers worked furiously over the keys:

Dear Hester,

Thanks again for sending that interesting article. Hope your cat had a clean bill of health at the vet.

Your Friend, Ruth

"Is that okay?" Ruth asked, eyes on the computer monitor.

"Yes, perfect," Gillian said impatiently. "Send it."

Ruth hit the Send key. "Do you have any dictation for me while you're at it?"

"Huh, no, thanks." Gillian patted her shoulder. "But could you print up that article she sent?"

While Ruth hunted for the article, her computer let out a tonal *ping*. The e-mail icon was flagged. "That couldn't be Hester replying *already*," Ruth murmured. She printed the news article from Montana, and then checked her current e-mail:

MAILER-DAEMON . . . Returned Mail: User Unknown

"Well, that's screwy," Ruth muttered. "Hester's e-mail address was working this morning. . . ."

"I was afraid of this," Gillian said. She pointed to the list she'd scribbled down at home. "I found out about the stabbing in New York from an article my agent *didn't* send. Someone phoned me and hung up four times from Dianne's place. I heard about the second murder when I called her back. Do you see what's happening? He's going through my friends to make sure I know about each killing."

"Oh, no," Ruth whispered. She rubbed her forehead. "The son of a bitch . . ."

"I don't think there ever was a Hester," Gillian said. She glanced at the news article. "See if you can dig up this article from yesterday's *Great Falls Tribune*."

Ruth resumed clicking away on the keyboard. "I know where you're going with this . . ."

Gillian was skimming over the article "Hester" had sent to Ruth:

MUTILATED CORPSE FOUND IN BILLINGS

Woman Makes Grisly, After-Hours Discovery in a Downtown Abandoned Lot

BILLINGS: After finishing up the late shift at Rudy's Golden Oldies Café at 1:30 Thursday morning, 22-year-old waitress Penny Storli made a grisly discovery in an abandoned lot by the restaurant in downtown Billings. Ms. Storli found the mutilated body of an unidentified white male, approximately 25–35 years old. The victim, possibly a drifter or a hitchhiker, was missing his entire lower jaw. His fingers had been severed, and his heart surgically removed. Early police reports indicate that the victim had been alive, but heavily sedated, at the time of this gruesome "operation." The estimated time of death was midnight, Thursday morning.

The removal of the entire lower jaw, teeth, and fingers will make identifying the victim extremely difficult, reported a police source.

Ms. Storli was on her way to her car when she first noticed activity in the lot beside Rudy's Golden Oldies Café. . . .

"I found something," Ruth announced, eyes riveted to her monitor. "But it isn't the same article."

Gillian glanced at the story from the *Great Falls Tribune* archive. The headline and subhead were identical. But there was no description of the corpse beyond "mutilated body of

an unidentified white male, approximately 25–35 years old."
None of the other details from the article "Hester" e-mailed
were there.

"A newspaper reporter wouldn't presume to call an unidentified victim a 'drifter or hitchhiker,' " Gillian said. "He
put that in to show the similarity to *Highway Hypnosis*. Obviously, he got the waitress's name from the original article.
But all the details . . ." She trailed off.

Ruth took "Hester's" article from Gillian and studied it.
"I kept wondering why the cops would allow them to print
such an exhaustive description of what he'd done to the
corpse. None of the articles I read today were this thorough."

Gillian nodded. "No, because what you got yesterday was
a first-hand account from the killer."

Ruth drummed her fingers on the desktop. "The son of a
bitch has been e-mailing back and forth with me for a month
now."

"That middle-aged, cat-loving lady in Montana just sprang
from his imagination," Gillian said. "Those e-mails, and that
article he wrote, he's good. He's a very, very creative writer."

"Which brings us back to that night class," Ruth said.
"But hell, I heard most of the stories from my classmates. I
don't think any of them were this polished, this *creative*."

"He's had two years to hone his craft." Gillian glanced at
"Hester's" news article again. "The computer gibberish above
the fake article attachment looks very real. And I'll bet you
anything we won't be able to trace Hester's e-mail account.
He's obviously very skilled with computers too."

Ruth turned in her desk chair. "Do you think . . ." She fell
silent.

"What? Go ahead."

"I'm wondering about that e-mail you got, the one you
couldn't trace or respond to."

Staring at her, Gillian swallowed hard. "As in, 'Gillian, I
found your husband'? That e-mail?"

Ruth just nodded. She had the saddest look on her face.

* * *

"You have to slow it down a little, Ethan," said Dr. Pickett. Ethan's violin teacher was a tall, gaunt man with a goatee and long, receding brown hair he kept in a ponytail. He always smelled like stale cigarettes. Small wonder, because he never made it through a fifty-minute tutorial without a cigarette break. The music rooms were little windowless boxes the size of walk-in closets. There was just enough room for a piano, a chair, and two people. The walls were padded with cushioned dark green faux leather that was perforated with big brass buttons. It did something to contain the sound, Ethan wasn't quite sure what.

"You're still too fast! Slow down that bow," Dr. Pickett told him. He'd been accompanying Ethan on the piano for a Bach Concerto, but now he'd stopped playing. "You're really wound up today. You're going at seventy-eight rpm's, Ethan. It's like I'm waiting for Alvin and the Chipmunks to come in and sing the chorus."

"Who?" Ethan asked. His violin tucked firmly under his chin, he glanced over at his tutor.

Dr. Pickett got to his feet. "Never mind. Johann is begging you from the grave to slow down. And I need a cigarette break." He headed toward the door. "Keep playing—slowly. It's not a race."

He left the door open a bit. Ethan could hear someone tinkling a piano down the hall, and another person singing. Sometimes, Dr. Pickett took as long as twenty minutes for his cigarette breaks. But he never seemed to miss anything. Whenever he returned to the little room, he would tell Ethan what he'd been doing right or when he'd screwed up—and he was usually on target. It was like he had the place bugged or something.

Ethan kept playing his violin. He tried to slow down, which was difficult, because he was so keyed up. Dr. Pickett was right about that. Ethan couldn't help it. Just two periods ago, he'd watched his nemesis, Tate Barringer, get the crap beaten out of him. Ethan wasn't a sadistic person, but it had been pretty damn wonderful to see.

It was all over school too—in record time. After the last period, on his way to the music wing, Ethan didn't have to avoid Tate in the hallways. In fact, he'd heard that Tate had been taken to the hospital with a broken nose and a cracked rib. Tate's buddy had been sent home with an ice pack on his crotch. At least, those were the stories going around. Ethan was stopped in the corridor several times. Did he know the guy who pounded the shit out of Tate Barringer? Was the guy a senior? Was it true that Tate was now in a coma? Had he hired a hood to beat up Tate? It seemed like everyone wanted to ask him about the incident. And not one person who stopped him in the hallway called him a fag.

Despite his stolen victory, Ethan couldn't shake an underlying feeling that he would somehow get in deep trouble for what had happened. Giddy and guilty, it was a weird combination—that didn't go well with Bach.

He tried to concentrate and slow down, almost dragging his bow across the strings.

"Hey, waddaya know, dude? It's you."

Ethan stopped playing, and turned toward the door.

The "mystery man" who had rescued him from Tate now stood in the doorway of the little rehearsal room. He was still wearing his brown leather jacket—along with a slightly goofy, crooked smile. "Damn, you really know how to play the shit out of that thing," he muttered.

"Thank you . . . I think," Ethan replied. He lowered his violin and bow.

The young man leaned against the doorway frame. "Looks like you got cleaned up okay."

Ethan smiled and nodded shyly. "Thanks to you."

"The prick had it coming. Am I right or am I right?"

Ethan nodded again.

"I'm Joe, by the way. Joe Pagani."

"Ethan Tanner. Are you—um, a new student here?"

Joe nodded. "I'm a senior. Just started yesterday. Still getting a feel for the dump."

"I thought you might even be in college. You look older."

"Yeah, I know. Before moving here, I lived in Portland, and my friends always had me buy the beer for parties. I practically never got carded. I was shaving by the time I was in eighth grade."

"Wow, cool," Ethan murmured. He was just starting to get armpit hair—finally. "I thought you might have gotten into some trouble."

"For buying beer? Hell, no. I told you, they never carded me—"

"No, for beating up that guy today."

"Oh, that." Joe shrugged. "Not yet. Why? Were you planning to turn me in or something?"

"Oh, God, no. I'm grateful. That guy's a real jerk."

"So what are you doing tomorrow, Ethan?"

"Tomorrow? Huh, well, I have to go to this football game. There's a charter bus to Ballard. We're all supposed to go."

"They're making you go on a Saturday? That totally sucks."

"The freshman team is playing." Ethan rolled his eyes. "It's a required 'school spirit' thing. My best friend is one of the star players."

"Really?" Joe squinted at him. "If your best friend is such a hotshot jock, why is he letting this asshole harass you?"

Ethan looked down at the tiled floor. "Well, I guess he *used to* be my best friend. Anyway, I have to go see him play against Ballard tomorrow."

"Listen, why don't you take this bus to Ballard, then blow off the game. I'll meet you there, and we can hang out. You can show me around."

Ethan grimaced a bit. "Well, I don't know. I—"

"C'mon, don't wuss out on me. I'm dying of boredom. Plus—you owe me, right?"

Ethan let out an uncertain laugh. "I'm just a freshman. Why do you want to hang out with me?"

"Because you're the first person I've met at this school who isn't an asshole. So—what time is the big game? I'll meet you there. We'll hang out, then I'll get you back to the bus before they load up again."

"The game is at one o'clock. I think we're supposed to be there at twelve-thirty."

Joe smiled and winked at him. "Then I'll see you at twelve-thirty, dude."

"Okay," Ethan managed to say. He felt a little short of breath.

Joe turned away and glanced down the corridor. "Hey, I'm looking for the bathroom," he said to someone in the hallway. "Is it around here?"

Ethan heard Dr. Pickett muttering something. Between the pianist and the singer down the hall, Ethan couldn't make out what his tutor had said. But Joe nodded. "Thanks a lot," he replied. Then he headed in the other direction.

Dr. Pickett stepped back into the tiny room. He smelled of cold air and fresh cigarette smoke. He frowned at Ethan. "Was that a friend of yours?"

"No, I don't know him," Ethan heard himself lie. "Some guy looking for the bathroom."

Dr. Pickett sat back down at the piano. "All right. Let's return to Mr. Bach, taking it from the top."

"Yes, sir," Ethan said, assuming the position and tucking his violin under his chin.

"And you'd do much better, Ethan, if you just slow down and give some careful thought as to what you're doing. Do you hear me?"

"Yes, Dr. Pickett," he said. But he wasn't listening at all.

Chapter 12

Parked behind three school buses, Gillian sat at the wheel of Ruth's Toyota Camry. She was early—and maybe a bit over-anxious. The high school wouldn't be getting out for another ten minutes.

If this copycat was indeed in Seattle, she didn't want to take any chances with Ethan's safety. Gillian stared at the front doors of the high school. A few raindrops hit the windshield, and she remembered that old Monte Carlo with its rain-beaded windows in the college's parking lot. She recalled Kelly Zinnemann slumped in the passenger seat, her blond hair drenched with blood on one side. It had stained the front of her Catholic schoolgirl uniform.

"The Schoolgirl Killer" had wasted no time finding another victim. Just days after Kelly Zinnemann's corpse had been discovered, he struck again. Twenty-eight-year-old Christine Cardiff, like so many women attending night classes at Seattle City College, had started carrying pepper spray in her purse. She carpooled with a girlfriend. They'd been planning a trip to Paris with their husbands, and decided to take French lessons in a night course offered by the Experimental College. After her class on Monday night, Christine ducked into the women's restroom while her girlfriend and some classmates waited outside for her.

They never saw her again—alive.

A janitor found Christine's body in a storage room behind the school's auditorium on Wednesday morning. She'd been shot in the head. Her body had been dumped on top of a stack of metal folding chairs. She was dressed in a dark blue blazer, a white blouse with a Peter Pan collar, madras kilt, knee socks, and saddle shoes.

ANOTHER 'SCHOOLGIRL' KILLING ON COLLEGE CAMPUS, read the headline in *The Seattle Post-Intelligencer*.

Gillian recalled Ruth remarking at the time, "If he wants publicity—and I think that's just what he thrives on—this perp sure knows what he's doing. They were already calling him the 'Schoolgirl Killer' after the very first murder. And now with victim number two, the son of a bitch has established his pattern and made himself a superstar."

The police didn't exactly have to wrack their brains searching for "similarities" to the first murder. Once again, investigators concluded the victim's "uniform" had been compiled from purchases made at several second-hand stores some time before her disappearance. The clothing and shoe size were a perfect fit. This was extremely unsettling news for women attending classes at Seattle City College. Any one of them could have already been scrutinized and "outfitted" by the Schoolgirl Killer. He was just waiting for his chance to dress her up.

The police questioned the owners of used-clothing stores and thrift shops all up and down Western Washington. They conducted interviews at over a dozen Seattle-area private schools where uniforms were required. They reopened the files on hundreds of "schoolyard incidents," every reported case of voyeurism, indecent exposure, lewd conduct, and molestation inflicted on a schoolgirl in uniform in the last five years.

Female attendance at Seattle City College had dropped by nearly thirty percent in both day and night classes. Two women in Gillian's creative writing course hadn't shown up for class on Thursday. Everyone in the class was probably wondering the same thing: Had both women been too afraid to come to class? Or maybe one of them had already been abducted by the Schoolgirl Killer?

In the absent women's place, Gillian had two uninvited guests. One of them was a tall, hulking bald man in a crew-neck sweater and suede jacket. Holding a cell phone to his ear, he stepped inside Gillian's classroom about ten minutes into the session. "Madame Professor?" he said, interrupting Gillian, who was reading aloud Jennifer Gilderhoff's latest cutesy "dating story."

Following him into the room was a short, homely woman with glasses and corkscrew-curly, light brown hair. She carried a notebook and small tape recorder. They came up the side aisle together. "Madame Professor, I'm Detective Dunbar," he said, still holding the phone to his ear.

"Um, I'm not a professor." Gillian tried to smile. "I'm not a madame either. You can call me Gillian."

The woman at Dunbar's side was a soft talker. Gillian just caught her first name, Teri. She was some kind of police reporter or something. Dunbar started talking over her to his friend on the cell phone. His eyes shifted toward Gillian. "We're investigating the recent murders here on campus, and—Madame Professor?"

Gillian blinked at him. "Oh, I'm sorry. Were you talking to me? I thought you—"

"We're investigating the homicides here on campus," he said, cutting her off. "I'll be talking to your students in the hallway one at a time. I want to start with you. C'mon."

Flustered, Gillian turned toward the class. "Um, I'll be right back—hopefully."

The detective and his friend followed her out to the hallway. He closed the door behind them. "Yeah, okay, okay," he said into his phone. "Bye." He snapped the little phone shut. He nodded at Gillian. "So who decorated your face?"

Though her bruises had faded and the cuts were healing over, Gillian still carried faint souvenirs from the beating she'd gotten the week before. She hesitated before answering. "That has nothing to do with your investigation," she said.

"Did your husband do that?" he pressed.

"No, he didn't. My husband has been missing for almost two weeks. The police know about it. That has nothing to do with your investigation either."

"What makes you so sure?" Detective Dunbar asked with a half smile. "The guy goes missing, and a few days later so does Kelly Zinnemann. Then she shows up dead in a Catholic schoolgirl's uniform. Was your husband Catholic?"

"Episcopalian," Gillian answered. "And I don't like where you're going with this. I'll be happy to cooperate with your investigation of these homicides, Detective. But if you have any more questions about my husband, I suggest you contact Lieutenant Brad Reece with the Seventh Precinct. He's already interviewed me at length about my missing husband."

The homely woman with the corkscrew hair looked a bit amused as she eyed her cohort.

The detective sighed. "Okay, *Madame Professor*," he said in a mocking tone. "Have you noticed anyone following you lately? Anyone hanging around outside the classroom or your home? Repeated hang-ups on your cell or home phone?"

"No," she lied. All of those things had been happening recently. But she'd attributed the incidents to the hoods—and cops—who had her under surveillance because of Barry.

"Okay, tell me about the guys in your class," he said,

glancing through the window in the door. "You can skip the old geezer, the black dude, and the Asian guy."

Gillian had done the research for her books, and statistics said most serial killers were white males between the ages of twenty and thirty-five. Old Glen Turlinger with his three-pronged cane was easy to disqualify. Age—along with race—eliminated Gary Connelly and Luke Huang as well. That left only two male students. "Todd Sorenson is the one seated by the windows," Gillian said. "Chase Scott is in the second row. What do you want to know about them?"

Dunbar checked a printout of the class list. "Is there any-thing—*peculiar* about either one of them? Quirky?"

"I'm not sure what you mean."

"I think you read me loud and clear. Now, c'mon, I'm tired. Tell me about these guys."

"Well, exactly what do you want to know?" she replied. She didn't like this guy, and didn't feel like cooperating.

"Well, for starters, is either one of these guys a swish?"

"A what?" she shot back.

He rolled his eyes. "Can you tell me if either one of these guys in your class is a queer?"

"No," Gillian said evenly. "But I can tell you the detective in the hallway is a jerk."

He let out an abrupt laugh. "Oh, really? Anything else I should know, Madame Professor?"

Gillian nodded. "Yes, if you're an example of the investi-gators on this case, you guys don't stand a chance of finding this killer. You're rude, and your methods are tactless. Is this how you're treating all your potential witnesses? Why should people cooperate if you're all acting like ill-mannered creeps?"

Snickering, the corkscrew-haired woman scribbled a few notes.

"Okay, you're done with me," he said, unfazed. "So—tell me about these two guys."

"I've only been teaching them for about six weeks now,"

she replied coolly. "I can't tell you much." That was untrue. She'd already formed opinions on Todd and Chase, but she wasn't about to share them with this oaf. "I can tell you what they're writing. Todd is working on a novel about a rock band, and Chase is writing a thriller set in the Bahamas."

"Anything kinky in their stories?"

"Not really. Some recreational drug use in both books and a couple of sex-on-the-beach scenes in Chase's thriller. But there's nothing to indicate a twisted mind at work—if that's what you're getting at. The books I write are far more twisted, and I haven't killed anyone. I don't think there's anything else I can tell you."

Detective Dunbar frowned at her. "Well, you've been a great big help, Madame Professor," he muttered. Then he nodded toward the door. "Go back to your class."

She opened the door, and stepped into the classroom. He came in after her with the printout in his hand. "Let's start with Donahue, Debi," he announced.

"She's not here today," Gillian said. "She—"

"Connelly, Vincent G.," the detective called out, reading from the class list.

Gary Connelly slowly got to his feet. Taking off his glasses, he scowled at the detective. With his huge frame, Gary could look pretty intimidating when he wanted. But Detective Dunbar stared right back at him.

"Um, the detective here just needs our cooperation for a few minutes," Gillian piped up. "I'm sure we all—"

"Hey, I don't need you to explain my job to these people, Madame Professor," Dunbar said, holding up his index finger as if to silence her. Then he pointed to Gary with the same finger and crooked it twice. "Mr. Connelly. Will you kindly step outside with me?"

Gary followed the man out the door. The woman with the corkscrew hair took a seat in the back of the class. As soon

as the detective closed the door, Todd Sorenson muttered—
just loud enough for everyone to hear: "What an asshole."

It was the only time Todd ever got a laugh out of his
classmates.

Gillian resumed reading Jennifer Gilderhoff's story aloud,
but no one seemed to be listening. They could all hear the
muffled voices on the other side of the door. And they kept
glancing over their shoulders at the strange woman in the
back of the classroom. After a few minutes, just when Gillian
thought she had recaptured the students' attention, the door
opened again. Gary lumbered back to his seat.

"Okay, Gilderhoff, Jennifer," the detective announced.

Jennifer turned toward him. "Actually, could I go last?
They're reading my story, and I wanted to get the reaction—"

"*Now,* ma'am," he said, impatiently motioning her to
stand.

Once Jennifer stepped outside the room and shut the
door, it was Chase Scott's turn for a quip. "Vee musn't keep
de Gestapo vaiting," he said with a bad German accent.

It seemed pointless to read Jennifer's work when Jennifer
wasn't in the room. So Gillian sighed and put down the
story. "We'll restart class in earnest when this police detective has finished his interrogations," she announced. "How
does that sound? Talk among yourselves."

"God, he's so rude!" Shauna Hendricks said. "I can't believe they're going around yanking people out of class like
this."

"I guess desperate times call for desperate measures—
and obviously they're pretty desperate right now." Gillian
locked eyes with the woman in the back of the room. "Still,
that's no excuse for *loutish* behavior."

The woman with the corkscrew hair smirked, and then
shifted in her chair. She seemed to enjoy watching her detective buddy spread misery wherever he went.

"So tell us." Chase Scott said, leaning forward in his desk

and grinning at Gillian. He was in his late twenties, and slightly beefy with receding brown hair, a swarthy complexion, and a cocky, impish quality. "Would you ever write a character like him into one of your books?"

Gillian managed a smile. "You mean someone who might alienate witnesses and bungle a case? I don't know. In detective novels, there's always some loudmouth, boorish cop who gets on the policeman hero's nerves—"

"Or the police*woman heroine's* nerves!" Shauna piped up.

Gillian nodded. "Until finally, in Chapter Fifteen, the hero or heroine cop punches his lights out."

Everyone laughed. But they fell silent when the door opened again, and Jennifer Gilderhoff walked back into the classroom. Red-eyed, she wiped the tears from her cheeks as she padded back to her seat.

"Hendricks, Shauna," the detective called.

Standing up, Shauna started toward the door with visible trepidation. She looked like a child walking into the doctor's office to get a shot. She kept glancing back at Jennifer. Everyone was probably wondering the same thing. What had the cop done to make Jennifer cry? What kind of questions was he asking?

Gary, Glen, and Edna were whispering to Jennifer, trying to comfort her. She dabbed her eyes and blew her nose with a Kleenex. "I feel so silly," she whispered. But the whole class could hear her. "I thought I was okay. But I keep seeing Kelly in that car—dead. I was hoping to forget about it, but all his questions . . ."

Gillian sat at her desk with her hands folded. She was thinking back to the third class session, when she'd invited Barry to come sit in for the period. He'd taken a seat in the back, and remained silent the whole time. Afterwards, driving home, Gillian had asked what he thought of everyone. His assessments had been amazingly on-target. Of Jennifer Gilderhoff, he'd said: "Cute, kind of self-absorbed, really loves getting attention—you can tell."

Even though Jennifer's tears seemed genuine, Gillian sensed that she was relishing this moment. She kept referring to *Kelly* as if Kelly Zinnemann had been her friend. She had everyone in the class focused on her—except Todd Sorenson. He sat in his usual spot by the windows, glancing down at his desktop with a cryptic little smile on his face.

"That one is trouble," Barry had said of Todd. "I have a bad feeling about him. He's like a time bomb waiting to go off."

The door opened, and Shauna returned, looking relieved. Detective Dunbar poked his head in the room. "Okay, now I need Langford, Ruth."

Ruth got to her feet and paused for a moment.

"C'mon, let's not take all day," he said.

Ruth smiled sweetly at him, and ambled out of the room. She closed the door behind her, but her big, booming voice still resonated in the classroom. "JUST WHO THE HELL DO YOU THINK YOU ARE, DETECTIVE?"

"Ruth is a force of nature," Barry had said.

"I wouldn't want to be in his flat-footed shoes right now," Chase Scott muttered, leaning back in his chair.

Jennifer, still dabbing her eyes, and Shauna both laughed extra loud at his comment. The two young women were clearly interested in Chase, who remained aloof to them. Sometimes, in his critiques of their work and the writing of his other classmates, he could be downright cruel. On a few occasions, Gillian had even intervened. "I don't think you're being helpful here, Chase," she'd say. He was a real snob, and yet he still managed to charm everyone—especially the women. It was amazing too, because Chase wasn't nearly as handsome as he thought he was.

"He's kind of a snake," had been Barry's assessment of him.

"So *Madame Professor,*" Chase went on. "You've written a couple of thrillers about serial killers. Do you think you'd ever write something based on these 'Schoolgirl Killings'?"

Gillian shook her head. "I don't think so, no."

"Really?" He didn't seem to understand, and the cocky grin fell off his face. "But don't you think this stuff could be the basis for a juicy thriller?"

Gillian shook her head again. "I don't think I could ever cash in on something like this. I deal in fiction."

"Well, maybe you'd change your mind in a few years, once—"

"No, Chase. I don't think so. It's in bad taste."

He let out a sigh, and pouted at her.

The door opened again, and Ruth reappeared. She patted the detective on the shoulder, then headed to her desk in the front row. "Excuse me, Gillian," the detective said—almost meekly. He glanced at the class list. "Could I talk with Edna McGovern for a couple of minutes?"

Edna got to her feet, and the detective worked up a smile for the old woman. "Edna? Hello . . ."

Edna shuffled outside, and people started whispering to each other again. Gillian shot a look at Ruth. "You do good work," she said under her breath.

Ruth just smiled and nodded.

The interviews with Chase Scott and Todd Sorenson took longer than the others. Chase returned from his session, announcing, "Well, he beat it out of me. I did it. I'm the killer. I'll send you guys the rest of my chapters from San Quentin." Both Jennifer and Shana laughed.

After his five minutes in the hallway, Todd silently lumbered into the room, and slumped back into his seat.

When Dunbar finished questioning the last student, he stuck his head in the classroom and thanked everyone for their cooperation. He even apologized for disrupting the class. Then he closed the door.

His friend with the notepad and the tape recorder remained in her seat in the back. Gillian waited until the break to talk with her. She found out Teri wasn't with the police department after all. She was a newspaper reporter, working on a story about how the Schoolgirl Killings affected the night classes on campus. She asked Gillian about *Killing Legend,* and her next book, *Highway Hypnosis,* which was already scheduled for release in three months.

Teri said she wanted to talk to a few students while they were still on their break. Before Teri left the room, Gillian pulled her aside. "I hope you aren't going to write about my discussion with Detective Dunbar in the hallway," she whispered. "That was private. I thought you were his partner. I didn't know you were a reporter. I don't want you mentioning my husband."

"Oh, don't worry," Teri assured her. "I won't write about your husband."

Thriller Author Slams Police Investigation of 'Schoolgirl' Murders

"They Don't Stand a Chance of Finding this Killer," She Says

SEATTLE—Local thriller-author and serial-killer expert Gillian McBride had some harsh comments Thursday night regarding the police investigation into the "Schoolgirl' murders at Seattle City College, where she teaches a night class in creative writing. "Obviously, they're pretty desperate right now," McBride said, angered after police questioned her and some students from her writing class. "Still, that's no excuse for loutish behavior. Their methods are tactless." She added

> that police investigators "don't stand a
> chance of finding this killer."
>
> Within the last ten days, Seattle City
> College has been the site for two star-
> tlingly similar murders. . . .

"Oh, my God, I sound like such an ass," Gillian said, rereading the article on the front page of the Metro Section. She sat at a table with Ruth in the Starbucks by Group Health Hospital. "She totally quoted me out of context. Look at this! She makes it seem like I accused the entire police force of 'alienating witnesses' and 'bungling the case.' "

Ruth gave her a sour smile. "Let's not forget the part when you seem to call all the investigators 'ill-mannered creeps.' "

"Oh, and what's with this 'serial-killer expert' bit? Where the hell did she get that?"

At least the reporter hadn't mention Barry. She devoted two paragraphs to Gillian's thriller, *Killing Legend*, and her upcoming *Highway Hypnosis*. But it almost sounded as if Gillian herself were using the Schoolgirl Murders as a forum to criticize the cops and plug her books.

She'd already been regarded as "uncooperative" by police investigating her husband's disappearance. This article made things even worse. Gillian came across as a cop-hating, self-promoting, smug bitch.

"Do you think I should write a letter to the editor?" she asked Ruth. "Maybe they'll print a retraction."

Ruth sipped her latte, and then shook her head. "If you do that, people who didn't see the article will want to read it. And then they'll believe the article. Everyone else will think you're protesting too much—or you're after even more publicity. Let it go, hon."

"But how do you think the police feel about me?"

"Well, good thing you no longer have a car, because it's not very likely you could charm your way out of a traffic ticket any time soon."

Even with Ruth trying to talk her up to all her friends on the force, Gillian's reputation as an uncooperative bitch with the police remained unshakable.

Thinking back to that night two years ago, when Dunbar had questioned everyone in her class, Gillian remembered the way Chase had egged her on—asking for her opinion of the rude detective, and if she planned to write her own version of the Schoolgirl Murders.

She remembered how his "erotic thriller" became more and more graphic as the semester progressed. He seemed to enjoy shocking the class with his overly descriptive scenes of sex and gore.

During one session, he followed her back to her office at the break. Reaching her doorway, Gillian turned around. "What are you doing, Chase?" she asked with a wry smile. "Stalking me?"

He chuckled. He had that impish, I'm-so-cute-you-can't-resist-me look on his face, the one Shauna and Jennifer fell for time after time. "Well, actually, I *am* sort of stalking you, Teach. I wanted to get together with you for coffee sometime—or maybe even a drink."

"Are you asking me out on a date?"

"I sure am." He grinned.

"Well, I'm flattered. But I'm almost ten years older than you, Chase—"

"I dig older women."

"I think Edna's available."

"Cute." Smirking, he leaned against the doorway to her office. "I dig *you*."

Gillian sat on the edge of her desk. She wondered if she was blushing. She also wondered if his ridiculously awful "I dig *you*" line had ever worked before. Still, she found herself strangely attracted to him at that moment—maybe because she was lonely.

"Chase, I'm married," she said finally.

186   *Kevin O'Brien*

"Yeah, but I hear he isn't around."

"That doesn't make any difference to me," Gillian said. "I'm still married. But thanks for the offer."

"Sure you won't change your mind?" he asked, his smile fading. "I never ask a girl twice, you know."

"That's a relief," Gillian replied.

She remembered thinking at the time that he took the rejection rather well. Rick in the administration office was a hell of a lot more pushy.

However, Chase did phone her three times the following week. But he hung up every time. During a break in the next class session, she asked him about the calls—and the hangups. He tried to deny it.

"Your name and phone number came up on my Caller ID box," she explained.

"Well, I didn't mean to call you," he insisted. "Your phone number's very similar to that of a friend of mine. It was an honest mistake, Teach. It won't happen again."

And as far as she knew, he was true to his word. It didn't happen again.

Or maybe it had. Maybe he hadn't completely stopped calling.

Gillian heard the school bell ring. From the driver's seat of Ruth's Toyota, she watched the main doors to the high school open. Students began to pour out.

Gillian grabbed her purse, and dug out the old class list. The number for Chase Scott was no longer good. He could have changed his phone number after finishing up the semester. He'd already changed his name once—from Scott Chase. Perhaps he'd changed his name again, to something totally different. He could still be calling her and hanging up—and he wouldn't have to worry about her seeing his name on her Caller ID box.

"He knows I have Caller ID," Gillian whispered aloud.

Had Chase Scott made all those aborted calls from Dianne's apartment the other day?

Someone let out a scream. It was a teenage girl. A bunch of them, talking at high volume, passed the car. Gillian looked toward the school's doors again and scanned the crowd for Ethan. She grabbed a pen, and with a shaky hand, she circled Chase's name on the old class list. Beside it, she scribbled: *"Knows I have Caller-ID—Good Writer—smart enough to trick Ruth w/ e-mail? Jennifer liked him."*

Gillian looked up again, focusing on the group of students lining up to board the buses. She still didn't see Ethan.

Like Detective Dunbar, she'd narrowed down her suspects from the class to the two white males between the ages of twenty and thirty-five. Todd Sorenson seemed dangerous, but his writing was a rambling mess. Gillian couldn't imagine him inventing "Hester" in Great Falls, Montana. He just didn't seem that clever and devious. But she could see him killing someone.

Chase may have telephoned her and hung up, but Todd Sorenson had stalked her and gone to her home. She jotted a few notes beside Todd's name on the list: *"Stalked me—Killer Potential—dangerous—seemed unfocused, but smart."*

She glanced up once more. "Oh, no," she muttered under her breath. Only a few stragglers wandered out of the main doorway now. The last few kids were boarding the buses. She didn't see Ethan among them.

Grabbing her purse, she climbed out of the car and hurried toward the door of the bus parked in front of her. "Excuse me," Gillian said to a thin girl with braces and a ponytail. She was the last student in line. "Is this the bus to Capitol Hill?"

The girl stopped biting her nails for a moment. "Nope, try one up," she muttered.

"Thanks." Gillian ran alongside the next bus, searching the faces of students seated on the other side of the windows.

Still no sign of Ethan. The bus started to move. Gillian frantically pounded on the door, and the bus ground to a halt.
The door opened with a whoosh. "Excuse me," she said, out
of breath. "Are you going to Capitol Hill?"

The driver, a chubby, black woman with dark copper-
colored hair, frowned at her. "Yeah . . ."

"Can I see if my son is on this bus, please?"

The driver nodded tiredly. "SHUT UP BACK THERE!"
she screamed.

Gillian climbed up the steps. The bus was warm and stuffy.
A few students were still chattering, despite the driver's com-
mand. Gillian scanned the faces of all the students. "Ethan?"
she called. "Is Ethan Tanner here?"

A few kids laughed.

"SHUT UP, I SAID!" the driver yelled. Then she turned
to Gillian. "You mean Ethan, the kid with the violin? Are
you his mother?"

Gillian nodded. "Yes. Do you know him?"

"Hm-hmmm, he's a doll. But I didn't see him get on the
bus." She glanced up at the rear view mirror. "ANYONE
KNOW WHAT HAPPENED TO ETHAN TANNER?"

There was some mumbling—and snickering. One girl had
an obnoxiously loud giggle. Biting her lip, Gillian looked
out at all the young faces again and waited for an answer.

"Check the principal's office," someone said. "I think he's
in trouble."

"Yeah, try the principal's office," somebody else piped up.

"Try the Girls' Glee Club," someone muttered. A bunch
of them laughed.

"C'mon, can we get going already?" another kid yelled.
They all started talking over each other again.

Gillian anxiously turned to the driver, who shrugged.
"You might want to go ahead and try the principal's office,"
the woman said. "If he's missing, that's the place to report it."

Gillian found the administration office on the first floor. A white-haired woman in a pale blue pantsuit was working the copy machine behind the long counter. "Pardon me," Gillian said. She couldn't control the panic-induced warble in her voice. "I came here to pick up my son, and he wasn't on the bus, and they told me to try here."

The woman adjusted her glasses and moseyed up to the counter. She still had some papers in her hand that she was about to copy. "What's your son's name?"

"Tanner, Ethan Tanner." Gillian nervously tapped her fingers on the countertop.

"Oh, Mrs. Tanner, we tried several times to get ahold of you. . . ."

"What?" A hand went over her heart. "What happened? Is Ethan okay?"

"I'm sure Principal Brickman would like to see you, Mrs. Tanner," she said, moving to the half door at the end of the counter and opening it for her. "The police were in there, too. They just left."

"Oh, no," Gillian murmured. She remembered all those mornings years ago when Ethan was a little boy; she would send him off to school, worried that he might never come back—or that the police would call, asking her to come identify his body. And now it was happening.

Her knees felt weak as she followed the woman behind the counter to a long hallway. "Could you—tell me what happened?"

"Well, I've heard a bunch of different stories," the woman sighed, waddling toward a door at the end of the hall. She didn't seem very concerned or compassionate. "They're still trying to get to the bottom of it."

The woman opened the door. Gillian stared into an office, where eight people turned to stare back at her. They stopped talking, and the scene seemed to freeze for a moment. The principal and some woman in a dark blue suit—maybe the vice-principal or a teacher—stood behind a big mahogany desk. Two more women sat in front of the desk, both looking over their shoulders at Gillian. One of them Gillian didn't recognize. The other was Stephanie Merchant, blond and perky with sun-wrinkled skin that was now pale. She wore jeans and a cowl-neck sweater. A leather coat was draped over her chair arm.

Their heads slightly bowed, two boys flanked each side of the principal's desk—like four meek shepherds in a Nativity set.

"Hey, Mom," said one of those boys.

"All of you, thanks very much for your cooperation," Principal Brickman said soberly. A tall, thin man in his mid-fifties with receding gray hair, he wore a rumpled brown suit and stood by the open door to his office. With a joyless smile, he nodded to the people as they started to file out of his work space. He'd asked Gillian and Ethan to stay on for another minute.

For the last half hour, Gillian had held her tongue while the principal—and the bookish-looking woman in the blue suit, who turned out to be a lawyer for the Barringer family—questioned the boys about an assault on a sophomore, Tate Barringer. Apparently, Tate and a friend of his named Don Woodruff had—either *"teased," "picked on,"* or *"kidded around with"*—Ethan after gym class both yesterday and this afternoon. It depended on the particular witness's testimony as to exactly what had gone on. Ethan was the one who claimed Tate and Don had merely been *"kidding around."* And during this afternoon's *"encounter"* (the word the lawyer insisted on using), an older boy interrupted them and proceeded to beat the ever-living crap out of Tate and Don. The victims had been taken by ambulance to the hospital, where Tate was treated for a broken nose, two cracked ribs, and other minor injuries. Don was sent home with a prescription for painkillers and an ice pack for his scrotum.

Principal Brickman and the lawyer were trying to determine the identity of this older boy, who had carried out the beatings. No one had ever seen him before.

Gillian also wanted to know who this young man was—so she could thank him for coming to Ethan's rescue. None of the three boys being questioned—including Craig Merchant—had bothered to help Ethan. Gillian was so angry, she wanted to scream at the lawyer, the principal, the boys, and their mothers. So a couple of bullies had gotten a little more than they'd deserved. Too bad. But they'd been picking on her son, who had never harmed a soul. Didn't anyone care about what Ethan had been going through?

She didn't say a word, because she knew Ethan was already humiliated enough. Obviously, that was why—more than anyone—he'd tried to play down the fact that these boys had been harassing him. Gillian couldn't help wishing Ethan had stood up for himself—even if it meant a black eye. At this point, the damage to his dignity had to be worse than the physical injury he might have endured.

The other two mothers hadn't said much. The lawyer had recommended that the boys' parents be present for the questioning. Throughout the session, Gillian had repeatedly looked at Stephanie Merchant, who had managed to avoid eye contact with her.

Gillian and Ethan stood near the door as the others filed out of Principal Brickman's office. Both Craig and Mrs. Merchant walked by, neither one even glancing their way. "Hello, Craig," Gillian said coolly. "How are you doing, Stephanie?"

"Hi," Craig sheepishly muttered back. That was all she got from either one of them.

They were the last ones out of the office. Principal Brickman closed the door, then let out a sigh. "Mrs. Tanner, Ethan," he said. "I'm very sorry this happened—and that you were being harassed by these boys. I didn't want the lawyer here for this, but I need to ask you something, Ethan. There's a rumor going around the school that you hired this young man to beat up Tate and Don for you. Is there any truth to that?"

"No, Dr. Brickman," Ethan replied, shaking his head. "Like I told you, I never saw him before today. I have no idea who he is."

"All right, thank you," the principal nodded. "In the future, if anyone gives you trouble, I want you to come to me about it. All right?"

"Yessir."

Gillian waited until they'd stepped out to the hallway before she turned to Ethan. "These boys, Tate and Don," she whispered. "Were they part of that group who were teasing you in front of the house the other afternoon?"

Ethan rolled his eyes. "Can't we just drop it, Mom?"

"No, we can't," she said.

"Okay, yeah," he muttered. "They were there. But I didn't hire anyone to beat them up. I didn't do *anything—anything at all.*"

"Okay," Gillian whispered, patting his shoulder. "I borrowed Ruth's car. Where's your coat?"

She waited in the corridor while Ethan ran up to the second floor to retrieve his coat, violin, and books from his locker. The stairwell door was still swinging back and forth when Gillian saw Craig emerge from the boys' lavatory.

He seemed to notice Gillian in the dim, otherwise empty hallway, and he quickly looked away. But he didn't move.

Gillian stepped up to him. "How have you been, Craig?"

"Fine," he said, glancing down at his feet—and then at the girls' restroom door. Gillian realized he was probably waiting for his mother.

"So—what's going on with you and Ethan?" she asked quietly. "Did you two have a falling-out or something?"

He shrugged evasively.

"Your mom told me yesterday that you weren't attending Ethan's birthday party next week. What's that about?"

"I—I'm just busy, that's all."

"Craig, you've been Ethan's best friend since the fourth grade. What's going on? The way you and the other boys were talking in the principal's office, I got the idea that those bullies were harassing Ethan, and you saw it. But you just walked right on by. How could you do that to your best friend?"

"He doesn't have to answer that," Stephanie Merchant said, pausing in the girls' restroom doorway.

"Yes, he does," Gillian shot back. She turned to Craig. "If Ethan ignored you when you were in trouble, I'd want your mother to be asking Ethan this same question. Why didn't you help him, Craig?"

He sighed. "It's for the same reason they were picking on him."

"And why were they picking on him, Craig?" She knew the answer, but had to ask.

"Because they—they think he's gay."

"Is that what you think?" she asked, trying to keep her voice steady.

He looked away and nodded.

"Are you satisfied?" Stephanie Merchant asked. She put her hand on Craig's shoulder.

Gillian scowled at her. "No, I'm not satisfied, Stephanie. So—big deal! Why should it matter all of a sudden? What the hell difference does it make?"

"You can't blame Craig if he isn't comfortable around Ethan anymore," Mrs. Merchant said.

"Why are you uncomfortable around him? Did he do something to make you feel that way, Craig? Tell me, and I'll shut up."

Wincing, Craig shook his head. "He didn't *do* anything. I just—if I keep hanging around with him, people will think I'm gay, too."

Gillian shook her head. "Lord, Craig, I thought you had more confidence than that. I thought you were better than that."

"I'm not making any judgments about how certain people choose to live their lives," Stephanie chimed in. "I just don't want it in my house, and I think you ought to respect that."

"By '*it*' do you mean my son?" Gillian retorted. "And I don't respect you very much at all right now, Stephanie. Ethan has been a good friend to your son. Craig, remember two years ago when you fell off your bike on Interlaken Drive and twisted your ankle? Ethan carried you home piggyback for a mile. And while you drove your son to the hospital, Stephanie, my son walked back to Interlaken Drive and carried Craig's broken bike to your house. Remember?" She turned to glare at Craig. "So where were you when my son was in trouble yesterday—and today?" Gillian shook her head. "Shame on you," she whispered. "Shame on you both."

Down the hallway, the stairwell door opened, and Ethan stepped out. He had on his jacket, and carried his books and violin case. He headed toward the school's main doors. Gillian noticed he didn't wave or nod at Craig and Mrs. Merchant. Perhaps he already knew they'd written him off.

Gillian met up with him by the front entrance. He didn't say anything, but obviously, he could see she was shaking and on the verge of tears. He held the door open for her. Outside, they walked down a few steps together, and then Ethan stopped at the bottom step.

Gillian turned up her coat collar and glanced up at the rain. Then she looked at him.

Ethan gave her a sad, crooked smile. "If we were in a TV commercial, this is when you'd take me to McDonald's for a Happy Meal."

Gillian laughed, and mussed his hair. They walked toward

Ruth's car together. "I wish you would have told me these bullies were bothering you, honey."

"Can we just forget about it, Mom? Please?"

"All right," she murmured. They climbed into the front seat of Ruth's Toyota. Gillian started up the engine; then she switched on the vent and the rear-window defogger. They sat idling for a minute. Rain tapped on the roof.

"Honey, do you know *why* they were picking on you?"

He squirmed in the passenger seat. "Mom, please—"

"Ethan, I . . ." She hesitated. "Honey, if you ever want to talk about it, I'll listen. I'll understand. Okay?"

"Fine," he said, nodding a few more times than necessary. "The windshield's clearing up. Can we go now?"

Before pulling away from the curb, Gillian checked the rear-view mirror. Through the semi-fogged rear window, she saw someone standing on the street about ten feet behind the car. He wore a stocking cap pulled down to his eyebrows—and sunglasses. The collar of his windbreaker was turned up to cover his mouth. He swayed from side to side—as if keeping rhythm with a slow tune. It was a creepy little dance. Though his body was moving, his gaze seemed locked on her and Ethan. The collar of his windbreaker dipped down for a moment, and she could see his mouth. He was grinning.

Gillian let out a gasp.

"What is it?" Ethan asked.

Gillian swiveled around in her seat. The rear window was still clouded with condensation in spots. The strange man with the sunglasses wasn't behind them anymore.

Baffled, Gillian glanced out Ethan's window—and her window, and at the side mirror. She took another look at the street in back of them. She didn't see the man anywhere. He'd vanished.

"What's wrong?" Ethan asked.

Gillian quickly pressed a switch by the gear shift between them. All the doors automatically locked. "Nothing," she said. "I—thought I saw someone." She took one more look in the rearview mirror, and then slowly pulled away from the curb.

"Huh." Ethan gave her a wary half smile. "Someone we know?"

Gillian eyed the road ahead. Her heart was still racing.

"Maybe," she murmured under her breath.

Chapter 13

He slowed down when he spotted the hitchhiker standing at the roadside on International Boulevard south of Sea-Tac Airport.

Instead of taking the Interstate back from Ethan Tanner's school in Seattle, he'd driven down the boulevard, where he was more likely to come across some hitchhikers. It couldn't be just any hitchhiker either. This person had to be a particular type, and finding him depended a lot on luck and timing.

So far this afternoon, his timing had been on the mark. He'd watched Gillian pick up her son. She'd been driving her friend Ruth Langford's car, the same old Toyota Camry Ruth had two years ago. He'd parked half a block behind Gillian on the other side of the street from Ethan's school. Then he'd waited for just the right moment to emerge from his car. He'd stepped up behind the Toyota for only a few seconds, but he was almost certain she'd seen him. Those sudden jerky movements of her head as she turned in the driver's seat had given her away.

He'd ducked in front of a parked SUV, and continued to

watch her. Gillian had kept glancing around. He'd imagined her telling the kid, *"I just saw him a second ago. . . ."*

All she'd caught was a glimpse of him, and that had been his plan. He'd wanted her to know he was near. He controlled the flow of information. Feeding her bits and pieces of knowledge was part of the thrill.

The stocking cap and sunglasses were now beside him on the passenger seat. He reached over and tossed them in the back. He had to make room for his passenger.

Visibility from inside his car was questionable. The rain had stopped, but it was getting dark. The hitchhiker wore a backpack and a ski jacket. He was about six feet tall with a medium build.

Pulling over to the shoulder, the driver reached over and unlocked the passenger door. He glanced in the rearview mirror, and smiled. His prey was hurrying toward the passenger side of the car. The door opened. "Looks like it's going to start raining again," the hitchhiker said. "Lucky for me you stopped."

"You can throw your stuff on the backseat."

The hitchhiker complied, then climbed into the car. Up close, he looked younger, maybe in his early twenties. He had dark brown hair and a narrow face with a slightly weak chin. He looked a bit like a farm boy.

"Where are you headed?" asked the driver.

"Portland." He shut the door and buckled his seat belt. "I'm Andy, by the way."

"Well, I can take you all the way to the end, Andy," the driver said. He glanced in his rearview mirror, then pulled onto the road again. "My name is Barry," he said, eyes on the road. "Barry Tanner."

"Ruth gave me the lowdown on what's been happening," Lynn Voorhees said, picking at the fries left on her plate. Ruth's police lieutenant friend was about forty-five, with a robust figure and a careworn face. Her mousy-brown hair was pulled back in a ponytail, and she wore jeans with a Seattle Seahawks sweatshirt.

She had to talk loudly over Elton John's "Crocodile Rock" on the jukebox, and all the chatter from the Friday night crowd at O'Reilly's Pizza & Burger Emporium. Framed travel posters decorated the brick walls, and plastic red-and-white checkered tablecloths covered the tables. Gillian and Ruth shared a six-top by the window with Lieutenant Voorhees. At the end of the meal the lieutenant had started talking about her hysterectomy. Ethan and Lynn's fifteen-year-old daughter, Jodi, had taken that as their cue to head for the pinball machine and video games near the door. The waitress still hadn't taken away the dirty plates or the pizza pans.

Jodi was skinny, with spiky mink-colored hair, and a stud in her right nostril. During dinner, she'd rolled her eyes at everything her mother had said, and done little to disguise the fact that she hated every minute of being there.

Apparently, Lynn Voorhees was divorced, and her ex-husband had custody of Jodi. This was the mother and daughter's "alternate weekend" together. Gillian didn't know much else about Lynn, except that she'd had a hysterectomy last year, she'd been in law enforcement for two decades, and Ruth had briefed her on the "copycat" killings.

"So—we have three murders in three different cities," Lynn continued, smearing a limp fry in some ketchup on the side of her plate. "And each murder is similar to a death scene in one of your novels. I'm sorry to say I haven't read any of your thrillers, Gillian—"

"Well, you should," Ruth cut in. "They're damn good, honey."

Lynn ate her fry. "I'll get around to them when I get a life." She sighed. "Anyway, Gillian, I understand someone has made it his job to notify you about these murders as they occur. Obviously, trying to track down this 'Hester' in Great Falls, Montana, is a dead end." She turned to Ruth and grinned.

"I know half the guys on the force think you're crazy, Ruth. Just wait until I tell them you had an imaginary friend. Ha!"

Gillian didn't laugh. Ruth just shook her head and sipped her beer.

"Oh, lighten up," Lynn said, munching on another fry. "Now, about your friend in Chicago, tell her to have the cops there check her phone records."

Gillian nodded. "I'll call her tonight."

"As for this bogus note from your agent," Lynn said. "The envelope was from the agency, but you say no one there sent it. Do you know if anyone has been by the agency recently? Maybe someone helped himself to a few envelopes off a secretary's desk. Have they had any temps or people coming in for job interviews in the last few weeks?"

Gillian shrugged. "They have people going in and out of there all the time—editors, other writers, delivery people. It would be tough to pinpoint one particular visitor. And for all we know, this guy could have gone there and helped himself to some envelopes five or six months ago."

Lieutenant Voorhees chuckled. "You really have this guy thinking ahead, don't you?"

"But that's what he does," Gillian replied. "He's a planner. That's obvious. He plots everything out in advance. He thinks like a writer. He's figured out all the action ahead of time. He knows his characters and how they will react. Look at this 'Hester' business he pulled on Ruth." Gillian turned to her friend. " 'Hester' first contacted you—what—a month ago?"

"More like five weeks," Ruth replied, frowning.

"That's how far in advance he knew he was going to mutilate some poor hitchhiker and dump the body in Montana. Do you know who he reminds me of?"

Frowning, Lynn shook her head.

"He's just like the Schoolgirl Killer," Gillian said. "Remember how the police determined that he'd bought all their 'school' clothes—including the saddle shoes—long before he abducted and killed them? The clothes and shoes were always a perfect fit, too. That's what I mean about him planning ahead."

Voorhees shoved her unfinished plate away, then sighed. "So are you implying that your copycat killer might have pulled off the Schoolgirl Murders as well? What? Do you think Boyd Farrow rose from the dead and started murdering people again? Or are you saying he had a disciple?"

"I think the police might have arrested the wrong man," Gillian replied.

"Gill, that case is closed," Ruth said. "The killings stopped once they arrested Boyd Farrow."

"Well, as long as you brought it up, Gillian," Voorhees sighed. "Some of the statements you made to the press at the time of the Schoolgirl Murders factor heavily into how my friends on the police force feel about this 'copycat' business, Gillian. I consulted a colleague about it. Right away, my friend asked me, 'Doesn't she have a new book out? Is this some kind of publicity stunt?' I know it's been almost two years, but that newspaper article about you—"

"I was misquoted," Gillian interrupted. "There's hardly any truth to—"

"I know," Voorhees cut in, tiredly waving her hand at Gillian. "Ruth told me. But the truth is you were critical of the police investigation of the Schoolgirl Murders. And hearing you talk tonight, it sounds like you still feel that way. Do you really think we arrested the wrong man?"

"It's possible." Gillian frowned at Ruth's friend. "So the police won't do anything to help me because of some stupid newspaper article two years ago?"

"Officially, we can't do much, Gillian. Not one of these murders occurred in Seattle or even in Washington State. None of the victims were from the state either. You should be talking to the investigating officers in New York, Chicago, and Billings. But I can pretty much tell you what they're gonna say."

" 'Thanks a lot for the tip, now get lost,' " Ruth interjected.

Voorhees nodded.

"I was hoping a word from someone like you might yield a better response from them," Gillian said glumly. She sipped what was left of her Diet Coke. It was flat and watery. "I think this copycat killer is in Seattle now. I might have even spotted him today, hanging around outside Ethan's high school. I couldn't see much of his face, but he scared the hell out of me."

Gillian glanced over at Ethan—with Jodi by the pinball machine. "I'm worried he'll come after my son next," she admitted. "And if something happens to Ethan, I want you to remember I came to you for help. I'll *make* you remember. I'll talk to the newspapers about it, and believe me, I'll see they get the quotes right this time. It'll make that article from two years ago read like a valentine."

"All right, all right, chill out," Voorhees groaned. "I'll see there's an extra patrol on your block. And I'll put in a word to the guys in charge of these homicide investigations. But you need to play ball with us, show you're willing to cooperate."

"Cooperate, how?"

"You weren't very helpful with the police when your husband went missing. And testimony from him could still put away a lot of people in local organized crime. If you have any idea where your husband is—"

"I don't," Gillian said, cutting her off. "I'm sorry, I can't help you. I really have no idea what happened to him."

The lieutenant sighed. "Well, Ruth said you've had some of these hoods hanging around your house lately. They're expecting Barry Tanner to pay his son a visit on his birthday? I find that very interesting."

Voorhees took her napkin off her lap, crumpled it up, and tossed it on the table. "You'll have an extra patrol on your block, all right," she said. "But I wouldn't expect any other special favors, Mrs. Tanner."

"You know what she meant about putting an extra patrol on our block, don't you?" Gillian whispered to Ruth. They were walking from the restaurant to the car. Ethan had run ahead of them. "They won't be there to protect us. They just want to see if Barry tries to pay us a visit."

"I'm really sorry, hon," Ruth said, shaking her head. "Lynn didn't tell me this was *Let's Make a Deal* night. I had no idea she was going to ask you to blow the whistle on Barry."

"Well, I can hardly 'blow the whistle' on him when I don't know where the hell he is," Gillian grumbled. "At least it's nice knowing my status with the Seattle Police as their Public Bitch Number One hasn't been compromised in the last couple of years."

"If it's any help, I have something for you." Ruth stopped and looked ahead at Ethan, who was now waiting by the car. "After I talked to Lynn today, I phoned another pal on the force. I asked for arrest records on two of your former students, Todd Sorenson and Chase Scott. All I came up with were a couple of traffic tickets for Chase, a possession bust for Todd, three traffic tickets, and an indecent exposure rap for skinny-dipping in the Arboretum. Nothing to write home about."

Ruth took a piece of paper out of her purse. "But I remembered how you needed new phone numbers for Chase and Todd—as well as Shauna Hendricks. So I got this buddy of mine to go through the Driver's License Registration files." She handed the piece of paper to Gillian. "We got two out of three. Chase now lives in Bremerton, and Shauna's in Bellingham. The addresses are there. I called Directory Assistance, and wrote down the phone numbers for you."

"God, thanks," Gillian said, studying Ruth's notes. "I

asked for an update this morning from the school administration office, but I have a feeling the idiot woman there won't ever be getting back to me. Nothing on Todd Sorenson, huh?"

"Bupkis," Ruth said. "The most current address my friend could find is the same old one you had—from two years ago. That means, either Todd Sorenson moved out of the state or he's dead."

Gillian sighed. "Or maybe he just doesn't want anyone to know where he is."

She was still out to dinner with the kid and her black friend. The upstairs neighbor was home—and getting some serious action tonight. He heard her panting and moaning as he crept around outside the duplex. Damn, she was a loud one. But all the love-noise she made assured him that she wasn't hearing any noise herself. So directly below all that rapture, he went to work on Gillian's bedroom window. It took a while, but with his switchblade, he managed to jimmy the lock.

The upstairs neighbor wasn't the only one in this dump who would be seeing some action tonight. He'd made up his mind. Before the evening was through, he would nail Barry Tanner's wife. Gillian wouldn't squeal and make all that noise, like her upstairs neighbor. He'd make sure she kept quiet. It wouldn't be the first time he held a gun on a woman while he did her.

He'd skipped Taco Bell this evening, and gone for a couple of drinks instead. Maybe that had been a mistake, because he'd started thinking about how fed up he'd gotten with this goddamn assignment—and with all her teasing. He'd been watching her for several days and nights now. He couldn't take it anymore, he couldn't just keep *looking* and nothing else.

He knew her routine. Whenever she came home at night,

she went into the bedroom and changed her clothes. That would be when he got her, a sneak attack. The kid wouldn't hear anything. The bathroom was between their bedrooms. After finishing with her, he'd keep the gun to her head and make the bitch tell him where Barry Tanner was hiding. He was sick of all this sneaking around. He'd force it out of her, and he'd be a hero with his cohorts.

He noticed that the upstairs neighbor had become awfully quiet, which allowed him to hear something else more clearly. A strange rustling came from the ravine area—along with a grunting noise that sounded almost human. He crept across the yard to the edge of the gulch. In the darkness it was hard to see anyone amid all those trees and bushes. But everything was perfectly still. There was no wind tonight. Yet he could hear those rustling sounds and someone breathing hard—and something else now, an intermittent tapping.

He ventured further down into the darkness, and made out a silhouette moving amid the foliage. "Jesus, what the hell?" he muttered to himself. The ravine leveled off at one spot, and on that little plateau, someone was digging a big hole in the ground. He could see the guy hitting the back of the shovel scoop with his heel—tap, tap, tap. He heard him grunting with every pile of earth he excavated. But he couldn't see who the crazy son of a bitch was. Twigs snapped and dried leaves crunched under his feet as he made his way further down the gully for a closer look. He wasn't afraid. He had his gun.

He reached the small ridge, where the crazy man had been digging just a minute ago. But there was no sign of the guy—or his shovel. He almost tripped over one of several mounds of scooped-out dirt. A five-by-three sheet of cheap wood paneling rested against a tree by the big crater.

It took him a moment to realize that it was a lid for the grave, something to cover the empty plot until he was ready to fill it with a body. The crazy bastard was going to bury

someone back here, but obviously not tonight. In the meantime, that panel of wood with a few scoops of dirt spread
over it would hide his work nicely.

He started to snicker. He'd stumbled upon someone in the
middle of an elaborate murder scheme. This was the final
resting place for an unwanted spouse or business partner or
whoever needed to die. He couldn't help laughing.

But then he heard a rustling noise again. It was just behind him.

"Shhhh!" He felt someone's breath on his ear.

Reaching for his gun, he started to swivel around. But a
hand came up over his mouth and snapped his head back.
His throat was exposed.

He saw the knife coming toward him, then felt the steely
sharp pain at the side of his neck. The blade raced across his
gullet, sending a jolt through his entire body.

He knew he was already dead.

Ethan didn't want to say anything, but his mother and
Ruth were starting to scare him.

"Blink the porch light a few times to let me know you're
okay," Ruth had told his mom when she'd dropped them off
at the duplex.

Stepping into the house, Ethan half-expected to find some
ax-wielding guy in a hockey mask. His mother checked the
kitchen, both bedrooms, and the bathroom. Then she returned
to the front door, and flicked the light switch several times.
Ethan watched the porch light blinking. His mom double-
locked the door, and then moved to the living room window,
where she waved to Ruth. The Camry's headlights blinked as
it pulled away from the curb.

"I gotta admit," Ethan finally said. "This is freaking me
out a little."

"I'm just being cautious," his mother said, hanging her
coat in the closet.

She'd told him about it in the car yesterday. Some "dangerous" weirdo fan might be stalking her. They had to be careful. Ethan didn't think his mother was famous enough to have stalker fans.

As he took off his jacket, Ethan heard footsteps above them. It sounded like Vicki had company. The thought that two more people were in the duplex made him feel safer. Ever since his dad had disappeared, Ethan had slept with a baseball bat by his bed. He didn't remember being scared at night when his dad had lived there. But now he always worried about someone breaking into the duplex and killing them. Having the bat close at hand gave him a sense of security. At least it was good for something, because he sucked at baseball.

"I'll need you to stick close to home for a while, at least until this blows over," his mother said, heading for the kitchen. "Maybe we can go buy you a cell phone tomorrow. I'd feel better knowing you can get ahold of me more easily."

"I'm supposed to go to a football game in Ballard tomorrow, remember? You signed the permission slip a couple of weeks ago. A bus is picking me up at ten forty-five."

At the refrigerator, his mother stopped to frown at him. "Oh, honey, I don't like the idea of you going off to some game when this—this wacko is on the loose. You don't really want to go, do you? I can tell them you're sick."

"No, I *want* to go," he protested. "There's only like—two hundred people going, Mom. I'll be okay."

"Well, do you have a friend you can stick close to? I don't want you to be by yourself—not for a minute. I'm serious, Ethan. I don't even want you going to the restroom by yourself."

"I have somebody I can hang with," he said. He was thinking of Joe Pagani. If anyone could protect him from some weirdo stalker, it was Joe Pagani. "I'll be fine, Mom."

His mother sighed, then reached into the refrigerator for her seltzer water. "I'll think about it."

Ethan retreated to his bedroom and closed the door. His walls were decorated with a couple of M. C. Escher posters, a beer sign, an autographed photo of Itzhak Perlman, and a Seattle Seahawks poster that he wasn't crazy about, but it helped make the room seem more masculine. Ethan figured it might help him feel more masculine too. So far, it wasn't really working. He had a lava lamp on his bookcase, and on his desk, a fiber-optic gizmo with a metal base sprouting iridescent-tipped stems.

Ethan kicked off his shoes, sat down, and opened the bottom drawer to his desk. He listened to his mother moving around in the kitchen. Her computer beeped on. She'd be busy for a while.

Reaching into the drawer, Ethan dug under a pile of papers and old music sheets to uncover a spiral notebook. He pulled out the book, and opened it to the first page:

WARNING: DO NOT READ THIS! This is my PRIVATE journal & no one should be looking at this except me. If you're still reading now, you should stop, because you're invading my privacy & that makes you a scumbag. This is NONE OF YOUR BUSINESS. Only a total asshole would keep looking at this & you are cursed to suffer for eternity. You suck if you're still reading this. . . .

Ethan figured it might have been easier if he'd just written, "Mom, please don't read this." But he was extremely nervous about someone finding his journal. He kept it stashed in a spot second only to his hiding place for the gay magazine he'd held onto for a while (until he'd destroyed it, that prize had been tucked beneath a loose section of carpet, under his bed). At the same time, he liked having the journal. He could be completely honest, and write things in it that he couldn't tell any human being. And it kept him from feeling so alone.

He paged through the journal, stopping to glance at bits and pieces from random entries:

. . . Dr. Pickett yelled at me today about not practicing enough & I guess he's right. It's just that I get pretty bored . . .

. . . came into the kitchen & saw Mom crying while she was doing the dishes. She tried to pretend she wasn't, but I saw her. I think she misses Dad. She never goes out or anything. Maybe it would help if I did the dishes once in a while so she doesn't have to . . .

. . . I'm really pissed at Craig. He thinks he's so cool now, just because he got stoned with a bunch of his burn-out friends last weekend. Plus he tongue-kissed Dakota Dillon. Big deal. She's kind of a skank. Of course, he didn't invite me to this party. I didn't hear about it until yesterday . . .

. . . I really miss Dad. I sometimes think I wouldn't be queer if he was around. But then, I know I was this way long before he left. But maybe if he was here, I would at least be more masculine like some of those juniors and seniors (John McCready & Rick Johnson) who are gay & comfortable about it & no one bugs them . . .

. . . for no reason, he called me a "fag" & I hardly even know him. I found out his name is Tate Barringer & he's a sophomore. I keep thinking maybe he caught me looking at him. He's kind of handsome in a weird way, even though he has bad pockmarks . . .

Ethan stopped reading when he heard his mother talking on the telephone. "Hi, Dianne," she was saying. "I hope you're doing all right. You might be in Milwaukee for Joyce's funeral. Anyway, when you get this message, call me, okay? I talked with this police lieutenant tonight, and she was con-

cerned about those four phone calls from your place after
Joyce was killed. She thinks you should have the investigating officers look into it. I'm sure dealing with the police
again is the last thing you want to do right now, but it's important. Anyway, I should hang up before your machine cuts
me off. I'm thinking of you. Take care. And call me."

Ethan heard some papers rustling. He wasn't sure what
his mother was talking about on the phone. Some friend of
his Aunt Dianne's was killed? He wondered if there was a
connection to his mother's weirdo fan and the death of this
Joyce person.

"Hello, is Shauna there, please?" his mother was saying.
She suddenly sounded more cheerful: "Oh, hi, Shauna. This
is Gillian McBride calling . . . yes, a voice from your past.
How are you?"

His mother started gabbing with this Shauna woman about
some class from two years ago. She didn't sound so grim anymore. Ethan figured she must be okay. He switched on the
radio. It drowned out the chatter, but he could still hear if his
mother was coming toward his bedroom. She always knocked
when he had the door closed. That gave him plenty of time
to stash the journal before she poked her head in.

He grabbed a pen, and started writing:

Friday, Nov. 9th:

*God, what a day! I got picked last for soccer during gym
class & wanted to slit my own throat. I was so humiliated. Now I know how Mark Phair feels. Anyway, so
much happened & I'll get to it later, but the main thing is
that I met this guy today. It was incredible. It's like he's
an answer to my prayers, because he showed up out of
nowhere when Tate & Don were giving me shit in front of
the locker room again. He totally kicked the crap out of
Tate & even put him in the hospital. This guy is older &
good-looking & he's really cool . . .*

Ethan stopped writing for a moment. He wasn't listening to his mother, who was still talking on the phone. He could barely hear her. He was thinking about his rendezvous with Joe Pagani tomorrow. For the first time in a long, long while, he actually looked forward to seeing that school bus in the morning.

"Oh gosh, no, I haven't seen anybody from that class since—like—two years ago when the semester ended," Shauna said to Gillian over the phone.

It wasn't what Gillian had wanted to hear. She'd figured Shauna was the type who kept in touch with classmates long after they'd stopped caring, the well-meaning busybody who circulated group e-mails and planned reunions. She'd hoped Shauna would know if Jennifer had recently been dating someone from the class—or perhaps another teacher from the college. She'd also wanted to hear updates on Chase and Todd.

Instead, she got an explanation from Shauna about what she'd been doing the last two years. Shauna had moved to Bellingham, found a features writing job for the *Bellingham Herald,* met a man, gotten married, and now she was going to have a baby.

Gillian listened to her former student, and thought about her own life these last two years: staying in the same place, writing "medium-selling" books, and waiting for a husband who was never coming back to her. She told Shauna how happy she was for her.

"How about you?" Shauna asked. "Seen any of the old gang? I know you're still writing, because I saw your new thriller at Village Books. Did anyone in the class ever get published?"

"As a matter of fact, Jennifer Gilderhoff has a collection of short stories coming out next month," Gillian said. "She— ah—"

"Oh, Jennifer, the flirt," Shauna said. "She drove me crazy sometimes. I'm sorry, but I didn't like her very much. I tried to make friends with her, but she was too busy throwing herself at the guys—especially Chase. Not that he paid any attention to her."

Gillian decided now wasn't a good time to tell her about the stabbing. "Yes, I don't remember Chase ever talking with her much. He was a—an *interesting* guy, wasn't he?"

"Well, he was an awful snob sometimes. But he could be a lot of fun too. I remember we were both reading your first book, *Killing Legend,* at the same time, and we kept comparing how far along we were on it. At the end of the semester, we exchanged e-mail addresses, and I wrote him a couple of times, but Chase never wrote back, the rat." She let out a sad little laugh.

"Do you remember Todd?" Gillian asked. "Todd Sorenson?"

"Oh, he was the crazy one, wasn't he? The very first day of class, when I saw him I thought he was so cute, very James Dean. Then I tried to talk with him, and forget about it! Remember how he yelled at everyone and quit before the end of the semester? I wonder what happened to him. He's probably in jail for murdering somebody or something. Talk about scary!"

"Well, that was a pretty scary time to be attending classes there," Gillian remarked.

"I'll say. I used to go to class with pepper spray, a whistle, *and* a switchblade in my purse."

"Did you ever discuss the Schoolgirl Murders with Chase?"

"I remember him saying it was too bad you didn't want to write about the Schoolgirl Murders. He said the killings had all the ingredients for a best-seller."

"Um, did you ever discuss the murders with Todd?"

"Oh, God, no," Shauna replied. "He never talked to me. He—" She trailed off.

"What is it?" Gillian asked.

"I just remembered something weird Todd did say. It was one night before class started, and I was chatting with Chase about *Killing Legend*. Out of nowhere, Todd let out this strange laugh. So Chase and I turned to look at him, and he was slouched in his chair like he always was. Todd said he'd read your book, and that you—well, sorry, but he said you weren't a very good thriller-writer."

"Really?" Gillian murmured.

"Yes. Chase said to him, 'Would you care to elaborate?' Then Todd, he smiled and said, 'She's no good, because she doesn't really know about killing people.' Isn't that a strange thing to say?"

Gillian studied Chase's phone number, scrawled in Ruth's scratchy handwriting. Then she glanced at her wristwatch: 10:10. If she waited any longer, it would be too late to call him.

She'd been on the phone with Shauna for twenty minutes. They'd promised to keep in touch, and Shauna had said she'd run out and buy *Black Ribbons,* even though she didn't like reading scary books while pregnant.

That call had been easy, because Shauna wasn't a suspect.

Not so with Chase. She had to be very careful with him. In fact, she was better off talking with him in person than discussing things over the telephone. She would learn more from him—from his reactions to questions, his facial expressions and body language—if she spoke with him face-to-face. But what could she say to lure him into a meeting? She thought of something, but it was awfully cruel. Still, it was the best incentive to get him to meet with her.

Gillian dialed the number in Bremerton. She started counting the ring tones. After the fourth, the answering machine clicked on. *"Hey, you almost got me,"* Chase's voice cooed. *"Try, try again or leave me a message. Ciao."*

Beep.

"Hi, Chase," Gillian said into the phone. "This is your old creative writing teacher, Gillian McBride, calling at around ten o'clock on Friday night. I was talking with my editor and my agent today, and I thought of you. They're looking for some new blood, and erotic thrillers are really hot right now. I remembered the book you were writing for class, and told them about you. Anyway, let's get together and talk. I happen to be free most of the day tomorrow. Give me a call, okay? My number is 206-555-5492. I hope you're doing well. Talk to you soon. Bye."

Gillian hung up. It was a horrible ploy, promising him a possible book deal. No aspiring writer could resist an offer like that. If he took the bait, and was remotely nice, she'd put in a word for him with her agent.

She was shaking a little. She realized there was a chance he wasn't nice at all. He was a suspect, and there was a chance she'd just left a message with the man who was using her books as blueprints for killing people.

Chapter 14

On the nineteen-inch TV screen, there was a helicopter explosion, followed by a buffed shirtless man brandishing a gun and kicking down a door, then a buxom blonde in a hot tub, removing her bikini top, followed by a truck explosion. . . .

A sultry woman's voice purred over the coming attractions, which promised plenty of sex and violence: *"Fuel-injected action is coming up next with Travis Rock, Shane Archer, and their bod squad of sexy sirens, Amber, Tarrin, and Latoya, taking on the bad guys in* Tahitian Dynamite! *Erotic pleasure and plenty of high-octane adventure are coming your way with Cinemax After Dark. Next!"*

Ethan was in heaven. His mom had gotten a bigger-screen TV with some royalty money about a year ago, and they'd moved the old television set into his bedroom. When the cable people hooked it up, his mother requested the parental-control option. The cable company screwed it up and put the controls—which his mom didn't know how to operate anyway—on the living room TV instead. His mom had never caught on to the mistake. So Ethan was always on the lookout for free Cinemax, Showtime, and HBO offers, so he could catch R-rated movies. Some of the ones on Cinemax After Dark were pretty close to X-rated. Craig always came over to spend the night when it was a free Cinemax weekend.

Sitting on the floor with a pillow between his back and the foot of the bed, Ethan watched the television set, and tried not to think about Craig. He didn't want to get depressed. Who needed him anyway? He was better off alone. Without his friend around, he didn't have to feign disinterest during those rare moments amid the bimbo-boob-and-beaver-fest when some hunky guy got naked and showed his butt. And hell, that was half the reason he watched this crap.

In the darkened window to the right of the TV, he saw rain pelting at the glass. He was snug in his bedroom, bathed in the flickering light from the TV. He knew his mother was in her writing nook, researching stuff on the Internet. He'd seen her a few minutes ago when he'd gotten a pack of Red Vines out of the kitchen cabinet. The remote was at his side; he could always switch channels if he heard her coming.

He tuned down the volume as the Viewer Advisory came on: *"This film has not been rated. It contains graphic violence, adult language, nudity, and strong sexual content. Adult Discretion Advised."*

"I'm going straight to hell," Ethan murmured, eyes glued to the screen. He munched on a Red Vine.

The titles to the movie were coming up when he saw something move outside his window. He stared at the window for a moment. Some bushes beside the house rustled. Maybe that was what had caught his eye. He kept staring— at his own reflection in the darkened, rain-beaded glass. He saw a skinny kid, sitting on the floor, looking stupid and scared. He imagined someone out there at the ravine's edge, staring at the exact same image right now.

Ethan squirmed a little, and wondered if someone saw that too. A chill raced through him. "Quit creeping yourself out," he muttered. He didn't notice anything outside. His mom's paranoia was contagious.

He reached for a Red Vine, and shifted his focus to the movie. The villain, an evil maharajah in bad brown makeup, wore a turban with his tie and white dinner jacket. He sat on his throne in the reception hall of his castle. An arms dealer, an Italian-looking dude with sunglasses, was having his sumo-wrestler henchman demonstrate different newfangled weapons for him.

Ethan saw something out of the corner of his eye again. He turned toward the window in time to see a man dart past the bushes. "Oh, shit," he murmured. He felt the hairs stand on the back of his neck. With a shaky hand, he fumbled for the remote and switched off the television. His room turned dark.

At least the guy outside couldn't see him now. Getting to his feet, Ethan felt his way to his nightstand. Blindly, he groped for the baseball bat he kept at his bedside. He almost knocked over his lamp.

"Mom?" he called out softly. Ethan could hardly breathe. His fingertips finally brushed against the bat, and then he grabbed hold of it. He didn't hear anything except the rain outside. He made his way toward the window. He could see the backyard more clearly now. The trees and bushes swayed in the heavy rain. Beyond the yard, the ravine was engulfed in blackness. Then he saw something emerge from the shadows—a man in a white T-shirt.

Ethan gasped. "Oh, Jesus . . ."

The man paused at the edge of the gully. He was tall, and he swayed a bit, like the trees behind him. He seemed to be staring back at Ethan.

"Mom?" Ethan called, louder this time. "Mom?"

He hurried toward the door. Stumbling over his pillow on the floor, he fell against the wall. But he didn't trip, and he didn't let go of the bat either. He felt around for the doorknob. As his hand fanned at the air, he glanced back toward the window. He saw the man outside, getting closer. He was approaching the house.

He found the knob and flung open the door. "Mom?" he called, racing down the short hallway.

"What is it?" his mother said, stepping out of her writer's nook. "Ethan—"

"Somebody's in the backyard," he said, the words rushing out of him. He tried to get a breath. "A tall guy. He's coming toward the house. . . ."

Wide-eyed, his mother stared at him for a moment. "Where? Where did you see him?"

"Out by the ravine." Ethan clung to the baseball bat. "I— I don't think he's one of those guys looking for Dad. He's wearing a T-shirt and jeans, and he looks kind of crazy. . . ."

"All right, calm down," his mother whispered. But a look of panic swept over her face. She headed for the kitchen sink and pulled a carving knife from the drain rack. Just then, they heard a noise on the front porch. Boards creaked. Footsteps.

His mother grabbed his arm and pulled him back behind her. Then she switched off the kitchen light. Ethan peeked over her shoulder toward the front window. The curtains were open. A shadow started to pass over the porch. Then they saw him.

His mother bolted toward her little office and snatched up the cordless phone.

Ethan edged closer to the kitchen door. He didn't recognize the man, who was soaked with rain. The T-shirt clung to his broad shoulders and muscular chest. Ethan could see he was breathing heavily. His dark hair was in wet ringlets and he had a strange snarl on his face. But he wasn't holding a gun or knife or anything. He stopped in front of the window and stared at them.

Then he smiled.

His mother still had the phone in one hand and the knife in the other. She seemed to freeze for a moment.

The man tapped on the glass and waved.

"What the hell?" his mother muttered.

"You must be Gillian and Ethan!" he called at them, his voice muffled by the glass. "I'm Jason . . . Vicki's friend!" He pointed up. "I'm friends with Vicki upstairs!"

"Vicki's friend," his mother repeated, almost under her breath. She set the knife down on the kitchen counter. "Oh, Lord . . ."

"I hope I didn't scare you!" he called.

Ethan came around the corner from the kitchen. He kept the baseball bat hidden behind him. His mother moved to the front door, and unlocked it. But she left the security chain fastened. She opened the door as far as the chain lock allowed.

"Hi, sorry if I gave you a fright," Ethan heard the man say. "I'm Jason Hurrell, Vicki's friend."

Ethan stepped up behind his mother and peeked through the gap in the door. The man was very handsome, with a friendly smile. He shivered and rubbed his brawny arms. "Vicki thought she saw someone in the yard. She sent me out to investigate," he explained. "Are you folks okay? Did you notice anything unusual outside?"

"Just you," his mother said warily.

He laughed. "Sorry. Anyway, I'm glad you're all right. Vicki was concerned. She said you've been having some prowlers—people hanging around outside the house."

"We're okay," Ethan piped up. "Thanks a lot for checking. It's very nice of you."

"No problem," he said, smiling at Ethan. The water dripping down his face caught in his thick eyelashes. The man looked at Gillian and shrugged. "I guess you can expect people hanging around outside your house when you're a famous author, huh?"

"Not really," Ethan heard his mother say. Her tone was flat and cold. And this handsome guy was being so nice.

"Listen, if you need to call and double-check with Vicki about me, I totally understand, Mrs. Tanner. I got in very late last night. I think you folks were in bed. Anyway, it's nice to meet you, and I'm sorry I disturbed you." He started to reach out to shake hands, but seemed to think better of it, and his hand dropped down to his side. He cleared his throat. "Well, good night."

His mother just nodded.

"Nice meeting you!" Ethan called. "Thanks for—"

His mother shut the door before Ethan finished. He watched Jason Hurrell slink across the porch. "God, Mom, did you have to be so rude to him?"

She double-locked the door. "What are you talking about?"

Ethan paused to listen to him go upstairs to Vicki's apartment. He frowned at his mother. "You practically slammed the door in his face. The way you acted—God, I'm so embarrassed. You didn't even let me say good-bye to him."

"Let you say good-bye?" she repeated, incredulous. "A minute ago you were ready to bash his brains in with your baseball bat."

"That's before I knew he was Vicki's friend. I can't believe you didn't even try to be friendly."

With a sigh, his mother brushed past him on her way into the kitchen. She switched on the light and put the knife back in the draining rack. "Well, I'm sorry," she said, shrugging. "I was just being cautious. Did you expect me to open the door and invite him in for coffee just because he's good-looking and acting friendly?"

Ethan scowled at her. "What do you mean? I didn't say he was *good-looking*. I didn't say anything like that! I hardly even noticed what he looked like. He's Vicki's friend. I just thought we should be nice to him. That's all. God!"

"Ethan, I didn't mean it like that—"

"What are you trying to say, Mom? Huh?"

He didn't wait to hear her answer. He swiveled around and stomped toward his room, baseball bat in tow. She'd practically called him a queer. She was almost as bad as Tate Barringer.

"No wonder Dad has never bothered to come back to you," he hissed.

Then Ethan ducked into his bedroom and slammed the door.

She heard a scream.

Gillian sat up in bed. She stared at the ceiling. It sounded like he was killing her up there. But no, Vicki and her stud of a boyfriend were just having a good time. Vicki the Vocalizer, Barry used to call her. There was a time when she and Barry used to lay in bed and listen—and giggle. "What can I do to you to make you moan like that?" Barry would whisper in her ear. Then his hand would glide up her thigh. Vicki's arias had instigated many a romantic interlude one floor down.

But at the moment, Gillian just felt lonely and bitter. The man who was bringing Vicki to the gates of ecstasy was indeed very handsome and sexy and charming. She couldn't help being cautious around him. Sixteen years ago, she'd fallen for a handsome, sexy, charming guy, and married the son of a bitch. And look where that had gotten her.

Had she really been rude to Jason Hurrell? When had she become so bitter? Some Adonis showed up at her front door, shivering in a wet T-shirt that showed off his gorgeous physique. He was friendly and sweet, and he kept smiling at her. All the while, she'd just snarled at him.

Well, why shouldn't she snarl? He wasn't interested in her. What was Jason Hurrell doing right now? No second-guessing, she could *hear* what he was doing.

"Damn it," Gillian muttered, throwing back the sheets. She glanced at the nightstand clock: 1:23 A.M. Putting on her robe, she wandered down the hallway. As she passed Ethan's door, she didn't see any light along the crack at the threshold. She'd tried to talk to him earlier. She'd given him a few minutes to cool off after he'd blown up at her. Then she'd tapped on his door. She'd seen his light was still on.

"Honey, I'm sorry," she'd called softly. "I'll apologize to Vicki's friend in the morning. Okay? Can I come in?"

"Mom, I'm trying to sleep," he'd replied. She'd heard the strain in his voice. "Could you please leave me alone?"

"All right. We'll talk in the morning, okay, honey?"

"G'night," he'd grumbled.

Well, at least one of them had been able to sleep.

She padded into the living room and stopped to stare out the front window. Was her copycat out there? Perhaps he'd seen Jason Hurrell on the front porch earlier tonight, and now he was keeping his distance.

She'd told Lieutenant Voorhees that he was a planner. No doubt, he'd already chosen his next victim—probably in Seattle. And he'd already selected a murder scene to emulate from one of her books. He was just waiting to make his move, so much like the Schoolgirl Killer.

Gillian remembered the MISSING posters that went up around the campus that week after Thanksgiving. On the bulletin that hung by the second floor vending machines, someone had scribbled *"#3?"* beside the woman's grainy photo. There was room for doubt this time. Valentina Tran was a petite, fifty-one-year-old, Vietnamese grandmother. She drove herself to an English as a Second Language course at the college three nights a week. According to her daughter, Valentina started carrying a canister of Mace in her purse after the Kelly Zinnemann murder. She'd left her North Seattle home for the campus on Monday evening, but never showed up for class. Her abandoned car was discovered, parked along a residential street half a mile from the college, on Tuesday morning. There had been no sign of a struggle.

"If Valentina is number three, the shrinks on this case will really be scratching their heads," Gillian recalled Ruth say-

ing. "He's breaking his pattern with the age and the race difference. It's not like him to be indiscriminate, not when he
outfits them in advance. If he chose this poor fifty-one-year-
old Asian woman, he might be sending a message. This
could be his way of saying, 'Watch out. No one's safe.' He
wants everyone scared."

Valentina Tran was still missing when Gillian's class con-
vened that Thursday night. It was about forty minutes into
the session, and Gillian was reading aloud a chapter from
Edna's historical romance novel, when they heard a commotion in the hallway. Gillian kept reading, but hardly anyone—
except Edna—was paying attention. Through the window in
the door, she noticed people running up and down the hallway, a couple of them policemen. Everyone was looking in
that direction. Gillian heard sirens outside the school. "Okay,"
she said, finally putting down Edna's story. "Ruth, could you
go check for us what's happening out there?"

Nodding, Ruth got to her feet and headed out of the classroom. For a moment, while the door was open, they got a
sample of all the noise in the hallway—and the fetid smell.
Gillian tried to maintain a discussion on what she'd read
from Edna's bodice-ripper so far. After ten minutes, the
chaos in the corridor had gotten worse, and Gillian thought
about having someone go check on what had happened to
Ruth. But then Ruth stepped back into the classroom.

She walked up to Gillian's desk. "They found Valentina,"
she whispered soberly.

In the second row, Shauna let out a gasp.

"The body's two doors down—in the janitor's closet,"
Ruth continued under her breath. "She's curled up under the
sink. It's the same MO. She was shot in the head, and dressed
in the schoolgirl outfit—the whole getup, right down to the
saddle shoes."

Gillian remembered glancing out at the class, with everyone leaning forward in their desk-chairs, trying to hear what
Ruth was saying. She remembered that Todd Sorenson was

the only one who didn't seem concerned. Slouched back in
his chair, he stared out the window.

That following week had been the last time she'd seen
him. It had been during the break in that session when he'd
lashed out at his classmates and never returned to class.

She'd hardly given Todd a sustained thought since then.
And now, as she stared out her front window, she wondered
if he'd been stalking her all this time.

The Schoolgirl Killer and Gillian's copycat were both
planners, both incredibly patient. Were they both the same
person? It took a hell of a lot of patience to stalk someone
for two years.

Gillian moved over to her study nook. She switched on
her computer. While it warmed up, she went to the refrigerator, took out a bottle of Chardonnay, and poured a glass. She
didn't turn on any other lights. The light from the computer
monitor was enough; it bathed the little room in an eerie
glow. She sat down with her wine, and her fingers started
tapping on the keyboard.

She pulled up Google.com and typed: *Boyd Farrow,
Seattle City College, Murders.*

She hit Enter, and glanced at the item at the top of the list,
a headline from *The Seattle Post-Intelligencer*:

Accused 'Schoolgirl' Killer, **Boyd Farrow** Commits
Suicide . . . **Boyd Farrow,** 43, a former priest and a
teacher at **Seattle City College** . . . accused of killing
three women in what have been called the 'Schoolgirl
Murders,' ended his own life . . .
www.seattlepi/news/bfarrow/122906.htm. – 13 k.

They'd arrested Boyd Farrow only a few days after the semester ended, around Christmastime. Gillian remembered
how it had looked like an open-and-shut case. Apparently,
Farrow had been at the college four years, teaching a class in

World Religions. Kelly Zinnemann had been one of his students a year before her murder. Farrow had asked out the pretty twenty-two-year-old blonde, but she'd politely turned him down. Most everyone who knew Farrow said he was quiet, well-mannered, and friendly, the same description given to most serial killers—until people discovered their true nature. Police investigators took a hair sample discovered on Kelly's madras "schoolgirl" dress, and it matched Farrow's. They also found a match with a single strand discovered in the palm of Christine Cardiff's hand. Another match came up with a hair sample discovered under Valentina's corpse—on the floor of the janitor's closet.

If there were any lingering doubts about Farrow's guilt, a scandal in his past seemed to seal the deal. It certainly explained the killer's penchant for schoolgirl uniforms. Fifteen years before the murders, Farrow had been a Catholic priest at St. Lambert Parish in Portland. He also taught religion at the grade school—until he was accused of molesting a fifth-grade girl during a school camping trip. Boyd Farrow left the parish and the priesthood. He moved to Seattle, and continued teaching courses in religion, but only at a college level.

Gillian remembered how they never found the .45 that had dispatched the three victims. Nor were they able to locate Farrow's "hideaway." The former priest had lived on a modest income in a small apartment building in Queen Anne, and all his neighbors knew him. There was no way he could have kept his victims alive—sometimes days at a time—without someone suspecting. So where had he kept his victims? Where had he dressed them and killed them?

At the time of his arrest, Boyd Farrow had maintained he was innocent. Many of his neighbors and friends talked to the press on his behalf. From everything Gillian had read about Boyd Farrow, the shy, modest man seemed a far cry from the Schoolgirl Killer, the monster with a flair for the dramatic who had made himself a serial-killing "superstar."

Ruth had said the Schoolgirl Killer had wanted publicity. But Boyd Farrow clearly loathed the headlines and all the attention.

Boyd and his friends hadn't been able to post bail. Eleven days after his incarceration, Boyd had complained of an upset stomach. A guard at the jail took pity on him and gave him a bottle of 7-Up. Boyd broke the bottle and slit his own throat with the jagged glass. One of the newspapers reporting Farrow's suicide mentioned that the guard was suspended for two weeks without pay. Gillian remembered the article quoting one of Farrow's friends: "If Boyd had left a suicide note, he probably would have included an apology to the guard for getting him into trouble. Boyd was that kind of guy."

The police still maintained that Boyd Farrow was guilty. After all, the Schoolgirl Murders had stopped once he'd been arrested.

Gillian had already read most of the news stories and articles listed by Google. She remembered many details. But what Gillian couldn't remember was the name of Boyd Farrow's friend, the one who had made the comment about him being the kind of guy who would have apologized to the guard in a suicide note.

Gillian scanned eleven articles—until she was blurry-eyed. Then she came across the quote in the second to last paragraph of an article in the *Seattle Weekly*. Funny, but she'd remembered it practically word for word:

. . . Boyd was that kind of guy," said Timothy Haworth, 40, of Seattle. Haworth was a longtime friend of the accused, and a former priest as well. "I'm convinced the police arrested the wrong man. Boyd's death is just one more senseless murder caused by this Schoolgirl Killer."

Gillian got up from her desk, headed into the kitchen, and pulled the phone book out of the junk drawer. She found the listing: *Haworth, Timothy—2552 NW Market . . . . 206-555-1907.*

She copied down the address and phone number, then sipped her Chardonnay. The clock on the stove said 3:42 A.M.

If this was the right Timothy Haworth, she wanted to meet with him tomorrow. She'd make time for him *and* Chase Scott if they'd see her. Gillian wasn't sure what Boyd Farrow's friend could tell her. But at dinner tonight with Ruth and her friend, they kept saying there was no connection between her copycat and the Schoolgirl Murders. They didn't see that both killings took a meticulous planner, an incredibly patient man—so patient he may have even waited two years before starting to kill again.

Ruth and her friend had insisted that the Schoolgirl Killer was dead.

Gillian needed to talk with someone else—someone who didn't agree with them.

Chapter 15

"Yes, this is Tim Haworth," said the voice on the other end of the line.

"The Tim Haworth who used to be a priest?" Gillian asked.

"Um, who's calling?"

"My name's Gillian McBride. I was hoping I could—"

"Gillian McBride the writer?" he interrupted.

Gillian was speechless for a moment. She didn't often run across strangers who knew her work. "Um, you've heard of me?"

"I certainly have," he said. "I remember that newspaper article where you really slammed the police for their shoddy investigation into the Schoolgirl Murders."

"Oh, that. Listen—"

"You spoke out and told it like it was. The cops really screwed that up. They arrested the wrong guy. Boyd Farrow was no killer."

For once, that stupid article was doing her some good. "Well, I'm glad we see eye to eye. Listen, Tim, would you have time to talk with me today?"

"Sure. Are you writing a nonfiction piece about the killings?"

"Yes, something like that."

Tim Haworth said he would be working all day in his plant shop, Ballard Botanical. The address he gave was the same one listed in the phone book. She could come in anytime.

After Gillian hung up the phone, she poured herself another cup of coffee and dug some bus schedules out of the junk drawer. She probably had to take a transfer to Ballard.

Operating on about four and a half hours of sleep, she was fatigued. At 8:30, she'd woken up to Vicki and Jason having another go at it upstairs. Later in the morning, she'd tried making amends with Ethan, but he'd said he just wanted to forget about it. He'd been listlessly polite and distant, passing on her offer to make him pancakes for breakfast. He'd fixed himself a bowl of Alphabits, and studied the back of the cereal box while eating.

Now he was in the bathroom, getting ready for the football game. The bus was due to pick him up soon.

Gillian had gotten dressed an hour ago: khaki slacks and a black sweater. There hadn't been any calls or messages. No response from her friend Dianne in Chicago, and nothing from Chase Scott.

From the bus schedules, she figured the ten-mile trip to Ballard would take her over an hour each way. Gillian considered springing for a cab. She still had a bus schedule in her hand when she heard someone knocking on the front door.

She glanced out the front window, and balked when she saw Jason Hurrell standing on the front porch. He wore a fisherman's sweater and jeans. His hair, when not wet, was light brown, almost a gold color, and wavy. For someone who had been having sex all night—and this morning—he looked disgustingly fresh and well-rested right now. Gillian felt the snarl already pulling at her upper lip as she opened the door.

"Hi, Gillian," he said. "I hope I didn't disturb you—again. I just wanted to say I'm sorry about giving you and Ethan a scare last night."

"We've gotten over it," she said coolly. "No need to apologize."

"Do you or Ethan need a ride someplace?"

She squinted at him. "What?"

He nodded at the bus schedule in her hand. "You don't need to take a bus. I happen to have a car, and lots of time on my hands. Vicki's at this spa appointment she didn't want to cancel. She'll be gone all day until four. I'm looking for something to do. I'd be happy to give you a lift if you're going someplace."

Gillian hesitated. She saw the chartered bus pull up for Ethan. "Just a minute," she said. Then she ducked back inside. "Ethan, your bus is here! Do you need any money?"

She heard the toilet flush, then he emerged from the bathroom. "I'm fine, thanks," he said, making a beeline to the front closet, where he took out his jacket.

"What's the name of this new friend you're going to hang out with at the game?" she asked.

Throwing on his jacket, he seemed to have to think for a moment before he answered, "Jim Munchel."

"Well, stick close to Jim today," she said. "I don't want you going off by yourself at any time. Understand?"

"Yeah, sure, Mom," he said, heading for the door.

She started outside after him. "What time are you supposed to be back?"

"I dunno, three-thirty or four," he called over his shoulder. "Bye."

Jason Hurrell had moved off the porch. He now stood by the curb, talking to the driver through the bus's open door. A boy on the bus had his head half out of the window. "C'mon, Tanner, move your ass! C'mon . . ."

Gillian saw Ethan's stride suddenly falter. He tripped and hit the ground hard.

Laughter erupted on the bus. Gillian came down the porch steps to make sure Ethan wasn't hurt. But her eyes met Jason Hurrell's, and he was shaking his head at her. She stopped in her tracks. She realized he knew better. Ethan would have been doubly humiliated if his *mommy* had helped him up.

"Nice going, spaz!" the same annoying kid called from the bus window. He was cackling.

While Ethan got himself to his feet, Jason Hurrell stepped over to the boy with his head out the window. "How would you like to shut the hell up?" he muttered.

Gillian just barely heard him. But Ethan obviously caught the whole thing. Brushing himself off, he paused for a moment, and glanced at Jason Hurrell. A smile flickered between the two of them, a look that used to pass between Ethan and his father.

The wise-ass kid ducked his head back inside, then quickly shut the window.

"So long," Ethan said to Jason Hurrell.

He nodded. "See you, Ethan."

Ethan boarded the bus, and the door shut. As the bus started down the street, Jason Hurrell turned to Gillian. "So— can I give you a lift someplace?"

"Vicki told me how you two met," Gillian said, sitting in the passenger seat of Jason's rented Taurus. At the wheel, Jason Hurrell wore sunglasses, so she couldn't quite read his expression whenever he took his eyes off the road and glanced at her. They were driving on Westlake Avenue along Lake Union. "She said you were a passenger on one of her flights, and you tracked her down through some friends of yours with the airline."

"That's right. I'm a charter pilot out of Missoula, so I knew some people."

"Missoula, Montana? Do you fly to Billings often?"

Staring at the traffic ahead, he nodded. "Often enough. Why? Do you know someone in Billings?"

"I might," Gillian said.

"Anyway, I was able to track her down."

Gillian stared out at the boats docked in Lake Union's harbor. "Well, Vicki certainly seems to like you," she said tonelessly.

"She's a lot of fun, a great kid."

What a horse's ass, Gillian thought. She just shook her head and continued to look out the window.

Jason cleared his throat. "I asked Vicki about your husband, and all she said was, 'He's been out of the picture for a couple of years.' "

"That's a good way to put it."

"Are you divorced?"

"No."

"Two years, that's a long time for a beautiful woman to be alone."

Gillian rolled her eyes. "I'm not alone. I have Ethan. Plus I'm very busy with my writing."

"So there aren't any boyfriends in the picture? You're not dating anyone?"

"No."

"Don't you get lonely?" he asked quietly.

"It passes," Gillian replied. She turned toward him. "Listen, why are you so interested in my personal life?"

He glanced at her, then let out an awkward laugh. "I'm just making conversation here, that's all."

"Well, if I knew you were going to get this personal, I'd have taken the bus." She pointed to a sign posted over the roadway. "Take the left lane to the Ballard Bridge—please."

Gillian felt bad for snapping at him, and she could see he looked slightly wounded. But she didn't trust him. He was Vicki's boyfriend. Why was he so interested in her? And she didn't like the way he was trying to get chummy with Ethan.

For the next few minutes in the car, she endured the uncomfortable silence, punctuating it with an occasional direction. They found Ballard Botanical on Market Street at the western edge of downtown Ballard. It was a sad-looking little stucco house with a big picture window on which BALLARD BOTANICAL was written in fancy silver script. Buckets of flowers and some plants placed around the door seemed to brighten up the depressing edifice.

Jason found parking in front of the store. He insisted on waiting for her.

"Well, that's very sweet of you," Gillian said. "But I might be a while. I don't want to take up any more of your time, Jason."

"Tell you what," he said. "If I get tired of waiting, I'll honk my horn, and then wait a couple of minutes before driving off. That will give you a chance to catch a ride, if you want one."

He shut off the engine and started to open his door. Gillian figured he was going to get the passenger door for her. She didn't want him doing her any more favors. "Thanks." She quickly opened her door. "Really, please, don't bother waiting."

A little bell attached to the door rang as Gillian stepped inside the store. For a flower and plant shop, it was rather gloomy. The tall, standing plants created a dense little jungle in the middle of the store. There were a couple of spin-racks of tacky-looking cards. Along one wall were the roses, in a refrigerated case, and the open door to a small greenhouse. It looked much brighter in there. She didn't see anyone behind the counter.

Gillian heard a car door slam, and an engine started up.

She turned and looked out the picture window. Jason Hurrell drove away in his Taurus.

Once again, she had mixed feelings about the way she'd behaved with him. Clearly, he was trying to be nice to her, but why? What was he after? The fact that he worked out of Missoula, and spent time in Billings, where they'd found that mutilated hitchhiker, was reason enough to be wary of him. But then, if he were the copycat killer, he wouldn't be giving out that information so freely. Or maybe he would. This killer seemed to enjoy pushing the envelope a little.

"Gillian?"

She gasped, and swiveled around.

Standing in the doorway to the greenhouse was a slightly pear-shaped, pale man with receding blond hair and a goatee. He wore a blue sweater, khakis, and blue Converse sneakers. He looked so gentle, Gillian immediately felt silly for being frightened. "Oh, I'm sorry," she said. "Hi. Are you Tim?"

Nodding, he shook her hand enthusiastically. "It's a pleasure to meet you, Gillian. I think what you're doing is great. Are you writing an article or a whole book?"

She shrugged. "I'm not quite sure yet. I've done some research, but you're the first person I'm interviewing. I thought I'd start with someone who believes Boyd Farrow was innocent. How long did you know him?"

A sad smile danced across his face, and he rested an elbow on top of the cash register. "Twenty-four years. He was my best friend. We met in the seminary back in 1980." He squinted at her. "Aren't you going to take notes or anything?"

"Um, not this time. I thought I'd just get some general background information for this session."

"Well, you know, after we spoke on the telephone, I got very nostalgic—I mean, about Boyd's and my days at the seminary. I started going through some old photos that used to belong to him. Would you like to see them?"

Tim Haworth opened the door behind the counter, and led her down a short hallway—past a bathroom and some stairs. Apparently, the rest of the living quarters were upstairs. But the kitchen was on the first floor. Tim said they could hear the bell ringing on the store's door just fine from there. The kitchen had a worn linoleum floor, an old, yellow dinette set, and over the sink, a crucifix. Tim Hawkins started to make a pot of coffee. A mangy-looking cat he called Oscar wandered in.

Gillian sat at the table and looked through a pile of old photographs. She'd seen photos of Boyd Farrow at the time of his arrest. She remembered him as a fairly attractive, middle-aged man who appeared more priestly than dangerous. Looking at photos of Boyd Farrow in his twenties, Gillian realized how his friend remembered him. "Isn't he handsome?" Tim asked.

"He's a stunner," Gillian murmured.

"And he didn't have a clue how good-looking he was."

She was staring at a photo of Boyd Farrow with his arm around Tim. They wore their priest collars and black jackets. With his wavy black hair, intense blue eyes, and a killer smile, Boyd Farrow looked like a model. He was even better-looking than Barry—and Jason Hurrell. And that was saying a lot.

"That was taken around the time I decided to leave the priesthood," Tim said, peeking over her shoulder. "It's when I told him I was gay. He wasn't. Believe me, I know, because three quarters of the guys at the seminary wanted him. But he wasn't interested. And he wasn't judgmental either. He understood why I had to give up the priesthood. I know a lot of priests who have their fun and rationalize their way around the celibacy issue. But I couldn't. Boyd, he had women coming on to him in droves. But he didn't give in to any of them."

He set a cup of coffee in front of her. "Cream or sugar?"

"Cream, please, thanks."

"Please don't twist this around to sound perverted," Tim continued, heading toward the refrigerator. "But Boyd loved teaching—and he loved kids. Kindergarten through eighth grade, they adored him. He was very athletic—you can tell in the pictures. He used to play sports with the boys, and he helped coach the girls' teams. If a student ever got sick, he'd go visit them at home—or in the hospital. God, they loved him."

Gillian was looking at one photo after another of this handsome priest—sometimes in regular clothes, sometimes in his clerical garb, and a couple of times in his altar vestments. In so many of the snapshots, he was surrounded by smiling people, children and adults alike, and he seemed to be the shy recipient of everyone's adoration.

Gillian looked up from the pile of photographs. "Something happened on a camping trip with a sixth-grade girl. None of the articles I read would elaborate."

Tim set a small carton of cream in front of her, then he sat down. He took a sip from his own cup. "That camping trip," he said, grimacing. "Some parents in the parish cooked it up for the sixth-graders. Boyd and one of the teachers, plus a couple of the mothers, ended up chaperoning. They had cabins for the boys and girls." He let out a sigh. It clearly pained him to explain it. "Boyd had his own room in the boys' cabin. These cabins had several kids in each room. Anyway, at lights out, Tim said good night to the boys; then he went to do the same thing in the girls' cabin. Well, the teacher in the girls' cabin had stuck one girl alone in a room, because she had a bad cold. There was talk about one of the parents driving her home. Anyway, Boyd had some Vick's Vaporub in his room, which was just like him. At the seminary, he was a walking pharmacy. I mean, if you needed something to cure Himalayan goat-bite, he had it in his travel kit. Anyway, this sick little girl was in bed coughing her lungs out. So Boyd fetched his

Vick's Vaporub, he unbuttoned a couple of buttons at the very top of her nightshirt, and he rubbed Vick's on her chest. And they talked until she fell asleep. I asked him later if he'd touched her breasts or anything. He told me no. He only rubbed the stuff on her upper chest, just below her neck, her *clavicle*. It was nothing, only—he told me—" Tim trailed off and shook his head. "It was totally innocent. The next day, the girl was actually feeling better. No one made a fuss. It wasn't until after the trip, when the girl got home and told her mother. That's when the shit hit the fan."

Gillian cocked her head to one side. "A moment ago, you started to say that Boyd told you something—"

He quickly shook his head again, then sipped his coffee. "It wasn't important. Anyway, this girl's mother was divorced and bitter, one of those high-maintenance types with lots of issues. You have to wonder about a mother who sends her daughter on a camping trip when the kid has a horrible cold and a fever. Boyd never said anything, but I heard from someone else in the parish that this lady had made a pass at him at one time. It's just hearsay, but you're not taking notes, so you won't quote me."

Gillian shook her head. "Oh, I won't quote you—not yet."

"Anyway, the mother went ballistic and raised a big stink with the archdiocese. Boyd had to go before the bishop. They felt he'd shown 'an error in judgment' tending to the girl the way he had. They officially censured him for it. He could have stayed in the priesthood. But Boyd quit. He was so hard on himself. He felt—well, he . . ." Tim trailed off and shook his head.

Eyes narrowed, Gillian stared him. This was the second time he'd stopped himself from saying something. "Go ahead," she whispered.

Tim sighed. "You know, he didn't feel sorry for himself at all. Boyd was more concerned about the girl, and how the other kids at school probably knew who she was. He even felt sorry for her mother. He said she was just so full of anger and bitterness about her marriage and her life that she had to take it out on somebody. He never complained. He took on all the blame for his 'error in judgment.' Anyway, he was never the same."

The cat, Oscar, sidled up to his leg. Tim picked him up and set him in his lap. "That was seventeen years ago," he said, stroking the cat's head. "Boyd started drinking, and it aged him so quickly. You can see it in the pictures. He was still a handsome guy, but he suddenly no longer had that same—beauty." He let out a sad little laugh. "Listen to me. I'm so pathetic. You can tell I had a crush on him."

"It sounded like everyone did," Gillian said, "for a while there, at least."

Tim nodded. "Anyway, Boyd worked in retail for a while. He dated. He moved to Seattle, and so I moved here, too, of course. Then he finally went back to teaching."

"But not kids," Gillian said. "I remember one of the newspapers hinted that he wasn't allowed to teach children after the camping incident."

Tim frowned. "That's bullshit—if you'll excuse me. It was Boyd's decision not to teach kids after that."

"But you told me earlier that he *loved* children. If he could have gone back to teaching kids, why didn't he?"

The cat jumped off Tim's lap. Standing up, Tim took his coffee cup to the sink, and turned on the water. "Boyd was very tough on himself. He felt he'd made one 'error in judgment,' and he didn't want to make another."

Gillian stared at his back as he hovered over the sink. "You make it sound like he thought he'd get into trouble again if he were around children."

Tim didn't respond. She noticed him lift his head a little, like he might have been staring at the crucifix over the sink.

"Tim, was he afraid of another 'incident' happening?"

He shut off the water, then turned around. Gillian could see tears welling in his eyes. He didn't look at her. He gazed down at the cat, rubbing its flank against his leg.

"Was there any truth in the accusations?" she pressed.

"Boyd was worried there might be," Tim murmured. "He confided in me that he got a feeling when he was touching the girl—"

"Oh, God, I don't want to hear any more," Gillian said, holding up her hand. "I'm sorry."

"Nothing happened," Tim said. "That girl wasn't molested in any way. . . ."

Gillian was staring down at photos of schoolchildren mixed in with the others of Boyd Farrow. The girls were in their school uniforms—including the saddle shoes. She felt so silly for trusting her gut instinct about Boyd Farrow's innocence. Now, it made sense that he was the Schoolgirl Killer. Depriving himself of the company of children, he abducted grown women, dressed them like little schoolgirls, then killed them. The only reason Tim Haworth defended Farrow was because he had been in love with the guy. Maybe he still was.

"Don't you see? He'd been celibate for so many years," Tim was explaining. "This was human contact—with a certain amount of intimacy. And even though it was perfectly innocent, it scared him. Boyd was always so tough on himself. He was horrified at just the—the *infinitesimal possibility* that it could be true . . ."

Tim pointed to a class photo—with about forty small individual portraits of the students on an eleven-by-fourteen glossy sheet. ST. LAMBERTS 6TH GRADE—1989 was written in fancy calligraphy across the top. "That's the class," he said. "The girl who had the cold is there, but I'm not going to show you which one she is. There's no point in it. She died from leukemia back in the mid-nineties. But this one . . ." Tim stabbed his finger on the portrait of a dark-haired girl

named Cynthia Siddons. "She's one of the liars who came
forward after Boyd was arrested for the Schoolgirl Murders.
There were three of them—her, another woman, and a man,
both from another class. They'd claimed Boyd had molested
them, *too*. As soon as the archdiocese told them they weren't
getting a dime, they dropped it. Everyone knew they were
lying. If Boyd had done anything to them at all, why didn't
they speak up after the camping trip incident? All the kids
knew about it—as much as their parents had tried to keep it
secret."

"I'm sorry," Gillian said, pushing her chair away from the
table. "But really, I don't think I'll be writing this piece after
all. I'm—"

"Damn it, sit down!" he yelled.

Gazing up at him, Gillian stayed in her chair.

"Please, please, listen to me," Tim whispered. "Boyd
never molested a child, and he never killed anyone—except
himself."

"If he was innocent, why did he commit suicide?" Gillian
dared to ask.

"It wasn't because of the Schoolgirl Murders. Boyd felt
they'd realize their mistake soon enough and clear him of
the charges. But he couldn't handle these former students
saying he'd molested them. It hit a nerve with him—because he'd always beaten himself up for that one incident.
None of their stories stood up to questioning. But by the
time everyone realized that, Boyd had already slit his own
throat."

"What about the hairs they found on all the Schoolgirl
victims?" Gillian argued. "Didn't they all match with Boyd's
hair?"

"You'll think I'm crazy," Tim said, sitting down again.
"But I'm almost positive Boyd was set up. About a month
before the first campus murder, someone broke into his apartment. Nothing was stolen, but they'd gone through his things—

including his journal. He'd written about Kelly Zinnemann in there. He told me about it at the time. It was just one date, and they didn't click. After the break-in, Boyd had his locks changed. But he didn't tell the police about it until his arrest. Naturally, the sons of bitches didn't follow it up." Tim's eyes wrestled with hers. "I think someone set him up. They knew he'd gone out with Kelly, and they could have easily taken hair samples from Boyd's apartment—off a comb or hairbrush, then planted them at the murder scenes."

Gillian frowned at him. "A month before Kelly was even killed?"

"I know, I know," Tim sighed. "Who would frame someone for a murder that far in advance?"

"He'd have had to pick Boyd as the fall guy a month before even killing anyone," Gillian pointed out.

"So—you don't believe it's possible someone could have planned something so far in advance?"

Gillian was thinking of her copycat killer, the planner. "No, I believe it's possible," she heard herself say. "I believe it's very, very possible."

She gazed down at the St. Lamberts sixth-grade class photo on the table. Among the individual portraits, a boy's name and photo caught her eye. He was a pudgy, slightly cocky-looking, brown-haired boy. The face was eerily familiar. His name was listed under his photo, his old name, before he'd changed it around: *Scott Chase.*

Gillian realized that she and Boyd Farrow had something in common. They'd had the same pupil.

"C'mon, Andy, c'mon," he grunted, lifting the half-frozen corpse from the large, horizontal deep freezer in his basement. Hoisting the dead hitchhiker out of his icy resting place was a hell of a lot more difficult than dumping him in there last night. He had to wear oven mitts to handle the body, it was so cold. Fortunately, Andy hadn't frozen solid, so his cadaver bent a bit—with some pushing and pulling and tugging.

"Son of a bitch!" he gasped, dropping his victim. Andy hit the cellar floor with a thud—facedown.

"Oops!" He chuckled. Bending forward, hands on his knees, he caught his breath.

He'd taken Andy as far south as Tacoma. Then he'd mentioned that the car didn't *feel right.* He'd gotten off the Interstate, and found an isolated road. "Don't you feel it, Andy?" he'd asked. "Something seems to be dragging on one of the rear tires. I have a crowbar on the backseat. Can you hand it to me? We might need it."

Andy had climbed out of the car with him, and bent over to check the tire. One blow to the back of his head had done it. Then he'd dumped Andy in the trunk, and headed for home.

He readjusted the oven mitts on his hands, then squatted down and rolled Andy onto his back. The corpse had been resting on top of an old bedsheet in the deep freeze. The section that had been under Andy's head was stained with his blood. The sheet had become hard, but still pliable. As he pulled at the stiff material, little rust-colored ice crystals broke off from where the blood had soaked through. He wrapped the sheet around Andy's head.

Closing the freezer lid, he reached for the shovel he'd brought down earlier.

"Don't worry, Andy," he muttered. "You won't feel a thing."

He raised the shovel over his head, and brought the back side of it down on Andy's shrouded head. He heard a crack. He'd knocked out several teeth, he was certain. That was the least of the damage.

He leaned on the shovel, giving himself a minute before

he took another whack at what was left of Andy's face. It occurred to him that Gillian had never written a scene like this in any of her books. No, she hadn't.

She just wasn't as clever as he was.

Chapter 16

The man was still staring at him.

He occupied a spot in the bleachers a few spaces down and one row back from where Ethan sat alone. The man was alone too. He was tall, with a solid build and black hair graying at the temples. There was nothing special about him—except his shirt. He wore it under a heavy-looking brown jacket that was unzipped and open in the front. The shirt had a gaudy, eye-catching print with gold-colored Roman gladiator helmets, swords, and tridents against a burgundy background.

Ethan had never seen a shirt like that before. He'd never seen the man before either. And the guy wouldn't stop staring.

His mom had freaked out about him going to this stupid football game, because of some stalker who was out there. Now Ethan wondered if she'd been right to worry. Was this guy planning to kill him or abduct him or something?

Another thing his mother had said was haunting him. She'd told him not to wander off alone, not even for a trip to the bathroom. He'd thought about that on the bus, and ever since, he'd desperately needed to pee.

Otherwise, the bus ride had been painless. Richard Marshall, who had been so obnoxious yelling at him from the bus window, hadn't bothered him during the trip. It was so cool, the way Jason had shut him up.

Ethan figured his mother must have apologized to Vicki's friend. Or maybe Jason Hurrell was just an incredibly nice guy, despite his mom being so rude. Ethan was still a little ticked off at her this morning. He wondered if she knew he'd lied about hanging around with Jim Munchel at this game today. Jim was a nice guy—and popular—but Ethan didn't know him very well.

He didn't know Joe Pagani very well either. Ethan was a little nervous about his secret rendezvous with the cool, edgy, handsome senior. Hell, his idea of a wild time was sitting at home and watching TV. This was a real adventure for him.

Stepping off the bus by Ballard High's football field, Ethan anxiously glanced around for Joe Pagani, but he didn't spot him anywhere. Ethan felt so disappointed. Maybe it was some kind of trick. Maybe Joe was having a good laugh about this with his pals.

Frowning, Ethan glanced around for a restroom. On the side of the school, there was a line of guys on a short, wrought-iron stairway leading up to a men's room door. "Damn," Ethan muttered. He was pee-shy. He'd have to wait to sneak away during the game, so he could pee without an audience in there.

Turning, he headed for the bleachers, and noticed a man coming toward him. The shirt caught Ethan's eye. It was kind of ugly, but cool at the same time—probably a vintage treasure from some thrift store. Ethan suddenly realized the man was staring back at him. He even smiled a tiny bit.

Ethan quickly looked away, then hurried toward the football field's bleachers. He took a spot by himself—a couple of seats down from the nosebleed top row. He didn't mind sitting alone at games. It beat eating by himself in the cafeteria at lunchtime; that really made him feel pathetic.

He hadn't been sitting there for even a minute when he glanced around, and over his shoulder, he noticed the man—one bench up and a few spaces away. The man's eyes locked with his.

Ethan's head snapped forward and he pretended to gaze at the field. All the while, he wondered how the man had gotten up there so fast. The guy must have followed him. Ethan kept thinking about his mother's stalker. Or was he one of those mobsters looking for his father? He remembered the black vintage Mustang from the day before yesterday. Maybe he was the driver. Vintage car, vintage shirt.

That had been twenty minutes ago, twenty minutes of agony, because on top of everything else, he still had to pee. Ethan had casually glanced over his shoulder on several occasions, and practically every time, he'd caught that man staring. He was afraid to go to the bathroom for fear that creepy guy might follow him in there.

Their team was getting slaughtered. Craig played miserably. From the bleachers, big-mouth Richard Marshall kept heckling him: "Nice going, Merchant, you pussy!" Ethan didn't enjoy seeing his friend perform so badly. Despite everything, he couldn't bring himself to hate him.

He turned his head ever so slightly and glanced back. He didn't see the man. Ethan swiveled around. The guy wasn't there. Ethan scanned the crowded bleachers and couldn't find him. From where he sat, he had a view of the side of the school. He didn't see Mr. Weird Shirt outside the men's room.

Ethan waited another minute before he got up. Making his way down the bleachers, he kept a lookout for the stalker man. But there was no sign of the guy.

He walked around the back of the bleachers to the side of

the school. A bunch of people in the stands let out a cheer about something. Ethan headed up the half-flight of wrought-iron stairs. They reminded him of a fire escape. His footsteps made strange hollow reverberations on the grating. At the top step, he hesitated and listened for a moment before opening the men's-room door.

The place stank, but at least it was empty. Graffiti was scrawled over the gray tiles on the wall; dirt and God only knows what else covered the cement floor. A bare fluorescent bulb hummed overhead. The bathroom only had a sink, one urinal, and one stall. Small wonder there had been a line to get in. Some clown had stuffed a wad of toilet paper in the urinal, and now it was yellow and soggy. "Gross," Ethan muttered, bypassing it for the stall.

At least no one had left any surprises in the toilet. He closed the stall door, lifted the toilet seat with his foot, then unzipped his fly. Sometimes, he got pee-shy even when he was alone in a public restroom. There was always a chance someone could walk in.

"C'mon," he muttered. "So go, already."

Then he heard the footsteps, they reverberated on the grated stairs. "C'mon, c'mon," Ethan whispered to himself.

The door squeaked open.

Ethan stood there in the stall. He glanced toward the gap between the bottom of the stall door and the dirty floor. He saw shadows moving.

"Shhh," someone whispered.

Ethan tucked his penis back inside his trousers, then quickly zipped up. He saw someone standing on the other side of the door. He wore jeans and boots.

"He's in there," someone murmured. "Let's get him. . . ."

Ethan froze.

All of the sudden, there was a loud pounding on the stall door. "You're a dead man, Tanner!" the guy shouted.

Ethan recoiled, his back against the grimy wall. "Leave me the hell alone!" he bellowed.

The pounding abruptly stopped. "Ethan?"

"Yeah?" he said, catching his breath. His heart was pounding furiously.

"I'm just screwing with you, dude. It's me, Joe. Sorry I'm late. I got held up with something at home. Are you coming out of there? Ethan?"

"I—I haven't gone yet," he replied finally.

"Well, go. I want to get out of here. This place stinks."

"I—um . . ."

"What? Are you pee-shy? I'll wait by the stairs outside. Take your time, sport."

Once alone, Ethan was able to go to the bathroom—at last. When he finished up, he met Joe at the bottom of the stairs. Grinning, Joe mussed his hair. "C'mon, let's get out of here. All these people are making me nervous."

As they walked toward Joe's car together, they passed by the football field. Ethan spotted the man with the weird shirt. He was down by the sidelines, talking to a kid on the other team. The guy must have been his dad or something.

Ethan felt silly for being so scared. He'd been perfectly safe all this time.

"C'mon, hurry up," Joe said, nudging him. "I don't want anyone seeing me here. That's my piece-of-shit Subaru up ahead."

Ethan eagerly picked up the pace, even though he had no idea where Joe was taking him.

Tim couldn't tell her anything about a St. Lambert's sixth-grader from 1989 named Scott Chase. Boyd had never mentioned the boy. And to Tim's knowledge, no one named Scott Chase—or Chase Scott, for that matter—had ever come forward with accusations of having been molested by Boyd Farrow or any other priest. He let Gillian take the St. Lamberts sixth-grade class composite—as long as she promised to return it.

Gillian had made him another promise. Even if she didn't write an article or a book about it, she swore she'd do her damnedest to find the real Schoolgirl Killer.

Stepping outside Ballard Botanical, Gillian pulled out her cell phone and dialed her home phone to check for messages. Nothing. Then she tried Ruth's number and got her machine.

"Hi, Ruth, it's me," she said after the beep. "I'm in Ballard, and it's around noon. I've uncovered an interesting connection between the Schoolgirl Murders and Chase Scott. I'm hoping to meet with him today, but I don't want to do it alone. I thought you could come along—if you're free. I phoned Chase and left him a message last night, but I still haven't heard back from him. I doubt I'll be able to get ahold of him today, but I'll give it a try. Buzz me on my cell if you get this any time soon. Thanks, Ruth."

Fishing into her purse again, Gillian pulled out the slip of paper with Chase's address and phone number on it. She dialed the number in Bremerton. It rang twice.

"Hello?"

She'd expected to get his machine again. "Um, is Chase there, please?"

"Is this Gillian McBride?" he asked.

"Yes—"

"I got your message last night, but it was too late to call you back. Are you serious? Do you really think your agent or your editor might be interested in my story?"

"Yes, it's worth a shot," Gillian said into the phone. She covered her other ear to block out traffic noise on the street. "I thought we could meet for coffee and discuss it sometime. Are you free tomorrow?"

"God, I'm sorry, no. I'm flying out to Boston on a red-eye late tonight. I'll be gone until next week. Could we meet when I get back?"

"Do you have time this afternoon?" Gillian asked.

"Well, I live in Bremerton, and that means taking a ferry

back and forth. I'm on kind of a tight schedule because of the trip. Would you mind coming out to see me?"

Gillian bit her lip for a moment. "Let me check the ferry schedule and get back to you, okay? Will you be home?"

"You bet, Teach. I'll just be here packing. Hey, you know, I've almost called you several times since that class wrapped up."

"Really?" she said.

"Yeah, but I felt too weird about it, because of that one weekend you busted me for phoning you and hanging up a few times."

"Oh, I—I hardly remember that," she lied.

"Well, you want to hear something strange? I almost called you about this because it happened right after the semester ended. You know the Schoolgirl Killer, Boyd Farrow? He was a priest in my parish when I was a kid. How about that for a bizarre coincidence? The guy used to coach my sixth-grade basketball team, and fifteen years later, he ends up teaching at the same community college where I'm taking your class. I had no idea. And then he turns out to be a serial killer."

"Yes, that is a coincidence," Gillian said carefully. She couldn't believe he was volunteering this information. She'd expected she would have to drag it out of him. Maybe he was just being very clever.

"Um, I read a lot about the case," Gillian said. "They quoted all these people who knew Boyd Farrow. But I never ran across your name, Chase."

"Well, I told the cops what I remembered from when I was eleven. I didn't know Farrow that well. He was supposed to have molested this classmate of mine on a camping trip. I always figured it was bullshit. But now, I'm thinking maybe there was some truth to that old story. Anyway, I guess we can talk about this over coffee, right? So—you'll call me back after you check the ferry schedule?"

"Yes, I'll do that, Chase," she said. Just a few minutes

ago, she'd been so convinced of his guilt. Now, she wasn't so sure. Nevertheless, she still didn't feel very safe going to meet him alone.

"If you get my machine, just keep talking," Chase said. "I'm screening lately. I've had some weird goings-on around here. It's like something out of one of your books."

"What do you mean?" Gillian asked.

"Oh, some crank with a blocked number keeps calling me up, saying he's *watching* me. The other night, I even had to call the cops, because I had a prowler outside my house."

"Did they catch him?"

"Nope. The son of a bitch got away."

"During these phone calls, has he said anything else?"

"Yeah—" Chase Scott started to answer, but someone nearby on the street honked his horn.

Gillian covered her other ear again. "I'm sorry, could your repeat that, Chase?"

The horn stopped blaring. "I said, yes, last time this guy called, he told me, 'You can go to the head of the class. You're next.' I don't know what the hell that's supposed to mean."

Gillian just shook her head.

"You still there?" Chase asked.

"Um, yes. I—"

"Listen, I found a ferry schedule. You can probably catch the one o'clock from Seattle. It'll get you into Bremerton at two. I can come pick you up at the ferry terminal."

"Oh, that's okay. I'll take a taxi. Where can I meet you?"

"Well, why don't you come to my place? I have the manuscript here."

"Manuscript?" she repeated.

"Yeah, my book—or the first eighteen chapters. I have an outline too. Maybe your agent or editor would like to see an outline first."

"Yes, of course," Gillian said. "Listen, Chase, I'll just come to your house. What's the address?"

Chase gave her the same address Ruth had written on the scrap of paper. Gillian said she'd have a taxi drop her off sometime after two. Then she clicked off the cell phone.

"Need another lift?" She felt someone touch her shoulder.

Gillian swiveled around and almost dropped her cell phone. She gaped at Jason Hurrell, who was smiling back at her. "God, you shouldn't do that!" she said, catching her breath. "You scared me."

He chuckled. "Sorry. That's the second time in twenty-four hours I've frightened you. I didn't know I was such a scary guy."

"I thought you'd driven off," Gillian said.

He held up a Bartell's Drugs bag. "I just needed some things from the drugstore. And look what I found." He pulled a copy of *Black Ribbons: A Maggie Dare Mystery* from the bag. "If you autograph it for me, I'll drive you to your next destination. No tipping necessary."

Gillian glanced at her watch. She had about forty-five minutes to catch the Bremerton ferry. She still didn't quite trust Jason Hurrell. But he'd driven her here to Ballard without any incident—except for her sniping at him. And she needed to get to the ferry as soon as possible.

She looked at Jason and worked up a smile. "How could I refuse such a generous offer?"

"Sounds like this guy wanted to get into your pants," Joe said.

He and Ethan were moving like tightrope walkers on the rails along the Burlington Northern tracks. Trees and bushes bordered the tracks, and on one side, beyond the wooded area, lay the beach at Golden Gardens Park. A chilly breeze rolled off Shilshole Bay, so Ethan and Joe kept their jackets buttoned up.

"Oh, I don't know," Ethan said. "The guy was talking to some kid on the other team when I left. So I think he's somebody's dad."

"Are you kidding? That doesn't make any difference." Joe grabbed hold of his hand.

It took Ethan by surprise, and he had to steady himself to keep from stumbling off the rail. Joe just smiled. Ethan suddenly felt warm inside. He wondered if he was blushing.

"If you fall, I fall," Joe said. He squeezed Ethan's hand. "Anyway, just because this guy with the gladiator shirt has a kid who plays football, it doesn't mean he's totally straight. He probably wanted to jump your bones. I know what I'm talking about because a few years ago, when I was a freshman, the father of this friend of mine made a pass at me. To look at the guy, you never would've guessed."

"Really? How did it happen?" Ethan wondered if Joe could feel his hand sweating.

"I was spending the night at their house. It was like two in the morning, and I went downstairs in my underwear to get a snack out of the refrigerator, and my buddy's old man showed up. He tried to grab me. Really freaked me out."

Ethan missed his footing and stumbled off the rail. But Joe didn't let go of his hand. He stopped and remained balanced on the rail. Ethan's eyes wrestled with his. "What did you do?" he asked. "When he tried to grab you, I mean."

"I told him, 'No, thanks, Mr. G., I don't go that way.'" Joe winked. "Then I went upstairs with my snack, and got back to messing around in bed with my buddy."

Dumbfounded, Ethan stared at him. "Um, by 'messing around,' do you mean—"

Grinning, Joe nodded. "Aren't you getting back up on the rail?"

Ethan couldn't move. For a moment, he became aware of the sound of waves on the beach nearby and the fall-colored leaves rustling on all the trees around them. They were alone. He'd never had anyone admit to him that he'd "messed around" with another guy, and Joe didn't seem one bit ashamed of it.

"You're trembling," Joe said, squeezing his hand again. "Are you cold?"

Ethan shook his head. "No, I'm fine." He climbed back up on the rail, and they resumed walking along the tracks. "Did you ever tell your friend about his dad?"

"Nope. His old man was so nervous about it, I felt sorry for him. He apologized all over the place, and said, 'Oh, I was just kidding, Joe,' and bullshit like that. Anyway, I didn't rat him out. I'm pretty good at keeping a secret. In fact, you're the first person I've told that story to." Joe paused and weaved a little on the rail. "So—it's your turn now. You have to tell me a secret."

Ethan continued walking. He gave him a wary sidelong glance. Did Joe want to know if he was gay? Was that what he was asking? "Um, what kind of secret do you want to hear?"

"A *secret*," Joe said. "Something you haven't told anyone—or something you're not *supposed* to tell anyone."

Ethan's mind was reeling with the possibilities: *I'm gay . . . I whack off a lot . . . I've had a semi-boner ever since you took hold of my hand.*

"God, I—I can't think of anything to say," he finally replied, his eyes looking down at the steel rail.

"Maybe there's a family skeleton," Joe said. "Tell me a family secret, like you saw your mother banging the meter guy, or your old man takes Viagra and cocaine, or—I don't know. Work with me on this, sport."

Ethan stepped down from the rail. "My dad ran away two years ago," he said quietly. "He had gambling debts and he was in trouble with the police. So he just—took off." Ethan felt his eyes tear up, and he shrugged awkwardly. "Anyway, I don't know where he is."

Joe slowly shook his head. "Oh, shit," he whispered. "That sucks." He hopped down from the rail.

Before Ethan knew what was happening, Joe slipped his arms around him. "I'm sorry, guy," he whispered. Ethan felt Joe's warm breath swirling in his ear. He hesitated, then brought his hands up to Joe's back.

After a moment, Joe chuckled. "Hey, I'm feeling something. Aren't you?"

"What?" Ethan murmured, his face pressed against Joe's neck.

Joe broke apart from him. "A train's coming, dude," he said, laughing. "Can't you feel the vibration?"

Suddenly, Ethan felt the tremors on the tracks, and he could hear the roar of the engine as it approached. He glanced over his shoulder at the length of tracks. In the distance, the locomotive was speeding toward them.

"Ha!" Joe yelled, as the train's horn threatened to drown him out. "I can see the *Seattle Times* headlines now! *Two High School Homos Squished to Smithereens by Freight Train!*"

He grabbed Ethan's hand again, and pulled him toward the beach side of the tracks. They staggered through the rocks around the rails, then leapt over a little creek at the bottom of the rock pile. Ethan stepped in the cold water and it splashed him. The train roared past them, and they laughed over all the noise—the engine's horn and the steel wheels grinding on the rails.

They found an opening in a barbed-wire fence, then made their way toward the beach, weaving through the bushes and trees. All the while, Ethan thought of what Joe had said about them being "two homos." For the first time in his life, it didn't hurt when someone referred to him as a "homo." That was because this handsome, fascinating guy was saying he was one too.

Through a clearing ahead, Ethan could see the beach and Shilshole Bay. His sneaker was soaked with creek water, but he didn't care. They ran toward the beach together. Joe took the lead, and Ethan followed.

As far as he was concerned, Joe Pagani could take him anywhere.

Gillian sat alone at a window table on the ferry, gazing out at the choppy gray waters of Puget Sound. She was nervous about the impending meeting in Bremerton with Chase Scott. But now there was someone else to worry and wonder about: Jason Hurrell.

Turning away from the window, she glanced at Jason. He was feeding a dollar into one of the vending machines. She noticed a few other women in the area, also checking him out. He seemed too good to be true, and that was just the problem. She still didn't completely trust Jason Hurrell.

While he'd driven her to the Seattle ferry terminal, Gillian had been the one asking all the personal questions. Jason had answered very candidly—unless of course, he'd been lying through his teeth the entire time, a possibility Gillian couldn't quite dismiss. He'd grown up in Clinton, Iowa. "I wanted to be a flyer back when I was just a little kid," he'd told her, eyes on the road. "I guess you could say I never really grew up. My ex-wife, Rachel, would probably back me on that statement. I got this high-paying, but tedious, engineering job in Denver, and we had a beautiful baby, Annie. On weekends, I took flying lessons in Pueblo. When I finally got my pilot's license, I really took off, flew all over. I went everywhere, except home. I was a lousy husband and a lousy dad. Rachel got custody of Annie. Three years ago, she remarried and moved to Missoula. I relocated there to be closer to Annie. She's eleven now. She has red hair and braces. On her days with me, I often take Annie and her friends up in my plane. They all seem to think I'm Super-Dad or something. Actually, I'm super-schmuck. It kills me to think Annie's stepfather is a better dad to her than I am. At best, I'm just like a fun uncle. Give her a few more years to wise up, and I won't even be that to her."

Sitting on the passenger side of his rental car, Gillian had found herself staring at Jason—and wondering if he was on the level. Did this nice-guy-baring-his-tortured-soul routine work on other women? Of course, it didn't hurt that he was so handsome.

He'd offered to take Gillian to her destination in Bremerton. She'd lied and said someone was picking her up at the ferry terminal. "Well, I don't get many opportunities to take a ferry ride in Montana," he'd said. "Do you mind if I come along?"

"Suit yourself," she'd replied, with a shrug.

And so Jason had accompanied her onto the ferry, and sat across from her at this table by the window. He said he'd started reading Vicki's copy of *Killing Legend* this morning, and he was really enjoying it. He asked her about her books, and what it was like to be a famous author.

Gillian let down her guard and opened up to him a little. Jason seemed fascinated by her tales of publishing highs and woes. He suggested buying them a "faux lunch" at the vending machines, and Gillian agreed.

As Jason got up from the table, Gillian realized she was gazing up at him and smiling. That was when a voice inside her head asked: *What are you doing? What the hell are you thinking?*

She'd been fighting an attraction to Jason ever since she'd set eyes on him—and for good reason. He was up to something. She remembered Vicki's orgasmic vocalizing last night—and the encore this morning.

Gillian watched him make his selection at the vending machine, and she found herself sneering at him again. Why was Vicki's boyfriend being so nice and attentive to her? What was his angle? The fact that Jason Hurrell suddenly wormed his way into her upstairs neighbor's life—and her bed—at this particular time was awfully suspicious. Gillian

wondered if he was somehow tied in with those hoods looking for Barry. Or was he connected to the copycat killings?

Jason returned to the table with his hands full of snack
packs, candy bars, and two cans of soda. He sat down and
carefully unloaded the makeshift feast onto the Formica-top
table. "I wasn't sure about the nutritional value of a Kit-Kat
bar versus Nestle's Crunch versus Animal Crackers, so I got
all three. I took a chance and bought you a Diet Coke." He
set the can of soda in front of her. "Unless you want this root
beer?" He hesitated before opening the other can of soda.

"No, Diet Coke is fine, thanks," Gillian said, not touching
it. "Is that what Vicki drinks?"

Jason shrugged. "I'm not sure, actually." He opened his
root beer.

"Why don't you know?" she asked, eyes narrowed at him.
"Why are you here with me, and not waiting for her at the
duplex?"

He let out a wary laugh. "Damn. I thought we were doing
so well. Now you seem angry all of a sudden. What's going
on? What did I do wrong?"

"Oh, you've done everything *right*," she replied coolly.
"Everything to sweep a girl off her feet. You've been very attentive toward me. And I'd really be flattered by all your attention—if you weren't having sex with my upstairs neighbor."

He sat back and crossed his arms. "So because I happen
to be dating Vicki, I can't be nice to you? Is that what you're
saying?"

"You're *overly* nice toward me, *overly* solicitous," Gillian
replied. "And it's fishy. I can't help wondering what your
angle is, Jason. Do you even care about Vicki?"

"Of course I care about her."

"Well, I'm sorry, but I don't believe you. And I don't trust
you."

He let out a sigh, and shook his head. "I give up," he muttered. "I thought we'd just gotten off on the wrong foot last

night. I've been trying to make it up to you. But I can see now that trying to be nice to you is pretty hopeless. And thankless too." He got to his feet. "I don't know what kind of number your husband pulled on you, lady. But he must have done a lot of damage if you're suspicious of every guy who has the unmitigated gall to show you a little kindness and attention."

He picked up his root beer can. "I'm going to sit somewhere else. If you still want a ride to this place in Bremerton, you can come to my car when we're ready to dock. Otherwise, I'll just take the next ferry back, and you're on your own."

Gillian slumped back in the seat and watched him walk away. She could tell he was still hiding something.

But he'd gotten in the last word. And he was right. Even if his anger was just a smoke screen, he was right about one thing.

Gillian sat there alone, feeling damaged.

"I wish *my* old man would run away," Joe said, skipping a stone on the rippled blue-gray water of Shilshole Bay. "The son of a bitch isn't even my real father. At least I can be glad for that. When he isn't knocking me around or getting shit-faced, he's always making it a point to remind that I'm a bastard."

"God, that sucks," Ethan said, trying not to throw like a girl as he hurled a pebble into the surf. "My dad never ever hit me."

Joe squinted at him. "Hey, did you hurt your foot? You're limping."

"Oh, it's just creek water in my sneaker. My sock's wet, that's all."

Joe pointed to a picnic table by the park area. "C'mon, let's sit over there and take care of that."

They started walking, and Ethan felt his sock releasing a bit of cold water with every step. "What was I saying?" Joe asked.

"You were saying that you're a—" Ethan hesitated. "That you're illegitimate, and your stepfather's a jerk."

"Yeah, I don't know who the hell my real father is. Could have been anybody passing through Sacramento. My mother was a cocktail waitress at a Ramada Inn there. When she married this asshole seven years ago, I refused to take his last name. I stuck with Pagani. It's her maiden name. Maybe 'Joe Ramada' would've been better."

Ethan sat down at the picnic table and pried off his damp sneaker.

"So I'm a bastard," Joe said. "That's another secret about me. It's your turn to tell one, dude. Make it good."

Ethan peeled off his wet sock and squeezed out some water. Joe picked up his sneaker, shook it, tapped it on the bench, then set it on the table. He took the damp sock out of Ethan's hand, and spread it out beside the shoe. "So—come on," he said. "If you can't think of anything juicy, tell me more about your old man."

Rubbing his cold, bare foot, Ethan shrugged. "Well, I miss him."

"So—you really haven't seen him in two whole friggin' years? No contact with him at all?"

"Nope, none," Ethan muttered.

"That sucks big-time, man." Joe reached out and took hold of Ethan's bare foot. Then he unzipped his own jacket, and guided Ethan's foot into the opening.

Ethan was startled, and so incredibly turned on. His foot immediately warmed up from Joe's body heat. Joe casually rested his hand on Ethan's leg, and rubbed it a little. Ethan couldn't help it. He was getting an erection. He squirmed on the bench to cover up what was happening at the front of his jeans. Joe didn't seem to notice.

"Haven't you ever tried to get in touch with the guy?" Joe asked.

"You—you mean with my dad? I wouldn't know how."

"Don't you think your old lady might know? I mean, maybe she's in secret contact with him, and she's not telling you. Ever think that?"

"I doubt it." Ethan shook his head. "No, she'd tell me if she knew."

"Yeah, you're probably right." Joe leaned forward a bit. Ethan could feel his heart beating against his toes. "Besides, if you really knew where your old man was, you wouldn't go blabbing it to me anyway. Am I right or am I right?"

"No, I—I'd tell you," Ethan replied. "I'd trust you to keep it secret."

Joe smiled. "Really? Well, I trust you too, Ethan." He rubbed Ethan's leg again. "Hey, are you cold? You're shaking again."

"No, I'm okay. I . . ." He trailed off as a young couple approached from the beach area. Ethan was about to pull his foot away, but Joe held it there under the folds of his jacket.

The couple was around college age. The guy had his arm around his girlfriend, and they were staring. The guy scowled at them, but the girl was giggling.

"What the fuck are you two looking at?" Joe growled. He kept his hand on Ethan's leg.

The girl shut up. The guy quickly shook his head. "Nothing, man. It's cool." They hurried toward the park area.

Joe sighed, then turned to Ethan. "Well, at least you knew your old man, and you liked the guy. That puts you one up on me." He patted Ethan's knee. "Okay, so it's your turn to ask me something."

Ethan wanted to ask what Joe and his friend had done when they'd been "messing around." Was that his first and only time? Did he think of himself as gay or bisexual? Did he always feel that way? Ethan had a wonderful, weird, scary

262   *Kevin O'Brien*

feeling in the pit of his stomach. Even though he felt so warm inside, he couldn't stop trembling.

"I can't think of anything to ask you," he lied.

Joe took his hand off Ethan's leg. He poked at the sneaker and sock on the picnic table. "Still damp," he said, frowning. He glanced over toward a public restroom at the edge of the park. "Hey, maybe there's a hand-dryer in the can. We could dry these out for you." He guided Ethan's foot out from the folds of his jacket. "Lean on me and we'll go check it out."

Ethan touched his toes—still warm from the inside of Joe's jacket. He grabbed his sock and sneaker. As he stood up, Joe took hold of his hand and slung it over his own shoulder. "C'mon, dude," he said. "I still owe you a secret. Ask me anything, and I'll tell you. Because we trust each other, right?"

Ethan leaned on Joe and hobbled on one foot along side him. "Right," he said nervously. "Um, Joe, when you—you messed around with your pal on that overnight at his house, was that the only time you—*experimented* with another guy?"

"Shit, no. I've done lots of experimenting—guys and chicks. Ha, guess I sound like this great big he-slut. But not really. Put it this way, I've had my fair share of messing around—and so far, it's been pretty fan-fucking-tastic."

"So—you think you might be bisexual?" Ethan asked.

"I'm not into labels, dude."

"Oh, yeah," Ethan said. "Me neither."

"That guy I told you about, the friend of mine my freshman year, his name was Chris. He was the first person I ever screwed around with. I was your age. You want details?"

"Oh, well." Ethan shrugged. "Sure, I mean, if you want to tell me, yeah, I guess."

Joe nudged him and chuckled. "Yes, you want details, you horny devil. I'll tell you what I did with Chris. Maybe I'll even *show* you."

Ethan let out a nervous little laugh. He wasn't exactly

sure what Joe meant, but he had an idea. The strange taut-
ness in his stomach got tighter.

They paused in front of the restrooms, which were
housed in a small brown and beige chalet-style cabin. A pay
phone and a drinking fountain were between the men's and
women's room doors. Inside the men's room, it smelled like
seawater, dead fish, and urine. All the fixtures were dull
stainless steel—including the blur-reflecting square that
passed for a mirror over the single sink. There was a hand-
dryer on the wall. Joe hit the button, and it let out a roar. "It's
working, dude," he said, waving his hand under it. "Hotter
than a hump in the backseat of my car. Go to town, sport. I'll
wait outside."

Leaning against the sink, Ethan kept his bare foot a few
inches from the dirty floor. He watched Joe saunter out the
door. His heart was racing. Did Joe really intend to *show*
him how he'd had sex with his freshman buddy, Chris? And
what did that mean exactly?

The hand-dryer ran out of air. Ethan hit the button, and it
started up again. He waved his damp sock under the heat. On
the other side of the dryer was a fogged window with criss-
crossed thin wires running through it. In the bottom corner
of the window, part of the glass had been broken, leaving a
tiny hole.

Ethan peeked out the hole at the parking lot behind the
lavatories. There weren't many cars, because of the time
of year. So the black vintage Mustang was very conspicu-
ous.

Ethan couldn't see if anyone was inside the car. It didn't
make sense. Joe had parked his Subaru at least a mile back—
off Seaview Avenue. How in the world had the Mustang
managed to follow them along railroad tracks and through
the woods?

His hand started burning. Ethan dropped the sock just as
the dryer stopped. He retrieved the sock, slipped it over his

foot, and went back to the little opening in the window. He
saw Joe stroll over toward the Mustang.

"Oh, my God," Ethan whispered. "No, no, no . . ."

He watched Joe step up to the driver's window. He leaned
one arm on the Mustang's roof and bent forward to talk to
the driver. He shook his head, and then glanced at his wristwatch.

Ethan grabbed his sneaker from the edge of the sink, then
slipped it on. It was still cold and damp, but that didn't matter. He quickly laced up his shoe. He was shaking again, and
the tightness in his stomach was even worse than before. But
this time, it had nothing to do with sexual tension. He was
terrified. Moving to the window again, he checked on Joe,
who was still conferring with his buddy in the Mustang.
"Son of a bitch," Ethan muttered, tears stinging his eyes.

The bathroom door and pay phone were on the other side
of the lavatory compound from the parking lot. Ethan checked
his pockets for change, and found a couple of quarters. He
peeked out the restroom doorway, then hurried to the pay
phone. Having been without a car for two years, he knew the
number for the taxi service by heart. He slipped the quarters
into the slot, and dialed. It rang three times. "Yellow Cab,"
the operator finally answered. "Your phone number please, area
code first."

"I'm calling from a pay phone," Ethan whispered. "Could
you please send a cab to Golden Gardens Park?"

"You'll have to speak up," the operator said. "I can't hear
you."

But Ethan couldn't talk. He froze.

Joe came around from the other side of the cabin. "Who
are you calling?" he asked, eyes narrowed.

Ethan shrugged. "A cab. I—I suddenly realized how late
it is. I need to get back to the high school. I'll catch hell if
I'm not on that bus. They're doing a head count. I thought I'd
take a cab—and—and drop you off at your car on the way, of
course."

He still had the phone to his ear, and he could hear the taxi dispatcher asking him to speak up again.

Joe smiled. "There's plenty of time, dude. The game's probably in the third quarter." He gently pried the receiver out of Ethan's hand and hung it up. "Besides, you can't cut out now. We're still telling secrets."

At the Bremerton ferry terminal, Gillian waved down a taxi. Before climbing into the backseat, she glanced over her shoulder at the cars lining up for the next outbound ferry. She noticed Jason's rented white Taurus joining them. She felt a pang of regret. What if she was wrong about him—and he was just a nice guy?

She had thought about seeking him out on the ferry again, and apologizing. But she'd remained seated alone at the table for the rest of the boat ride. She had no idea where Jason had gone to. This glimpse of his car in the distance was the closest she'd come to seeing him in the last hour.

Gillian gave the taxi driver Chase's address on Overlook Drive. She'd phoned Chase from the ferry to say she was on her way. Chase said he'd been to the local Kinko's to make copies of his outline and the first eighteen chapters of his erotic thriller. Gillian couldn't help wondering if she was wasting her time and his.

Still, maybe Chase could give her more information about that prowler and those strange phone calls he was getting. It was a good thing he was headed out of town tonight. Maybe it would get him out of harm's way.

There was also the possibility that he'd made it all up, and this was a trap.

The cab ride took less than ten minutes—all uphill—before they turned onto Overlook Drive. They came to a curve in the road and a little lookout point with two park benches and a tourist's telescope. The spot had an expansive view of Port Orchard and Bainbridge Island. As they drove on, the houses they passed were set back from the road, old-money estates and some new-money monstrosities on big, wooded lots. Gillian wondered how Chase Scott could afford to live in this prime real-estate area. She'd been reading the numbers along the way, and knew his address was coming up.

"I need to catch the three-thirty ferry back to Seattle," Gillian told the driver. "Could you come back for me here in about a half hour?"

She saw him check his wristwatch. "Pickup at two-forty-five? I can do that." He reached for something by the gear shift, then glanced back at Gillian and handed her a business card. "Just call that number in case you need to cancel."

"Thanks," Gillian said. "This might sound odd, but if a man calls and cancels for me, then something's wrong. If that happens, send the police here, okay?"

The driver's eyes shifted to the rearview mirror. "You want I should stick around?" he asked.

Gillian hesitated. If he left his meter running, it would cost her at least another forty dollars. But she didn't quite know what she was walking into with Chase.

The driver's cell phone went off just as he turned into a driveway. Gillian noticed Chase's address on the mailbox. The long driveway wound through a wooded lot. The driver mumbled into the phone while he drove. Gillian saw the house ahead—a surprisingly modest ranch house. It was even a bit dilapidated, and in need of a paint job. The lawn was patchy and brown in spots, and the bushes around the house needed trimming.

"I'm sorry, but I have another fare to pick up," the driver said, pulling in front of the house. "I can't stay. But I can pick you up. You sure you'll be okay?"

"Yes, thanks." Gillian saw the meter on the dash, and then she fished some money out of her purse, throwing in a five-dollar tip. "So I'll see you in a half hour?"

"You bet. Thanks." The driver took the money.

Gillian climbed out of the cab and approached Chase's front door. She rang the bell. She waited a moment, and glanced back as the taxi turned around. Then it started down the driveway. After *"You sure you'll be okay?"* and *"You want I should stick around?"* she thought the cabbie might have at least waited until someone answered the front door. Gillian rang again, then knocked. Still no answer.

She peeked into a tall, thin window by the door. She saw a hallway with stone tiles and a mission-style dresser. But there wasn't anyone in sight.

She took another glance over her shoulder. The cab was now at the other end of the driveway. It turned on to Overlook Drive and disappeared. Gillian suddenly felt very alone—and stranded.

She rang the bell again. After a few moments, she tried the doorknob. It was locked. Just as well, she figured; she wouldn't have wanted to walk in there by herself.

Stepping away from the door, she dug into her purse. She pulled out her cell phone and the business card the cabbie had given her. Gillian dialed the number. She was uncertain about the reception up on this bluff. She hoped to God the call would go through. It rang several times.

"Bremerton Taxi," a dispatcher answered—at last.

"Hi, yes," Gillian said. She nervously eyed the wooded lot in front of her. "I just got dropped off at 1954 Overlook Drive, and no one's home. The driver pulled out of the driveway only a minute ago. Could you get him to turn back and pick me up?"

There was a pause. "We can have someone there in—twenty-five minutes."

"Yes, I know. The driver said he'd be back in a half hour to pick me up. But he just left, you see. If you radio him now, he could turn around and be here right away. If he could just come get me, I'd appreciate it. I really can't stay here. I—"

"Twenty-five minutes is the soonest we can have someone there," the dispatcher repeated.

"All right," Gillian muttered. "Thank you." She clicked off the phone.

She'd spoken with Chase only forty minutes ago, and told him she was on her way. It didn't make sense that he wasn't here. She clicked the phone back on, and dialed his number. From inside the house, she could hear the muted ringing. Then it stopped. On the cell phone, she listened to Chase's machine click on: *"Hey, you almost got me. Try, try again or leave me a message. Ciao."*

"Hello, Chase?" she said after the beep. "It's Gillian, and I'm here outside your house. It's about twenty after two. Where are you? Call me as soon as you get this message, okay?" She left her cell phone number, then clicked off the line.

Gillian kept the phone in her hand—in case he called back, or in case she had to dial 911. With trepidation, she walked around toward the back of his house. All the while, she wondered what could have happened to Chase. Why wasn't he answering his door—or his phone?

The backyard had a sweeping view of the water. Dark gray clouds moved across the horizon. The wind kicked up. Trees and bushes around the house rustled. She remembered what Chase had said about the "weird goings-on around here." Someone claimed to be watching him. Was that same someone watching her now? Was Chase's "prowler" back?

"Quit spooking yourself out," she muttered.

She approached the house, her eyes fixed on the back door—with a little diamond-shaped window in it. She figured this was the kitchen entrance. Gillian paused at the three steps leading up to the door. What if Chase was dead in there? She realized it would have to match a scene from one of her books—a murder in a kitchen. She remembered a grisly murder scene in her fourth book, *Flowers for Her Grave*. A charming gardener used a sickle to hack up his employer, a young widow. The scene had occurred in her kitchen. Gillian remembered her own description of the blood beading up on the Spanish tiles. Her villain had dug a grave for his victim ahead of time, in her dahlia garden.

Gillian ascended those three steps, wondering if she'd see Chase's hacked-up remains on his kitchen floor. *You're the one who came up with the idea,* she told herself. Her copycat was simply making it real.

Gillian nervously peeked through the diamond-shaped window in the door. It was a modern kitchen with granite countertops, shiny white appliances, and a black-and-white tiled floor. There was no corpse lying on it, thank God.

She sighed, and then tried the doorknob. Locked, just like the front door.

Gillian backed away, and moved toward the garage—attached to the other side of the house. All the while, she couldn't shake the feeling that someone was watching her. She was uncertain whether it was Chase or his "prowler." But someone else was there, she could feel it.

She hadn't noticed a car in Chase's driveway earlier. She wandered over to the side of the garage, and peeked in the window. It took her a moment to focus past the dirty glass on anything in the darkened garage. There was no car, just a couple of bikes, some scuba gear, an outboard motor for a boat, a lawn mower, and other yard equipment. It didn't make any sense that he'd driven off somewhere.

Gillian heard a twig snap—and then another. She swiveled around. No one. Still, with all the trees and bushes bordering Chase's yard, it would be easy for somebody to hide. "Hello?" Gillian called. "Chase? Who's there?"

The wind blew, and a few leaves scattered across the patchy, brown lawn at the side of the garage. Gillian quickly wound her way around to the driveway in front. She wasn't going to stay there another minute. She couldn't wait around for the cab.

Gillian started up the driveway toward the road. If she

ended up walking all the way to the ferry, she would. She kept glancing around, expecting to spot someone in the wooded lot. She was shaking inside.

She just couldn't get away from there fast enough.

"I can't exactly *show* you what Chris and I did, not here," Joe said, grinning. "There are people around. Want me to fucking get arrested for lewd conduct and indecent exposure?"

Ethan leaned against a railing to some steps that went from the park restrooms down to the beach area. Glancing around, he noticed two couples on the beach—and a group of kids, playing in the sand. Only a few minutes ago, he'd relished being alone with Joe. But now, he wasn't going to let that happen.

Joe had suggested a stroll through the woods—and then they could follow the railroad tracks back to his car.

"I screwed up my foot," Ethan lied. "It hurts now when I put weight on it. I really think we should take a cab back to your car—and then I can go on and catch the game before it ends."

Joe nudged him. "You don't want to go into the woods with me?"

Ethan pulled away. "Sorry. I need to get back, I really do." He glanced over toward the parking lot.

"What's wrong with you all of a sudden?"

"Nothing." Ethan couldn't look at him. He knew what Joe was trying to do. He knew what he'd been trying to do most of the afternoon. It was all about flirting with him and telling secrets—so Joe and his mobster buddies could find out where his dad was. Ethan realized now that the Mustang hadn't followed them to this beach. Joe must have told them ahead of time where to meet him. The Mustang was still in the lot. Were they giving Joe a few more minutes at the seduction route? Then what were they going to do? Ethan wondered if Joe would turn him over to his pals so they could try beating the information out of him.

Joe touched his arm. "Are you pissed at me or something?"

Ethan shrugged. "Of course not—"

A car engine started up. Ethan turned in time to see the black Mustang pull out of the lot.

"Do you recognize that car?" Joe asked.

Ethan didn't answer.

"The driver was asking me for directions earlier—while you were in the can."

Ethan gave him a wary sidelong glance. "What did you say to the guy? Did you ask him for a few more minutes alone with me—so you can find out more about my dad?"

Joe stared back at him, then chuckled. "Then you *have* seen that car before. When?"

"The day before yesterday," Ethan said. "It drove by my bus stop a couple of times in the morning. Then it showed up again near the playfield during my gym class."

Joe kicked at a little stone on the steps. "I told that idiot he was driving too close the other day, the dumb shit." He let out long sigh. "Okay, kid, here's the deal. You know what I'm after. Just tell me where Daddy is, and we can still take that walk in the woods. I'll put on a private little show for you. How does that sound?"

Ethan scowled. "Do you really think I'm so sleazy I'd sell out my father for a—a lap dance in the woods?"

"Don't act so goddamn high-and-mighty. I know you want it. And what the hell has your old man done for you lately? They don't want to hurt him. They just want to talk with him."

"Really? They don't want to hurt anybody?" Ethan said, deadpan. "Well, a couple of years ago, one of your buddies beat up my mother. He beat her up bad."

"Well, maybe she mouthed off to him. Do you know who it was? Did you see what the guy looked like?"

"He was short with black hair and a goatee."

"Perfect!" Joe let out an abrupt laugh. "That was Leo. How's this for karmic retribution? Old Leo hasn't been doing so hot since his girlfriend shot him in the balls last year. I never could stand that son of a bitch. Anyway, if she has a grudge, tell Mama her prayers have been answered." Joe's hand came up around his shoulder. "Now, how about it, Ethan? How about some answers for me?"

Ethan wiggled away. "Quit trying to act like you're my friend," he muttered. His voice cracked a little. He hated that his eyes were tearing up, because he didn't want this jerk to know how hurt he was. "What were you planning to do to me in the woods? Why were you so anxious to get me there alone? Were you going to kill me?"

"You're no good to anybody dead—unless your old man would get lured back to the funeral." Joe slowly shook his head. "No, I was just going to lean on you a little bit, kid."

He'd seen what Joe had done to Tate Barringer. He knew what he was capable of. He'd never been in a fight before. He didn't know what it was like to get hit in the face—or punched in the gut. But he figured he would be finding out very, very soon. He quickly wiped his eyes, and stared at Joe. But he was shaking. "I already told you, I don't have any idea where my dad is. You know I wasn't lying before. I trusted you—up until just a few minutes ago. And I liked you, Joe—if that's your name. I liked you a lot."

"You know something, dude? I believe you."

"I was telling you the truth about my mother too," Ethan said, still trembling. "She doesn't know where my dad is any more than I do."

"I believe you there too. You can relax, sport. I'm through with you." He slapped Ethan on the shoulder. "We're through with both you and Mama—for a while."

But Ethan couldn't relax. He couldn't stop shaking. "All those stories you told were lies, weren't they?"

Joe nodded. "Yeah, except for the story about my prick of a stepfather. That's true."

"I guess you figured it was pretty funny—leading me on like that, making me think you really liked me."

Joe shook his head. "It wasn't funny at all. I didn't like this assignment, kid. In fact, I was pretty disgusted with myself—and how I acted with you."

Ethan could see that Joe was being honest with him now. He seemed genuinely ashamed. A tiny smile came to Ethan's face. He almost reached out to touch Joe's arm. But he hesitated. "Really? You felt bad?"

"Of course I felt bad," Joe replied. "How would you expect me to feel? I had to hang around with you all afternoon and pretend I like you." With his lip curled in disgust, he glared at him. "Sorry, kid, but I fucking can't stand queers. I'm glad as hell this is over. I couldn't take another minute with you."

Joe started up the steps toward the parking area. "I'd punch your faggoty face in, but I don't want to touch you again. You make me sick."

Devastated, Ethan clung to the railing and watched him walk away. Joe might as well have sucker-punched him in the stomach.

It couldn't have hurt any worse.

"Hi, honey," Gillian said into her cell phone, a little out of breath. She was hiking along the roadside of Overlook Drive, about two blocks from Chase's house. She glanced over her shoulder to make sure no one was behind her. "I'm in Bremerton, following up a—a story idea," she continued for the answering machine. "I'm catching the three-thirty ferry, and should be home before five. You'll get there before me. Could you do me a big favor and just stay put and keep the door double-locked? I know it's a drag, honey, but I'm worried about this stalker. We're still on alert. Okay? See you soon. I love you."

Gillian clicked off her cell phone, and slipped it inside her purse. A loud flapping noise made her stop in her tracks. She glanced over at a newly built monster of a house, half of it on support beams, poised on the edge of the bluff. It was shrouded in black plastic tarp, with scaffolding along its front side. The tarp flapped in the breeze. It sounded like a ship's sail during a storm at sea.

Gillian stared at the house. The place looked deserted. In her neighborhood, dozens of condominiums and apartment buildings built only a few years ago were getting the same repair treatment, due to faulty siding or something. She didn't know much about it, except that a lot of new-home-buyers had gotten screwed.

From the looks of things, the displaced owners of this monstrosity probably weren't moving back any time soon. In two blocks, there were only a few homes between Chase's little ranch house and this deserted mansion. And so far, not a single car had passed her on the road. Gillian kept thinking that if she'd screamed for help earlier, no one would have heard her.

She moved on, picking up the pace a little. She wondered what had happened to Chase. She couldn't help feeling as if she'd narrowly avoided some kind of trap back there at his house. Chase was still the most likely suspect in the copycat murders—with Todd Sorenson running a close second. Who else was there?

At the little lookout point with the park benches and the tourist telescope, Gillian stopped and caught her breath. She gazed out at the water, and noticed the outbound ferry—a little speck in the distance. Jason Hurrell was on that boat.

Gillian pulled out her cell phone and dialed home again. The answering machine clicked on. "Hi, Ethan," she said, after the beep. "It's Mom again. Listen, I don't want you answering the door for anyone—except maybe Vicki or Ruth. If Jason stops by, don't open the door for him. I know you think he's a nice guy, but please, if he comes to the door, don't let him in. Ruth's number is there by the phone. And you have my cell. If Jason comes by, call one of us. Okay? Thanks, honey. See you soon."

Biting her lip, she clicked off the line, and watched the ferry disappear on the horizon.

Jason Hurrell sat at a window table on the ferry's main level. He'd taken his laptop computer out of the trunk of his car, and he now had it in front of him. He'd pulled up Amazon.com to check out Gillian's first book. He'd told her that he'd started reading it this morning, but that was a lie. He'd read *Killing Legend* almost a month ago, along with most of her other books.

Gillian already seemed to be putting it together that he'd started up with Vicki merely to get to her. He had to be very, very careful. He couldn't quite remember which one of Gillian's books was *Killing Legend*. He hoped one of the Amazon.com reviews would refresh his memory.

A reader with the user name *dgotlieb* bestowed four stars on the book, and gave it the headline **A Fast, Fun, Page-turner.**

I loved the heroine of this book. Struggling actress Rachel Porter is gorgeous, smart, funny, down-to-earth & she makes a great amateur sleuth! After her ex-boyfriend, an actor & overnight sensation, is suddenly "killed" in an auto accident, Rachel starts her own investigation. She begins to suspect he's really alive & the culprit behind several recent murders. The closer she comes to finding the truth, the closer she comes to getting herself killed. One scene in which a bitchy, back-stabbing actress dies from drinking some poisoned milk is so horrifying I was

off dairy for a week! I couldn't put this book down! Gillian
McBride, you have a new fan!

Someone called *imalegend2* gave the book three stars and
the review blurb **Sporadic Thrills amid the Clichés.**

There are certainly worse ways to kill a few hours than to
spend them reading Gillian McBride's debut thriller. It's
about a "hot hunk" of a movie star who is disfigured in an
auto accident. Everyone thinks he's dead, and he likes it
that way. All the better for him to go around bumping off
those Hollywood heels who hindered his quest for star-
dom. These predators-turned-victims are all cardboard
characters and some of their dialogue reads like it's from
a bad episode of DYNASTY. But it's fun to see how this
hot hunk sets up his victims. One scene has him poisoning a bitchy actress with tainted milk; in another, he
bashes a slimy producer's brains out against the edge of
his Olympic-size swimming pool; and in another, he
knocks out the hunk who stole "the role of a lifetime"
from him, tosses the guy in a car, and rigs it to career off
a bluff into a lake below (one problem, Ms. McBride, Los
Angeles isn't exactly the Land of 1000 Lakes, where is
this body of water with its "murky depths"?). This is the
literary equivalent of junk food, but still, pretty tasty.

Jason had read enough. The reviews had jarred his memory of what *Killing Legend* was about. As snotty as the last
reader was, he or she had made a good point. Gillian's books
were like tasty junk food that went down well. Maybe that
was why he'd had a hard time recalling which one was which.
Still, she was a good writer. And much like her "down to
earth" heroines, Gillian was pretty damn smart.

Jason had a feeling she saw right through him.

He got out of Amazon.com and brought up his e-mail account. He started composing an e-mail to *Nowagers@yahoo.
com.*

Hey, Buddy,

So far, she doesn't like me much. In fact, we had a fight about an hour ago. But I think she might come around & start trusting me. I'm lucky that way. Vicki is a bit of a problem, very clingy & sort of in the way now. But I can handle that. Rest assured, I'll carry out my mission. Talk with you later.

Stay Cool & Take Care,
Jason.

Vicki unlocked her door, and started up the stairs to her apartment. It was already getting dark, and the steps were hard to navigate. Fresh from her pedicure, manicure, facial, and massage, she felt revitalized and relaxed. She was also ready to jump on Jason the minute she saw him. She'd been thinking about him all day at the spa.

But he didn't seem to be home. There weren't any lights on. Then again, maybe he was napping. They'd been very busy last night—and this morning. Vicki smiled as she recalled all their hot, passionate lovemaking—the kisses, caresses, and love bites. He was a marvelous lover.

The smile faded from her face as she stepped into the living room. The only light came from the computer screen on her desk. She set down her purse, peeled off her coat, and read what was written on the monitor:

Darling—They called me to replace someone on a flight going out this afternoon. I may be gone a couple of days. So sorry to rush off like this. Be sure to tell Gillian that I'll be away & tell Ethan happy birthday from me. Call you tonight. Love U—Vicki.

Vicki was baffled that someone had typed up this note. Why were they pretending to be her? She wasn't going anywhere, not that she knew of. It didn't make any sense.

The stove light flickered on in the kitchen. It was an old stove, and the light always blinked a few times whenever she first turned it on. Vicki swiveled around and noticed a plastic tarp covering her kitchen floor. "Jason?" she called. "Honey, is that you?"

"Yeah?" he replied from somewhere in the kitchen.

"What are you doing?" she asked with puzzled half smile. "Are you painting in there?" Warily, she moved toward the kitchen, where she saw his shadow sweep across the wall. "Did you write this note on my computer?"

"Uh-huh," he replied.

The baffled smile frozen on her face, Vicki looked at that shadow on the wall. He was holding something in his hand. "What's going on, honey?"

The phone rang. She hesitated, and then glanced back at the telephone on her desk.

"Don't pick it up," he said, his voice muffled.

"What?"

The answering machine clicked on—along with her cheerful recording: *"Hi, you got my dumb machine. But leave me a message, and I'll get back to you as soon as I can. Bye!"*

The beep sounded.

"Hi, Vicki, it's Gill. Are you home yet? I need to ask for another favor. I'm in Bremerton, and won't be home until after four-thirty. Ethan should be returning from a football game around three-fifteen. Would you mind checking in on him?"

Vicki glanced toward the kitchen again, and saw his shadow on the cabinet. He was still hovering there. He hadn't moved. What did he have in his hand?

"I know this sounds strange," Gillian continued on the machine. *"But I'd rather you check in on Ethan than have your friend, Jason, do it. I have reason to believe Jason isn't very—um, trustworthy. You probably think I'm nuts, but I'll explain when I see you, Vicki. In the meantime, please, be careful around him. . . ."*

Vicki squinted at the answering machine and shook her head. Gillian didn't make any sense. But then, neither did that bizarre note Jason had left on her computer. *Jason isn't very trustworthy?*

"Honey?" she called over Gillian's voice on the machine. "What's going on? Do you know what she's talking about?"

". . . I hope I'm wrong, Vicki, and we'll have a good laugh about this later. . . ."

There was no answer from him.

Heading into the kitchen, Vicki stepped onto the tarp. It was slippery, and she glanced down at the floor for a second.

"Thanks a lot," Gillian was saying.

When Vicki looked up again, he was coming at her. She started to reel back, but the plastic sheet slid beneath her feet. She started to lose her balance.

". . . Bye, Vicki."

He grabbed her arm. But she still felt as if she were falling. He yanked her toward him. His face was just a blur as Vicki's head snapped back. She was looking up toward the ceiling.

The last thing she saw was the garden sickle in his raised hand. It was coming down at her.

Chapter 17

"Hey, Tanner."

Ethan paid no attention. He sat alone and stared out the window of the bus. Across the aisle from him was that loud-mouth idiot, Richard Marshall. In addition to ragging on him earlier today (before Jason had shut him up), Richard had called him a *fag* last week. The bus had just pulled out of the parking lot by Ballard High School's football field.

From Golden Gardens Park, Ethan had taken a taxi and made it back in time to see Craig Merchant lead their fresh-man team to a humiliating defeat. The mood on the bus was somber. Ethan didn't say a word to anyone.

"So—Tanner, where's your bodyguard?"

Ethan kept gazing out the window.

"Hey, I'm talking to you," Richard said, louder this time. "Where did you go during the game?"

Ethan closed his eyes. *Shut up, shut up, shut up . . .*

"Tanner?"

Finally, Ethan turned and glared at him. "Fuck off, ass-hole," he growled.

Richard Marshall's eyes widened for a moment.

Ethan was ready for him to leap across the aisle and start punching. He almost *wanted* it. He continued to stare at Richard, just waiting for him to lunge. *Go ahead, beat the crap out of me. I don't care. I don't care about anything anymore.*

Richard Marshall let out an abrupt laugh. "Jesus, chill out, Tanner. I was just making conversation." Shaking his head, he squirmed closer to his own window. "God, touchy!"

Ethan felt a bit disappointed Richard had backed down. He'd had no idea it could be so easy to stifle the jerk. Richard Marshall didn't say another word to him for the rest of way.

Ethan stepped off the bus two stops before his own. Belmont Avenue and Lakeview intersected at the end of a tall viaduct over the Interstate. Ethan had walked the vertigo-inducing overpass several times with Craig. It had a low guard-rail, and at one point, stood several stories above the freeway.

Hell, if he missed the highway and landed on the ground below, it was even further down. Certain death.

Ethan stared at the traffic on the Interstate—all those cars zooming below him, the long stream of headlights piercing through the murky dusk. Did he really want to screw up everyone's Saturday afternoon commute? And what if his body hit a car? He could kill someone. That was no way to make his exit—with a bunch of people pissed off at him.

Ethan didn't really want to kill himself anyway. Still, he'd fantasized about it a lot recently. Contemplating suicide gave him a strange sense of control over his situation. And for a while, it seemed like the only way to escape from all the treatment he was getting at school. He pictured his funeral, and thought about how sorry his former tormentors would be. He imagined Craig wishing he hadn't pulled away, and telling everyone that they were best friends up until the very end. But he also thought of his mother, and how it would destroy her if he killed himself. She'd been through enough. Still, maybe she'd write a book about him, and it would be a best-seller. Too bad he wouldn't be around to attend the funeral or read the book. No, suicide wasn't the answer—as much as he flirted with the notion.

He headed for home. Approaching the duplex, he didn't see any lights on. It looked like no one was home—both upstairs and down. But then Ethan thought he saw a curtain move in Vicki's living room window. He stared up at the window for a moment, and figured it had just been something reflecting off the glass.

Pulling his key out of his pocket, he let himself in, switched on the light, and took off his jacket. He kicked off his shoes. The right one was still a little damp. He thought about how Joe had taken his foot and tucked it under the folds of his jacket. Ethan felt so disgusted with himself for having gotten turned on by that—and for having had a little crush on Joe.

They'd set him up. He'd figured it out on the bus. One of their guys, casing the house, had found what was left of that half-burnt, sleazy *Stallion* magazine. They'd had his number right there. The following morning, the vintage Mustang had started following him around. They'd seen how Tate and his buddy had picked on him in front of the boys' locker room. *"Hey, Tanner! You can't go in there! No fags allowed!"* With Tate's big mouth, everyone within a block's radius had probably heard him. So the next day, Joe had shown up to save him—and he'd beaten the crap out of Tate. They'd given him a hero with Joe.

Ethan had trusted him. He kept thinking that if he actually knew where his dad had gone, he might have told Joe. That was how weak and stupid he was. He deserved to die. That was why he'd practically invited Richard Marshall to slug him on the bus—and why he'd thought about jumping off the viaduct. He wanted to punish himself.

While Ethan made a peanut butter and jelly sandwich in the kitchen, he heard footsteps above. He'd thought no one was home upstairs. Now he wondered what Vicki and Jason were doing up there with all the lights off.

"Duh," he muttered to himself—after a moment. "What do you think they're doing?"

He had a little crush on Jason. He was so sexy—and nice. Ethan still couldn't understand why his mom had been so cold toward Jason. Maybe she was just mad because he was Vicki's boyfriend. He probably reminded her of how lonely she was. Ethan suddenly felt awful for getting so snotty with his mom last night. What had he said? *"No wonder Dad has never bothered to come back to you."*

God, what a horrible thing to say.

While leaning against the counter and eating his sandwich, Ethan started to think about his mother, and her life these last two years without his dad. She'd gotten a pretty raw deal, but he'd never heard her complain. He'd never heard her bad-mouth his dad. Ethan remembered her after that *Leo* creep had beaten her, and how she'd tried to convince him—despite her swollen, battered face—she was okay. Her only concern seemed to have been about him.

Ethan couldn't eat any more of his sandwich because he was crying. He heard the footsteps overhead again. They were moving toward the stairs. It didn't sound like two people—just one. And that one person was coming down the steps.

Ethan listened to Vicki's door open and shut, then the footsteps again—this time on the front porch.

He emerged from the kitchen in time to see a shadow pass across the thin drapes at the living room window. A moment later, someone knocked on the door.

Ethan wiped the tears from his eyes, and then he headed toward the door to answer it.

* * *

"It's just up ahead, the gray house on your right," Gillian said, staring out the taxicab window. "Right by—where those guys are playing Frisbee," she added, not sure she liked what she saw.

Gillian had caught a taxi at the Seattle Ferry Terminal. She'd tried calling Ethan, but had gotten the machine. He certainly should have been home by four-thirty. During the taxi ride, she'd tried not to panic.

Now, she realized Ethan must not have listened to her messages—or he'd just blatantly disobeyed them. He was tossing the Frisbee to Jason on the grassy parkway in front of the duplex. She could hear them as the taxi approached the house.

"God, you think *you* stink at this?" Jason called, after his wild toss sent Ethan digging the Frisbee out of the bushes by the porch. "I totally suck! Sorry, Ethan!"

"That's okay!" Ethan yelled back, waving the Frisbee at him to show he'd recovered it. He was laughing. Then he stopped to stare at the taxi.

A tiny smile flickered on Gillian's face. Ethan looked like he was having fun; and it had been a long time since she'd seen him laughing and playing like this. She almost hated to interrupt them, but she didn't trust the man who was making her son so happy.

Gillian paid the driver and climbed out of the cab. Ethan tossed the Frisbee to Jason one last time, and they both started toward her. The taxicab drove off.

"Your timing's perfect," Jason said, tapping the Frisbee against the side of his leg as if it were a tambourine. "We were just about to call it quits on account of darkness—and on account of the fact that I haven't touched a Frisbee since college and I'm terrible. How was your ferry ride?"

"Fine, thanks," Gillian said cordially. She glanced at Ethan. "Did you get my phone messages?"

He shook his head. "No. I didn't check. Why? Is everything okay?"

"Everything's fine. I was just over in Bremerton, following up a story idea. I phoned to say I might be late. It's nothing." She turned toward Jason. "Isn't Vicki back yet?"

"Actually, Vicki had to work. She left me a note. They needed a replacement on a flight going out this afternoon. She'll be gone for the next two or three days. She told me to be sure and let you know. And she also wished Ethan a happy birthday." He smiled at Ethan. "I already passed that message along."

Gillian stared at him. She was thinking about the phone message she'd left for Vicki ninety minutes ago. "Um, did you check her answering machine for a follow-up message?" Gillian asked. "Sometimes, at the last minute, it turns out they don't need her after all."

Jason nodded. "Yeah, I checked her machine. No messages."

"How long ago did you get back?"

"Oh, about an hour ago."

Gillian mulled it over. It was possible that Vicki had gotten her message and erased it before leaving for the airport. But there was something wrong with what Jason was telling her about Vicki's note. Vicki never bothered to let her know about her work schedule unless she'd planned to be gone over a week. Another thing. How did Vicki know about Ethan's birthday on Tuesday?

"I asked Jason if he'll have dinner with us," Ethan announced.

Jason was shaking his head. "I told you, Ethan, I can't. I need to go hunt down a hotel tonight. But thanks anyway." He handed the Frisbee to Ethan. "Hey, didn't you say you'd get on the Net and look up some places for me?"

"You bet!" Ethan replied, a bit starry-eyed. "Hold on, be right back."

Gillian watched him hurry up the porch steps and duck inside the apartment.

"Listen, I'm sorry about earlier—on the ferry," Jason whispered. "From the look on your face when you got out of the cab, I'm guessing you weren't pleased to see me with Ethan. But I heard him come home while I was upstairs earlier, and I wanted to pass along Vicki's message before I took off."

Gillian just nodded. Part of her wanted to apologize for being so awful to him. Another part of her still didn't trust him at all.

Jason gave an awkward shrug. "It's none of my business, but I thought you should know. When Ethan answered the door, it looked as if he'd been crying. I figured he didn't want to be alone. I hope it's okay that I asked him to step out and toss around the Frisbee with me."

Dazed, Gillian stared at him. It broke her heart to think of her son sitting alone at home, crying. She wondered what had happened at that game in Ballard. She managed to smile at him. "That was very nice of you," she murmured. "Thank you, Jason." Then she retreated inside the apartment.

Ethan was at her computer, eyes glued to the screen and fingers working the keyboard.

"How was the game?" Gillian asked, trying to sound nonchalant.

"They creamed us," Ethan replied, wrapped up in his task for Jason.

"Did you have an okay time?"

Ethan didn't answer. He hit a key and the printer started up.

"Honey, you didn't have anyone—*harassing* you at the game, did you? Did anything happen?"

"No, Mom, nothing happened," he said. He briefly glanced up at her, then went back to work.

Gillian studied his face for another moment, then she

took off her coat. She opened the curtains to the front window. Jason was waiting in front of the duplex, his back to her. The polite thing to do would have been to ask him in for a cup of coffee. But she wasn't going to cave in and do it. Gillian turned from the window. "Did you have fun with Mr. Hurrell?"

"Yeah, he's a nice guy. Why don't you ask him in?"

"Um, I think he'd rather wait outside. Honey, did you mention anything to Vicki about your birthday coming up?"

"Nope, I thought you did."

"No, I haven't," she murmured. Gillian glanced out at Jason again. "What did you and Jason talk about?"

"I dunno, stuff," he answered distractedly. "Mom, I'm trying to get this done. Okay? He's waiting."

Gillian just nodded, even though Ethan wasn't looking at her. She walked past him, and checked the answering machine. Skipping through her messages for Ethan, she listened to one from Ruth: *"Sorry I missed you, hon. Call me as soon as you get this. I want to know how it went in Bremerton. Bye."*

There weren't any other messages, nothing from Chase Scott.

Ethan printed up about a dozen pages' worth of local hotel information for Jason; then he ran outside with the papers in tow. He looked like a kid, eager to show his dad a composition he'd written. Gillian watched from the living room window as Ethan went over the selections with him. She watched Jason take the papers. He shook Ethan's hand, and then pulled him in for a hug. He patted Ethan's back a few times.

Gillian had such mixed feelings as she watched Ethan embracing this man—this *father fill-in* who was being way too nice to them both.

When Ethan came back inside alone, he had a sad, goofy smile on his face. "Jason says he'll probably stay at the Best

Western Loyal Inn, because it's close." Ethan peeled off his jacket. "Mom, if Vickie isn't back by Tuesday, and we're doing something for my birthday—like going out to dinner or something—could Jason come?"

Gillian worked up a smile. "We'll see, honey."

She asked him if Chinese or Thai would be all right for tonight's dinner. Ethan was leaning toward Chinese. As Gillian wandered toward her bedroom to change into sweatpants and a pullover, she liked the idea of this night with Ethan. He spent way too much time alone. She'd let him choose something on Pay-per-View, and they'd watch TV together—unless of course, Saturday night at home with Mom was just about the worst thing she could inflict on him. She imagined how much better it would have been for Ethan if Jason Hurrell were part of this equation. Saturday night at home with Mom and *this real cool guy* didn't seem so pathetic. There would have been more dignity in that.

With a sigh, Gillian kicked off her shoes and opened the closet door. Then she froze. She saw something on the floor of her closet, something that didn't belong there.

For a moment, she couldn't breathe. Tears welled in her eyes, and she shook her head over and over again. "No," she whispered. "God, no . . . no . . ."

He'd been inside her home—in her bedroom. And he wanted her to know.

Lined up with her shoes on the floor was a pair of saddle shoes, the kind Catholic schoolgirls wore.

They looked like a perfect fit.

Gillian watched from the front window. Outside, Ruth was talking to two policemen. Her arms folded, she leaned against their patrol car. One of the cops was smoking a cigarette, and the other was on his cell phone.

They'd already combed through the duplex—including

Vicki's unit upstairs. Gillian had let them in with her key. Nothing had been stolen or disturbed in either apartment. They'd inspected the basement laundry room too. Gillian was grateful for that. It was creepy enough going down to that dank little cellar during the day—no less at night, right after a break-in. With their flashlights, they also checked around the yard—and even walked a few feet down into the ravine. They hadn't stumbled across anything except a family of raccoons.

Ethan had used his key to get in when he'd come home around four o'clock, but he couldn't say for certain whether or not the front door had been locked. And no, he hadn't invited Jason Hurrell inside. Jason had never set foot in the apartment.

Gillian told the policemen that if they wanted to speak with Jason, he could be reached at the Loyal Inn downtown.

They bagged the saddle shoes—and double-checked her bedroom for any other surprises. Gillian stripped her bed while they were there. The cops probably thought she was crazy. But she didn't want to uncover another gift from her copycat sometime later. She'd been wondering what he'd done with the heart of that "drifter" in Montana. She didn't want to discover it tonight, tucked under her pillow.

Gillian decided she couldn't sleep in her bedroom tonight. She felt so violated. He'd probably been through all her things. She imagined him peeking into closets and drawers and touching her clothes.

The police had promised to have the saddle shoes analyzed and compared to the shoes found on the Schoolgirl Murder victims.

Gillian watched them talking with Ruth by their patrol car. Ruth patted one of them on the arm, and then sauntered toward the front porch. "Okay, thanks, guys!" she called over her shoulder.

Gillian shot a look back toward Ethan's room, where he

was watching TV. Then she let Ruth in. "So—are they taking me seriously or do they think I planted those saddle shoes in my closet for publicity or something?"

"The question did come up," Ruth admitted. "There aren't many folks besides you eager to see the Schoolgirl Murders case reopened after two years. But these are good guys. They'll make sure those shoes get to the lab. Don't sweat it, hon. By the way, they struck out with your pal at the Loyal Inn. There's no Jason Hurrell registered there."

Gillian wasn't very surprised. "Of course not," she muttered, almost to herself.

Ruth started to take off her coat, then put it back on again. "Listen, I've handled enough break-ins to know how you feel right now. You probably want the place fumigated, and your wardrobe cleaned and burned."

Gillian nodded. "For starters, yes."

"Do you want me to spend the night? I can go home and come back in fifteen with Eustace, my .45, a nightgown, and enough Jack Daniel's to make us both feel okay."

Gillian smiled. "Thanks, that sounds great. We're ordering Chinese. Do you want anything?"

"Sweet-and-sour pork. And you can tell me how it went today with Chase Scott." She started toward the door again.

"He wasn't home," Gillian said.

Ruth hesitated and turned to her. "Really?"

"I talked to him about forty-five minutes before showing up there. He said he'd be waiting. But no one came to the door. I knocked. I called him on my cell. Nothing."

Ruth reached for the doorknob. "We'll talk about it when I get back," she said. "See you in fifteen minutes. Double-lock this. Okay?"

After Ruth left, Gillian closed the door and double-locked it. She tried to ignore the voice inside her head, telling her: *That won't do any good at all. If he wants to get in, he will. . . .*

* * *

The last ferry out of Bremerton was almost empty. Danielle had a large window table all to herself. She could see the lights from the Seattle skyline in the far distance. She was on her way back from a birthday party for her dad. There were only a few other passengers on this deck, and maybe a dozen more on the upper tier. Some others were probably napping in their vehicles.

Danielle was twenty-four years old, and pretty, with wavy black hair. She'd taken this ferry ride often enough, and enjoyed the quiet, lonely night trips like this. But tonight, Danielle was reading an Ann Rule book about the Green River Killer, and she was a little spooked out.

Not helping matters was a man who had passed by her table twice—and by her window three more times as he paced around the deck outside. He kept looking at her whenever he walked by. At first, Danielle thought he was kind of cute with his athletic-husky build, receding sandy-colored hair, and that impish baby face. But as they drew closer to Seattle, he seemed more and more agitated each time he passed.

Danielle saw him outside the window again, and he locked eyes with her. She quickly looked away and picked up her book. After a few moments, she felt a blast of cold air sweep down the aisle. Glancing up, she saw him approaching. The doors to the outside deck were swinging back and forth behind him.

Danielle hoped he would just pass by again. She kept her nose in her book.

"Excuse me," she heard him say, out of breath. "Sorry to bother you . . ."

Reluctantly, she looked up. This close she could see he was sweating—and trembling. "Do you have a cell phone?" he asked.

Danielle hesitated. "Um—"

"I don't need to borrow one," he explained, still catching his breath. "I just—I need someone to call the cops for me if it becomes necessary. Do you mind if I sit down?"

Danielle balked again. "I—I'm sorry . . ."

He let out a skittish laugh. "Of course you mind. I'm a total stranger. Listen, my name's Chase—Chase Scott. I live in Bremerton. This sounds crazy, but for the last few days, someone's been following me around. And this afternoon, it got worse. I swear, every time I turned around . . ."

He took a couple of deep breaths. "I know he followed me onto this ferry. I tried to tell the old security guy here, but he thinks I'm nuts. Have you seen a fairly tall man in a gray raincoat that goes down to about here?" He tapped his upper thigh. "I know he's on this boat."

Danielle started to shake her head, but then she remembered seeing someone on the deck outside, and he'd had on a gray raincoat. He'd passed her window.

Chase let out a sigh, and ran a hand through his receding hair. "Damn, I wish I could give you a better description, but this guy is like a phantom. He's always in the shadows. I don't know why this is happening. . . ."

"I saw someone like that," Danielle said. "Someone tall in a gray raincoat."

Chase's face lit up. "You did? Oh, thank God! At least I know I'm not crazy. Did you see his face? What did he look like?"

Danielle shook her head. "I'm sorry, I can't tell you. He passed by the window pretty fast. It was dark, and he had the collar up on his raincoat."

"Shit," Chase muttered. He suddenly plopped down across from her, and the table shook. Danielle recoiled a bit. He looked over his shoulder and outside the window. Danielle followed his gaze. The cityscape loomed closer, the lights reflected on the dark water. "We're almost in Seattle," he said, turning toward her again. "Listen, if you could just do me a favor, and go to the upper bow before we get to the dock. I'd feel a lot better if I knew someone was watching out for me."

Danielle shrugged helplessly. "I don't understand what you want me to do—"

"I'm driving a red Ford Probe with a broken back antenna," he went on. "I'm at the front of the line. Mine should be one of the first cars to drive off the boat when we dock. You won't even have to wait very long. If you could just make sure I get off the boat okay—"

"How?" she asked, shaking her head. "Listen, I'm sorry—"

"Please! All you have to do is look for my car. I'll flash my headlights or wave to show you I'm okay. But if you don't see my car—or—or if I don't signal to you, you'll know something's wrong. Then I'll need you to call the police. That's all I'm asking, just delay leaving the ferry for a few minutes so you can make sure I get out of here all right."

Danielle squirmed in the seat. He seemed to read her reluctance.

"Listen, I'll pay you if you'd like—"

"No, I don't want your money," she said. "I'll do it."

"Thank you," he gasped. "It's a red Ford Probe, and the license plate number is AOB829. In case you need to call the police, you should give that to them."

Danielle took a pen out of her coat pocket and scribbled the number on the inside cover of her paperback.

"I'll blink my headlights to let you know everything's okay."

She nodded. "I understand."

He let out a nervous, little laugh. He had a cute smile. "You must think I'm nuts."

"No, I just think you're very scared," Danielle replied. "I'll keep watch for you."

"Thanks," he said, grinning at her. He glanced over his shoulder again, then quickly got to his feet. "What's your name, by the way?"

"Danielle."

"I'm Chase," he said, shaking her hand. "Danielle, you're literally a lifesaver." He turned and headed for the stairwell that led to the parking level.

For a few minutes, Danielle sat there in a stupor. What if this man following Chase Scott saw them sitting together and talking? Would he come after her now? She took her cell phone from her purse and checked the battery. It was charged up. She could call the police if she had to.

She noticed a few other passengers getting to their feet and putting on their coats. They headed into the same stairwell Chase had used. They were going to their cars. Danielle peeked out the window. The Seattle skyline was just ahead. They'd be docked in five minutes.

Danielle felt scared. She knew it was silly. All she had to do was watch for his car—and the blinking headlights. She really wasn't in any kind of danger. She'd laugh about this when she got home in a half hour.

Standing, Danielle threw on her coat and grabbed her purse. She stuffed her cell phone and the book into her coat pockets, then headed for the stairway. Danielle took a deep breath, and opened the door to the stairs. She didn't know why she was so nervous. She'd been up and down these dim, narrow stairwells on the ferry countless times. It had never made her claustrophobic before. But now she felt as if the walls were closing in. She hurried up the steps toward the top level. Suddenly, the door opened.

Danielle froze, and a shadow swept over her. It was another passenger, an older woman. The lady came down the

stairs. Danielle pressed her back against the wall to let the
lady pass. Then she continued up the steps to the upper deck.
Everyone else had left. She was alone as she hurried up the
aisle to the double doors that led to the bow outside.

A gust of cold air hit her as she pushed through the
doors. No one else was out there. The brilliant skyline was
so close, it seemed ready to swallow her up. She could see
the dock ahead. Danielle clutched the guardrail and peered
over the edge at the car deck. A security chain ran across the
open end. A couple of ferry workers prepped the boat for
docking.

Past the howling wind, Danielle thought she heard something behind her. She glanced over her shoulder. The doors
to the passenger area were swinging back and forth. Danielle
panicked for a moment. Had someone else stepped out
there? She didn't see anybody in the smoking area, a shel-
tered section with rows of benches. No one seemed to be
hiding behind the lifeboats. She told herself that she was
alone out there, but her heart was still beating furiously.

Danielle reached for the cell phone in her pocket.

A loud squealing noise from below made her swivel
around. It sounded like tires screeching. But she was almost
certain she heard someone scream, too. Danielle stared down
at the parking deck.

All at once, a red car shot forward and burst through the
security chain. A spray of metal links exploded in the
air. The ferry workers leapt out of the way. Smoke from
the car tires rose up from the deck. The Ford Probe ca-
reened off the front of the boat—and dove into the murky
sound.

Danielle screamed. But the ferry whistle drowned her
out. Chase Scott's car flailed in the water for a moment.
Danielle glimpsed the broken antenna in back. The silvery
water started to swallow up the car, and then the boat was on
top of it.

A loud alarm went off. It was deafening. Danielle couldn't imagine hearing anything beyond that blaring horn.

But then, she couldn't have imagined the sound of the ferry's propellers grinding up that automobile—and the man inside it.

Chapter 18

"We recently discovered in our records here at the college that Mr. Sorenson didn't complete the semester," Ruth was saying into the cell phone. She paced around Gillian's living room. "We're required by Washington State law to give Todd a full refund for the night course, plus interest. That comes to exactly eighty-six dollars and twenty-two cents. Do you know how we can get in touch with Todd?" Ruth stopped pacing and listened for a moment. "The Whispering Brook Retirement Home? Is he an employee there or a resident, hon? Well, no, this Todd is a few years younger than that. But thanks anyway for your time."

Ruth clicked off the line, and rolled her eyes. "God, I may blow my brains out. We got the right name, but he's the wrong age."

Sitting by her computer with the cordless phone in her hand, Gillian squinted at Ruth. "Is there really a state law on refund policies?"

Ruth shook her head. "God, no, I was just getting bored giving them the same old routine. How many Sorensons have we called so far?"

Gillian consulted the list they'd gathered from Directory Assistance and the Internet. There were fifty-nine Sorensons in the Fort Lewis and Tacoma area.

"We've had ten hang-ups, eleven I've-Never-Heard-of-Hims, nine messages left on answering machines, and one right-name-wrong-age. That's thirty-one calls so far, with twenty-eight to go."

The time was 9:40 in the morning. Ethan was still asleep. Gillian had heard his TV going at 3:00 A.M. when she'd nodded off on the living room sofa with Eustace nearby. Ruth hadn't had any qualms about sleeping in Gillian's bedroom after her uninvited guest had been in there. With a couple of shots of Jack Daniel's, she'd gone to bed at one in the morning, and just minutes later, Gillian had heard her snoring.

They still hadn't heard from Chase Scott. Gillian had left another message on his answering machine this morning. Ruth had phoned a friend on the Bremerton Police Force to look into Chase's sudden disappearance.

Either he was dead, or he was playing games with her. Since they couldn't get ahold of him, Gillian had decided this morning to track down Chase's classmate, Todd Sorenson.

She remembered Todd's rambling novel about a teenage "garage band" in the Fort Lewis and Tacoma area. That was all she had to go on. She figured Todd might still have family there, someone who could tell her where he was. So she and Ruth had gathered the list and started making simultaneous calls on her cell and home phones.

So far, thirty-one Sorensons hadn't been any help at all.

"Do you want another cup of coffee?" Gillian asked.

"Honey, I'd rather drink phlegm," Ruth said wearily. "You're a wonderful person, but your coffee is the absolute worst."

Gillian rolled her eyes. Since leaving the police force, Ruth had become a coffee connoisseur. Gillian, forever on a budget, settled for whatever coffee was the least expensive.

Ruth reached for her coat. "I'm going down the block to the Top Pot Café. I'll bring back some *good* coffee—and doughnuts. Eustace could use the exercise. You'll be okay here for fifteen minutes, won't you?"

Slumping back in her desk chair, Gillian nodded. "Bring back a couple of chocolate doughnuts for Ethan, okay? I'll pay you back."

Ruth tied the leash on Eustace, then slipped Gillian's cell phone in her coat pocket. "I have your cell with me. Call yourself if anything happens."

Gillian watched her leave with the dog. Then she picked up the cordless phone and dialed the next Sorenson on the list. It rang twice before a woman picked up: "Yes, hello?"

"Hi, I'm trying to track down someone named Todd Sorenson. He has a refund coming for a night class he—"

"*Todd* Sorenson?" the woman interrupted. "My God, it's been a dozen years since I've heard that name."

"Um, are we talking about the same Todd Sorenson?" Gillian asked, sitting up. "He's in his late twenties, kind of good-looking, and he's from Fort Lewis—"

"Actually, he's from Tacoma."

"So you know him?"

"Oh, yeah. My son, Tom, and Todd were in the same class in high school. Practically every time *T. Sorenson* got in trouble, they called me by mistake. It was always Todd, not my Tommy. And Todd got into trouble a lot."

"Really? What kind of trouble?"

"Are you a friend of Todd's?" the woman asked warily.

"No. Actually, I'm trying to track him down for someone. Anything you could tell me about Todd—good or bad— would be helpful. You said he was always getting into trouble. Could you elaborate on that?"

"You got an hour? Drugs, beating up other kids, stealing—he was into all sorts of things, all bad. His father was a captain at Fort Lewis, and they kept giving Todd a break— even after he killed a neighbor's cat. He tortured the poor thing. I hear the captain whaled the daylights out of him for that little caper."

"Um, do you—or Tommy—know how I might get in touch with Todd now?"

"I haven't a clue where he is. His father died about six or seven years ago. And his mom, the poor thing, she moved to Phoenix—or Tucson, someplace in Arizona."

"Do you remember Mrs. Sorenson's first name?"

"Sure, it's Christine."

Gillian scribbled it down on the listing: "Christine Sorenson—Phoenix—Maybe Tucson?"

"So—um, why exactly are you trying to track down Todd?" the woman asked. "Is he in trouble again? Did he murder somebody or something?"

Gillian put down the pen. "That's what I'm trying to find out."

She thanked the woman, and while hanging up the phone, she noticed the Mail icon blinking on her computer screen. Gillian pulled up her mail. The new correspondence showed "No Subject." Gillian didn't recognize the sender's address: *nmbr1fan@yahoo.com*.

She hesitated, then opened the e-mail:

Dear Gillian,

I have now made contact with your long-lost husband. We've talked & gotten along quite well. We're supposed to meet again tonight. He doesn't know I'm going to kill him. For now, that's a secret between you and me. I'll be sure to do it just the way you wrote it down.

See You Soon.

"Oh, my God," Gillian whispered.

With shaky hands, she hit the Reply key and typed up a brief note: "Who are you?" She hit the Send key, knowing what would happen. A moment later, she got a message back: "MAILER-DAEMON . . . Returned Mail: User Unknown."

"Damn," Gillian muttered. She pulled the e-mail back up.

A knock on her front door startled her. Then she realized it was probably Ruth. She hurried to the door and opened it.

Jason Hurrell stood on her front porch. He was wearing an aviator jacket over a white oxford shirt and khakis. Gillian almost shut the door in his face, but she froze up.

"I'm sorry to bother you," he said. "Have you heard from Vicki?"

Gillian shook her head. "No. Why?"

"She gave my cell phone number as an alternate contact to the scheduler with her airline." He scratched his head. "It's kind of weird she'd list me for that—so soon. But that's not why I'm here."

"Yes?" Gillian stared at him.

"They called me an hour ago. They want Vicki to substitute on a noon flight today."

"But she's already subbing for someone—"

"That's what I told them," Jason said. "They don't have any record of it. They didn't call her yesterday, Gillian. That note she left me on her computer, it doesn't make sense."

"The note was on her *computer*?" Gillian repeated, backing away from the door.

Jason nodded. "Yes. Her fish-tank screen saver was the only light on when I came into her apartment yesterday afternoon. I touched the mouse, and up came the note. Why? What's going on?"

Gillian just shook her head. She was thinking about her book, *Killing Legend*. The ex-movie star hunk on a murder spree had written a suicide note on a victim's computer before poisoning her.

All at once, Gillian realized why in her note "Vicki" had asked Jason to pass along the news that she'd be away for a couple of days—when Vicki never bothered telling her about short trips before. Vicki didn't know Ethan had a birthday coming up, and yet it was mentioned in the note.

Gillian was thinking about the phony note from her agent,

those hang-ups from Dianne's home phone, and the fake e-mails to Ruth from "Hester." The copycat was once again letting her know—through someone else—that he'd killed again.

Jason took a step into the apartment. "Gillian, are you all right?"

Gillian retreated to the kitchen, opened the refrigerator, and pulled out the filtered-water pitcher. Her hands trembled and water sluiced over the glass as she poured. A little puddle formed on the countertop. Gillian didn't really notice. She took a few gulps from the glass.

"Would you please tell me what's going on?" Jason asked.

Gillian shook her head over and over again. "Vicki didn't write that note."

"Then who did?"

She took another swallow of water, then stepped closer to her desk. Gillian nodded at the e-mail on her computer screen. "The same person who just sent me that."

Jason squinted at the screen for a few moments. "Is this for real?"

"I think so," Gillian replied.

He glanced up at the photos above her desk, and seemed to focus on one of her and Barry in front of the Pike Street Market sign. He looked at the computer screen again. "May I have a glass of water too, please?" he murmured.

She retrieved a tumbler from the cupboard, and poured some water into it. Her hands were still shaking. She gave him the glass of water.

"Vicki hinted that your husband was in trouble with the cops—and some mob types. Is that what this is about?"

"Yes, there are some people who want my husband dead," Gillian heard herself say. She was searching his eyes. "But this is something else."

"What is it?"

"Someone's been copying the murders from my books," she answered carefully. "He's killing people I know. I—I'm pretty sure he's already murdered Vicki. And it looks like he's going after my husband next. . . ."

Gillian told him everything, and with each detail she divulged there was a nagging dread that confiding in Jason Hurrell was the wrong thing. She knew in her gut that he wasn't being completely open and honest with her. He was hiding something. She hated herself for letting down her guard with him. But she couldn't help it.

Jason listened intently, and every once in a while he blinked and shook his head. When she finished, he looked at the e-mail on her computer again. "Listen, I think I can help," he said. "But it means I'll be gone until tonight—at least. I don't know you well enough to tell you what to do, Gillian. But could you and Ethan stick close to home—and keep your friend, Ruth, nearby? If you do go out—well, better give me your cell phone number. Is it okay to use this pad to write on?"

Gillian nodded and told him her cell phone number.

Bent over her desk, he scribbled it on the notepad, then tore off the top sheet. "I'll call you and explain as soon as I get anything." He zipped up his jacket and headed for the door.

Gillian trailed after him, but he got to the door first and let himself out. From the front porch, Gillian watched him hop into his rental car and drive away.

"Was that Jason? I thought I heard his voice."

Gillian swiveled around.

Rubbing the sleep from his eyes, Ethan stood in the living room in his pajama bottoms and T-shirt.

Gillian stepped inside. "Yes, he's coming back tonight," she said numbly.

She suddenly remembered the e-mail on her computer. She didn't want Ethan seeing it, and brushed past him on her

way to her study nook. "Um, Ruth's getting you some doughnuts," she said, pressing the key to close the e-mail display.
The note forecasting Barry's death was wiped off the screen.

Gillian caught her breath, then looked up at the family
photos on the wall of her study nook. The framed snapshot
of her and Barry at the Pike Street Market was gone.

Ruth started up the stairwell to Vicki's apartment. She
sipped her extra-large-coffee-to-go from the Top Pot Café.
Gillian was behind her, amazed at how blasé Ruth seemed
while checking a potential murder site. Of course, the police
had briefly looked through the apartment last night, and found
nothing. But they'd merely been checking to make sure the
apartment was empty. At the time, they'd had no reason to
suspect someone had been murdered there.

She and Ruth had left Ethan downstairs with his chocolate doughnuts and Eustace. Ruth's dog would bark if anyone got near the duplex.

"Try not to touch anything," Ruth said, stepping from the
stairwell into the living room.

The drapes were shut, but a dim light filtered through the
windows. Hanging on the wall above Vicki's mauve sofa
were several framed Matisse prints. A bouquet of flowers,
obviously from Jason, sat in a vase on the coffee table. The
room looked undisturbed, almost pristine.

Gillian smelled something she hadn't detected last night
while going through the apartment with the police. She
smelled pine-scented disinfectant. If any blood was spilt, the
killer must have cleaned up afterward.

The idea that Vicki might have been murdered here turned
Gillian's stomach. She wondered if the killer had stopped by
downstairs and planted the saddle shoes before or after
killing her neighbor. Vicki had never done a thing to hurt
anyone. And she'd been mercilessly killed.

Sunlight came through the window above the kitchen sink. The pine scent was stronger in there.

"Your neighbor's dead, Gill," Ruth said, standing in the middle of the kitchen. She glanced around the room. "He killed her in here. I can feel it."

Rubbing her forearms, Gillian walked around the room. She stared at the tiled floor, the cabinets and countertops, searching for signs of blood. Everything was spotless.

"I can't remember right now," Ruth said, sipping her coffee. "In your books, are there any murders that occur in a kitchen—in the victim's home?"

Gillian didn't want to think of how she'd contributed to Vicki's death. She felt sick. "Um, *Flowers for Her Grave,*" she said. "The gardener uses a sickle to kill one of his victims in her kitchen."

"Yes, I remember that scene now," Ruth muttered. "It was awfully bloody."

Gillian thought she might have to run to the bathroom and throw up. She clutched her stomach and glanced down at the floor. "But it's spotless," she managed to say. "He cleaned everything."

"Not quite everything." Ruth was gazing up at the kitchen ceiling.

Gillian saw what she was looking at: the dark red stains on the white ceiling—a pattern of two long streaks and several little dots.

"I think that's off the murder weapon, not the victim," Ruth said, frowning. "He hit her at least a few times. He was standing just about where I am now. That's blood from the sickle when he raised it in the air for the second and third hit."

Gillian was sick in Vicki's bathroom.

After flushing the toilet, she slurped some water from the faucet and splashed some more on her face.

In Vicki's kitchen, Ruth had used Gillian's cell phone to call the police.

"Well, hon, more bad news," she said, clicking off the line. She met Gillian in Vicki's living room. "We'll have quite a wait before the forensics gang can come in and take samples off the ceiling. Doesn't your landlord live in California?"

"Yes. Why?"

"Well, without his written permission—and without Vicki to allow it, the cops can't come in here and collect evidence. It's got to be official, which means a search warrant, which means a great big delay—especially on a Sunday."

"But the police were just in here last night," Gillian argued.

Ruth shook her head. "That was a favor to me. Officially, they never set foot in this place. Got that? And for the record, I told them you and I came up here just a few minutes ago, because it sounded like she'd left the water running."

Ruth glanced over her shoulder toward the ceiling in the kitchen. "The detectives might not even get in here until tomorrow. But don't worry. Those bloodstains aren't going anywhere."

She started down the stairs, and Gillian followed her. "I think we can definitely add to our list of suspects this Jason character I've yet to meet," Ruth said. "He had at least an hour here yesterday afternoon. That's enough time for him to kill your neighbor, clean up the mess, and leave those schoolgirl shoes in your closet."

At the bottom of the stairs, Gillian stopped and shook her head. "I don't know. He drove me around yesterday—and spent time alone with Ethan. If Jason wanted to kill either one of us, he had a chance."

Ruth stepped out to the front porch, and then headed toward the side yard. The cellar light went on as they walked past the stairs down to the laundry room. The dog started barking. "Shut up, Eustace!" Ruth called. The barking ceased from inside the house. "Thank you, baby!"

"About this copycat," she continued, her voice dropping to a whisper. "It's not about killing you, Gill. It may ultimately lead to that. But right now, this is a game for him. It's kind of a twisted courtship. He enjoys terrorizing you. He might be close by, all the better to watch you squirm. I wouldn't eliminate Vicki's boyfriend from our short list of suspects—just because he's been a perfect gentleman so far."

Gillian had been focusing on Chase Scott and Todd Sorenson. She figured the copycat killer had to be someone from that class with Jennifer, someone she knew. Until the night before last, she'd never set eyes on Jason Hurrell.

But he could have very well been watching her for a long, long time.

Ruth sipped her coffee, and winced a little. "Hmm, cold," she muttered. "Well, you're the expert, hon. What do you think he did with the body?"

Gillian felt a chill, and she rubbed her arms. "In *Flowers for Her Grave,* the killer buried his victims in their backyards." She gazed out at the ravine.

"Then it's going to take a while to find your neighbor, Gill," she heard Ruth say. "You have an awfully big backyard."

After a while, Ethan realized he'd just been shaking his head over and over, and repeating practically everything his mother was telling him: *"This stalker guy has been killing people? He was actually in the house yesterday? That wasn't just an attempted break-in? What do you mean, he probably killed Vicki? How would he know where Dad is?"*

Apparently to keep from upsetting him, his mother had soft-pedaled everything about this psycho-case. Ethan had thought the dinner at O'Reilly's with that policewoman had been about researching a book. He'd figured all his mother's precautions were due to those hoods hanging around—and a few weird e-mails from some faraway stalker fan. Ethan had no idea it was this serious—and this terrible.

He sat at the kitchen table with his mother, while Ruth paced around the living room, mumbling into the cell phone. Ruth's Jack Russell terrier kept his head and paws propped up on Ethan's thigh. Ethan absently stroked the dog's head while his mother carefully explained everything to him.

He started to tear up thinking about Vicki. She used to bring him these cheap little snow globes from different cities whenever she returned from her trips. He'd had a collection for a while. "That's for guarding my home and all my priceless treasures, Ethan," she'd say, handing him a new snow globe from a new city.

He couldn't believe she was dead.

And now this killer was going after his father.

In so many ways, it didn't seem real. It was like something was about to happen on the other side of the world somewhere. His father had been gone for two years. Part of Ethan had already given up hope that he'd ever see his dad again.

"Honey, in his e-mail, he talked about killing Dad *tonight*," his mother was saying. "I wouldn't expect you to break a confidence, but this is an emergency. If your father has been secretly communicating with you in any way, you need to tell me. It could save his life—"

"Oh, Mom," Ethan whispered. "I haven't heard from him at all since he left, I swear."

She touched the side of his face. "Are you sure? I promise I won't be upset with you if you've been keeping this a secret. We need to get to your father and warn him."

"Honest, I don't know where he is."

He saw her eyes water up as she sat back in the kitchen chair. She looked so hopeless.

"Mom, I need to tell you something," Ethan said. "I wasn't at that football game yesterday. The guy who beat up Tate Barringer and that other kid? Well, I'd never seen him before until Friday. His name is Joe Pagani, and he wanted to get together and hang out. So he met me at the high school and we drove to Golden Gardens."

His mother bit her lip as she looked at him.

"Anyway, it turned out Joe was just pretending to be my friend so he could pump me about where Dad might be hiding. He's with that group Dad owes money to. He said they weren't going to hurt him, just *talk* to him—or something like that."

"What did you tell this Joe?" his mother asked.

Ethan shrugged. "I told him that I didn't know where Dad was, and that you didn't either."

His mother shot a look across the room at Ruth, who was now off the phone and standing by the kitchen door. She'd obviously heard everything he'd just said.

"There could be a connection between this Joe and our copycat," Ruth said. "But didn't that e-mail this morning say he'd already talked with Barry? And yesterday afternoon, these hoods were still trying to track him down through Ethan—and with no luck."

"Still, do you think it's at least *possible* the copycat could be one of these hoods looking for Barry?" Gillian asked.

Ruth nodded glumly. "Yes, I suppose it's possible—especially when you take into account that our list of potential suspects just got shorter."

"What do you mean?"

Ruth sighed. "I just got off the horn with my friend in Bremerton. Now I know why you couldn't get hold of Chase Scott today. He's dead."

Standing on a stepladder, Gillian searched for the small Tupperware container in the back of her bedroom closet. She knew it was there on the top shelf, somewhere amid the stacks of Barry's old sweaters, some board games, and boxes of memorabilia.

She'd left Ethan in the kitchen with Eustace. Ruth was on the cell phone with her police connections, trying to get an update on Chase's death.

Gillian had created his murder in *Killing Legend,* when the killer knocked out a colleague, dumped him in a car—then sent the vehicle careening off a bluff into a lake. She remembered questioning a car mechanic about how it could be done: rigging the gas pedal, blocking and unblocking the wheels, releasing the parking brake. She'd wanted to make it as real as possible.

And now it was.

Her copycat had taken it one better, with Chase's car sailing off the front of a ferry. According to Ruth's sources, there had been several witnesses to the "accident." One ferry passenger, a young woman, had talked briefly with Chase. He'd claimed someone was following him and he was afraid for his life. But the police were still calling it an accident. No one on the car deck had seen anything suspicious.

The ferry had run over Chase's car in the water. His Ford Probe was sliced up, and so was its passenger. So far, divers had recovered from Puget Sound several pieces of the automobile—along with a severed leg.

It was obvious to Gillian that Todd Sorenson was her copycat. The little bits she'd learned about his background today were right out of a serial killer's profile: a trouble-prone teenager; a penchant for torturing pets; the abusive father. He'd stalked her, seemed smugly amused by the Schoolgirl Murders, and felt no one appreciated his genius. Now one of his classmates was lying in a coma with stab wounds, and the other was in pieces at the bottom of Puget Sound.

Something else besides Todd's culpability was obvious to Gillian. She was almost certain that Barry was in Seattle.

She found the Tupperware container, and climbed down from the stepladder. Opening the container, Gillian spilled its contents on her bed. She looked at the sticks of gum, Lifesavers, Starlight mints, old *Racing Forms,* cocktail napkins, poker chips, matchbooks, and a couple of pens. Shortly after Barry's disappearance, she'd collected all of these items from the pockets of his clothes. At the time, she'd been looking for clues to where he might have gone. But most of the paraphernalia came from local casinos, and she didn't think he would be staying close to home with the police and those mobsters after him.

A couple of those cocktail napkins had women's names and phone numbers on them: *Megan* on one; *Jamie* on another. Long ago, she'd wrestled with the notion that Barry might have been seeing other women as part of his secret life. Maybe it was another one of his *addictions,* she couldn't be sure. At least the handwriting on the cocktail napkins wasn't his. Maybe he hadn't solicited the phone numbers, or perhaps he had. It didn't matter anymore.

Gillian reexamined the cocktail napkins, poker chips, and matchbooks. Barry seemed to have a preference for three gambling spots in the area: the Emerald Queen Casino in Tacoma; the Tulalip Casino just north of Everett, and Club Royale Casino-Resort in Anacortes, Washington. She wondered if someone working at one of these casinos—a manager, doorman, dealer, or waitress—had seen Barry recently. He had to be nearby. The copycat killer had told her so.

Gillian had tracked his killing spree from New York to Chicago to Billings. And yesterday, he'd killed twice—in Seattle. He wasn't about to backtrack and go to Las Vegas or Reno so he could murder her estranged husband. He'd talked with Barry recently, gained his trust, and made an appointment to get together with him tonight. That could have only happened someplace near Seattle.

Barry was somewhere in the area, within driving distance.

That was what Gillian had ahead of her, a lot of driving. She would start thirty miles south at the Emerald Queen in Tacoma, then work her way north again to Everett, then up to Anacortes. It would take at least four hours, but she might save Barry's life.

Returning to the kitchen, Gillian grabbed the refrigerator magnet for Redi-Rental.

"You can take my car, hon," Ruth said. "But I think your luck at those casinos will be about as good as ninety percent of their customers, which is slim to none."

"I have to go," Gillian explained. "Even if there's just the *slightest* possibility I can get to Barry before this killer does. I have to try."

"Can I come with you?" Ethan asked.

She shook her head. "I'm sorry, sweetie. Most of these places don't allow anyone under twenty-one in the casinos. Besides, I'll need you to keep Ruth company. Someone has to be here to let the police into Vicki's apartment."

As she got ready to leave, Gillian felt optimistic. After two years, there was a chance she might see Barry again. If only she could get to him in time.

She had a few last-minute instructions for Ruth. "Todd has a mother named Christine. She lives in Arizona—Phoenix or Tucson, my source wasn't sure. I wrote it down on the list we made. Anyway, Todd's mother might know where he is— if you can track her down."

"Will do," Ruth said, handing Gillian her cell phone. "Keep us posted."

"Another call I'd like you to make," Gillian said in a low voice. She slipped the cell phone into her purse, then buttoned up her coat. "Could you phone your friend, Lynn Voorhees, and tell her about Vicki and Chase? Tell her those two people were murdered yesterday—one day after she refused to help us. Will you do that?"

"Yes, I'd like very much to make that call," Ruth said. She

handed Gillian her car keys. "Do you have a photo of Barry to show people?"

Gillian slapped her forehead. "God, I'm such an idiot. Thanks, Ruth. I didn't even think of that." She went back to her study nook and grabbed a framed photo of Barry off the wall. Suddenly, she realized why Jason Hurrell had done the same thing. And it was for the very same reason. He wanted to track down Barry. Obviously, he had an idea where Barry might be, too. Was he hoping to get to her husband before anyone else? And why was that so important to him?

Tucking the framed photo in her purse, Gillian kissed Ethan good-bye. "I'll see you in a few hours."

Ethan nodded. "Say hi to Dad for me, okay?"

Gillian gave him a hug, and then headed for the door.

Chapter 19

"Excuse me, have you seen this man?"

The waitress was young and pretty with a trim, toned figure. Of course, all the waitresses in the grand ballroom of the Golden Eagle Casino in Auburn had to be in good shape considering their uniform: a high-waisted tuxedo blouse, glittery bow tie, spandex miniskirt, and black stockings. Balancing a tray-load of drinks, she paused to glance at the framed photo of Barry for only a moment. "Cute, but no, he doesn't look familiar at all."

"Are you sure?" Gillian asked, talking loudly over all the noise and the music. But the waitress had already moved on.

This wasn't working. Gillian had already spent thirty minutes over at the Emerald Queen Casino, trying to get one of their waitresses or floor people to give her a minute of their time—all to no avail. She'd tried a couple of the cash windows, and a few of the dealers between games. Finally, some big, albino-looking man in a navy blue suit with the casino logo on his breast pocket had approached her, saying he would escort her to the parking lot and she wasn't welcome back.

From the highway, she'd spotted a billboard for the Golden Eagle, and decided to give it a try. She'd been here for twenty minutes now, and it was just like the other casino—except the music was louder, the main room smaller and more crowded, and some woman had accidentally spilled a rum and Coke on her. Fortunately, it didn't show up that much on Gillian's black-slacks-and-sweater ensemble, but she now smelled like a distillery.

She spotted another cocktail waitress. "Excuse me," she said. "I hate to bother you, but could you take a look at this picture and tell me if you—"

"You asked me that fifteen minutes ago!" hissed the brunette with the heavy eyeliner. She carried a tray full of dirty glasses. "The answer's still no. Now, would you please get out of my way?"

"I'm sorry," Gillian said, stepping to the side.

She felt someone touch her arm. She turned to see a tall, formidable-looking man in a security guard's uniform. He had straight brown hair, piercing blue eyes, and only one ear. On the right side of his head, there was a hole and a bunch of pinkish scars where his ear should have been. "Excuse me, ma'am, the manager would like to see you."

"Um, I'm sorry," she said. "I don't mean to bother any-one—"

"You can tell that to Albert," the guard said, leading her away from the tables. "He's the manager, and he wants to talk with you."

She tried to show him the photo of Barry. "If you wouldn't mind—"

"I'm not interested," he grumbled, not even casting a glance at the picture. He took her to a door marked PRIVATE, punched in a security code on the number-pad under the handle, then pushed the door open. After the plush green and gold carpeting and all the gaudy trimmings of the main ball-room, the cement-and-cinder-block stairwell was stark and cold.

The guard wordlessly led her up two flights of stairs. Gillian caught a glimpse of the gold name tag on his navy blue uniform shirt: CHAD. She figured it should have said, MR. PERSONALITY.

She followed him through a series of narrow, slightly grimy corridors to the manager's office. The door was open. Behind the big mahogany desk, a chubby man with a gray comb-over smiled and waved them in while he chatted into the telephone. The office had thick green carpeting, a wall with about a dozen built-in closed-circuit TVs, another wall full of framed licenses, a third wall that was gold-foil-mirrored—and finally, behind the manager's desk, one long window with a view of the casino's main ballroom. Gillian figured he'd seen her down there, and that was how she'd been busted.

Chad, aka Mr. Personality, pointed to one of the two black leather upholstered chairs in front of the manager's desk. "Sit down," he grumbled.

Gillian obeyed. She watched the chubby man on the phone. He was laughing—a jolly chortle. "Oh, that's just like him! Ha!" he bellowed. His laughing turned into a coughing fit; then once he caught his breath, he said, "Listen, I have a pretty lady sitting here, waiting to talk with me. I gotta go."

Gillian figured if she apologized nicely enough, this man might take pity on her. These casinos had detectives and floorwalkers all over the place, and one of them might know Barry. Her husband was very friendly, the type of guy who knew all the clerks' names whenever they went to the supermarket. Certainly, people knew him here. This manager would only have to make a couple of calls.

He hung up the telephone, cocked his head to one side, and smiled at her. "Well, I'm Albert, and I'm the manager here at the Golden Eagle. It looks like you're running some interference with our girls taking the drink orders, and that clogs up the works here."

"I'm very sorry," Gillian said. "I'm trying to track down

my husband, who's been missing for a while. His name is Barry Tanner, and he—"

"Excuse me, excuse me," he said, waving his hand and shaking his head at her. "Mrs. Tanner, I'd like you to take a look at my friend Chad here." He pointed to the security guard.

Gillian turned in her chair, and suddenly a flash went off, blinding her.

It took her a moment to realize what had just happened. Once she could focus on the security guard, Gillian saw the Polaroid camera in his hands. It spit out a photo, which he tossed on the manager's desk.

"This picture of you will go out to our doormen and floor people," Albert announced. "It's SOP with all undesirables. You're bad for business. We get this shit all the time, people looking for missing spouses or kids. And I'm sick of it. If we see you in here again, Mrs. Tanner, you'll be arrested for trespassing."

"Sir, I'm just trying to find my husband," Gillian pleaded. There were still spots in her vision, and she kept blinking. "This is an emergency, a life-or-death situation, and I'm not exaggerating—"

"I don't give a flying fuck about your problems, lady," he cut in. "You're out of here." He nodded at the tall man with one ear. "Take this sorry bitch out the side door. I don't want her going through the casino again."

The guard took hold of her arm and led her out of the office. In the hallway, Gillian wrenched away from him. "Get your hands off me," she growled.

Stone-faced, he pointed her down another hallway, then another. He led her to a different stairwell, but it was just like the other one, all cinder block and cement. She almost stumbled on a step, and grabbed the banister. The photo fell onto the landing. The glass in the frame broke. Chad picked it up and glanced at the picture.

"Give that to me!" Gillian said, tears in her eyes. She didn't want to cry in front of this big creep. But she felt so defeated.

He handed the framed photo back to her, then opened a metal door.

Clutching the broken picture, Gillian paused in the doorway. It led to an alley—with four big Dumpsters along the side of the building. "Where's the parking lot from here?" she asked, unable to look at the guard. She just wanted to get out of there.

"Ma'am, I know him," she heard the guard say.

Gillian turned and stared at the man.

He nodded. "I recognized him in the picture. He's a really nice guy—only I know him as Frank. Frank Dorsett."

"Have you—have you seen him recently?" Gillian asked. "Do you know where he is?"

"Last time he was in here was almost two years ago. But he was a regular here for a while. You told Asshole Albert upstairs this is a matter of life and death. Is that true?"

Gillian anxiously nodded.

"C'mon, I'll walk you to your car," Chad said. "I know someone who saw him not too long ago. But I'm not sure you want to hear about it."

"Go ahead," Gillian said. "I'd be grateful for anything you can tell me."

"This cocktail waitress who used to work here, her name's Andrea, she and Frank—your husband—they had kind of a thing going on a while back. If it's any consolation, I don't think it was anything too serious."

Gillian didn't break her stride as they walked down the alley together. She'd been in such deep denial during her years with Barry. It had taken his leaving for her to realize— along with all his other secrets—he'd probably strayed too. She swallowed hard, and told herself that it didn't matter anymore. "Go on," she said.

"Andrea eighty-sixed this dump a while back. She works

at the Club Royale up in Anacortes now, but we still talk. She told me she ran into Frank about six weeks ago."

"In Anacortes? He was in Anacortes?"

Chad nodded. "Want me to call her?"

At the end of the alley, they came to the parking lot. Music churning over a speaker system by the entrance competed with traffic noise from the nearby freeway. "Hold on for a second, okay?" Chad took out his cell phone and backtracked into the alley.

Gillian remained at the edge of the alleyway, watching him talk on his cell phone. He cupped a hand over the hole where he once might have had an ear. Gillian glanced at the photo of Barry again—behind the cracked glass of the frame. She couldn't believe he'd been in Anacortes—only eighty miles away—just six weeks ago. The copycat killer wasn't lying to her about finding Barry. Her husband was still alive— and not so far away. Even if she had to find him through some woman he'd been sleeping with, Gillian was ready do whatever it took. She had to get to him before this killer did.

Tucking the phone in his pocket, Chad lumbered up to her. "Do you mind driving up to Anacortes today?"

"No, not at all," Gillian said.

"Andrea works the main room. She's not there yet. Her shift starts at two today. But when you get there, ask for Paul Dwoskin. He's expecting you. He's a floorwalker there, nice guy. He knows your husband too. He'll hook you up with Andrea."

Gillian nodded. "Thank you, thank you very much."

"I hope you find your husband, ma'am," Chad said. "It's none of my business, but I hope you can forgive him too. He's a pretty damn nice guy. Tell him old One-Ear-Chad said hello, okay?"

Gillian impulsively hugged him, and kissed him on the cheek. Still holding Barry's picture to her chest, she hurried toward the car.

* * *

He showed the photo of Barry and Gillian to the desk clerk. She was a thin, brown-haired woman in her late thirties with lipstick on her teeth and a green cardigan over her T-shirt. The lobby was tiny—with room for two orange plastic bucket-style chairs and a Formica table, which supported a Mr. Coffee machine, a stack of Styrofoam cups, a bowl of sugar packets, and a canister of Coffeemate. He'd torn the clerk away from the TV behind the counter. Right now, Paul Newman was talking with Eva Marie Saint, but they were on mute.

Jason drummed his fingers on the countertop while the woman studied the photo. "Yeah, I know him," she said at last. "He stayed here for a few weeks a while back—maybe four or five months ago."

"Does the name Barry Tanner ring a bell?"

She snuck a peek at her TV, then shook her head. "No. I think this guy's name was Frank."

"Could you check your registration records?"

She shook her head. "Everything before last month is in the basement, and I don't have a key. You could ask the owner, but he'll probably tell you to get lost—unless you're a cop. You aren't a cop, are you?"

Sighing, Jason took the framed photo from her. "No, I'm not with the police."

"What do you want to see this guy for anyway?" the woman asked.

"I owe him some money," Jason lied. He headed for the lobby door. "Thanks for your time."

He would try the next hotel down the road.

"Anyway, this person saw Barry only six weeks ago," Gillian said into her cell phone. She had just passed a sign along the Interstate that read: ANACORTES FERRIES—17 MILES "I'm on my way to this casino in Anacortes so I can talk to her."

"*Her?*" Ruth repeated.

"Yes, *her*, and at this point, it doesn't matter." Gillian sighed. "Put Ethan on, okay?"

"He can't talk right now. He decided to give Eustace a bath and he's up to his elbows in suds and dog. What do you want me to tell him?"

"Just say what I told you, and that I think we may be close to getting in touch with his dad. So maybe something good might come out of all this."

Gillian heard water splashing on the other end of the line, then Ruth explaining to Ethan that his father had been in Anacortes only a few weeks ago. *"Really?"* he kept asking while Ruth relayed the information to him. "And your mom says maybe some good might come from all this," she heard Ruth finish up.

"God, that's fantastic! Awesome, Mom!" Ethan shouted.

"Watch the dog, honey," Ruth said, her voice a little muffled. "Eustace, stay! Gill, we're going through all your towels here. I'm going to put a load in your wash. Is there anything else you need cleaned while I'm at it?"

"I got stuff!" Ethan piped up.

"No, and please, don't do my laundry," Gillian said, glancing in her rearview mirror.

"It's no sweat. Listen, I connected with Todd's mother in Tucson. I just got off the horn with her about an hour ago. Don't drive off the road when you hear this. . . ."

"I'm listening," Gillian said.

"Todd died from a drug overdose eight months ago. He was living in Los Angeles. No foul play as far as they know. You don't have anyone dying of a drug overdose in any of your books, do you?"

"No, I—I don't," Gillian answered numbly.

"Then I don't think our copycat had anything to do with it."

"Where does this leave us—suspect-wise?" Gillian said. "Do you really think it's Jason?"

"Well, he's in the lead by default."

"In the lead over whom?" Gillian asked. "Who else is there?"

"There's . . ." Ruth trailed off.

"There's who? Go ahead, say it."

"You know who I'm thinking about," Ruth whispered. "You've considered the possibility too, I know you have."

Gillian sighed. "It's not Barry."

"I'm not going to say anything else—except you've always been in denial when it comes to him, hon. And now you're on your way to go see him. I keep thinking you're walking into a trap—or *driving* to one. Just be careful and make sure no one's following you. Okay?"

"Okay," she said. "But it's not Barry. And don't do my laundry—please."

"Call me in an hour with an update," Ruth said. "And don't call again while you're driving my car. I can't stand cell phone drivers. My car, my rules. Bye, hon." She hung up.

Gillian clicked off the line, then stashed the phone back in her purse. She checked her rearview mirror again—looking for any familiar cars. She'd been checking routinely ever since she'd left the house this morning. She was pretty certain no one was following her.

One thing she was more certain about was Barry's innocence. He was capable of a lot of things, but he could never murder anyone.

Still, she understood why Ruth might have suspected him. Barry certainly fit the bill. The copycat killer had to be charming; otherwise he couldn't have gotten close to his victims. And he obviously knew Gillian very well. But it wasn't Barry, damn it.

No, the killer was connected to that class or the school, and Barry had visited the school only once. This person knew the place inside out. He was the Schoolgirl Killer. He'd left the saddle shoes for her yesterday. It was his way of telling her, *"Yes, I'm the one who killed before."* And maybe he'd done it for her.

"What will the famous and beautiful mystery author do for me?"

She remembered his coy little grin when he'd asked her that question, and she shuddered.

Why hadn't she thought of him before? She'd been focusing on that one particular class. But he was at the college; he'd been there when those three women were murdered, his three "schoolgirls."

"How come you've never written a mystery based on that? The Schoolgirl Murders, it would make a good one."

He knew the students in her class—and in every class. He knew when people were coming and going there, because that information was always at his fingertips.

Gillian clutched the steering wheel tightly. "Oh, my God," she muttered to herself. It all made sense.

Rick in Administration had always been coming on to her. She'd even gotten a little snippy with him for flirting so much the other night. She'd apologized a minute later.

She remembered Rick smiling at her and saying, *"That's okay. I'll see you make it up to me."*

"Hon, you better hold onto him, or he'll run right outside."

Ethan grabbed Eustace by the collar, then opened the door for Ruth. She was carrying a laundry basket full of damp and dirty towels. "You sure I can't carry that for you?" he asked.

"I'm fine. Just hold onto His Nibs."

"Where do you want me to hold him?"

"By the collar, honey," Ruth said, waddling out the door. "You're doing fine."

She carried the towels, which smelled appropriately enough

like wet dog, down the porch steps. As she turned the corner, the light went on above the cellar door. Ethan had given her the keys. At the bottom of the narrow cement steps to the basement, Ruth paused and balanced the laundry basket against her hip while she fished the keys out of her pocket. She unlocked the door. She'd been in the dungeonlike little cellar for the first time just last night—when the cops had gone over the place. It was pretty damn creepy, and she didn't creep out easily. There were no windows at all. It was just an unfinished wood and cement hole with enough room for a furnace, hot-water heater, some gardening tools, and the washer and dryer. The ceiling was only a few inches above her head, and she felt inclined to duck while in there. Hoisting the laundry basket to the washer, Ruth had to step aside to avoid the glaring bare lightbulb that dangled from a cord in the ceiling. She loaded the damp towels into the washer, but suddenly stopped.

Eustace let out a few yelps upstairs.

She listened for a moment, waiting for him to quiet down. But he kept barking.

Someone was coming toward the house.

Ruth put down a towel and moved toward the door. She brushed against the hanging lightbulb, and it swung from side to side. The cramped little room seemed to spin as shadows raced around the unfinished walls. Just as she reached the door, Ruth froze.

Someone stood at the bottom of the cement stairs, blocking her only exit. His back was to the sun. She couldn't see his face.

Before Ruth could move again, he slammed the door shut.

Ruth rattled the knob and pushed. But the door didn't budge. Past Eustace's relentless barking, she heard an object scraping against the cement. He'd propped a shovel or something against the door, she could tell. There was no way she could get out.

"Ethan?" she heard him call in a soft, singsong voice. "Ethan? Can you come out and play?"

Eustace was going berserk, running back and forth from the living room window to the front door. He wouldn't stop barking.

Ethan could hear a pounding below. For a moment, he thought the washing machine had malfunctioned. Then he realized it was Ruth downstairs, banging on the cellar door. He saw a shadow pass across the living room drapes. Someone was on the porch.

Past all Eustace's barking, and that hammering downstairs, he heard Ruth screaming: *"Ethan, call 911! Ethan? Ethan?"*

He ran into his bedroom and grabbed the baseball bat from his bedside. His heart was racing. The way Ruth was screaming scared him more than anything else. She'd always seemed so tough and unflappable. *This is it,* he thought. Someone was here to kill them.

Listen to her . . . get to a phone . . . call the police . . .

Clutching the bat, he hurried out of the bedroom. Eustace scurried into his path, and Ethan tripped over him. The dog let out a yelp as Ethan slammed against the wall and knocked over a picture. The glass in the frame shattered. The baseball bat flew out of his hands and Ethan hit the floor—hard. But he barely felt it. In a daze, he watched the bat roll to one side of the couch.

Blinking, he glanced over toward the front door. He hadn't locked it, because he'd thought Ruth would be back from the basement in a minute.

He could still hear her screaming at him to call the police. He started to get to his feet, but then he saw the door open. Ethan froze.

Barking furiously, Eustace charged the intruder. The man darted to one side and kicked the dog in its ribs. Eustace gave out a shrill bark and recoiled. The man kicked him again—this time, out the door.

Ethan could tell he'd hurt the dog. The man was wearing the same boots he'd had on two days ago when he'd kicked the crap out of Tate Barringer.

Joe stepped in and slammed the door before Eustace could lunge at him again. "Hey, dude," he said, with a lop-sided grin. "We didn't finish telling secrets yesterday. You owe me one."

"What are you talking about?" Ethan asked, out of breath.

"Ethan? Ethan!" Ruth cried out. She continued to bang on the cellar door.

Eustace couldn't have been too hurt, because he was still barking—and scratching at the front door. Together, Ruth and Eustace were making so much noise, nearly everyone on the block could have heard them.

Joe stomped on the floor with his boot. "Hey, you, down in the basement!" he yelled. "If you don't shut the fuck up, I'm going to hurt this kid! I mean it!"

Ethan started to get to his feet. "What do you want?"

Joe came toward him. "Tell her to shut up," he growled.

"What—"

Joe hauled back, then slapped him across the face with such force, it sent him crashing to the floor again. For a moment, Ethan couldn't see anything. His ears were ringing, yet he could still hear the banging downstairs and Eustace yelping. Joe was screaming at him to shut up his dog.

Ethan's head was throbbing. Dazed, he tried to focus on Joe, who hovered over him with his fist clenched. "Want another?"

"Ruth!" Ethan called. He was surprised his mouth was still working. It felt like his jaw had been unhinged. "Ruth . . . please . . . stop! Tell, Eustace to be quiet! Please!"

All at once, the pounded ceased. *"Eustace, shut up!"* she shouted from the cellar. The dog let out one more bark, then fell silent. *"Good boy,"* Ruth called more softly.

Joe stood over him. "Where's your old lady?"

Ethan was still trying to get his breath. The left side of his face seemed to be burning up. "She—she's out. She won't be back until later."

"Where's Al?" he asked.

"Who?"

"Al. He's one of my buddies. He's been watching your place for over a week—waiting for your daddy to make a return engagement. Al's been missing since Friday night. He checked in saying he was here, casing the place. This afternoon, they found his car off Rainer Avenue—all picked apart. Where the fuck is he, kid? Did somebody whack him? Did Daddy come back and decide to be a hero?"

Ethan started to shake his head, but it hurt. "No. I—I don't know what you're talking about."

"Who's the bitch downstairs?" Joe asked.

"She's a friend of my mom's."

Joe grinned. "Think maybe if I worked her over, she'd tell me something?"

"Tell you what? She—she doesn't know anything either. Please . . ." He squirmed away, dragging himself across the floor until his shoulders were against the wall. He glanced down at his shirt and saw blood. Then he touched his mouth. He hadn't realized his lip was bleeding until now. "Listen, if this—this—Al guy was watching the house, none of us saw him. I swear. Friday night we went out to eat. Nothing happened when we came home. We didn't see anyone. We—"

Ethan stopped himself. He remembered seeing Jason Hurrell come up from the ravine late that night. He'd said Vickie had seen someone in the yard.

"What?" Joe pressed.

Ethan faked a coughing fit. "Nothing," he said. "We didn't see anyone. And even if we did, do you really think my mom or I could have killed your friend?"

"That's why I was asking if your daddy came back, smart-ass."

"I told you—"

The telephone rang, and Ethan immediately shut up.

Joe looked over toward the phone in the study nook. Ethan quickly glanced around for the baseball bat. It was by the sofa—behind Joe. Ethan couldn't hope to reach it.

The answering machine clicked on. The beep sounded. *"Hi, one of you must be on the phone,"* his mother said. *"You'll be happy to know, Ruth, I'm not calling from the car. I'm on foot—in the parking lot of the casino. I'm about to talk with this woman who knows Barry. . . ."*

Joe let out a surprised laugh.

"I'll give you another shout when I'm finished here. In fact—Ruth, I need you to check something out for me, a new lead. So call me when you get this. Okay? Wish me luck. Love you guys."

There was a click, and then the answering machine let out a beep.

Joe grinned at Ethan. "So—Mama's at a casino, following a new lead? She's talking to Daddy's lady friend?" Joe leaned in toward him. "Something's going on, something about your old man and where he's hiding. Why aren't you sharing this with your good buddy?" His hand came up to Ethan's neck. He pushed him against the wall. "You still owe me a secret, Ethan."

Chapter 20

Gillian waited by the dollar slot machines at the lobby's edge in the Club Royale Casino Resort. She'd spoken with Paul Dwoskin, a handsome man in a navy blue suit. He was kind of a throwback to the seventies with his handlebar mustache and sideburns. He had a lot of nice things to say about *Frank,* but seemed ill at ease. Small wonder. In a few moments, he would be introducing *Frank's* wife to *Frank's* girlfriend. He'd left Gillian there while he navigated through the crowded main room to find Andrea.

Gillian glanced at her wristwatch: 2:25. She'd thought Ruth would have phoned her right back after she'd left that message fifteen minutes ago. They couldn't have stepped out. She would call home again as soon as she finished here. Maybe Ruth could get one of her detective friends to check on Rick's background, and find out what he'd been doing the past few days. Had he had time for trips to New York, Chicago, or Montana during the last two weeks?

She wondered about two years ago. Certainly, they would have questioned Rick about the Schoolgirl Murders. All the male faculty and administration staff at the college had been under heavy scrutiny. What kind of alibi had he given the cops?

"Gillian?"

She hadn't even seen her coming. Gillian turned to her left, a cordial smile already plastered on her face. Barry's girlfriend was pretty, with a pale complexion and wavy red hair. Her skimpy waitress uniform—a form-fitting, black tuxedo jacket with emerald-green lapels—showed off her long legs and statuesque figure. She was almost as tall as Paul, standing behind her.

"Well, I'll leave you two at it," he said, retreating back into the noisy chaos of the main room.

"Andrea . . . hi." Gillian extended her hand. "Thanks for agreeing to see me. I know this is pretty awkward."

"No kidding." Andrea shook hands with her. "Listen, I can't talk long. We're kind of swamped right now." She tucked her empty tray under her arm, then glanced back at the main room for a moment. She turned to Gillian again. "So—Paul told me that Frank—um, well, your husband—he's in some kind of trouble. Is that true? Or are you just pissed off? I mean, if you've come here to bitch-slap me or something, then let's get it over with."

"I'm not mad at you," Gillian heard herself say. "I was telling Paul the truth. My husband's in trouble. I need to get to him before someone else does. And his real name's Barry, by the way."

"Barry, huh?" A wistful smile came to her face. "Suits him. He told me his name wasn't really Frank. A lot of these closet gamblers keep different identities. A lot of them are in trouble too. I knew your husband was in way over his head. But that's been going on for a few years now. This 'trouble' you're talking about, is it something new?"

Gillian nodded. "He might be dead by tonight if I don't get to him in time."

Andrea's eyes searched hers for a moment. Finally, she took a deep breath. "Listen—Gillian, you should know, he loves you. What he and I had was physical, yeah. But we were mostly friends. He helped me out when I got into this mess with this guy a while back. Never mind the details. But I won't forget how Frank—*Barry* was there for me."

"Well, I'm glad he was there for *someone*," Gillian murmured. Then she quickly shook her head. "I'm sorry. This is very difficult for me. It—it's good Barry was able to help you when you needed help. And now maybe you can return the favor. I understand you saw him here about six weeks ago."

Andrea nodded. "It was more like five weeks, but yes, he paid me a visit."

Gillian didn't say anything. She wondered why Barry would visit his old girlfriend, but not bother to contact his wife and son. She told herself once more that it didn't matter. "Um, did he say where he's living now? Do you know how I could get in touch with him?"

"No. He just kind of showed up out of the blue. He took me out for a couple of drinks after my shift ended. He didn't say where he's been living. It's still not safe for him to show his face in Seattle or anywhere around there. Then again, you already know that."

Gillian just nodded.

"If it's any help, he was driving an old Nissan with Montana plates. I don't remember the number. I asked him whose car it was, and he said it was his. So my guess is he's living there. And if it's any consolation to you, all we did during this visit was share a couple of drinks together. Nothing else happened."

"He drove all the way from Montana just to take you out for a couple of drinks?"

Andrea shook her head and let out a little laugh. "God, no. He made the trip for *you*."

"What are you talking about? I haven't seen him in almost two years."

"You write some kind of mysteries, right? Frank—*Barry*

never told me any of the titles. I guess he was afraid of me finding out his real name through one of your books. Anyway, you just published a new book five weeks ago, right?"

Gillian nodded.

"That's why he took a chance and drove to Seattle. He's come back twice that I know of. Both times, it's been to see you. Doesn't some bookstore in your neighborhood always throw a 'signing party' for you?"

Gillian nodded. "Broadway Books."

"Well, your husband was there for at least two of them. He watched through the store window. You had about twenty people attending the last time, and your son was there too. Barry said you both looked like you were doing okay. He's really proud of you and your books."

Gillian just shook her head. She couldn't believe Barry had gotten so close to her—and didn't let her know.

"Anyway, he saw you that night, and then drove up here to say hi to me. He told me he was headed home early the next day." Andrea reached into the pocket of her tuxedo jacket. "Chad from the Golden Eagle gave me a call about an hour ago and told me you might be coming. So I remembered to bring this."

She handed Gillian a business card:

SALVADOR ("SAL") SALGADO
Private Investigations
PROFESSIONAL, CONFIDENTIAL & EXPERIENCED

There was a Portland address and phone number on the card.

"Did you hire this guy to find Barry?" Andrea asked.

Mystified, Gillian looked up from the card and shook her head. "I've never heard of him."

"Well, this joker—very slick, Vegas is full of characters like him—he came into the casino a few nights after—um, *Barry,*" Andrea explained. "He asked all sorts of questions.

He had your husband's photo and asked if I knew Frank Dorsett. I told him yes, but I hadn't seen him in a couple of years. Then he read off about five other aliases. Now that I'm thinking back, *Barry* was one of them. Y'know, when your husband first disappeared two years ago, I had some of these low-life types waltzing in here making inquiries about him. But I could tell they were clueless, chasing down any lead they could. This Sal Salgado character was different. I had the feeling he was closing in on Barry. I remember wishing I knew how to get in touch with your husband, because I wanted to warn him about this guy."

Gillian glanced at the business card again. "Can I keep this?"

"Sure. The only reason I saved it was to give it to Barry if he ever showed up again."

"Did this Sal Salgado mention the people who had hired him?"

Andrea nodded. "I was getting to that. See, I said to this private dick: 'Who are these people you work for anyway? They've been looking for Frank for two years now. Why don't they just give up already?' And he told me that he wasn't working for Frank's 'business associates.' He knew all about them. He'd been employed by someone else. And this part really stuck with me. He said, 'Her reasons for wanting to find this man are very personal.' "

"*Her* reasons?" Gillian repeated, making sure she'd heard right.

Andrea nodded. "That's why I asked earlier if you were the one who hired him."

"Hello, Mr. Salgado?" she said after the beep. Gillian stood by Ruth's Toyota in the parking lot of the Club Royale Casino. She had the cell phone to her ear. "My name is Gillian Tanner. I understand you may have located my husband, Barry, for someone. I'm prepared to pay double whatever this other client paid you—for the same information. I can assure you, I'd keep it totally confidential. The hitch is, you need to get back to me right away. This is a one-time offer, Mr. Salgado. Please, call me on my cell phone at 206-555-1771. I hope to hear from you."

She clicked off the line, then checked her cell phone again to see if Ruth or Ethan had returned her call. It had been almost a half hour, and they hadn't gotten back to her yet.

Gillian hit the speed dial for her home number, then counted the ring tones. After four rings, the machine picked up—and she felt her heart sink a little.

Ruth heard the phone ringing again upstairs.

She'd been listening to Ethan and that man, but what they said was muffled and indecipherable. Occasionally, the man had raised his voice: *"I'm not fucking kidding you!"* he'd bellowed at one point.

All the while, she'd heard Eustace's paws clicking against the front porch floor as he paced back and forth. He'd whimpered—and every few minutes let out a single bark.

Ruth figured the intruder upstairs must not have been listening too carefully. For the last ten minutes, she'd been gnawing away at a section of the old cellar door with a garden spade. She'd dodged the flying splinters of wood as she repeatedly hit the same spot with a series of quick little jabs and scrapes. It seemed to be taking forever, and she was sweating. But she saw a tiny crack of daylight in the area she'd been working on.

Still, she guessed it might be another twenty minutes before she'd made a hole big enough to reach through the door and move that damn shovel. By then, Ethan could be dead.

Upstairs, the phone stopped ringing. She heard a distant mechanical beep, and then a voice—muffled, but recognizable. It was Gillian.

* * *

"Hi, it's me again," his mother was saying on the answering machine.

Ethan sat on the floor, with his back to the wall and his knees up to his chest. Joe pulled over a chair and sat down in front of him.

"Listen, I'm worried because I haven't heard back from you," Ethan's mother said. *"So call me. Ethan, I really think we're close to finding out where Dad is. Anyway, give me a call as soon as you get this. Bye."*

Joe nodded pensively. "Y'know, I believed you yesterday when you told me you had no idea where your dad was. But it looks like things have changed in the last twenty-four hours. Let me give you a little background information, so you know the score as far as your old man is concerned. Okay, Ethan?"

Ethan just nodded.

"This big shot in my organization has a fuck-up son, who did a really stupid thing when he arranged a little heist with one of your dad's trucks. A guy got killed, and your dad's testimony could put this kid away for a long, long time. Actually, I don't give a crap what happens to this big shot's son. The guy's an asshole. But his father doesn't want to see him go to jail. That's why they haven't given up on your daddy. He's a bad loose end. I'd be a real hero in the organization if I could track him down. No more shit-assignments like when they stuck me with you. I could write my own ticket. Now, how about if you do your buddy, Joe, a favor and tell me where I can find your old man."

Ethan stole another glance at the baseball bat on the floor over by the sofa. If Joe had noticed it at all, he didn't seem very concerned about it. Ethan's eyes met Joe's. "I don't know any more than you do," he said, shrugging. That was the truth. He could tell this bastard everything he knew—

and none of it would help. "My mother went looking for my dad at a bunch of casinos today. You heard what she said on the first message. I don't know anything else, I swear."

Frowning, Joe heaved a sigh. "Well, I believe you, Ethan. That's why you're going to do what Mama told you. You're going to call her back, and find out exactly where she is and what she knows."

Ethan automatically shook his head. "I—I can't do that. It won't work. She'll know something's wrong. She'll hear it in my voice. Besides—"

"Goddamn it, Ethan!" he roared. Joe quickly shot out of the chair, which tipped over behind him. "You saw what I did to that clown in front of the locker room the other day. I didn't even break a sweat. Hell, I wasn't even mad at the guy. But you're pissing me off, Ethan." He moved toward the cordless phone in the study nook. "Now, you're going to be a good little faggot and call your mommy."

As soon as Joe's back was turned, Ethan started to go for the baseball bat.

But Joe swiveled around. All at once, he was coming at him, ready to kick. Ethan felt a powerful, hammerlike blow to his stomach. He hit the floor with a thud.

"Shit, Ethan, now look what you made me do," Joe said.

Ethan couldn't breathe. He curled up on the floor, feeling sick.

Joe bent over him, and stroked his hair. "Now, I want you to lie there and think about the fact that I'm merely starting with you, kid. I ain't leaving here without the information I want. And you're going to help me. Otherwise, I'll put you in the hospital. And before I'm done with you, I'll take a little break, and go to work on the cunt downstairs. You lie there and think about that, Ethan."

Ruth heard the loud thump overhead. A bit of dust plumed from the basement ceiling. She stopped whittling away at the door for a moment. Someone had been knocked to the floor upstairs, and she was pretty certain it had been Ethan. The son of a bitch was beating him.

She stared at the little crevice she'd made in the door, barely enough room for her to fit her fingers through it. "The hell with this," she grumbled, dropping the spade. There were a bunch of other garden tools against the wall. Ruth grabbed a pitchfork. With a firm grasp on the handle, she slammed into the spot on which she'd been working. The thick prongs made a crack in the door. She gave it another hit, and a section of wood split. She felt the shovel give a little on the other side of the door; its blade scraped against the concrete steps. Ruth bashed the door again and again. Splinters of wood flew—and the gap in the door became wider.

Eustace started barking again.

Ruth kept slamming away at the door. Covered in sweat, she tried to get her breath. The air in the dank little cellar was bad. But daylight—and fresh air—poured through the opening. She could see the shovel propped up against the door handle.

She stopped and reached her hand through the hole. Frantically, she groped for the shovel handle. At last, she knocked the shovel to the side. It clattered as it hit the concrete.

She heard footsteps—and the man yelling upstairs.

"Goddamn it!" Joe bellowed. He abruptly pulled away from Ethan, and gave the back of his head a swat.

It hurt, but Ethan barely felt it compared to the lingering agony from being kicked in the gut a minute ago. He managed to sit up. He'd gotten his breath back a little. Blinking, he tried to focus on Joe, who was pulling out a gun from inside his leather jacket. He stomped toward the window and peered outside. He'd clearly become unnerved by all the pounding on the door again. Eustace's barking seemed even

louder and more frenzied than before. And just a moment
ago, there was a loud clang as something hit the basement
steps.

"Pain-in-the-ass bitch," Joe growled. He turned away
from the window and started for the front door.

Ethan grabbed the baseball bat, and got up from the floor.
But he'd stood up too quick. The room was spinning and he
felt nauseous. He could barely see anything—except Joe with
his back to him. Even Joe was sort of blurry. Still, Ethan didn't
hesitate. He kept moving.

He already had the baseball bat raised in the air when Joe
turned around. With all his might, Ethan swung the bat and
clipped the side of Joe's head. There was a loud snap. Joe let
out a sharp cry, then he fell back against the door. The gun
flew out of his hand. He crumpled to the floor.

Ethan was barely aware of footsteps on the front porch.
He hardly noticed that Eustace had stopped barking. But
then he heard Ruth's voice. "Good boy," she said to the dog.

The front door opened—as far as it could. Joe's crumpled
body blocked the threshold.

Ethan spotted Ruth on the front porch. She had the pitchfork in her hands. Eustace was behind her. She glanced
down at Joe, lying in her path. Then she looked at Ethan.
Catching her breath, she nodded and gave him a little smile.
"Good boy," she whispered.

Gillian's cell phone rang just as she climbed into the
Toyota. "Oh, thank God," she murmured, reaching into her
purse. It had to be Ruth or Ethan calling back. She clicked
on the phone without checking the caller identification.
"Hello?" she said anxiously.

"Is this Gillian Tanner?" someone asked.

Crestfallen, she slumped back in the driver's seat and
rubbed her forehead. "Yes. Who's calling?"

"Sal Salgado calling. Listen, Mrs. Tanner, I need to know.

Does this 'one time only' offer you're throwing at me in-
clude a free toaster-oven?"

Gillian frowned. "I was serious, Mr. Salgado."

"Okay, lighten up, jeez. I'm willing to talk—but not on
the phone."

"Well, I don't think I can make it down to Portland
today," Gillian said. "I'm kind of pressed for time."

"I happen to be in Seattle right now. Where are you?
Sounds like you're in a car."

"I'm in the parking lot of a casino in—" Gillian stopped
herself. She remembered what Ruth had said about walking—or *driving*—into a trap by trying to track down Barry.
"Um, I'm about two hours from Seattle. I can meet you
someplace in the city."

"Well, I've never been on top of the Space Needle. I understand there's a bar up there. I'll see you there at six-thirty.
Come alone, and bring your checkbook."

"How will I know you?"

"Oh, I'll know you, Gillian. I like mysteries. I'm a big
fan. See you at six-thirty."

"Wait. Before you hang up, tell me this much. Did you locate my husband?"

"Yes, ma'am, I certainly did."

Behind the registration desk there was a small, handwritten
cardboard sign taped to a shelf displaying a collection of
troll dolls: NOT 4 SALE! The sale items—dust-covered overnight kits, gum, Rolaids, condoms, and car deodorizers—
were crammed onto the shelf below the troll collection.

The desk clerk was a big oafish-looking man in his thirties. He had receding blond hair, and wore a purple bowling
shirt. He kept wheezing as he studied the framed photo of
Barry and Gillian in front of Pike Street Market.

Jason bit his lip and waited patiently. The Tuck-U Inn was

the twentieth motel he'd visited this afternoon—and one of the cheesiest.

"Yeah, I know this guy," the desk clerk said at last. "He stayed with us—hmmm, back in September for a few weeks. He was casino-crazy, coming and going at all hours. His name's Garner, Frank Garner. I always thought he was a nice enough guy. But he really ticked off the manager, because he smuggled a hot plate and a microwave into his room. So they gave him the boot."

"Have you seen him at all since?" Jason asked.

"Nope. But some private detective was snooping around here looking for Frank about five weeks ago."

"Did he say why he was looking for Frank?"

The desk clerk shook his head. "No. But I'll tell you what I told this private eye guy. All you have to do is go to all the casinos in the area, and if you don't find Frank Garner, then he's moved on to another city." He sighed and nodded. "Y'know, I'll bet he's done just that. I have a feeling, mister. You might be wasting your time looking for him here in Missoula."

"Are you sure everything's all right?" Gillian asked. She was on her cell phone, and stuck in bumper-to-bumper traffic about thirty miles north of Seattle.

The last hour and a half had been sheer agony while she'd waited to hear back from Ruth and Ethan. Two more calls to the house had gone unanswered. She'd been convinced something awful had happened at home. She'd started speeding toward Seattle—until hitting this traffic jam a half hour ago. Gillian had been thinking about calling the police when her cell phone had rung.

"Ethan's fine, hon," Ruth had assured her. She'd said she was calling from a pay phone in the police station, and suggested Gillian pull over to hear what she had to tell her.

"I haven't moved in the last ten minutes," Gillian had

replied. "So I'm not about to swerve off the road or anything. What's going on? Why are you at the police station? Are you sure Ethan's okay?"

Ruth had told her about the unexpected visit from Joe Pagani, who was now in Harborview Hospital with a mild concussion—and under police guard. Ethan had a cut lip and a bruised rib. Eustace, who yelped in pain every time Ruth touched his side, would be spending the night at the vet's. And Gillian's landlord probably wouldn't be too happy about the broken door to the cellar.

"You're not just telling me this now and saving the real bad news for later?" Gillian asked warily.

"No. The bad news is you have about two more hours to track down Barry before the cops and these hoods start putting the pressure on. I pulled some strings, and the detectives with this Joe Pagani character aren't letting him make any calls for a while. Like I say, I figure two hours. As soon as he talks to his lawyer or anyone else, these mobsters are going to know you're on the verge of tracking down Barry."

"What about the police?" Gillian asked.

"Well, Joe ain't gonna say anything to them. His buddies want to get to Barry before the police do."

"No, I meant, do the police know what I'm doing?" Gillian asked.

"Ethan and I got it covered, hon," Ruth said. "We erased your phone messages. And Ethan's talking to a couple of detectives right now. The story he and I agreed on is that you took my car to chase down a new lead in the copycat killings. And we haven't been able to get ahold of you since. It's more or less the truth."

"I need to see Ethan."

"You'd just be an extra body here. You need to find out where Barry is, and you have to act fast. Ethan's fine. He's better than fine. He's the hero of the hour. The other good news is my buddies in blue seem to be taking this copycat business more seriously. I had Lynn Voorhees eating a hearty helping of crow earlier. On the downside, they probably won't have the paperwork to go through Vicki's apartment until tomorrow morning. And divers in Elliott Bay came up with a few more pieces of Chase's car and an arm."

Gillian winced at the news. "Ruth, could you do me another favor? I thought of someone who might be our man. Could you use your connections to get some information about this guy Rick? He works in Administration at the college. Among other things, he handles student and class records, which gives him access to information on everyone's comings and goings at the school."

"Hmmm, so he would have known when all his *schoolgirls* had their classes. . . ."

"Bingo. Also, he'd be well acquainted with the layout of the college."

"All those creative places he'd left the bodies, I hear you."

"And I've never had a single conversation with Rick in which he hasn't come on to me."

"Does this Rick have a last name?"

Gillian didn't know it. "Just a second." She dropped the cell phone in her lap for a moment while she searched through her purse. Finally, she found the old class printout. On the top left corner was some computer-related gibberish, which included the job name and the administrative employee who had executed it: R. SLAUGHTER.

Gillian got back on her cell phone. "His name's Rick—I'm guessing *Richard*—Slaughter."

"*Slaughter,* well, that's appropriate. I'll check if he has a rap sheet here, and then do some more digging. What about your expedition? Did you dig up anything about Barry?"

Gillian told her about the Space Needle meeting with Sal Salgado. "He claims he found Barry."

"Well, you be careful with him, hon. I'll poke around here and find out if this Salgado is a legitimate PI. Even if he is, it doesn't make him a boy scout. Proceed with caution."

"According to his business card, he works out of Portland," Gillian said. "Um, did Jason Hurrell ever call the house?"

"Not that I know of," Ruth replied. "At least, he didn't leave any messages. Listen, I need to hang up. There's a cop down the hallway looking at me funny. They think I'm on the phone with my sister."

"You sure Ethan's okay?" Gillian asked one more time before Ruth hung up.

"He's peachy. We both are. Just look out for your own ass for the next couple of hours."

After Gillian clicked off the line, she let out a sigh. Yet she still felt horribly tense and clenched. She glanced at her watch, and then at the gridlock ahead. The car in front of her crawled forward a few feet, and she followed suit. Some of the other cars were actually moving too. There was a good chance she'd get to the Space Needle in time for her 6:30 meeting with Sal Salgado.

But her chances for getting to Barry in time still seemed very, very uncertain.

Gillian parked in a pay lot across the street from the Seattle Center. It began to drizzle as she walked two blocks to the Space Needle. The Experience Music Project nearby was already closed for the night, but a few stragglers were still hanging around. Gillian glanced at their faces. She didn't recognize anyone—and no one seemed to be watching her. She kept thinking about Ruth's warning to proceed with caution. Ruth still hadn't gotten back to her about Sal Salgado, but it had been only forty minutes since Gillian had last talked to her.

Gillian stepped in the ticket line for the Space Needle's scenic elevator. She remembered Ruth's other warning—earlier today. What if that e-mail forecasting Barry's death was some kind of trick? Someone could be following her, hoping she'd lead them to Barry. Or perhaps this was all an elaborate trap, and it was *her* death someone had planned for tonight.

Gillian took some solace in the fact that none of her books featured a murder scene in or around the Space Needle.

She got to the ticket window and pulled out her wallet. A group had gathered for the next elevator ride.

"Gillian? Mrs. Tanner?"

She turned to see a lean, swarthy-looking Latino man with a goatee and perfectly groomed, moussed hair that miraculously resisted the light rain. He wore a brown leather jacket and tight black jeans. "Put your money away!" he said loudly, getting the attention of the ticket seller and a few different families waiting for the elevator. "I was misinformed. They had a bar on the observation deck, but it closed in 2000. Do you know what's up there now?"

Gillian shrugged. "No."

"Several screaming babies, about three dozen kids running amok, their stupid parents, and another fifty morons all on their cell phones, talking over one other and saying the same thing: *'Guess where I'm calling you from!'* Christ, spare me. I'd rather be staked to an anthill naked than go up there again. What a rip-off!"

Gillian tried to ignore the icy, contemptuous stares from the ticket-seller and the folks waiting for the elevator. Her head down, she quickly stepped out of line. "You must be Sal Salgado," she muttered. "Maybe we can move away from all these people."

"That's cool with me," he said. "Want to check out this amusement park?"

"Sure," Gillian said. She'd been to the Seattle Center amusement park on a warm summer night four years ago. She, Barry, and Ethan had taken in all the rides and galleries. The place had been overflowing with people and noise. The smell of hot dogs, chili, and popcorn had filled the air. Tonight it was deserted, due to the rain and cold. But the unoccupied Ferris wheel, gilded with bright colored lights, kept revolving anyway.

"I lied to you on the phone, Mrs. Tanner," Sal said, shoving his hands in his pockets. "I'm not a mystery fan. I don't have any of your books. I know your face because I had you under surveillance a while back. But I didn't want to creep you out by telling you that over the phone."

"Well, thank you for your honesty—I guess. Did you see anything interesting?"

"Just you," he replied with a wicked, little smile. "I find you very interesting to look at."

"Sal, you know what you just said about not wanting to creep me out? Well, you're kind of doing that now."

"The charm ain't working, huh?" He let out a little laugh. "Sure you're not in the market for a little Sal action? No extra charge. Comes with the *one-time-only* deal."

"No, thanks," Gillian said.

"Well, you're breaking my heart, Mrs. T." He glanced up at the empty conglomeration of girders and rails that was the Wild Mouse. "I might as well tell you, I wasn't the only one checking you out. I noticed this other guy around your place. But he was a slippery son of a bitch. I never got a good look at his face."

Gillian frowned at him. "When was this?"

"About six weeks ago."

She didn't think this elusive Peeping Tom could have been with the mobsters looking for Barry, not five weeks ago. She was pretty certain they'd only recently restarted their surveillance. Was this *slippery son of a bitch* her copycat?

"What really drove me nuts about this yo-yo was he seemed to be eyeballing me as much as he was eyeballing you. It was like his idea of a game or something. He was there for a while, and then just disappeared. Pretty soon, I figured out your old man wasn't sneaking back to you any time soon, so I beat it out of there."

"Where did you go?" Gillian asked.

"Missoula, Montana. It's where I tracked him down—about five weeks ago. He was staying in a dump called the Aces High Motor Inn, registered under the name Frank Carmichael."

Beneath the blinking neon sign for the Aces High Motor Inn, Jason noticed the "perks" listed on a yellow billboard with movie theater marquee lettering: POOL—FREE MOVIES—HBO—ROOMS WITH KITCHENS!

He remembered the oafish night clerk at the last motel telling him that *Frank Garner* had been evicted for trying to smuggle a hot plate and microwave into his room. Perhaps *Frank* had moved on to a motel where he didn't have to cook in secret. Jason pulled into the parking lot of the Aces High Motor Inn.

It was one of those sprawling two-story motels from the sixties—with outside entrances to each room, pale-blue-painted cinder block with black doors. Tiki torches adorned the lobby entrance.

Like so many of the other lobbies, this one smelled of stale coffee. It was mostly windows—and that ugly blue cinder block. Three slot machines were lined against one wall, along with—for the kiddies—one of those games with the claw-on-a-crane picking up prizes in the glass case. The stocky, thirtyish brunette behind the registration desk wore a white shirt, black pants, and a vest that had hearts, spades, diamonds, and aces on it.

Jason asked her if they had a *Frank Garner* or *Barry Tanner* registered there. "Frank and Barry and I are getting together for a reunion," he explained. "They said they might be staying here."

The desk clerk checked her computer and shook her head. "Sorry, sir. I don't show either one."

He pulled out the photo of Barry and Gillian. "Barry might have registered under another name. This is his picture. You don't recognize him by any chance, do you?"

The clerk's eyes widened as she looked at the photograph. "Oh, my God," she murmured. "It's Mr. Carmichael. . . ."

"Mr. Carmichael?" Jason repeated. "Then you know him?"

She nodded. "Yes, I *knew* him. He's been staying with us since early October, and then . . ." The woman trailed off. She was still staring at the picture.

"Go on," Jason said.

She clicked her tongue against her teeth and shook her head. "There was an accident a few nights ago. Mr. Carmichael, he—fell. He was out on our patio. They think he might have had too much to drink. . . ." She shook her head again. "God, it was pretty awful. The pool's still empty. We—we had to drain it to get rid of all the blood. . . ."

"It's still ringing," Gillian said to Sal Salgado. She had her cell phone to her ear.

"I had the same problem calling that hotel," he explained. "They have only one desk clerk, and if he's busy or out for a smoke or in the can, you can just forget about getting through."

Gillian had given up counting after the first dozen ring tones. They stood by the motionless merry-go-round in the deserted amusement park. The Space Needle loomed above them. "How did you find out Barry was staying at this hotel?" she asked, still listening to the ring tones.

"Probably the same way you found me," Sal answered. "Did you go asking around at the local casinos? And did one of the hotter-looking waitresses tell you that I was snooping around asking about your hubby?"

Gillian nodded. She clicked off the line, and decided to try again in a few minutes.

"Well, ol' Barry had a thing for the girls in uniform—waitresses, I mean—wherever there were casinos and race tracks. I'm sure you've figured out the guy hasn't exactly been a choirboy while AWOL these two years. Good-looking guy like that. How can you blame him? I know how he feels."

Gillian sighed. "All right, so Barry got around a little."

"*Got around a little?* Lady, he did more banging than a screen door in a cyclone. I just followed the trail of satisfied waitresses, and ended up in Missoula, Montana. I got lucky with a few of them myself, all in the line of duty, of course."

"Of course," Gillian said with a tiny sneer.

"Cut your old man a break. He's an addict. These guys spill over from one addiction to another—babes, booze, betting. FYI, all the honeys I talked with said your old man was a real gentleman. Quite a few of them even wanted to get serious with him, but he always told them the same thing—that he was in love with his wife."

"That's nice to hear, thanks," she said tonelessly. She gazed down at the Space Needle lights reflected in the wet, dark pavement. She had such mixed feelings about Barry right now. She hit redial on her cell phone, and started listening to the ring tones again. She shot Sal a look. "Was this woman who hired you one of Barry's *honeys*?"

"I guess she wouldn't mind if I told you," Sal replied. "Hell, seeing as she's in a coma, she won't be objecting to anything."

Gillian took the phone away from her ear and stared at him. "She's in a coma?"

He nodded. "Been that way since Halloween night. She was visiting New York, and some scumbag stabbed her. You know her. She took a night class from you a while back."

"Jennifer Gilderhoff?" Gillian said. "Jennifer hired you to track down my husband?"

Sal nodded again. "She was one of the babes who wanted to get serious with your wandering old man—at least, it seemed that way to me. They had a little fling shortly before Barry went on the lam. She said they met when Barry came to your class one night. He stayed in touch with her after he disappeared. So that gave me an edge over these *Goodfella* types who have been after him for a while. Jennifer knew where he was hiding for those first few weeks. Apparently, Barry kept asking her how *you* were doing, which really put a bug up her ass. When she didn't sign up for your class again, Barry gave Jennifer the old heave-ho. That was like—eighteen months since she'd seen him."

Gillian still wasn't getting an answer from the Aces High Motor Inn. She gave a vexed look at her cell phone, then clicked off the line. She frowned at Sal. "Did Jennifer say why she suddenly wanted to find my husband after eighteen months? Was she still in love with him?"

"She said it was for *'closure.'* I think that was the word she used. It's one of those words only someone with a uterus uses. I don't pay much attention to the why when a client hires me for a job. I dug up the information and gave it to her five weeks ago."

"Do you know if she went to Missoula to see Barry?"

"Your guess is as good as mine, Mrs. T."

"Do you think—" Gillian hesitated. "Do you think it's possible my husband had anything to do with her stabbing?"

"A *real gentleman* like your husband? I feel I've gotten to know the guy and all his aliases. He's definitely screwed up with his addictions—the gambling and the babes. But is he a killer? I wouldn't bet on it, lady."

Gillian's cell phone rang in her hand. She quickly clicked it on. "Yes, hello?"

"Gillian? It's Jason Hurrell."

"Yes?" she said. She was about to ask him to clear the line, but something strange about his tone made her hesitate. "What is it?"

"I tried to get you at home, but the machine answered. I didn't want to tell you this on a machine."

"Tell me what?" Gillian asked. She had an awful feeling in her gut. "Where are you?"

"I—I'm calling from a police station in Missoula, Montana. There was an accident. At least, they're calling it an accident. I'm sorry, Gillian. . . ."

Chapter 21

Apparently, the Missoula Police couldn't find any identification on the man floating in the pool at the Aces High Motor Inn near dawn on Friday. He'd been registered at the motel under a possible alias, *Frank Carmichael*. They surmised that he'd been drinking heavily on Thursday night, and on his way to his room, he'd tripped and split his head open on the edge of the motel's pool.

Frank Carmichael was now a "John Doe," lying in the Missoula police morgue.

His poor wife, thought Gillian, though she knew it was Barry in the morgue.

Everything seemed to be coming at her in a fog once she heard Jason say Barry was dead. All of it seemed to be happening to someone else. *Poor Mrs. Carmichael.*

"Barry was my friend," Jason told her on the phone. "But I really didn't know him very well. In fact, I didn't even know where he was staying. We were in Gamblers Anonymous together. Sorry I couldn't tell you anything earlier. He didn't want me to. I can explain it to you tomorrow. They'll need you here in Missoula to identify Barry's body. It's him, Gillian. I saw him. But you need to come here so it's official. I can make your travel arrangements for you. If you flew here in the morning, you could be back home by mid-afternoon."

"That's fine. Thank you very much," she said numbly.

"They have the cause of death down as an accident. But you and I know what really happened."

She knew exactly what had happened. She'd written that murder scene by the pool in *Killing Legend*. She'd told her husband's killer how to do everything.

"You never heard from Vicki, did you?" Jason asked.

"No," she said—almost distractedly. "I think Vicki's dead too."

"Jesus, why is this happening?" he whispered.

They didn't talk much longer after that. Jason promised to call her later in the evening with her travel itinerary. Once Gillian switched off her cell phone, Sal cleared his throat. "Did somebody die?" he asked apprehensively.

She just nodded.

"Is it your husband?"

She nodded again. "Could you walk me to my car, please?"

He just put his hand on her arm and said nothing. On their way to the parking lot, the light drizzle turned to rain. Gillian glanced back at the wet, lonely amusement park. She remembered that warm summer night they'd come here as a family. Barry had won a three-foot-tall stuffed gorilla in a ring toss, and Ethan had named him Pete. That had been a lovely night. But from now on, this sweet little park in the shadow of the Space Needle would be the place where she found out her husband was dead.

When they reached Ruth's car, Gillian remembered to take out her checkbook for Sal Salgado. "How much did I owe you?" she murmured.

He shook his head. "No charge, Mrs. Tanner. You—you've paid enough already."

She drove Ruth's car home. But the trip was all just a blur. She didn't cry. The only thing she thought about was how she would tell Ethan his father was dead.

Gillian found a parking spot in front of the duplex. Dazed, she sat inside the car for a while. She didn't know how long. But suddenly, someone was tapping on the window. Gillian gasped, then stared up at Ruth on the other side of the rain-beaded glass.

She climbed out of the car and started to cry.

"Oh, no," Ruth whispered, shaking her head over and over.

Gillian heard the front door slam. She glanced toward the porch. Ethan walked down the steps and came toward her. "Dad's dead, isn't he?" he asked, his voice cracking.

Gillian nodded. He threw his arms around her. She'd expected him to fall apart, but he was the one comforting her.

After all the tears, the explanations, and mutual consoling, Ruth went out and brought back some food from a teriyaki place. It was strange that they could sit down and eat after everything that had happened. Then again, maybe they'd been unconsciously preparing for this night for the last two years. During their dinner, the phone had rung. It was Lieutenant Lynn Voorhees, asking if she could stop by.

Ruth had put some pressure on her friend earlier in the evening, lighting a fire under Lynn that couldn't be lit two nights ago when they'd first told her about the copycat killings. At Ruth's urging, Lynn had run some unofficial checks on their one remaining suspect, Rick Slaughter.

Lynn had been at it for only three hours. She hadn't spoken with Rick yet. In fact, none of Rick's neighbors had seen him since Friday. Still, the lieutenant had said she'd uncovered some "interesting information" about Rick.

Gillian told her to come over. They were washing the dishes when they heard a knock on the door.

"Is there someplace where we can talk?" Lynn Voorhees

asked after Gillian showed her into the living room. Taking off her trench coat, Voorhees shot a look in Ethan's direction.

"Right here is fine," Gillian said, hanging up the lieutenant's coat for her. "Ethan can hear whatever you have to tell us."

Ethan gave her a furtive smile, and sat down in the easy chair.

Lynn Voorhees wore an ice-blue sweater set, and her mousy brown hair was swept down around her shoulders. She joined Ruth on the sofa. "Well, okay, that's fine. Listen, I'm sorry about—your loss."

Gillian sat across from her in the club chair. "Thank you."

She turned to Ethan. "You know, Jodi really enjoyed meeting you. In fact, next time she's staying with me, she might just give you a call. She has a lot of gay friends."

There were two seconds of dead silence that seemed to last forever. The only one not looking down at the floor was Lynn Voorhees, who didn't seem to realize she'd said the wrong thing.

"Okay, so you were checking on Rick Slaughter for us," Ruth chimed in. "What did you come up with?"

"Well, for starters, no one has seen him since Friday. I talked to his neighbors and his landlord. They seem to think he's a nice enough guy. He goes off on bike trips now and then." Lynn pulled a notebook from her purse and checked some of her scribbling. "He was away on a trip at Halloween and the following week. I haven't been able to confirm where he was during this period."

"So he could have been in New York and Chicago," Ruth said.

Lynn shrugged. "It's possible. I spoke with a neighbor who saw him early Thursday morning."

"Thursday morning?" Gillian said. "Then he could have killed that man in Montana too."

"The one who was *operated* on? Yes. And Rick was back at work on Thursday."

Gillian nodded. "I know, I saw him."

"So in order for him to kill your husband in Missoula late Thursday night or early Friday morning, Rick would have had to fly to Montana—again—right after punching out at the college on Thursday. He'd have had to cut it really close—time-wise."

"Still, it's possible," Ruth said.

"I suppose." Lynn nodded. "Rick came into the office on Friday afternoon to pick up his check. According to his boss, he got into an altercation with one of his coworkers." She looked at Gillian and cocked her head to one side. "The fight was about you, Gillian. Apparently, this coworker was supposed to have looked something up for you, and she didn't. Rick saw your name and phone number jotted down on her desk blotter. He asked her what business she had going on with you. The coworker told him to butt out or something along those lines, and this led to some harsh words. Rick got pretty abusive. They both ended up bitching to their boss about it."

"Do you know *when* this happened on Friday afternoon?" Gillian asked.

"Sometime between two and three."

Gillian was thinking about Friday afternoon in front of Ethan's school. She'd spotted that man in her rearview mirror, the one with the sunglasses and stocking cap. It could have been Rick. But the timing might have been too close to when he'd been at the college.

"I got the landlord to let me into his apartment tonight," Lynn continued. "That could land me in a pile of trouble, so keep it on the QT. Anyway, Rick has a porn collection like you wouldn't believe—videos, DVDs, and magazines. Real kinky stuff, too. After leaving that place, I wanted to take a shower. Along with his extensive porn collection, Mr. Slaughter does have a handful of 'normal' books. Three guesses who his favorite author seems to be."

"Pearl Buck?" Ruth chimed in.

Lynn threw her a deadpan look. "Gillian McBride, with Henry Miller running a close second." She closed her notebook and stuck it back in her purse. "That's all I have for now. It's going to take a lot more digging to find out what kind of alibi Rick Slaughter gave investigators of the schoolgirl killings. I'll be honest, Gillian. I still don't see a connection between what's happening with this copycat and those murders from two years ago. Ruth told me about the saddle shoes in your closet, but I think that's someone just playing around with you."

"Playing around?" Gillian repeated.

"I'm not saying it's harmless, Gillian. But from everything Ruth tells me, this guy likes to play games. And he isn't above sending you on a wild-goose chase for his own amusement."

"You mean like what he did to me today?" Gillian asked. "Telling me he was going to kill my husband tonight when he'd already murdered him three nights ago?"

Lynn nodded glumly. "It's all a game to him, a very evil game."

"You're not going to keep your underwear on, are you?"

Craig stood on the other side of the high school's indoor swimming pool. It was nighttime, and they were alone. One of the overhead lights flickered. Craig took off his sweater and tossed it behind him. Then he pulled his T-shirt over his head. "God, Ethan, what's the point in pool-crashing if you won't skinny-dip?"

Ethan tentatively stood by the edge of the shallow end in only his boxer shorts. He felt self-conscious about his body. And he didn't want to be the first one to get naked. Besides, he didn't trust Craig. He was still kind of mad at him for being so creepy lately.

"C'mon, lose the shorts!" Craig hopped on one foot as he

pried off a Chuck Taylor Converse sneaker, and then he went through the same ritual removing the other shoe.

Ethan couldn't help admiring Craig's athletic physique—the defined chest and wiry torso. Craig started to unzip his jeans. Ethan could see he wasn't wearing underpants.

Ethan didn't want to be caught gawking, so he glanced down at the water in the pool. A moment later, Craig let out a yell, and then there was a splash.

Ethan watched the rippling blue water, and Craig—naked—moving like a torpedo under the surface. But he stopped moving as he reached the shallow end. He stayed motionless underwater for a minute.

"Craig?" he called, starting to panic.

Ethan watched him ascend to the surface. All at once, he was semi-dressed—in a white T-shirt and khakis. And it wasn't Craig in the water. A lifeless body floated to the top of the pool.

Ethan's dead father stared back at him, and then his eyes rolled back in their sockets. His mouth yawned open. A gash in his forehead started oozing blood that rapidly spread across the blue water.

Ethan suddenly bolted up in bed, gasping.

He wasn't sure if he'd screamed out loud or not. He blindly reached for the lamp on his nightstand and his hand fanned the air until he found the switch. The digital clock read 2:47 A.M. Catching his breath, Ethan realized he was covered in sweat. He climbed out of bed and changed his T-shirt.

He wouldn't feel better until he checked the rest of the house. He pulled a pair of sweatpants over his boxer shorts. Opening his bedroom door, he heard Ruth snoring in his mother's bedroom. It was a reassuring sound. He saw the kitchen light was on, and padded down the hall to find his mother in her robe, sitting at the breakfast table. She had a glass of white wine in front of her. She seemed only mildly startled to see him. "Oh, hi, honey," she murmured. "Couldn't you sleep either?"

"Not too well," he mumbled, touching her shoulder on the way to the sink. He turned on the cold water and slurped from the faucet.

"Ethan, you'll give yourself a stomach cramp. Use a glass."

"It's okay, I'm done." Wiping his mouth, he shut off the water. "I feel kind of dumb. I should have taken the couch tonight."

"Don't worry about it. I can't sleep a wink anyway. Sit down for a second."

Ethan plopped down next to her at the table. She patted his arm.

"That cut on your lip doesn't look so bad, thank goodness," she said. "I was very proud of you tonight, Ethan. In the course of one day my little boy has become a man. I know that sounds corny, but it's true."

He shrugged. "I didn't do much. His back was turned, I hit him with the bat, and he went down. Hell, anybody could have done it."

"I'm not talking about that, Ethan. I'm talking about how you were there for me tonight. It made me realize that you've grown up. Your dad would have been proud of you, too."

Ethan glanced down at the tabletop. He wondered what his father would think about having a *queer* for a son. At the same time, he felt awful his dad had died before he'd gotten a chance to talk with him about it.

"I'm not sure Dad would be all that proud," he muttered finally.

"Sweetie," she said, squeezing his arm. "Your father knew you a lot better than you think. And he was very happy to have you for a son."

Ethan felt his stomach tighten. He knew what she was trying to say. His mother wasn't stupid. She'd been there when Tate and those guys had been taunting him in front of the house on Wednesday afternoon. She'd been there earlier to-night when Ruth's friend had practically said, *"You're gay."* His mother knew. And she was still there—for him.

"Mom, I think I might be gay," he said quietly. "In fact, I'm pretty sure of it."

"I know, honey," she whispered. Her eyes filled with tears, but she smiled. "And I have a pretty good idea how hard that was for you to tell me."

"And Dad knew?" he asked.

His mother nodded, and then hugged him. "My word, Ethan," he heard her whisper. "You certainly have grown up today, haven't you?"

From the edge of the ravine, he watched them through a pair of binoculars. They were sitting at the kitchen table, talking. Gillian suddenly hugged her kid. After a few moments, somebody must have said something funny, because they both started laughing.

It was a very tender, sweet scene, this moment between mother and son.

If things were going according to his plan, Gillian would leave in a few hours to identify her husband's body in Missoula, Montana. He'd expected her to travel alone. In fact, he'd counted on it. He needed to separate them, so he could get to the son.

He studied them some more, and smiled. Yes, it was a very sweet scene at the kitchen table. In fact, the writer in him would call this mother-son moment *bittersweet.*

After all, neither of them knew this was their last night together.

"You're the expert," Gillian said. "Does it look like it's been washed off recently?"

She and Ruth were in the cellar, standing in front of the unfinished wall where some garden tools hung from nails. Ruth handed Gillian her coffee-to-go from the Top Pot, and then shined a flashlight on the sickle. She carefully examined the blade.

"He washed it off, all right," Ruth murmured. She took back her coffee container and had a sip. "There's no dirt or rust. But I bet they'll still find traces of blood on there. They always do."

In *Flowers for Her Grave,* the killer had used a sickle to hack up a woman in her kitchen. Gillian had figured that was how Vicki had been murdered. It had occurred to her last night—along with all the other thoughts racing through her head—that her copycat might have borrowed the weapon from the duplex's cellar.

"I'll have our boys in blue bag this very carefully," Ruth said, switching off the flashlight. "Good thing you thought of it. I was locked down here for fifteen minutes yesterday and it never occurred to me—idiot that I am."

The search warrant papers had gone through, and the investigating team was due to arrive any minute. Two patrol cars had already shown up. The cops had put up some barricades outside the duplex and cordoned off the backyard with yellow Crime Scene tape. Ruth had already told them that they might find a body buried in the ravine.

Ethan was still asleep. He'd had an emotionally draining, long, late night. Gillian had stayed up talking with him until nearly four o'clock. She'd told Ruth about Ethan's not-so-startling revelation. "No wonder he's sleeping through all this," Ruth had said. "That's quite a lot for a fourteen-year-old to unload. You know, I've been on the receiving end of a lot of prejudice and ignorance from people I don't give a damn about. But I never had to sit down with *my parents* and tell them, 'Hey, I'm black. Are you still going to love me?' Anyway, good for him."

They emerged from the little cellar with its broken door, and then came up the cement steps. Gillian glanced at the yellow tape looped around tree trunks, sectioning off part of the ravine. "I know you'd like to stick it out for the Grand Guignol finale," she said. "But Ethan was fond of Vicki. I don't want him seeing her excavated from our backyard. Could you take him to your place—sometime before they bring up her body?"

"No sweat. We'll come pick you up at the airport this afternoon. I'll call you on your cell if they find anything. And Lynn Voorhees is still trying to track down Rick Slaughter. I'll keep you posted on that too."

"Thanks, Ruth. Thanks for everything."

Gillian glanced at her wristwatch: 7:25. Ruth had arranged for an off-duty policeman friend to drive her to Sea-Tac, and then see her onto the plane. He was due in five minutes. It felt strange going to the airport to catch a flight—and not having a suitcase with her. She was wearing a black sweater and gray slacks for her "reunion" with Barry.

"Ruth, I need to ask you something, and I want you to be your usual blunt self with your answer."

"Go ahead," Ruth said over her coffee container.

"Did you have any idea Barry was seeing Jennifer Gilderhoff?"

"Honey, I was clueless. I don't think anyone in the class knew either. But now that you've brought it up, I'll tell you something that's been sticking in my craw since you told me last night about Jennifer's extracurricular activities. What did this Sal character say Jennifer's reason was for hiring him to look for Barry?"

"Closure," Gillian said, with a roll of the eyes.

Frowning, Ruth nodded. "Yeah, my sentiments exactly. Two years after her affair with a married man goes down the toilet, she's looking for *closure*? Do you buy that?"

Gillian shrugged. "I'm really not sure."

"Well, knock this around during the plane ride," Ruth said. "I think the key to this thing is finding out *why* she suddenly hired this guy to find Barry. It wasn't long after this detective went to work for Jennifer that the killing started."

Chapter 22

She was lying on a four-poster bed with a frilly white canopy. A pair of pink ballet slippers was tied to one of the posts. A stuffed, smiling orange giraffe—about half the size of a body pillow—was lying beside her. Above the bed, a big poster of Orlando Bloom looked over her. Through the lacy curtains, she had a spectacular view of the mountains.

Gillian had fallen asleep in the bedroom of Jason's eleven-year-old daughter, Annie. She glanced at the alarm clock on the nightstand: 1:50 P.M. She'd actually slept over an hour. Of course, now Gillian was so groggy, she felt as if a truck had hit her. But she'd needed the nap.

She'd identified Barry's corpse this morning. In the two years since his disappearance, Gillian had often daydreamed about what it would be like to see Barry again. But she hadn't allowed herself to imagine this reunion scenario.

She'd tried to brace herself for it on the Seattle-to-Missoula flight. She'd barely slept at all during the trip. And she'd had other concerns. Though she knew Ethan was in good hands with Ruth—and the duplex was surrounded by cops—she couldn't help worrying. Even with Ruth's friend,

Lynn Voorhees, hot on Rick Slaughter's trail, she still felt so uncertain.

Any lingering suspicions she had about Jason Hurrell vanished when she saw him waiting for her at the arrival gate in the Missoula airport. He looked so handsome in his brown leather jacket, blue oxford shirt, and khakis. Now that she knew he was Barry's friend, his overly solicitous behavior the past few days suddenly made more sense. She could let down her guard a little.

They talked in the car on their way to the police station. Jason's story was quite similar to Barry's. For years, his wife, Rachel, had put up with his lies, the unexplained absences, the debts, and the shady debt-collectors—until she'd kicked him out of the house. For a while after that, he'd become a stranger to his wife and daughter. The only difference between him and Barry was that Jason had managed to quit gambling and Barry couldn't. As much as Jason had tried to help his Gamblers Anonymous buddy, Barry couldn't stay out of the casinos. They'd lost touch until about three weeks ago, when Barry had asked Jason to check on his wife and son for him. He'd wanted Jason to handle it very discreetly.

"So you agreed to fly to Seattle and do this for him?" Gillian asked, incredulous. "To hear you explain it, you weren't even that close to Barry."

"Well, see, in most of these Gamblers or Alcoholics Anonymous chapters, there's always some pain-in-the-ass do-gooder who wants to *save* everyone—whether they want help or not." Jason kept his eyes on the road while he spoke, but he smiled a little. "And that pain-in-the-ass guy is me. I just had to do what I could. Besides, I knew what Barry was going through. I lost my family too."

Jason glanced at her for a moment. "Barry never stayed in one place too long. He was hiding out at some motel, and wouldn't tell me where. He was so afraid someone might connect me to him. But I had an e-mail address so I could write to him. I had a feeling something was wrong when he didn't respond to my last few e-mails."

"What about Vicki?" Gillian asked.

"Vicki was Barry's suggestion. He thought if I ingratiated myself to her, I could get close to you and Ethan without raising any suspicions. It wasn't hard tracking down Vicki through some friends with the airline. I liked her when I met her. But I hadn't counted on her becoming so attached to me so quickly." He sighed. "Are you—sure she's dead?"

"I'm waiting for Ruth to call with confirmation."

"Jesus," he whispered. "I feel awful about how I treated Vicki. I mean, I *used* her. What's worse, I think she knew— once I met you—I think she knew I had feelings for you."

Gillian stared at him. She had no idea what to say. She'd been fighting an attraction to Jason ever since she'd set eyes on him. She suddenly felt embarrassed. "I'm not sure we should be talking about this right now," she murmured.

He took his eyes off the road for a moment, and shook his head at her. "I'm sorry. But I want you to know I didn't do all this just for Barry. After I met you and Ethan, I began to care about you both."

"Well, thank you, Jason," she said, unable to look at him.

"I should tell you what the police have so far. They got some of Barry's things from the hotel room. But his wallet and laptop were both missing. I'm guessing the killer got away with those. Even with his wallet missing, the cops are still calling Barry's death an accident. I've kept my mouth shut about the homicide angle. Unless you want to spend the night here in Missoula, I suggest you do the same thing—for now at least. But it's your call, Gillian."

She dreaded the idea of answering questions all night at the Missoula police headquarters when she could be back home in Seattle with Ethan. It made more sense to wait until she returned home to contact the Missoula police about the copycat killings. After that, they could work it out with the Seattle police, as well as the authorities in Billings, Chicago, and New York. Maybe by then, they would have already arrested Rick Slaughter.

"I think we should keep our mouths shut," she finally replied.

"You should know what to expect, Gillian," he said solemnly. "Of course, Barry doesn't look the same. He's kind of—bloated. He was in that pool for two hours before they found him. . . ."

Though Jason had tried to prepare her, it was still a shock to see her dead husband. A cop stood by her in a dark little alcove on the second floor of police headquarters. The closet-like area had a wide picture window looking into another room, brightly lit with a platform at one end, and lines indicating feet and inches on the wall. It was the police lineup room. Apparently, it doubled for identifying victims as well as suspects.

Directly on the other side of that window, a thin college-age man in a white coat stood beside a gurney. If not for the glass partition, Gillian could almost reach out and touch what was under a white sheet on the gurney. The cop at her side pressed an intercom button. "We're ready, Clay," he said.

The young man peeled back the sheet.

Gillian stared at Barry's once-handsome face. Jason was right. He looked bloated. His complexion was splotchy—almost purple in spots. Someone had slipped a surgeon's cap over his hair. Gillian figured they were trying to cover up the gash. She nodded. "Yes, that's my husband," she whispered. *Now, cover him . . . please cover him up.*

"Thank you, Clay," the cop said.

The young man quickly pulled the sheet over Barry's face again.

Yes, thank you, Clay, Gillian thought. But when she stared at the white sheet and the outline of Barry's body on that gurney, it broke her heart. How could he look so small? The man who had shared her bed for sixteen years had seemed so much taller.

She didn't want to cry in the police station. Gillian managed to keep it together until she and Jason stepped outside and headed for his car. He was opening the door for her when she let out a sharp cry, and then burst into tears. Jason wrapped his arms around her. "I'm sorry, Gillian," he whispered. "I'm so sorry."

She just clung to him and sobbed.

It wasn't exactly a *good cry.* She felt utterly miserable afterward. Her head throbbed, her eyes were stinging, and her throat felt raw. She went through several Kleenexes in the car. That was when Jason suggested she come by his house to have something to eat—and perhaps take a nap before catching her flight back to Seattle. He would be flying back with her.

He lived in a ranch house on a cul-de-sac with a dozen other middle-income family homes. It looked like a development from the late nineties. For a single man's home, the place was surprisingly neat and well-furnished.

Jason had made her a grilled cheese sandwich. Then he'd shown her into his daughter's room and pulled an extra blanket out of the closet for her. Gillian hadn't expected to fall asleep.

Now that she was awake, she didn't want to get up. She didn't want to move. She lay back on Annie Hurrell's comfortable bed, beside her stuffed giraffe, and under the gaze of Orlando Bloom.

But then her cell phone went off.

Startled, Gillian climbed off the bed and went to the desk chair, where she'd left her trench coat and purse. She dug the phone out of her bag and clicked it on. "Yes, hello?"

"Hi, Mom," Ethan said. "Have you seen him yet?"

She closed her eyes. "Yes, honey. It's Dad."

"I knew it," Ethan said listlessly. She heard him sigh on the other end of the line. "Are you okay, Mom?"

"I'm hanging in there. How about you? Are *you* okay?"

"Not really," he said, his voice cracking. "I—I better go. . . ."

Hearing him, Gillian started to cry herself. "Oh, Ethan . . ."

"Hon?" Ruth got on the phone. "He'll be all right. He just needs a few minutes by himself. How are you holding up?"

"I was okay until about a minute ago," she replied with a shaky voice.

"Well, you don't have to talk. Just listen. They tracked down Rick Slaughter. You can scratch him off the list. He's been laid up at Valley Medical Center in Renton since late Friday afternoon. He fell off his bicycle on one of the trails down there and shattered his leg in several places. Anyway, he was in surgery on Saturday, which means he couldn't have killed Vicki or Chase. Unless he had a proxy pulling off those two murders, Rick Slaughter is not our guy."

Gillian wiped her eyes. She felt numb. If Rick wasn't the killer, she had no idea who it could be. They'd run out of suspects.

"Are you—alone?" Ruth asked.

"Yes. Why?"

"My pals here would like to talk to Vicki's boyfriend."

"Well, I'm sure Jason would be happy to cooperate. He's coming back with me on the plane."

There was a silence on the other end. "Ruth? Are you there?"

"Honey, I don't know about him. Ethan says Jason was in the duplex when he got home around four o'clock yesterday afternoon. For all we know, he might have just finished cleaning up the mess in Vicki's kitchen. Ethan also said he first spotted Jason standing out by the ravine late Friday night—"

"Ethan was telling the police all this?" Gillian cut in.

"God, no. Ethan wouldn't want to get him in trouble. He thinks the guy walks on water. No, *I've* been pumping it out of Ethan. Anyway, I can't help thinking Jason might have been down in the ravine Friday, digging a grave."

"No, you're way off base, Ruth."

"They found something that looks like a grave about

halfway down the ravine. They're excavating as we speak. If your copycat planned on killing and burying Vicki on Saturday afternoon, he probably dug the grave ahead of time—like Friday night, while we were out to dinner with Lynn. Didn't the killer in *Flowers for Her Grave* dig the graves in their gardens ahead of time?"

"Yes, I suppose what you're saying makes sense. But it isn't Jason. You don't know him. He wouldn't—"

"Where was he on Saturday night when Chase's car took that dive off the ferry? He told you he'd be at the Loyal Inn. But he wasn't there. Do *you* know where he was?"

"No, but I'm sure he has a perfectly good explanation."

"Just the same, do me a favor and give that guy a wide berth. Don't take any chances with him. Where are you now?"

Gillian hesitated. "I'm at Jason's."

"What? For God's sakes, get out of there—"

"Ruth, I'm fine—"

There was a knock on Annie Hurrell's bedroom door, then Jason poked his head in. "Oh, you're awake," he said. "We should take off for the airport in a few minutes, okay?"

Gillian nodded. "Thanks."

"Are you talking to Ethan?" he whispered.

"No, it—it's Ruth. I'll be ready in a minute, Jason."

Nodding, he ducked back out and closed the door.

"Ruth, I'm perfectly safe," she whispered into the phone. "I've been napping in his daughter's bedroom for the last hour. Before that, he was with me all day. We went to the police station together, for God's sakes."

"Serial killers *love* hanging out at police stations. I thought you knew that from all your research. They like to see how they're pulling one over on the cops. It's a real kick to them. My God, just imagine how he felt driving the wife of his victim to police headquarters so she could identify the body. He was probably lapping it up."

Gillian didn't want to hear any more. "We're headed to

the airport, and we'll see you in about two and a half hours. You're wrong about Jason. He's a nice guy."

"Honey, I know your track record with *nice guys*. I'm telling you to be careful with him. I'll call you in fifteen minutes. If something's wrong, mention the weather, okay? Then I'll phone the Missoula Police. What kind of car does he drive?"

"A dark red Infiniti," Gillian replied, rolling her eyes. "And don't bother asking me for the license plate number, because I don't know it. Now, are you sure Ethan is okay? Can I talk to him again?"

"Yeah, here he is," Ruth said. "I'll get back to you in fifteen."

Ethan came on the line. "Sorry I lost it for a minute there. I'm all right now. Hurry home, Mom."

"I will, honey. You take care."

"I will. So long." There was a click on the other end of the line.

Sighing, Gillian switched off the cell phone, and then stashed it in her purse. She really couldn't be angry at Ruth. After all, they'd run out of suspects. And Ruth didn't know Jason.

Gillian smoothed out the wrinkles on Annie Hurrell's bedspread. Then she folded up the blanket and went to return it to the closet's upper shelf. As she opened the closet door, Gillian saw something that made her stop. For a moment, she couldn't breathe.

She stared at the pair of saddle shoes on the closet floor. They seemed too big for an eleven-year-old girl.

Gillian put her foot beside one shoe. It looked like it would fit her. She picked up the shoe and compared it to one of the ballet slippers hanging from Annie Hurrell's bedpost. The slipper was at least two sizes smaller.

Returning to the closet, Gillian set the saddle shoe back down on the floor. There was no other footwear in Annie Hurrell's closet. Gillian sifted thought the hangers, checking the pants and blouses, a very limited hodge-podge of garments that looked new and unworn.

She checked the desk drawers: some pens and two blank writing tablets. Nothing else. It might as well have been a desk in a hotel room. Annie's dresser drawers had two pair of socks and a few Gap T-shirts that looked brand-new.

Jason knocked on the door again. "Gillian?"

"I'll be out in a minute!" she called nervously.

Gillian closed the last empty dresser drawer. There were photos in the kitchen and family room of a redheaded girl. In some, she was with Jason; and in others, she was alone. Was that girl really his daughter? Maybe the photos were of his niece or a neighbor's daughter.

Gillian had a horrible thought. If her copycat killer had fooled Ruth by inventing a Montana woman named Hester, he certainly could have invented a daughter named Annie, too.

"They found the girl from upstairs," a policewoman told Ruth. They stood on the front porch.

Ethan was inside, by the living room window, but he heard them through the glass.

For the last few hours, about a dozen people—half of them cops in uniform—had been stomping through the backyard, taking trips up and down the ravine. The first wave had gone down carrying shovels or picks. Someone had placed an ice chest full of bottled water by the edge of the ravine, and that was where a lot of them stopped to take a break. Ethan had watched from the windows in his bedroom and the kitchen.

A few neighbors and passersby had gathered to see what all the commotion was about. But no one was telling them anything, so most of the people moved on. Ruth said they were lucky no reporters or TV news crews had shown up yet.

About ten minutes after he'd talked to his mother on the phone, Ethan had witnessed a flurry of activity in the backyard. A couple of the diggers had come up to talk to their pals on a break. From what Ethan could tell, they'd made a discovery down in the wooded gulch.

Now the short, husky policewoman was confirming it with Ruth. They'd found Vicki.

"Are they sure it's her?" Ruth asked.

The policewoman nodded. "At least she looks a helluva lot like the woman in the pictures we took from the photo album upstairs. She's pretty hacked up. . . ."

Hearing that, Ethan winced. But he wasn't going to cry. He needed to stand here and listen—no matter how much it hurt.

"You think the perp used a sickle?" Ruth asked.

"Or something like it. There's another body with her."

"What?" Ruth murmured.

The cop nodded. "She's sharing the grave with some guy. She's lying on top of him. His throat's slit."

"So is your daughter tall—like you?" Gillian asked. She sat in the passenger seat of Jason's dark red Infiniti. She noticed the sign for the airport at a busy intersection near a shopping mall.

"I'm glad Annie's not around to hear you ask that," Jason said, his eyes on the road. "I think she must have grown ten inches over the summer. Now she towers above all the girls and most of the boys in her class. Between that and her braces and just about everything else, she's so sensitive—like a raw nerve. During her last visit, I made the mistake of saying she looked like she was starting to get a figure. Oh, God, what a mistake that was. She wouldn't talk to me for half a day. I guess I came too close to mentioning her breasts, and even the most remote reference to them is strictly taboo."

Gillian stared at him and wondered if he was making it all

up. "Does Annie go to a private school? I noticed the saddle shoes in her closet."

"Yeah. She packed her uniform but forgot the shoes during a visit last month. Those are her second pair. Most of her stuff is at her mom's and stepfather's. I bought a few things for her, sort of a back-up wardrobe, but apparently I have no idea what's hip and what's not in the preteen fashion world."

Gillian just nodded. He was saying all the right things—as usual. "When you were driving me around the other day, you said it was your flying from place to place that put a crimp in your marriage. But today, you told me it was your gambling that ruined things. Which is the truth, Jason?"

Eyes narrowed, he glanced at her for a moment. "I haven't heard that tone from you since Saturday on the ferry. What happened all of a sudden?"

"Nothing happened. Could you answer the question, please?"

He shrugged. "The truth is, I was flying from place to place gambling. The racetracks around Los Angeles were my favorite. But I also liked the casinos in Las Vegas and Reno. Anyway, I only gave you half the story the other day. I couldn't have told you about my gambling; otherwise, you'd have connected me to Barry. And he didn't want you to know he'd sent me."

As he spoke, Gillian noticed they'd picked up speed. She saw a sign ahead with a left arrow, indicating the turn for Highway 10 and Missoula International Airport. "Well, you sure had me convinced that I was getting the whole story on Saturday," she said, a bit distracted by the sign. "Aren't you going to slow down?"

He didn't. A moment later, he sailed by the turnoff.

"Hey—hey, you just missed the airport!" she said, leaning forward in the passenger seat.

"Relax. This way is faster, fewer stoplights."

Gillian glanced over her shoulder—out the rear window.

Almost everyone else behind them was taking the turnoff. She looked at the backseat. No bags or suitcases. Nothing. He'd said he was flying to Seattle with her. Didn't he plan to stay a day or two?

"Are you upset with me again, Gillian?" he asked. "I'm getting this vibe. . . ."

"No. I'm just tired, that's all," she lied. She kept looking for where the airport might be. She didn't see any planes taking off or landing in the vicinity. Then again, Missoula wasn't exactly an international hub. She couldn't expect much air traffic. The road narrowed down to one lane each way. There weren't any signs for hotels or gas stations—none of the usual indications that they were destined for an airport. From what Gillian could see of the road stretching in front of them, they were headed for a forest—and the mountain range.

"Are you spending the night in Seattle?" she asked.

"Yes, I'm going to see if they can take me at the Executive Inn again. I stayed there Saturday night."

"So you weren't at the Loyal Inn?" Gillian asked, though she already knew the answer.

"No, they were booked. And the Executive was on Ethan's list."

"You—um, don't have any luggage," she said, trying to sound unconcerned about it. "Not even a carry-on."

"I keep an overnight bag in my locker at the airport," he replied "My laptop is in the trunk. I'm taking it, too."

Switching on his indicator, Jason slowed down and turned left onto a narrow road that wound through a forest.

Gillian's cell phone went off. Her hands were shaking as she dug it out of her purse. She hoped Jason didn't notice. She switched on the phone. "Yes, hello?"

"Gill, it's me," Ruth said—her voice chopped up by static.

Gillian glanced out the window at all the trees. "Hi, Ruth. Can you hear me all right?"

"Just barely."

She shot a look at Jason, whose eyes were on the road. "Um, we're driving through some woods," she said into the phone. "According to Jason, it's a shortcut to the airport. I—ah, can see some dark clouds. I'm hoping we don't have a bumpy flight. The weather looks a little iffy."

Jason frowned at her. "What are you talking about? I don't see any clouds."

"Gillian, I only got the very first part of that," Ruth was saying. "This connection is awful. I"—Ruth's voice skipped out for a moment—"tell me again. Are you all right?"

"I was talking about the *weather,*" Gillian said.

"Hon, I still"—another break—"maybe call you back? Or should I phone the police in Missoula?"

Jason took a curve in the road, and the forest area abruptly stopped. The land flattened out, and Gillian saw the airport tower directly ahead. She let out a sigh.

"Gillian, are you there?" Ruth asked, panic in her voice.

"Yes. I can hear you now," she said into the phone. "It's much better."

"Are you okay?"

"So far, so good," she replied. "It might be too soon to tell for sure."

"Is there any news on Vicki?" Jason asked.

"Did you hear that? Jason wants to know—"

"I heard him, loud and clear. The concern in his voice is a nice touch. I almost believe him myself. Just the same, I'm going to arrange a welcoming committee for Mr. Hurrell when you two arrive at Sea-Tac. Our boys in blue will be waiting at the arrival gate."

They turned onto Highway 10 and drove alongside a chain-link fence bordering the airport.

"You could be wrong, Ruth," Gillian said into the phone. "As I pointed out, it's too soon to tell. Now, what about Vicki?"

"They found her, Gill, buried in the ravine. She was pretty hacked up. They think you're right about the murder weapon. Looks like he used a sickle on her." Ruth let out a sigh. "And brace yourself. They found another body in the grave with her."

"What?" Gillian murmured.

"Maybe your pal there knows who it is," Ruth remarked. "Everyone around here was scratching their heads about it— including yours truly. Then your smart son came up with a very tangible lead. That creep, Joe, who paid us an unexpected visit yesterday, was asking about his friend *Al.* You know, the one who was last heard from on Friday night, when he was here, watching the house? Anyway, we're following it up. In the meantime, I want to remind you that Ethan says the first time he saw Jason was late Friday night, and he was standing at the edge of the ravine. I mean, c'mon, you do the math."

They were slowing down. Gillian noticed a sign on the chain-link fence: AUTHORIZED ACCESS ONLY. Jason lowered his window and turned into a little driveway. There was a break in the fence, and an electronic gate. He dug a card out of his wallet and swiped it in a machine by the gate, then punched some numbers on a keypad. The gate opened.

"Gill, are you still there?" Ruth asked.

"Yes. We're just pulling into the airport right now."

"I'm a gnat's eyelash away from calling the Missoula Police. But I don't think they'd hold onto him for very long. If you bring him here, we'll have a better shot at nailing the SOB. Just—please, be careful on that plane with him. I keep thinking about *For Everyone to See,* when you had that charmer who liked to kill women in public places. He strangled a woman on a plane, hon. Remember?"

The scene took place on a red-eye flight in an airplane restroom. The killer trapped the woman he was stalking just as she emerged from the lavatory. He pushed her back in, locked the door, and strangled her. The woman's corpse wasn't discovered until the plane had already unloaded after landing. Gillian received about a dozen e-mails from people saying that could never really happen.

Now she hoped they were right. "I'll be careful," she said into the phone.

Jason pulled into a parking spot, cut off the motor, and then stuck an employee tag on the dashboard.

"So, hon, you wanted me to get Ethan out of here before they bring up the body—though I guess now it's *bodies*. Anyway, I'll take him to my place for lunch. I'll give you another call right before we leave here. It should be in about fifteen minutes."

"Thanks, Ruth," Gillian said. She clicked off the phone.

Jason was staring at her. He looked so worried. "Did she have any news about Vicki?"

Gillian just stared back at him for a moment. He was so convincing. And she wanted very much to believe him.

"Yes, Jason," she said finally. "I'm so sorry. . . ."

"It's getting a little bumpy, folks, so we're turning on the seat belt signs. Please remain seated with your seat belts fastened until we get through this patch of turbulence."

The fortysomething blond flight attendant, who reminded Gillian a bit of Vicki, maneuvered her way down the aisle of the seventy-seat plane.

Clutching her armrests, Gillian rode the bumps and sudden dips. She chewed gum to combat nausea. Some idiot cowboy in the back wasn't helping with his loud "Whoowee!" every time the plane took a jolt.

Gillian resisted the urge to grab onto Jason's arm. Sitting beside her, the experienced charter plane pilot seemed unfazed by the turbulence. Through all the rolling and bobbing, his eyes stayed riveted on the laptop in front of him.

An hour ago, when she'd passed along the news about Vicki, Jason had almost started to cry. She'd seen the tears well in his eyes, and he'd shaken his head. "Who is this son of a bitch?" he'd murmured.

If it was all an act, it was a damn good one.

In the airport, everyone in a uniform seemed to know him—and like him. He reminded her of Barry that way, always charming people wherever he went. Jason put on a friendly smile for all those who said hello. Gillian caught a few of Jason's female friends sizing her up and frowning a bit.

If he'd hoped to murder her on the plane as in *For Everyone to See,* he was leaving behind a lot of witnesses who had seen them together. Though her suspicions about Jason had eased, she remained guarded around him.

Ruth phoned again just as they'd boarded the plane. She and Ethan were about to head to her place for lunch. At one point during her brief conversation with Ruth on the phone, Jason interrupted: "You know, Ruth should tell the police about me. Remember, I was there on Saturday. I was probably one of the last people to see Vicki alive. They might want to talk to me."

"That's a good idea," Gillian had replied. "Did you hear that, Ruth?"

She'd told Ruth they would meet her and Ethan at the arrival gate. At the time, Gillian had thought she would be safe for the next ninety minutes in the air. But she hadn't counted on this turbulence.

"Flight attendants, please take your seats," the captain announced calmly.

Gillian watched the poor attendant struggle up the aisle, grabbing hold of every seat back she passed to keep her balance. That did it. Gillian finally grabbed Jason's arm. "Aren't you even a little concerned?"

"This is nothing," he said, taking his eyes off the computer screen to look at her for a moment. "Don't worry about it. I'm looking at some of your reviews on Amazon.com. Do you ever look them up or Google yourself?"

"Only four or five times a week—for the sales rank mostly."

"When Barry asked me to pay you a visit, I picked up a few of your books and read them. I couldn't tell you earlier. Anyway, I'm trying to refresh my memory what each one was about."

Before the plane had started bobbing up and down, Jason had asked her for more details about the schoolgirl killings and her copycat. Then he'd gone online.

"A lot of these readers on Amazon.com keep coming back to review each one of your books," he pointed out.

Gillian nodded. "Yes, it's the same way on the Barnes and Noble site. If they like one book, they check out the others."

"But a few of these readers keep reviewing you even when they're not crazy about your work."

He tilted the laptop so she could see the screen. Then he scrolled down the reviews for *For Everyone to See*. Gillian got a bit nauseous as she rode the bumps and tried to read the starred reviews and the reviewers' computer names: four stars from *msnancyabbe*; one star from *bookworm85*; five stars from *dgotlieb*; *imalegend2* dished out two stars for it; *chadshclund* and *jbchurch* both gave her five stars. Gillian knew what Jason was talking about. *Bookworm857* and *imalegend2* were always pretty damn critical, but usually provided a begrudging compliment or two.

"It's kind of like a creative writing class—in reverse," Jason said. "These reviewers grade your work. I think you're right about this copycat. He must have been your pupil once, but he's turning it around and showing the teacher how it's really done." Jason readjusted the laptop so it was facing him again. He had to hold onto the little computer to keep it from bouncing off his tray table. "You said the woman stabbed in New York and this Chase person on the ferry were both in that same class?"

"That's right."

"And the schoolgirl murders were going on during that

particular semester? Are you sure you've considered *every-one* from that class?"

She rolled her eyes. "Yes, I've been over and over the class list. The two most likely suspects were Chase and Todd. And they're both dead."

Jason wasn't saying anything she didn't already know and hadn't already considered. It was a bit presumptuous of him to think at this point in time he could ask a few questions, reacquaint himself with her books, and suddenly come to some startling new conclusion about this copycat killer. Gillian had to give him credit for trying, at least. But he was grasping at straws.

The plane took another sudden plunge. The idiot cowboy in the back let out a "Yahoo!" A few other passengers screamed. Gillian kept chewing her gum and clutching Jason's arm.

"What do you think his next move will be?" he asked.

"I'm afraid he might go after Ethan—or Ruth," she admitted. She hated even saying it out loud.

The plane wobbled a bit, then seemed to hit an even patch. The sudden calm left Gillian feeling grateful but still uncertain.

"I just started reading *Black Ribbons* this afternoon while you were napping. It's the only one of your books he hasn't *paid homage* to yet, isn't it?"

Gillian nodded. He'd lifted murders from the other five, but hadn't gotten around to copying *Black Ribbons*. That was what Jason had meant when he'd asked what the killer's next move might be. She thought about her latest publication—with its serial killer abducting his victims and leaving a black ribbon behind on a nearby streetlight or signpost. Within twenty-four hours, each victim was found dead—and naked, except for a black ribbon tied around her neck. Was this her copycat's next move?

The seat belt sign went off. *"Looks like we're through the worst of it, folks,"* the captain said over the speaker. *"Feel free to get up and move around the cabin. We'll be starting our descent for Seattle in about twenty minutes."*

Gillian was still thinking about her copycat, and how he might be planning his next kill. She barely heard the captain's announcement. And she didn't notice the flight attendant coming down the aisle—or some of the other passengers who had gotten out of their seats. Gillian still expected more turbulence—all the jolts and dips, and that awful sensation of the floor dropping out beneath her.

She held onto Jason's arm.

"What if this copycat has a disciple doing a lot of the killing?" he asked. "After all, you've got this killer going from one city to another pretty quickly. Maybe someone you know is pulling the strings, someone with authority and experience, an older person from that class. . . ."

Gillian just shook her head. She was thinking of Glen with his three-pronged cane, affable Gary Connelly, and Luke Huang with his broken English and polite manner. It seemed Jason was still grasping at straws.

"There's no one," she started to say.

"What about your friend, Ruth? Is it possible she—"

Gillian quickly shook her head again. "No, not Ruth. That's crazy."

Ruth was her friend. She'd been there for her ever since Barry left. She'd been driving her to and from class for two years now. Ruth had helped her with the last four books. And she'd stood by her throughout this whole copycat nightmare, for God's sakes. Ruth was her rock. Gillian trusted her implicitly.

Yet a sudden panic surged through her. Gillian remembered asking Ruth to take Ethan to her house—away from all the police activity around the duplex. Ruth was alone with Ethan this very minute. "It's not true," Gillian whispered.

Still, she felt as if the floor had just dropped out from beneath her.

Ethan missed Ruth's dog. He'd been to Ruth's house about a dozen times, and Eustace had always been there to entertain him. But his canine pal was still at the vet's.

He'd never been to Ruth's house without his mom either. It felt strange, sitting alone at Ruth's kitchen table, trying to eat a peanut butter and jelly sandwich. She was at the stove, pouring herself her umpteenth cup of coffee for the day. They were supposed to leave for the airport in a few minutes to pick up Jason and his mom. Ethan wished they could just leave now. In the last couple of hours it had been confirmed for him that his father was dead and his upstairs neighbor had been hacked to pieces. Ethan didn't think he'd start to feel even halfway right again until he saw his mother—and Jason.

Ruth had been asking him a ton of questions about Jason. Apparently, she must have considered him a suspect. But it didn't make sense to Ethan that his mother and Jason were flying back to Seattle together if they really thought he'd murdered somebody.

Another thing that didn't make sense to him was coming back here to Ruth's house for lunch. They could have swung by a McDonald's or Arby's on the way to the airport. There were a lot of places to eat in the main terminal too. Why make this special side trip for a bad PB & J?

The peanut butter tasted stale, like it had been opened, resealed, and stuck back on the shelf sometime in 2005. And the milk had a bitter aftertaste. It was making him a bit nauseous. Still, when Ruth asked him how he liked his lunch, Ethan tried to be polite, and lied.

"Great, really great, thanks, Ruth," he said, nibbling at his sandwich.

She poured some milk into her coffee and sat down at the table with him. "Listen, kiddo. You've had enough surprises for the day, so I'll tell you what the plan is. We're going to head back to your house right after this. Your mom thought it best that you not be around when they bring the bodies up from the ravine, and I quite agree with her."

Frowning, Ethan stared at her and blinked a few times. Something weird was happening. Her voice seemed to be coming in and out of a fog.

"We're going to hitch a ride to SeaTac with Patti," Ruth continued. "She's the stocky policewoman we were talking with earlier. I've decided some police presence at the airport might be the insurance we need to make sure nothing goes wrong. I know you think the world of this Jason fella, but personally, I'd trust him about as far as I could throw him. I'll feel a helluva lot better about him once he's answered some questions the police have. Anyway, you, Patti, and I will be meeting Jason and your mom at the arrival gate. On the plus side, you'll get to ride in a police car. How about that?"

Ethan numbly glanced around the kitchen. He suddenly felt so tired. He was wondering where the dog had gone. But he knew that already. Of course, Eustace was at the vet's. Ruth was supposed to pick him up tomorrow.

Squinting at him, Ruth leaned forward. "Honey, what's wrong with you?"

"I'm dizzy," he muttered, trying to focus on Ruth.

"You're probably just stressed out—and hungry," Ruth replied. She pushed the glass of milk at him. "Here, drink your milk. Eat."

He sipped his milk. It still tasted funny. He stared down at the glass. "Did you—did you put something in this?"

"What are you talking about?"

Ruth got to her feet. Ethan glanced up at her. The room started spinning. "My God . . ." he murmured.

"Ethan?"

He felt the chair tipping out from under him. He tried to grab at the table, but he swiped at the air. He tried again, and knocked over the sandwich plate and the glass. They flew off the tabletop, and went crashing to the tiled floor.

He felt so helpless as he toppled onto the floor just a second later. He hit his head against the chair leg.

Then Ethan didn't feel anything at all.

Chapter 23

A woman with ash-blond hair and designer glasses was blocking the aisle. She struggled with her carry-on bag in the overhead bin while holding onto a shopping bag and talking on her cell phone. The gap in the aisle widened between her and the disembarking passengers at the front of the plane. At least thirty people were trapped behind her. Gillian and Jason were among them.

"I hate about half of the people I see on cell phones," Jason said. He had only one foot in the crowded aisle.

Her back hunched to avoid bumping her head against the overhead, Gillian stood in front of her seat. She watched the plane empty out ahead of the woman, who seemed oblivious to everyone behind her.

Though she was dying inside, Gillian didn't say anything. Ruth and Ethan were supposed to be waiting for them at the arrival gate. Ruth had said she was bringing the police along to question Jason about Vicki's murder—among other things. Gillian had told Jason this, and he didn't object. "Hey, if you think it might help the investigation, I'll talk to the cops or anyone you want," he'd said.

Gillian had tried phoning Ruth's house about forty minutes ago, but no one had picked up. She told herself that Ruth and Ethan had probably already left for the airport. They were both fine—and waiting for her and Jason at the gate. She would see them in just a few minutes—as soon as this stupid woman on the phone moved her ass.

A middle-aged man behind the woman finally helped her with her carry-on, and people started moving. Jason cleared a spot in front of him, and Gillian was able to straighten up and step into the aisle.

She refused to believe Ruth was somehow behind the copycat killings. How could she even think her dear friend had orchestrated those murders? She'd told Jason he was way off base suggesting such a thing. It was ridiculous.

Of course, only two hours ago, she'd been convinced Jason was the killer. She'd even thought that in order to gain her trust, he'd *pretended* to have a daughter. Good Lord, what had she been thinking? They'd run out of suspects, and she was just so tired and frayed. The only thing that made sense to her right now was seeing Ethan again.

They stepped off the plane, and hurried past several passengers on the jetway. "Excuse me . . . excuse me," Gillian said over and over again. Her tone became more anxious and edgy with each person she passed. She could see the terminal just ahead.

No one was waiting for them at the end of the jetway. She'd figured Ethan, Ruth, and the cop should have gotten beyond the security checkpoint. Ruth had said she would meet them at the arrival gate. But there was no one.

Gillian was suddenly stricken with an overwhelming dread. It made her sick to her stomach. She somehow knew—they could check the security point, the main terminal area, baggage claim, and the arrivals area outside, and no one would be waiting for them.

She wasn't going to see Ethan or Ruth here. In fact, Gillian had a horrible feeling she might not see Ethan or Ruth ever again.

The 911 operator kept interrupting and telling her to calm down. He had an *I'm the Voice of Authority* tone, and it didn't seem to matter to him that she'd had the police excavating two dead bodies from her backyard today. He treated her as if she were just another crackpot 911 caller. Gillian had told him about Ruth's and Lieutenant Lynn Voorhees's involvement in the case, and said she was worried about her son. Couldn't he connect her to someone who *knew something*?

He finally put her through to a detective, who didn't know a damn thing about what was going on. But from him, Gillian got Lynn Voorhees's number. Of course, Lynn Voorhees wasn't picking up the phone. Gillian left her a message: "Lynn, this is Gillian McBride. I'm in a taxi on my way from Sea-Tac. Ruth, my son, and someone from the police department were supposed to meet us there at the airport, and they didn't show. We had them paged and everything. Ruth's not answering her home phone either. I know something's wrong. We're on our way to Ruth's house right now. It's—um, 816 Sixteenth Avenue. We should be there in about fifteen minutes. Could you call me as soon as you hear anything?"

Gillian left her cell phone number. Jason had given the taxi driver forty dollars to go over the speed limit. So the guy was driving like a maniac—weaving through traffic and speeding in the HOV lane on Interstate 5.

Gillian stashed her phone in her purse. "Do you have a cell phone?" she asked Jason. "Can I borrow it? I need to call 911 again, and I don't want them to know it's me calling back."

With a baffled look on his face, Jason dug a cell phone out of his jacket pocket and handed it to her.

Gillian switched it on and dialed 911. A female operator came on the line this time.

"Yes, hello," Gillian said. "I was walking my dog on Sixteenth Avenue in Capitol Hill—near Group Health Hospital, and I heard screams and gunshots. It sounded like it was coming from this yellow house. The address is 816 Sixteenth Avenue. I thought you might send a patrol car over to investigate."

"816 Sixteenth Avenue?" the operator repeated.

"Yes," Gillian said. "I heard the shots just a little while ago—"

"Your name?"

"Stephanie Merchant. Could you send someone over to check it out—"

"There are officers on the scene, ma'am."

"Officers on the scene?" Gillian echoed. "The police are already there?"

"Yes, ma'am."

"Is anyone hurt? Can you tell me what happened?"

"All I can tell you is that there are officers on the scene."

"I know people in that house," Gillian said, her voice trembling. "Can't you please tell me what happened?"

"I don't have that information, ma'am."

From inside the cab, two blocks away, Gillian could see four squad cars parked in front of Ruth's house. An ambulance was in Ruth's driveway, behind her Toyota. It was dusk, and all the red flashing lights seemed to illuminate the block.

As soon as the cab pulled over, Gillian jumped out of the backseat and ran toward the house. A stocky young policeman tried to stop her. "My friend, Ruth Langford, lives here," she explained. "She's got my son. . . ."

He let Gillian pass, but ran alongside her as she hurried to the front door. Gillian almost plowed into the paramedics. They were carrying Ruth out on a portable gurney. She looked dazed, and half-dead. "Please, step aside," one of the paramedics said. He was monitoring Ruth's pulse.

But Ruth spotted Gillian and her eyes lit up for a second. She waved away the paramedic hovering over her. She tried to say something to Gillian, but could barely talk above a whisper.

As Gillian moved closer, she saw brown stains on the front of Ruth's blouse. She could smell the vomit.

"I'm sorry, hon," Ruth said weakly. "He's got Ethan. It was the poison milk scene from *Killing Legend,* only he used some kind of sleeping narcotic."

"Did you see who it was?"

Ruth shook her head. "Ethan drank the milk—and just collapsed. I went down right after him. I don't know, Gill. I'm still a little out of it, I'm sorry. They pumped my stomach." She squinted at Jason, who stood behind Gillian with his laptop case. "Are you Jason?"

He nodded.

Ruth seemed to have trouble focusing on Gillian again. "If he's been with you all this time, he's off the hook. It's somebody else."

Gillian just stared at her. She couldn't talk.

The paramedics started pushing the gurney toward the ambulance again, but Ruth grabbed Gillian's sleeve. "Wait," she said, her voice still raspy. "Gill, remember what I said this morning about Jennifer hiring a detective to find Barry— eighteen months after they broke up? Why did she do that, Gill? Why?"

The paramedics continued on. Numbly, Gillian watched them load Ruth into the back of the ambulance.

A plainclothes detective with a pale complexion and re- ceding reddish hair approached her and Jason. He said he was the officer in charge. Gillian didn't really hear his name. Jason was answering his questions and explaining as much as he knew. Gillian watched the ambulance back out of the driveway.

She heard the detective say something about an Officer Patti Renner, who apparently had been at the duplex with

Ruth this morning. She was supposed to have driven Ruth and Ethan to the airport after they'd returned from lunch at Ruth's house. But Ruth had never come back to the duplex. When Officer Renner couldn't get ahold of her, she had checked Ruth's house and found Ruth unconscious. There had been no sign of Ethan Tanner.

While the detective was talking, Gillian kept staring at this one cop, who stood by himself on the parkway. He looked bored. Someone had taken her son, and this cop wasn't doing anything. Then again, what did she expect him to do? No one had a clue who this killer was—or where he'd taken Ethan.

She couldn't just stand here wringing her hands and waiting for the police to find Ethan. She had to *do something*. More than anyone, she knew what this killer was like. Ethan's survival was up to her.

She thought about what Ruth had said. Why had Jennifer hired a private investigator to track down Barry—eighteen months after breaking up with him? Had someone put her up to it?

The bored-looking cop on the parkway lit up a cigarette.

Gillian kept staring at him and remembered Jennifer's friend, April, lighting up a cigarette outside the Seattle Aquarium.

That woman knew something. Gillian recalled how April had been ready for a cigarette break, but as soon as Gillian had said she was Jennifer's teacher, April suddenly hadn't any time for her—or a cigarette. It made sense now. Jennifer's friend knew about the affair with Barry.

"We talked to some of Ruth's neighbors," the officer in charge was telling Jason. "One of them saw a dark green SUV pull into the driveway here a little over an hour ago. We're still interviewing other people on the block. . . ."

Stepping away from them, Gillian pulled out her cell phone. She got the number of the Seattle Aquarium from Directory Assistance, and then called the Aquarium. After listening to the automated voice menu for what seemed like forever, Gillian finally got through to a real person. She asked if April Tomlinson was working today—and when they were closing.

April was there; and Gillian had thirty-five minutes to make it down to the Waterfront area and talk with her. This time, she was determined to get some answers.

Putting her phone away, she stepped up to Jason and the detective. "We—we have to go," she said, taking hold of Jason's arm. "Now, we have to go *now*."

The detective gave Jason his card, and then he waved over the stocky, young cop—the one who had tried to keep Gillian from going into Ruth's house. The two policemen spoke in hushed tones for a few moments. The young cop nodded, and then broke away from his superior. "I can take you wherever you need to go," he said to Gillian.

"Can you make it to the Aquarium in thirty minutes?" Gillian asked anxiously.

The young cop nodded. "You bet."

He led them toward his patrol car, parked near the start of Ruth's driveway. Nearby, there was a small light post—with a shingle that had Ruth's address number on it. The light wasn't on. Maybe that was why Gillian hadn't really noticed what was different about it tonight. But now, on her way to the patrol car, she saw the light post in front of her. She stopped in her tracks.

"What is it?" Jason asked.

Tears in her eyes, she stared at the post. "Ethan will be dead in twenty-four hours if we don't find him."

"How do you know for sure?"

"Because I wrote it that way," Gillian whispered.

Tied to the lamppost, a black ribbon fluttered in the wind.

"I think she might freeze up and not say anything if there's a policeman with us," Gillian told the young cop as they pulled into a loading zone in front of the Seattle Aquarium. "You understand, don't you?"

He glanced at Jason in the front passenger seat, and then at her in the rearview mirror. "Sure, no problem. I'll wait here."

"Thanks very much."

Jason climbed out of the front, and then opened the door for her. It was rush hour, and the sidewalk was jammed with tourists and people rushing to make the ferry. Weaving through the crowd, Gillian and Jason hurried toward the Aquarium entrance, only to find the ticket window closed. They tried the main doors, but got no further than the foyer. The same thin Asian man who had taken her ticket a few days ago stopped them. "I'm sorry, but we're closing in ten minutes."

"I'm here to see April—April Tomlinson," Gillian said. "It's kind of an emergency."

The ticket-taker shook his head. "You just missed her. She got some bad news this afternoon, and they let her go home a little early."

"What kind of bad news?" Gillian said. "It's all right, I'm family."

"Well, I heard a friend of hers died today. A woman in New York, she's been in a coma for a while."

"Oh, my God, no," Gillian whispered.

Jason gently took hold of her arm, and she squeezed his hand.

"I'm sorry," the man said. "Listen, you still might be able to catch April. As I said, she just left. The employee entrance is on the right side of the building—along the pier."

Outside, Gillian held onto Jason's hand as they merged with people on the crowded sidewalk.

Gillian spotted April just where she'd seen her a few days ago. Standing on the pier, April stared out at the water and smoked a cigarette. The cold wind swept through her hair. As Gillian approached her, she could see April was crying.

Jennifer's friend glanced her way, then she smiled sadly and shook her head. "So—you must have heard the news," she said, wiping her eyes.

Gillian nodded. "Yes, we just found out. I'm sorry, April." She touched Jason's shoulder. "This is Jason, a friend of my husband's."

He nodded. "How do you do?"

April shrugged. "Not so hot." She nervously puffed on her cigarette.

"April, I know Jennifer was seeing my husband," Gillian said. "I understand why you couldn't tell me anything the other day. Since then, I've found out my husband is dead, too. The same person who stabbed Jennifer murdered him last week. And now, this killer has my son."

April stared at her. "You're joking," she murmured.

"I wish I were," Gillian replied gravely. "I talked with a private investigator yesterday. Jennifer hired him about a month ago to find Barry. Do you know anything about that?"

April took one last drag off her cigarette, then tossed it on the pier and ground it out with her foot. "Yeah, I knew about it," she muttered. "The thing between Jennifer and your husband had been kaput for almost two years. Jennifer was over him, I know she was. But about six weeks ago, she met some guy. Jennifer was never good at keeping secrets, but she kept her relationship with this guy under wraps—but good."

"Did she tell you his name?" Gillian asked.

April shook her head. "Nope. That's just it. She was very hush-hush about who he was. He swore her to secrecy or something. I figured she must have hooked up with another married one, but she claimed he was single. Everything she told me about their relationship I practically had to browbeat out of her."

"What exactly did you find out?" Gillian pressed.

"Well, for one, hiring the detective was *his* idea. Apparently, he knew about her and Barry, and he wanted to make sure she was really over him."

"Eighteen months after they'd broken up?"

April nodded. "It struck me as weird too. Jenny had been in other relationships since Barry. One of them was a lot more intense than what went on with—your husband."

April suddenly seemed embarrassed. Reaching into her purse, she fished out another cigarette and lit it.

"How did this new boyfriend find out about Jennifer's affair with Barry?" Gillian asked.

Taking a long drag from her new cigarette, April shook her head. "I have no idea how the guy knew. But he insisted that Jenny track Barry down and see him again."

"For *closure*?" Gillian said.

"That's right. The guy even gave Jenny the money to pay this private investigator. But once the detective finally located Barry someplace in Montana, Jennifer's boyfriend suddenly dropped the whole thing. And not long after that, he suddenly dropped Jennifer. At least, that's what she told me."

"It sounds like there's room for doubt."

"Well, one of the things I put together on my own was that this mystery man lives somewhere in this neighborhood. And Jenny admitted as much to me."

Gillian glanced up at the cluster of high-rises—most of them fairly new—along the waterfront and in nearby Belltown.

"While she was seeing him, I happened to run into Jenny a few times around here—and she hadn't even told me she was coming to town. That's how I figured he must live around here. She was alone each time, but I realized she was probably on her way to see this guy or coming back from some rendezvous with him. The last time was after they were supposed to have broken up, just a week before she went to New York."

April shrugged. "I know Jenny went on a few dates with different guys after officially splitting with this mystery man. That was about three weeks before her trip. So maybe it *was* over. I can't say for sure. I didn't mention anything to the police or Jennifer's family about him when they asked about current boyfriends. They didn't press it. Everyone seemed so sure the guy who stabbed her was someone she picked up at that bar in New York."

She dropped her cigarette on the pier and squished it with the heel of her shoe. "Anyway, that's all I know, I swear. I've really got to go. I need to catch my bus." She touched Gillian's arm. "I—I'm sorry about your husband, Mrs. Tanner. And I hope you get your son back."

Gillian just nodded, and then watched April retreat toward the sidewalk. She disappeared in the crowd.

"Do have any idea who this mystery man could be?" Jason asked.

Tears stung her eyes and she shook her head. Gillian turned toward the choppy gray water of Elliott Bay, and saw the ferry approaching the terminal.

"Jennifer could have been here to catch the ferry," she murmured. "Maybe he lives on one of the islands." She wiped the tears from her eyes, and sighed. "Damn it, I keep thinking about Chase Scott. All signs point to him. He was my student. He might have known about Barry and Jennifer. I remember how disappointed he was that I didn't want to write about the Schoolgirl Murders. He acted as if I were passing up this golden opportunity. He seemed to take it personally—as if I were snubbing him or—"

"Or refusing a gift he was offering you?" Jason cut in.

Gillian stared at him. It was a strange way to put it—yet very on target.

"From everything you've told me about the Schoolgirl Murders," he continued, "they sound like something out of one of your books, Gillian. Do you think it's possible he killed those girls so you could write about it? Maybe he wanted you to immortalize him."

Biting her lip, Gillian considered what he was saying. In some awful, twisted way, it made sense. Chase knew Boyd Farrow, and he could have set up the former priest to take the blame for those murders.

They started back toward the front of the Aquarium. "It can't be Chase," she sighed.

"I know, I know," Jason muttered, walking alongside her. "They're still fishing pieces of him out of the Puget Sound. Do you know if Chase had any friends who could have . . ." He trailed off. He seemed to know they'd run out of possibilities.

Gillian stared down at the sidewalk. Their chances of finding Ethan in time seemed more and more hopeless. They'd reached another dead-end.

Someone screamed. Gillian and Jason stopped in their tracks. A man burst out of the doors to a souvenir shop near the Aquarium. He had something wrapped up in a coat tucked under his arm. He knocked down a tourist, and kept running.

"My camera got you!" yelled the store owner, a balding, Middle Eastern–looking man with a mustache. He shook his fist in the doorway of his shop. "Go ahead and run, you son of a bitch! I've got you on videotape!"

The young cop who had driven Gillian and Jason to the Aquarium jumped out of his patrol car. He pointed to them. "Stay right here," he said hurriedly. Then he took off after the shoplifter. "Hold it! Police!"

But the thief kept on running. The cop chased after him.

Dazed, Gillian—along with everyone else in the area—watched the young policeman pursue the man. It took her a moment to realize Jason was no longer beside her. She glanced around, a bit panicked, but then she spotted him by the side of the Aquarium. He seemed totally oblivious to the little drama that had just unfolded in front of them. He was writing something on the Aquarium's dirty window. Gillian stepped closer, and saw what it said: *IMALEGEND2.*

"Your reviewer online," Jason whispered. "He's been telling you all along who he is."

"What do you mean?"

"What's the plot of *Killing Legend*?"

Gillian frowned at him. "Well, you know. You said you've read it."

"Tell me anyway."

Gillian sighed. "It's about this movie star who is in a terrible car accident. Everyone thinks he's dead, but he isn't. He's killing . . ." Gillian didn't say any more. She stared at Jason.

"Maybe Chase Scott didn't die when his car went off the ferry. Maybe that's another man's remains they're fishing out of the Puget Sound." Jason pointed to the writing on the window. *"I'm a Legend Too."*

Chapter 24

Ethan woke up in a stupor. He had an awful, sour taste in his mouth, and couldn't stop shivering. Someone had taken most of his clothes. Dressed in only his jeans, he was lying on a cold, hardwood floor. It was coated with sawdust and grit. He felt it on his hands, his bare chest, and his feet. He couldn't move. Someone had tied his feet together, and his hands were bound behind him. Thick duct tape covered his mouth. There was also something tied around his neck, but Ethan didn't know what it was.

He heard a strange flapping sound, like a ship's sail in the wind. He didn't know where he was or how he'd gotten there. But the place was dark and damp and freezing. His fingers and toes were like ice.

"You're awake," someone said in a soft, friendly voice.

Ethan saw the shadowy figure of a man sitting on the floor across from him in the gloomy, barren room. There was another weird sound—something crunching. As his eyes adjusted to the lack of light, Ethan realized the man was eating an apple. There was a big, army-type knapsack at his side.

"You must be cold," the man said. "If it's any consolation,

I'll let you keep your pants on until the very last minute. I'm just doing it the way your mother wrote it."

Grabbing a flashlight, the man switched it on and shined it in Ethan's face. Blinded by the glare, Ethan could only see the spot moving against the pitch black and nothing else. But he heard the man getting to his feet. He was still eating that apple too. The light came toward him. He heard something hard hit the wood floor, and realized the man had tossed aside his apple.

He still couldn't see his abductor's face—though the man hovered over him. He took hold of Ethan's arm, and then pulled him up.

With his ankles bound and his hands tied behind him, Ethan had to twist around to keep from falling back. He suddenly felt dizzy and nauseous. The man maintained a tight grip on his arm, and shined the flashlight under Ethan's face.

"Your mother decided you should be naked," the man whispered. "At least, that's how she wrote it. The victims were all naked—except for the killer's trademark, his calling card."

Ethan gazed ahead at a sliding glass door. There was a dark tarp covering the other side of it. The plastic sheet flapped in the wind. The darkened glass was almost like a mirror. Ethan could see himself, propped up by this still-faceless stranger. He stared at the silver-gray tape over his mouth. He was shirtless and shivering in the man's grasp. And he saw the thing tied around his neck.

It was a black ribbon.

Gillian watched the ferry pulling up to the pier next door to the Aquarium. She could see the lower level where the cars were parked.

She had a pretty good idea of how Chase must have faked his death. She remembered peeking into the garage by his house in Bremerton, and seeing the scuba gear. The erotic thriller he'd written in her class had included some sea-diving sequences amid all the sex and violence. He must have had his scuba gear in the car—along with the corpse of someone who resembled him. Security people and bomb-sniffing dogs checked out all the cars departing from the Seattle side during rush hour. But late at night—from the other side? She wasn't sure. Chase would have had to be first in line on the ferry. He would have had to practice putting on his underwater gear within the confines of a small car—and in a hurry too. He probably enjoyed the challenge. He must have gotten a thrill from the dangerous stunt-dive off the ferry, and his escape from the sinking vehicle. But he couldn't have planned on the ferry propeller chopping up his car and the dead man inside it. Chase must have done something to the corpse ahead of time to make it unrecognizable, especially the face. Gillian cringed at the thought.

The same person who had done all this now had her son.

She and Jason stood by the empty squad car. The cop hadn't yet returned from chasing down the shoplifter. Every few moments, someone ran by them—obviously on their way to catch the ferry. Gillian wondered if it was the Bremerton ferry.

"Twenty-four hours," she murmured. "That's how long the killer in *Black Ribbons* kept his victims alive."

"Where does he take them after he abducts them?" Jason asked.

For the killer's holding area, Gillian had thought about the scene near the end of *Rebel Without a Cause,* when James Dean, Natalie Wood, and Sal Mineo explore a deserted mansion. She'd decided her *Black Ribbons* killer would keep his victims in a similarly remote, gloomy estate not far from his own one-bedroom carriage-house apartment.

"He takes them to an old deserted house, just walking distance from where he lives," Gillian explained. "There are a lot of isolated, old-money homes in Chase's neighborhood—in Bremerton. In fact, there's a big, empty house undergoing some repairs just down the block from him." She glanced at the ferry again. The next one wouldn't be for at least another hour, maybe two.

"You think Chase did the same thing with Ethan?" Jason asked. "I mean, he must know you're going to figure him out. It's kind of a risk for him, going exactly by the book."

"But that's just what he does," Gillian said. "He thrives on the risk. He *wants* me to figure out his next move. You said so yourself, he's been telling me all along who he is."

Imalegend2's critiques always affected her more than any of the other online reviewers, because he was so critical. Funny, how the bad reviews were the ones that stuck with her. And he was never very kind. But he always mentioned the murders. He seemed to dwell on them. Now that she thought of it, each one of the killings he'd copied had been cited in his reviews.

The last time she'd checked Amazon.com—a few days ago—there hadn't been any comments from *imalegend2* about *Black Ribbons*.

"When you were reading my reviews on the plane this afternoon, did you notice if *I'm a Legend Too* critiqued *Black Ribbons*?"

Jason nodded. "Yeah, he did, but I didn't read it."

"I need to know what he said, and what he's going to copy from the book. His plans for Ethan could be in that review."

Jason tried to open the passenger door of the police car. It was locked. He tugged at the handle to the back door—to no avail. "Dammit, my laptop is in there," he muttered.

A few passersby gave him strange looks as he ran around the unoccupied patrol car and tried to open the driver's door. Gillian anxiously scanned the street for the young cop. But there was no sign of him.

A man in a gray suit, carrying a briefcase, raced toward her. Gillian stepped out of his way. "Excuse me!" she called. "Are you heading for the ferry?"

"Yeah! Coming through!" he grunted, rushing by her.

"Where? Where's the ferry going?" she called.

"Bremerton!" he yelled back over his shoulder.

She turned to Jason. "I think we should go," she said. "We need to catch that ferry. It's obvious he's holding Ethan somewhere near his house in Bremerton. We'll go to his neighborhood, and look for a green SUV. Forget about looking up the review. We'll just call the police from the ferry, and . . ."

Gillian fell silent as she watched Jason stoop down and pick up a big chunk of concrete that had cracked off the curb. All at once, he smashed the patrol car's passenger window with it. The glass shattered into pieces.

A woman on the sidewalk screamed, but Jason didn't even look up. He reached though the broken window and opened the door. Then he grabbed his laptop computer from the floor, and shut the car door.

"C'mon, let's try to catch this ferry," he said, grabbing Gillian's hand. And they started running.

Imalegend2 gave *Black Ribbons: A Maggie Dare Mystery* only two stars in his Amazon.com review. It had yesterday's date. Apparently, Chase wanted to submit his critique before he carried out his next copycat killing.

Gillian sat beside Jason in a row of seats on the crowded ferry. Just in their vicinity, she noticed several other passengers with laptop computers or carrying cases for laptops. Breaking into that squad car really hadn't been necessary. They could have borrowed a computer from any one of these people. But she didn't say anything. The fact that Jason had broken that window for her was rather sweet—if willful destruction of police property could somehow be construed as *sweet*. It made for a charming story anyway, one she hoped to tell Ethan—once they found him. And she prayed they'd find him.

"Is Gillian McBride Losing Her Touch?" was Chase's headline.

This time around, Gillian McBride comes up with a tormented serial killer who abducts "nice girls" so he can confess his sexual fantasies to them. Gradually cutting away their clothes during these confessions, he works himself into a frenzy, and kills his objects of lust. The unmolested, naked body of each victim is found—with a black ribbon around her neck (a symbol of regret or mourning?)—not far from where she was abducted (and where he has also left his black ribbon calling card). More regret and/or mourning or just plain overkill, Ms. McBride? This villain almost wants to get caught. He takes his victims to a deserted mansion just a few doors down from his humble pad. It's there he talks their ears off before shooting them (usually in the head). There's some nice irony as McBride contrasts the villain's shame over his ho-hum sexual hang-ups with the blithe way he bumps off these women—along with a host of cops. (His house and his hideaway are both booby-trapped for the police pursuing him, and subsequently, the body count for those not-so-bright boys in blue is very high indeed.) The cops—except for Maggie Dare, of course—are pretty stupid in this one. This is McBride's second Maggie Dare Mystery, and I hope her last. She's not a very interesting protagonist. In this book, McBride seems more focused on Psychology 101 than producing gooseflesh. While the scenes with her tortured killer and his victims in the abandoned mansion pack some punch, the rest of this thriller just doesn't thrill very much.

"We can't let the police know where we are or what we're doing," Gillian said. "Not until we try to do this on our own." She looked at Jason and shrugged. "I guess it's presumptuous of me to say 'we.' You don't have to be involved, Jason. You've already helped so much—"

"Oh, shut up," he whispered, putting his arm around her

for a moment. "You know you can't get rid of me that easily. You've tried."

She smiled. "Thank you, Jason."

"You don't want the police rushing into a booby-trapped hideaway. Is that it?"

She nodded. The *Black Ribbons* killer had rigged a detonating device in his home, killing two SWAT members and wounding several others. He'd also planted mines and exploding devices in a warehouse where the police thought he might be hiding. Three more policemen perished—along with one of the killer's recently abducted victims. Gillian had no problem creating these six fictional deaths, but she didn't want any more real murders on her conscience.

It wasn't just the cops' lives that were at risk either. She didn't want Chase's recently abducted victim dying in an explosion during some ill-planned police operation. She wasn't going to be the author of her son's death.

"If we can't find Ethan within ninety minutes," Gillian said, "we'll tell the police everything. But we have to try it alone first."

She imagined Ethan, bound and gagged like one of her *Black Ribbons* victims. The young woman left alone in that abandoned wired-for-detonation warehouse hadn't known she was going to die. Gillian couldn't have been that cruel, not even to a fictional character. Was Chase as merciful? Or was he telling Ethan his plans right now?

Gillian remembered another scene in her book, between the killer and one of his victims. The exchange between the sweet, doomed young captive and the killer was both creepy and heartbreaking. At least, that was what Gillian had been going for when she'd written it. He was sitting with her in a second-floor bedroom of the old, abandoned mansion near his apartment. The young woman's hands and feet were tied. He'd removed her blouse and shoes while she'd been unconscious. She was wearing her bra and a pair of jeans when she woke up. He'd put tape over her mouth to keep her quiet.

He took a pair of shears out of his case, and told her not to squirm. He started to cut at the jeans—beginning at the cuff, by her ankle. He worked his way up to her thigh—exposing her creamy skin. "If you promise not to scream, I'll take the tape off your mouth," he said.

The girl had been very obedient. She hadn't squirmed or kicked. She nodded.

The *Black Ribbons* killer reached for the tape.

When the man ripped the tape off Ethan's mouth, it hurt like hell. But Ethan didn't cry out. He gasped for air, and then thanked the man. He'd decided he might live longer if he was cooperative. Besides, the more docile he seemed, the less guarded this guy might become—and the better his chances for escape. His abductor had already cut along one side of his jeans with a pair of scissors, and Ethan hadn't tried to pull away. In fact, he'd stayed perfectly still for the ordeal, like he was getting a shot from the doctor.

"This is the part in your mother's book when the hero caresses the girl's hair." He laughed. "Did you hear that? Freudian slip. Actually, he's the *villain,* but to me, her villains are always the heroes. Anyway, it's at this point in *Black Ribbons* when he caresses the girl's hair and tells her his sexual fantasies. But I'm not doing that with you. Then again, maybe you'd like it if I did, since you're gay."

"No, I wouldn't like it," Ethan said quietly.

"Well, don't try to tell me you like girls, because I've seen you at school. I've heard them calling you a *fag* in the playfield. I've watched you when you thought no one was watching, Ethan Tanner. I've followed you into bookstores, and magazine stores, and card shops. I've noticed the kind of things that catch your eye in those places. I've seen you look at other guys when you thought no one else could see you. I know you better than anyone."

Ethan felt so exposed and humiliated. He stared at the

man, sitting close by him on the floor. Ethan's eyes had adjusted to the darkness, and he could see his face now. He was in his late twenties, with receding hair, and a handsome, but kind of smarmy, dumb-jock look to him.

Though chilled to the bone, Ethan tried not to tremble. He listened to the tarp flapping in the wind outside. It became particularly loud during strong gusts, and the room seemed to sway a tiny bit. Beyond the heavy fluttering sound, he couldn't hear anything else at all—no people talking, no traffic in the distance. Ethan wondered if they were out somewhere in the country.

The guy talked about seeing so much. But he couldn't see behind Ethan's back. He couldn't see how Ethan was trying to loosen the rope around his wrists.

"What are you going to do to me?" Ethan asked, eyeing the scissors in the man's hand.

"If you have to ask that, you haven't read your mommy's new book." The man laughed. "It's trite and very clichéd in spots, but not so bad. I certainly don't see a best-seller there. You know, she could have had one two years ago. I gave her a chance for a runaway hit, but she turned it down. I thought we could be a team—write together, fuck together. I created the Schoolgirl Murders for her."

Ethan squinted at him. "I thought some ex-priest killed those women."

"No, but he was the perfect patsy. I picked him to take the fall before I even picked out any of the victims. I broke into his place a month before my first kill. I gathered hair samples from his hairbrush, and even took some fibers from a mat in front of his door so I could plant them at the crime scenes. I really knew this schmuck. I knew his past too. Hell, if your mother bothered to research for her books as much as I have for my kills, she'd be putting out fucking masterpieces. I found out about this girl old Father Farrow dated from one of his classes. I knew if she ended up dead in a certain way, he'd eventually take the rap. It was beautiful. And I did it all for your mother. I thought it would inspire her. I thought she was the only one worthy of documenting my work. But she shot me down. Stupid, stupid bitch . . ."

Ethan kept tugging and twisting at the rope. The skin around his wrists burned from all the friction, but he didn't stop.

"I tell you, Ethan, it pisses me off when I think about doing all that for her." He shook the scissors at him as he spoke. "She told me I had talent. But she was saying the same thing to my idiot classmates. Goddamn liar. Did you know that about your mother, Ethan? She's a goddamn, fucking liar. She told me if I kept writing and worked hard, I could get published. So I figured I'd show her. I'd show them all. Success is the best revenge, you know. I was going to finish my novel and get it published."

Ethan nodded attentively. All the while, he kept wringing his hands and pulling at the rope around his wrists. Maybe it was just his imagination, but the rope seemed to be loosening, stretching a bit.

"Well, I guess the joke was on me, because no one wanted to buy my book. They wouldn't even fucking look at the outline. Meanwhile, your mother continued to churn out that crap every seven or eight months."

"You know, it took her a really long time to publish her first book," Ethan said, rushing to her defense. "It wasn't easy for her—"

"Oh, blah, blah, blah. You sound just like her. She said I could get published if I worked hard enough. She led me on—in every way. Goddamn tease. How much rejection and humiliation is a guy supposed to take? I suffered, and your mother needs to be accountable for that. She has to suffer too, and realize her actions have consequences. The *words* she writes have consequences."

Ethan tried not to shake. "Did you kill my father?"

He nodded. "Your mother told me how to do it—in one of her books. You see, Ethan, she needs to understand just who her best pupil is. It's me." The man scooted closer, and tickled Ethan's throat with the scissors point. "And now, I have a question for you."

Ethan stared at him apprehensively.

The man grinned. "Doesn't it chafe your wrists when you try to wiggle out of the ropes like that?"

"I wasn't trying to wiggle out of the ropes," Ethan said. "I'm cold, and I'm trying not to shiver, that's all. I don't want those scissors to nick me. What—what's this book of yours about anyway?"

Chuckling, the man pulled the shears away from Ethan's neck. "Huh, smart kid. But your stall tactic isn't going to work, Ethan. I have a schedule to keep tonight." He pushed at Ethan's shoulder. "Now, I need you to lie down and roll over on your stomach for me."

Ethan couldn't help recoiling a bit at the man's touch. He heard himself whimper for a second. His whole body stiffened as the man pushed him down to the floor and rolled him over onto his stomach. In this dark, empty room—in a house in the middle of nowhere—he knew he was going to die.

"I know you're scared and uncomfortable, Ethan," he heard the man say. "I'm sorry. I really am. You can blame your mother for this. It was all her idea."

"Please, don't spend any of your time or manpower looking for us," Gillian told Detective Wright. He'd been the officer in charge outside Ruth's house, and this was his second call to Jason's cell phone. "I'd rather you focus on trying to find *my son*. We're sorry about the patrol car window. We'll pay for it. I have a lead I'm going to follow, but I need to do it alone. Just give me an hour. Then I'll call and tell you everything. Please don't phone us again unless you have some news about my son."

"Mrs. Tanner, I can't let you—"

Gillian clicked off the line, then handed the phone back to Jason. From the crowded passenger area on the ferry's upper tier, they stepped out to the bow. A cold gust of wind hit them, and Gillian automatically put her arm around Jason. They could see the city lights, and Bremerton ferry terminal ahead. They could also see some police cars parked near the harbor.

"Do you think those are for us?" Gillian asked. Detective Wright hadn't let on that he knew they were on the Bremerton ferry.

"I'm sure someone back in Seattle saw us running for the ferry terminal, and told our driver. Thanks to me, we didn't make a very subtle exit."

Gillian counted three police cars. It was possible they were there for routine security, but she hadn't noticed this kind of police presence in the Bremerton terminal when she'd come back from Chase's house on Saturday afternoon.

She glanced toward the passenger seating area behind them. Through the windows in the doors, she saw people heading for the stairwells to go down to their cars.

She turned to Jason. "The police will be looking for us on foot, won't they?"

Ten minutes later, the ferry was pulling into Bremerton. Gillian and Jason walked through the ferry's vehicle level, a floating parking lot—with very little room to navigate between the cars. Exhaust fumes mingled with the fishy odor from the harbor. Gillian passed several cars before she spotted the two young men in the front seat of a slightly beat-up Geo. They looked like they were in their twenties. It was a safe bet that two young men wouldn't be worried about giving a ride to a couple. Gillian pulled a twenty out of her purse, and knocked on the driver's window.

The window came down, and the young man with a blond crew cut glanced up at her. "Hey, what's going on?" he asked.

"My boyfriend hurt his foot, and he doesn't want to hobble off the boat. Could you guys maybe give us a lift—just a couple of blocks to town? We'd really appreciate it. There's a twenty in it for you."

The two men in the Geo were near the front of the line. They were both in the Navy, and very polite. They had "Bruce Springsteen's Greatest Hits" on the CD player. Gillian sat in the backseat with Jason. She kept her feet to one side to avoid stepping on the twelve-pack of beer. As they rolled off the ferry onto the pier, she spied the police checking the line of passengers at the terminal gate. A secret look passed between her and Jason.

"We can drive you folks wherever you need to go," the sailor at the wheel told them. "We're not in a hurry."

"The center of town is fine, thanks very much," Gillian said.

Traffic moved at a crawl due to everyone pouring off the ferry. They inched through a section of town that was all taverns, greasy spoons, and pawnshops. "Actually, right here is perfect," Jason said, pointing to a pub called The Meet Market.

As they climbed out of the car, Gillian tried to give the driver the twenty-dollar bill. But he refused it. "Thank you, guys," she said. Gillian didn't want to say anything in front of them, but she wondered why Jason wanted to be let out at this crummy-looking bar.

He waved to the young men in the Geo as they drove off. Then Jason nodded at the store next to the tavern. On the window, there was a very detailed rendering of a United States flag rippling in the breeze, and above it in silver letters: MILT'S GUNS & AMMO CENTER. "If you really think Chase is expecting us," Jason whispered, "we better not come looking for him empty-handed."

With all the hunting in Montana, Jason knew something about guns. The long, narrow shop was lined with glass cases full of handguns and knives. The walls displayed scores of rifles on brackets. Gillian remained behind Jason while he quickly looked over the merchandise. The place smelled a

bit like old fried chicken. Country-and-western music sere-
naded them over the radio. The people who ran Milt's were
sticklers about the five-day waiting period for handguns. But
after a glance at Jason's out-of-state license, they sold him a
Winchester Marlin 30-30 rifle and a box of ammunition for
$229. They dug a box out of the stockroom for him to carry
it in. At Gillian's suggestion, he also bought a flashlight.

They had been in the gun store for only ten minutes. But
for Gillian, it seemed to be taking forever. She'd felt the same
way on the ferry. Every minute counted. Ethan had been
Chase's hostage for over three hours now.

She wondered if they were really doing the smart thing by
not letting the police handle this. She knew what Ruth would
tell her to do. Still, Gillian had written the book Chase was
using for his guidelines. He would be prepared for the police, and many people could die. She couldn't have that on
her conscience. Ethan wouldn't want it either.

While the man behind the counter at Milt's gave Jason his
gun, ammunition, and all the paperwork, Gillian phoned for
a taxi to take them to Chase Scott's house on Overlook Drive.
If she didn't see what she expected to find near Chase's
house, she would call the police.

Their plan was vague and haphazard at best. They were
going to look for a dark green SUV parked somewhere near
an abandoned mansion in Chase's neighborhood. That one
recently built house now under repair was the most likely
spot for Chase's *holding area*. But she might be wrong.
Their search could waste hours of valuable time. And the
brief presence of a dark green SUV in Ruth's driveway was
something unsubstantiated from one of Ruth's neighbors.
Even if Chase had packed Ethan away in that SUV over
three hours ago, he could have switched cars since then. She
was operating on a hunch—and a lot of hope.

The ferry traffic through town had subsided a bit, and the
cab arrived within five minutes. Gillian had thought the driver
might balk at someone coming out of a gun store with a

rifle—even if it was in a box. But it didn't seem to faze him. He took them up to Overlook Drive.

Gillian squeezed Jason's hand as they passed the little lookout point. Her stomach was in knots. She had the window cracked open, and could hear a flapping sound as they approached the big house on stilts, half-covered in tarps. "Could you slow down here, please?" she asked the driver. She rolled down the window and gazed out at the house. It was completely dark, without any sign of activity. She'd hoped against hope to see a dark green SUV in the driveway, but there was nothing.

Her heart sank a little. This wasn't going to be an easy search. They would need to take a closer look around the house—but not now.

"Thank you, driver," she said. He continued on up the street. Gillian spotted Chase's address ahead. "It's on the right, but you can just pull over and let us out on the road."

The driver slowed down and turned into Chase's driveway. "No, please! Stop!" Gillian cried, leaning forward. "Just—just right here is fine, thanks."

He stopped at the end of Chase's driveway. "You sure you don't want me to take you up to the house? I need to turn around anyway."

"Could you do that in another driveway?" Gillian asked. Ignoring his vexed look in the rearview mirror, she gave him a twenty, and then opened the taxi door. "Thank you. Keep the change."

Jason climbed out after her, and closed the door. The taxi pulled away. They stood at the end of Chase's long, winding driveway. But they could see his little ranch house, and some lights on inside. They could also see a dark green SUV parked in front of the house.

"My God, you were right," Jason murmured. He took the Winchester out of its box, and loaded it. He tossed the rifle box in the bushes, and took a step into the driveway.

"Stop," Gillian whispered.

He froze. Gillian switched on the flashlight.

"What are you doing?" Jason hissed. "Turn off that light. He'll see us."

"I don't think he's home," Gillian said. She shined the light along the paved driveway. A near-invisible wire ran across it—about ten feet in front of them—at knee level. "It's a trip wire," she whispered. "It's how the *Black Ribbons* killer rigged his house for detonation. The doors and first-floor windows are probably wired too."

"My God," Jason muttered.

She wondered if he'd left Ethan bound and gagged—and alone—inside this booby-trapped house. But no, he wouldn't do that. She couldn't see Chase setting up a *Black Ribbons* kill so that his most important victim could die in some explosion. This was a trap for the police.

"Do you think the house is empty?" Jason asked.

She nodded. "He has Ethan somewhere else, I'm almost sure of it. I want to go back down the road to that house on stilts."

He nicked Ethan's leg with the scissors. Ethan flinched and let out a little cry.

"Now look what you made me do," he said, clicking his tongue against his teeth.

Ethan couldn't stop shaking. It was so cold, and he was so scared. He'd been lying on his stomach while the man cut from the cuff of his jeans up along the side of his leg. He'd jabbed him just above the knee. Ethan could feel the blood trickling down and soaking his jeans.

Now both legs of his jeans were sheared on the sides. The man was working his way up toward Ethan's hip. He explained that this was how it was done in *Black Ribbons*. The killer liked to cut the clothes off his victims. To tease himself, he took long pauses between each *cutting* session—until they were naked. "That's when he killed them, Ethan," the man said. "How does it feel to have a mother who dreams up things like that?"

Ethan didn't answer. He felt the sawdust and grit on the floor against his bare stomach. He wasn't going to cry in front of the man. But his nose was running, and he couldn't wipe it.

"Do you know what that bitch did to me?" the man asked. "She called me up the other day with this lie about her editor and her agent wanting to see my book. I knew it was a scam. Still, she's a smart one—just not quite as smart as I thought. See, I had a feeling she'd show up here tonight—to save her little boy. I was almost positive she would figure me out. But maybe I was wrong. Either way, I'm ready for her. I've made a lot of preparations. In fact, I'd really hate to see all that hard work go to waste. You should see how I've got this place wired."

"What do you mean?" Ethan asked.

"Oh, I have all sorts of surprises rigged up. You might still be alive to see some of my genius at work. You might not believe this, Ethan, but I'm hoping just as much as you that your mommy shows up here tonight."

As she and Jason walked along Overlook Drive, Gillian still had these terrible knots in her stomach, and they were tightening. She glanced back toward Chase's driveway. "Could you call Detective Wright for me, please?"

Jason paused on the roadside "Are you ready to turn this over to him?"

"Not yet," Gillian said.

He handed her the rifle, then pulled out his cell phone and hit the last call return button. "Detective Wright?" he said into the phone. "It's Jason Hurrell. Just a second, please." He gave the phone to Gillian.

She handed the rifle back to him. "Detective, it's Gillian

McBride," she said, continuing down Overlook Drive. "I need to ask you—"

"I don't appreciate being hung up on," he cut in. "Are you all right?"

"Okay, considering," she replied quickly. "I'm sorry about hanging up on you. I need to ask, have you or anyone else on the force received an anonymous tip in connection with this case?"

"An anonymous tip?" he echoed. "No. We haven't had anyone calling in with a *tip*."

It was how her *Black Ribbons* killer had lured a SWAT team to his house—and how Gillian had increased the body count in her book. "It's important you call us before acting on any tips someone might phone in," Gillian said into the phone. "I'm talking *life-or-death* important. Could you check with the Bremerton Police, too?"

"Check with them about what?" the detective asked. *"Anonymous tips?"*

"Yes, regarding this case, exactly. I'll call you back in a half hour to explain everything."

"Now, wait a minute, Mrs. Tanner—"

"Detective, I'm sorry, but I'm hanging up on you again." She clicked off the line, and handed the phone back to Jason.

A gust blew off the water. The trees swayed around them, and shadows moved in the darkness. Shuddering, Gillian rubbed her arms. Jason pulled her toward him and she slid her arm around his waist. She knew they were getting close to the house under repair. Though she couldn't see it, Gillian heard that tarp flapping in the wind. She wondered if Ethan was listening to the same sound.

As they passed a huge evergreen, the house on the bluff came into view. The dull, black plastic covering seemed to catch the moonlight only when it rippled in the wind. The scaffolding on the far side of the edifice looked steadier than the rickety support beams under the back side of the house.

Maybe it was just the plastic cover fluttering, but Gillian swore that monstrosity of a house seemed to sway a little with the wind gusts. The surrounding lot was somewhat barren, with only a few patches of green on the strips of recently planted sod. Some scrawny bushes lined the deserted driveway that curved into a three-car-garage. The taller trees and thicker shrubs bordered both sides of the yard, which seemed to drop off in back.

Gillian thought about her *Black Ribbons* killer. His *holding area,* the sacred spot for him and his victims, had been safeguarded against invaders. A hidden land mine—one of a dozen—killed a policeman. And a device attached to the front door detonated a bomb, killing two more. If Chase was here, he certainly would be expecting them.

She and Jason stayed close to the trees and shrubbery along the side of the yard as they skulked toward the house. Gillian kept looking down at the ground for any telltale bumps or thin wires stretched across their path. She couldn't help wondering if the place was indeed empty. They could be wasting these precious minutes on some stupid hunch she had. For all she knew, Ethan could be dead.

"Can you hear someone talking?" Jason whispered.

All Gillian heard was the wind—along with that tarp flapping.

"I thought I heard someone laugh," he said.

Gillian suddenly stopped. She saw a little device on the ground—only a few feet away. It was a box, with a tiny nailhead of a red light, planted under a bush. She wondered if it was some kind of electronic eye or sensor. Was it something the owners had installed before they'd vacated the place? Or had Chase prepared for unannounced visitors?

Hesitant, Gillian reached out for Jason's hand. As they moved closer to the structure half-shrouded in black plastic tarp, she couldn't help feeling the house was waiting for them.

*   *   *

A beeper went off amid the things in the man's army-issue backpack. "Company!" he said with grin.

Ethan rolled over on his side. "HELP!" he yelled. "HELP ME!"

Checking some device in his knapsack, the man chuckled. "That's right, Ethan. Go ahead and scream. Lure them in here."

"WATCH OUT! HE'S GOT THE PLACE RIGGED! HE'S—"

Ethan shut up as soon as the man grabbed him by the scalp. He lifted Ethan's head up, and then slammed it on the floor.

Chase had done the same thing to Ethan's father, cracking his head against the edge of the pool at the Aces High Inn in Missoula.

Ethan lay still and silent.

"Like father, like son," Chase muttered.

Gillian had heard his voice. It was unmistakably Ethan, crying for help.

From the trees and bushes at the side of the yard, she started to run out of the shadows—toward the house. For a moment, she forgot to look for trip wires or potential land mines.

"Wait!" Jason whispered. Grabbing her arm, he pulled her back toward the trees.

A loud shot rang out, and a tuft of dirt exploded at their feet. Jason shielded her, putting himself between her and the house.

Gillian glanced up at the half-shrouded mansion. She spotted an open window on the second floor—along one section that was uncovered. Chase was using it as a sniper's nest.

Another shot went off, and another little burst of dirt came from the ground.

They ducked under a tree. Jason took out his cell phone

and handed it to her. "Better call the police, Gill." Gazing up at the window, Jason readied his rifle.

There was another blast of gunfire. Gillian almost dropped the phone.

Jason recoiled and bumped against her. The rifle fell out of his hands. His legs just seemed to give out from under him, and he went down.

He hadn't uttered a sound.

Through the night-vision telescopic sight of his sniper rifle, Chase watched Gillian hovering over the crumpled form of her fallen boyfriend. She dragged the body behind the tree—out of his range. He couldn't help chuckling at the way she struggled. She looked slow and silly in the night-vision scope, a little green-neon figure shaking with terror. He watched her retrieve the cell phone, and then she ducked behind the tree.

A few moments later, she reemerged from the shadows. With the rifle in her hand, she zigzagged toward the house.

He kept her in the crosshairs. He could have shot her right there, if he wanted. He could have watched that small, green, cartoonlike thing stop and fall in its tracks. But he was enjoying this too much. From that second-floor window, he felt Godlike, looking down on poor, pathetic Gillian.

Firing repeatedly, he shot at the ground near her feet. He smirked as she darted around the spray from each bullet. He was only playing around with her, of course. He wouldn't shoot her now.

He wanted to see Gillian's face when he killed her.

His head throbbing, Ethan felt nauseous when he sat up. He was alone in the big, dark room. He pulled and tugged at the binding around his wrists behind him. He didn't see the scissors anywhere. The knapsack was gone too.

Ethan heard a few shots go off. The blasts sounded like they were coming from a room down the hall. Was the man shooting at the police?

Ethan noticed his T-shirt and shoes in a heap on the floor. He scooted over toward them, then twisted around and grabbed his shirt. He continued to crawl toward the wall, and then braced himself against it so he could stand up. As best he could, he wrapped the shirt around his hands.

Another two shots rang out. Ethan thought he heard the man chuckling.

Hopping over to one of the smaller windows, Ethan turned his back to it, and then punched at the glass with his covered hands. Nothing. Ethan tried it again, and again. He couldn't get much momentum with his hands tied behind him. He had to settle for a few short jabs—until he heard a crack. He wondered if the man could hear it too.

Ethan hit the window again, and his shrouded fists penetrated the glass. Blindly moving his hands, he tried to cut at the rope with a piece of glass stuck in the corner of the broken window. He nicked his arm and felt the blood seeping onto his wadded-up shirt.

"Please, God, please," he whispered, awkwardly twisting to one side. A tear ran down his cheek as he kept rubbing the rope against the shard of glass. He tried to pull his wrists apart to keep them from getting cut—and to make the rope more taut. The guy had looped the cord around twice, so Ethan wasn't sure if he was slashing at the same spot over and over again. His eyes stayed riveted on the doorway. Any minute now, he expected the man to come back.

At last, he felt the frayed rope break apart. Ethan's arms ached sweetly as he moved them from behind his back. He tossed aside the wadded-up, bloodstained shirt. Damp with blood and sweat, the rope still clung to the chafed skin around his wrist. At a certain angle, the rope looked as if it were still tightly tied around his one wrist. Ethan had to peel it off.

At long last he was able to wipe his nose.

Ethan snatched a piece of glass off the floor, then braced himself against the wall, and carefully cut at the cord round his ankles. The guy had double-looped the cord here too. Once his feet were free, he used the shard of glass to slice a hole in the black plastic tarp outside the broken window.

He couldn't expect to defend himself against this man who was almost a head taller than him and outweighed him by at least sixty pounds. Plus the guy had a gun—and in that knapsack maybe a whole arsenal. Ethan needed to find a way of escape. But as he peeled back a section of the dirt-coated tarp and peeked outside, he realized he couldn't climb out the window. It was a sheer drop, with nothing to break his fall except some trees and bushes a hundred feet below. "Oh, shit," he muttered. The place must have been built on a cliff.

He was about to start toward the sliding door, but then he remembered, and glanced down at the shattered glass around his bare feet. The bloodied shirt was nearby, along with the discarded rope. Ethan picked up a piece of the frayed rope. It was soaked with sweat, and almost stuck to his fingertips.

The plastic sheet outside the broken window flapped loudly. Past all that noise, Ethan thought he heard footsteps coming down the hallway.

Clutching the rifle close to her chest, Gillian inched alongside the house. She quickly wiped the tears from her eyes. She couldn't think of anything right now except saving her son.

She'd managed to make a brief call to the police after dragging Jason behind the tree. He'd been shot in the stomach, but he was still breathing—a raspy, labored rattle. He'd barely opened his eyes to look at her.

She'd told Detective Wright where they were. She'd said Jason was shot, and they needed an ambulance. "The killer has a sniper's nest on the second floor. And he has my son in there with him. You need to be very, very careful. The whole place could be rigged with explosive devices."

"All right, Gillian, now just stay on the line," the detective had told her. "Don't try to do anything—"

She couldn't just sit there and do nothing while her son was trapped in that place. "I'm sorry to do this to you again," she'd said, switching off the phone. Then she'd retrieved the Winchester. Sprinting toward the house, she'd dodged bullets with practically every step. The closer she'd gotten to the mansion, the wilder his shots became.

Gillian realized that if she stayed against the side of the house, he couldn't shoot at her unless he hung out the second-floor window. Past the loud fluttering from the tarp, she could hear him laughing up there. He stuck his head out and grinned down at her.

It was Chase, all right. Gillian fired at him. She'd never shot a gun in her life, and the force of it almost knocked her down. She didn't hit anything. She only succeeded in hurting her shoulder with the recoil. He was laughing even louder now, a smug cackle.

She retreated toward the back of the house, out of his range. Gillian pulled aside the plastic covering to check every window she passed. All of them were locked. If Chase was true to his *Black Ribbons* counterpart, he'd fixed detonating devices to the front and back doors. Her only chance was climbing through a window. She had to move fast too. If Chase couldn't take potshots at her, he'd turn his attention to Ethan.

The further Gillian crept toward the backyard, the more the ground dipped down. She glanced at the support beams holding up the back half of the house. There was no way she could climb them.

Gillian found a basement door near the rear of the house, but didn't dare try it. Nearby, a tall aluminum ladder rested against a balcony off the first floor. The plastic covering had become loose in one section. As it flapped out, Gillian caught a glimpse of a partially open window—not far from the balcony's ledge. Tucking the Winchester under her arm, she started to climb the tall ladder. A gust of wind came up, and the ladder wobbled, but Gillian kept climbing until she reached the balcony ledge.

Suddenly, she lost her footing on the last rung. In a panic, she grabbed at one of the ropes holding down the tarp. The rifle fell out from under her arm. Clinging to the rope, Gillian stared down at the weapon on the ground below her. It was all she could do to keep from crying. She managed to hoist herself up on the ledge.

Someone had left a few bricks at the corner of the ledge to weigh down the loose tarp. Gillian grabbed a brick, and then peered into the open window. All she could see was a murky blackness.

Setting a brick on the far side of the sill, Gillian reached inside the window and pulled herself in. Every sound she made seemed to echo in the huge, cold empty house. She retrieved the brick, and then glanced around. She couldn't see a damn thing. For all she knew, Chase could be in the room with her.

The wind howled, and the tarp billowed out—allowing Gillian a momentary glimpse of her surroundings. She was standing in a living room, stark and modern with hardwood floors and a characterless fireplace.

Above her, she heard footsteps.

Suddenly, she heard Ethan cry out: *"No, no, no! Wait, please—"*

And then, a gunshot. Gillian froze.

"Gillian!" Chase called in a teasing voice. *"There's somebody up here who needs his mommy! Hurry on up, now. He's hurt. We're waiting."*

Trembling, Gillian blindly waved a hand in front of her and started toward the sound of his voice. She could barely walk, she was so unnerved. She kept hoping Ethan would cry out again; at least then she'd know he was still alive.

Eventually, her fingertips brushed against the wall and she felt her way toward the front hallway. In her other hand, she clutched the brick.

She began to see dim shapes and images. Gillian wasn't sure if she was moving toward a light source, or if it was just her vision adjusting to the darkness. But she found the front stairs, which curved up to the second floor.

"C'mon, Teach," Chase called. *"Hurry up. Your little boy's asking for you."*

Gillian started up the stairs. She glanced at the brick in her hand. It seemed so useless against someone with a gun.

"Ethan wants to see you before he dies, Gillian! He's asking for you. . . ."

Tears in her eyes, she continued up the steps to the second floor.

"I knew you'd find me eventually. . . ."

Gillian followed the sound of his voice and moved toward a bedroom. A faint light showed through the doorway. Stepping into the room, Gillian saw the light source: a flashlight on the floor. It lay beside a big, army-camouflage-pattern knapsack.

"Come on in, Gillian."

She turned toward Chase. But he was just a shadowy outline, standing over something on the other side of the bedroom. It took her a moment to see that he had his sniper's rifle pointed down at Ethan. Shirtless and barefoot, her son was lying on his side on the hardwood floor. It looked like his ankles were bound, and his hands must have been tied in back of him. His jeans were all sheared at the sides. Then she noticed the black ribbon tied around his neck. He was shivering.

He's still alive, she thought.

"Toss in that Winchester, Teach," Chase said. "Gently now."

"I dropped the gun climbing into a window downstairs," Gillian said, a tremor in her voice. "All I have is this." She lobbed the brick into the center of the room. She took a step toward them. "Ethan . . ."

"Hold it right there, Mommy," Chase said, jabbing at Ethan with the barrel of his sniper's rifle.

"I'm all right, Mom," Ethan whispered.

"You didn't think I'd really shoot him, did you?" Chase asked. "C'mon, Gillian, you should know better than that. As long as he's alive, you'll cooperate. Isn't that right?"

"Yes, I'll do whatever you want. Just please let him go."

Chase backed away from Ethan. But he still kept the rifle pointed at him. He was moving toward the large knapsack on the other side of the room, near a sliding glass door. "You got yourself all messy for nothing. You didn't have to go through any windows, Gillian. I left all the doors open for you."

"I thought—" She swallowed hard. "I thought you might have copied the *Black Ribbons* killer, and set detonating devices at all the entries."

He snickered. "Oh, I did. I set up several. I just didn't switch them on." He squatted down by the open knapsack and reached into it. He took his eyes off her for only a few seconds. "And now they're switched on." With his foot, he nudged the backpack until she could see a mechanism in there with a tiny, glowing green light. "I've become quite a demolition expert—as you'll soon find out. You called the police, didn't you?"

"How do you plan to get out, Chase?" she asked, gazing at the sniper's rifle pointed at Ethan.

"I have an escape route, a window to the side yard. My car is parked in the driveway two doors down. The people who live in the house are in Paris right now."

"The police will see you."

"Not when I'm controlling the fireworks, Gillian. I'm saving the bigger blasts and the higher body count for when I'm leaving here. They won't notice me."

She bit her lip. "Listen, Chase, let's you and I go someplace. You don't need to kill all these people. It's just me you want. Just switch that—*that thing* off. Leave my son here.

You and I can take your escape route—now, before anyone gets here. We can—"

"Oh, Gillian," he groaned, shaking his head and clicking his tongue against his teeth. "That tactic never works for *anyone* in your books. What makes you think it'll work now? I should be insulted. Besides, we're not going anywhere until you change out of those dirty clothes." He picked up the flashlight and shined it in her face. "There's a closet in back of you—to the right."

Turning, Gillian stepped toward the closet. She hesitated, and then opened the door. He directed the flashlight toward the large walk-in closet. "Oh God," she murmured.

Only three items hung in the closet—each one on its own hanger: a dark blue blazer, a madras kilt, and a white shirt with a Peter Pan collar. The saddle shoes were on the closet floor, the white knee socks neatly rolled up inside them.

"Put on the uniform, Gillian," he whispered.

Gillian turned toward him, and shook her head.

"Do it," he said. All at once, he raised the rifle, pointed it toward Ethan and fired.

Gillian screamed. She saw Ethan recoil. The bullet missed him by inches.

"NOW!" Chase barked. "I want to see you naked. I don't want anything between you and the uniform."

Shaking violently, Gillian pulled her sweater up over her head. She had a T-shirt on beneath it. Chase was playing with the flashlight—directing the beam across her torso. Gillian stole a glance toward Ethan, curled up on the floor. His eyes locked with hers. Then, in the darkness, she saw one of his hands move out from behind his back. A piece of rope fell off his wrist. He uncrossed his feet, and the cord stayed tied around just one ankle.

"Keep going," Chase said to her. "Never mind about Sonny Boy seeing you naked. He won't be carrying around the emotional scars for very long."

Gillian slowly pulled up her T-shirt, and took a step closer to Chase, drawing his attention away from Ethan. Chase followed her with the flashlight. Gillian pulled the white T-shirt over her head. She was wearing a bra, but modestly clutched the T-shirt to her breasts. She swept her hair back from her face.

Chase sighed. "Oh, yeah, c'mon, keep going. That's right. . . ."

Out of the corner of her eye, she watched Ethan carefully, silently, get to his feet. Gillian wandered toward the other side of the room. The flashlight followed her every move. She took another step. Something crunched under the heel of her shoe.

Suddenly, the flashlight's beam was at her feet. Shards of glass were illuminated on the hardwood floor. Then the beam seemed to bounce up and reflect on glass fragments still lodged in the broken window.

"What the hell?" Chase muttered. He started to turn the flashlight toward the spot where he'd left Ethan tied up on the floor.

Ethan charged him.

When the man had returned to the bedroom, he'd found Ethan lying on the floor. Ethan had the loose rope wrapped around one wrist, which he crossed over the other. He'd pulled the same trick with the cord coiled around only one ankle. The man had quickly scanned over him with the flashlight, and said something like, *"You're working up quite a sweat there, kid."*

Obviously, he hadn't noticed the broken window. And he couldn't have seen that Ethan had been lying on top of his wadded-up shirt. It was protecting him from the sharp piece of broken glass on the floor underneath him.

Now Ethan ran at him with that shard of glass raised in his hand. He plunged it into Chase Scott, just missing his neck. Blood spurted from Chase's shoulder. He dropped the flashlight. Ethan cut his hand. But he barely felt it. He stopped to stare at the hunk of glass embedded in his abductor's shoulder—and the blood gushing out around it.

Chase seemed stunned. He fired his rifle—twice.

Ethan glanced toward his mother to see if she was hit.

The flashlight rolled across the hardwood floor until it bumped against the brick Gillian had taken from the ledge outside.

Two shots went off, echoing through the room.

Gillian grabbed the brick and hurled it at Chase with all her might. The brick just grazed his head and continued on through the sliding glass door. "Goddamn it!" he howled.

But the loud explosion of glass drowned him out. The brick and broken glass tore through the tarp. The tattered plastic covering billowed out with the breeze, and moonlight poured into the room. Chase blinked over and over again as blood trickled down the side of his face.

Ethan lunged toward the gun, knocking it out of Chase's hand.

"Son of a bitch!" Chase grabbed Ethan by the hair. He yanked his head back. For a moment, Gillian thought he might have broken her son's neck. For a moment, she couldn't move.

Chase had him in a choke hold. As much as Ethan squirmed and kicked, Chase wouldn't let go. He backed into the sliding glass door. A few large pieces of glass broke off and fell onto a tiny balcony off the bedroom. The black plastic covering fluttered in the breeze like an open curtain.

Gillian could see the moon and stars in the sky behind Chase as he held onto her son. He grinned at her. Ethan tried to struggle free as Chase held him by the scalp with one hand. He tipped back Ethan's head, exposing the boy's throat—with the black ribbon decorating it.

Paralyzed, Gillian watched in horror as Chase plucked

the piece of glass from his shoulder. Blood bubbled up from the wound and gushed out even more. He brought the sharp, bloodied shard of glass to Ethan's throat. "Watch this, Gillian," he said over the flapping noise from the tarp. In the distance, police sirens wailed.

Gillian stole a glance at the sniper's rifle on the floor—too far away. Helpless, she locked eyes with Chase and shook her head. "No, please . . ."

He gave Ethan's hair another tug. "I don't think this is in any of your books, Gillian. Watch your little boy die. You—"

A shot suddenly rang out. Chase dropped the piece of glass, and looked at her, stunned. His grip on Ethan's scalp seemed to slacken. He opened his mouth, and blood poured over his lower lip.

Ethan broke away from him. Chase staggered back, entangling himself in the black tarp. He grabbed at it, and tore off a few huge pieces as he went hurtling off the small balcony.

There was a loud thud. They could hear it over the police sirens.

Ethan rushed into his mother's outstretched arms. They clung to each other, unable to talk for a moment.

The sirens' pitch became louder. Fragments of glass left in the sliding door reflected a swirling red light. "The police," Gillian gasped. "He wired all the doors. . . ."

Ethan broke away from her and hurried across the room toward Chase's knapsack. Glass crunched under his bare feet, and he winced in pain. But he didn't hesitate. His last few steps to the large canvas bag were imprinted in blood on the hardwood floor. Biting his lip, Ethan reached into the sack, but then he hesitated. He seemed perplexed for a moment. Finally, he flicked one of the switches on the detonation device. He stared at it for another few seconds. "It's off, Mom," he said, at last. "Everything's okay." He plopped down on the floor, and reached for his shoes.

Gillian moved toward the sliding doors. Beyond the small

balcony's railing, she saw the yard bathed in a red glow. The police had arrived.

Jason stood alone near the bluff's edge, leaning against a tree. He lowered the Winchester from his shoulder. He looked ready to collapse, but he still managed to smile up at her.

Gratefully, Gillian smiled back at him. Then she carefully opened the sliding door, and peered down over the railing.

Chase was sprawled on the stone tiles of an elevated terrace directly below. His foot had somehow caught on the railing so it was raised and oddly twisted away from his body. Beneath him, a dark pool of blood began to bloom on the stone tiles. Long pieces of tarp were tangled around his lifeless body. They fluttered in the wind.

Like black ribbons.

Epilogue

It wasn't much of a birthday for Ethan. The fat lip from Joe Pagani and the quarter-size discolored bump on his fore-head—courtesy of the late Chase Scott—were both less than forty-eight hours old. And he felt miserable.

After everything that had happened Monday night, he'd spent two hours at Harborview Medical Center's Emergency Ward, where a nice East Indian doctor with a white streak in her hair had carefully removed seventeen pieces of glass from the soles of his feet. Even with a local anesthetic, it had still hurt like hell. She'd ordered him to stay off his feet for the next few days.

Jason had gone into surgery Monday night at the same hospital.

In still another part of Harborview that night, in a room guarded by a police officer, Joe Pagani, recovering from a substantial head trauma, was ratting on his cohorts. He cut a deal with authorities, naming names and citing enough incidents to put his associates away for years and years.

"Well, the heat's off you guys," Ruth had said. She'd also logged in some time at the hospital, after having had her stomach pumped earlier in the evening. "It's another story with our pal Joe. If he lives to testify, Joe's probably going into the witness protection program. And I can assure you, that son of a bitch will be looking over his shoulder for the rest of his life."

On Ethan's birthday, Jason was moved from the Intensive Care Unit to a regular room. Ethan wanted to visit him, but was still convalescing. Ruth and his mom spent most of the day talking with cops and FBI agents. The duplex was surrounded by reporters, TV news camera crews, and curiosity-seekers. Everyone wanted a peek at the ravine where the two bodies had been buried. Everyone wanted a statement from the suddenly famous author and her son. The story had gained national attention. Overnight, Gillian's book sales shot through the roof. Her Amazon.com listing had thousands of hits in less than twenty-four hours. Everyone wanted to read the killer's reviews. Chase Scott had a readership at last.

Gillian McBride books were suddenly hot properties, and Hollywood came knocking. How the hell the film people had managed to read any of his mom's books in less than twenty-four hours was a mystery to Ethan. They were also bidding for the rights to his mom's story. Was she interested in writing a screenplay about what had happened?

She wasn't.

His mom said she was grateful to see Boyd Farrow cleared of all murder charges. But she refused to write his story or any other story having to do with the Schoolgirl Murders. She didn't care how much money they offered her. Chase Scott had wanted her to write about those murders, and that was reason enough for her not to do it.

His mom managed to break away on Tuesday and pay Jason a brief visit in the hospital. But she said he was pretty doped up when she saw him.

Ethan didn't want her making a big deal out of his birthday. He didn't even want any cake or presents. They agreed to celebrate his birthday on Saturday, when he was feeling better. He had the next few days to think about what he wanted to do. He hoped Jason would be out of the hospital by then.

So it was a very low-key birthday. They ordered pizza Tuesday night. The poor Pagliacci Pizza delivery guy got mobbed by reporters, but his mom gave him a big tip for his troubles. They took the phone off the hook and ate in front of *October Sky* on cable. Ethan realized pizza and a movie with his mother was a pretty damn pathetic way to spend his fourteenth birthday. But hell, he was *recuperating*. Besides, it was a good movie, and Jake Gyllenhaal was in it.

By the next day, Ethan was hobbling around a little—in some old fleece-lined slippers that had belonged to his dad. He asked his mom if he could come with her to visit Jason in the hospital that afternoon.

But his mom took a look at the bottoms of his feet and vetoed the idea. "Maybe tomorrow," she suggested. "There's a phone in Jason's room. Why don't you call him? I'm sure he'd like to hear from you."

When he asked the Harborview operator for Jason Hurrell in Room 201-C, the woman on the other end of the line said something that made Ethan's heart stop. "I'm sorry," she replied solemnly. "He's gone."

Ethan's eyes welled with tears. "What—what happened?"

"The patient checked out this morning."

He let out a tiny, grateful laugh.

"Is there anything else?" the hospital operator asked.

"Um, yes. Do you know where he went? I'm trying to get ahold of him."

"One minute, I'll transfer you."

One minute became several, and his mom got on the line. She was put on hold twice, and had to explain three times that she was trying to get in touch with their former patient, Jason Hurrell. When she finally hung up the phone, his mom was frowning. "He went back to Montana," she said. "His— ah, ex-wife signed him out. At least, she's supposed to be his ex-wife. I'm not so sure anymore. I guess she flew in from Missoula early this morning." His mother tried to smile. "Anyway, I guess the good news is—he's out of the hospital."

Ethan felt gypped. Jason had been sent here by his dad, and he'd ended up saving their lives. Yet he'd gone away without even saying good-bye.

His mom left Jason messages at his home in Missoula. Ethan even left a message too, letting him know they'd planned a quiet, little memorial service for his dad on Friday morning at St. Mark's across the ravine. But Jason never called them back.

They didn't expect much of a crowd on Friday morning. None of the news stories about the murders mentioned the service. Only people turning to the obituary page would have known about it. His mom figured a few reporters might show up, but there wouldn't be much for them to see. His dad was getting cremated, so there wouldn't be a coffin. The only one talking would be the priest conducting the service, and he barely knew Ethan's dad.

To their astonishment, the large cathedral was nearly full. Sitting in the front pew with his mother, Ethan wondered if all these people really knew his dad. Some of them must have, because he noticed several people crying during the service. Afterward, he and his mother stood in the vestibule, thanking people as they filed outside. "I work at a Safeway in Ballard," one middle-aged woman told him. "It was on your father's delivery route. Everyone in the store just loved him. I was so sorry to hear he passed away. . . ."

A lot of the mourners were like her, store employees on

his dad's truck route. A few of them were handicapped or challenged in some way. There were fellow truckers from his union, wait staff from truck stops, and people he knew from casinos. His dad had turned many of them into Gillian McBride mystery fans. Several strangers asked Ethan if he still played the violin. His dad had been so proud. He heard it over and over again. Ethan couldn't believe these people still cared about his father after two years. He hadn't realized how many lives his father had touched.

Everyone had a little story about his dad. Saying goodbye to members of the congregation took longer than the service itself. It was overwhelming—especially for his mom. When they returned home, she hugged him for a long time, then went into her bedroom and cried.

Ethan had been moved as well, but a little disappointed, too. No one from his school had shown up at the service. Of course, maybe they couldn't get out of their classes. But the big letdown had been Jason pulling a no-show. Ethan had kept looking for him in the crowd, even as it had panned out to a few people.

His mom offered to take him out for a birthday dinner on Saturday, but Ethan had visions of the waitstaff making a big deal of it, bringing a cake to their table for two and singing "Happy Birthday" to him. He might as well go there wearing a sign: I'M A FRIENDLESS LOSER.

Ethan opted to stay home. He liked his mom's lasagna. She could cook that. In honor of his dad, they'd watch his favorite movie, *The Great Escape*. His mom asked if he wouldn't mind having Ruth and Eustace over too. That was fine by him. Considering what they'd gone through together, he felt like a war buddy with Ruth and Eustace.

Present-wise, he'd made out pretty well. His mom had just taken the lasagna out of the oven to cool when Eustace started barking, and someone knocked on the front door.

Ethan immediately thought of Jason. He raced Eustace to the door, grabbed his collar to hold him back, and then flung open the door.

Looking sheepish, Craig Merchant stood on the front porch. He was kind of dressed up with jeans, a button-down shirt, and a corduroy jacket. He had a gift-wrapped CD in his hand.

"Oh, hi," Ethan said, trying not to seem disappointed.

"Did you get a dog?" Craig asked, eying Eustace.

"No, this is Eustace. He belongs to my mom's friend." Ethan led the dog back into the house; then he stepped out to the porch and closed the door behind him.

"Sorry I missed your dad's memorial thing yesterday," Craig said. "A bunch of people wanted to go, but they wouldn't let us out of school. Everyone's been asking about you."

"What have you been telling them?"

Craig shrugged. "I tell them I haven't seen you in a while, because you're probably pissed off at me for acting like such an asshole."

Ethan grinned. "Do you really tell them that?"

"Sure, more or less."

"I'm not so pissed off." Ethan frowned at him. "Is that why you're here? Because suddenly everybody's interested in me?"

"No." Craig rolled his eyes. "I'm here because I miss you, man."

Ethan couldn't quite let down his guard. "What about all your other friends?"

Craig curled his lip. "They're okay in a group. But you're the only person I can really talk to."

"If that's true, why didn't you talk to me about what's been bugging you?"

"Jesus," Craig muttered. "You're not making this easy for me, are you? So—what was I supposed to do? Everyone in school and all my other friends kept on asking me, 'Is

Tanner gay? Is he a homo?' And I'd tell them it was none of their goddamn business, or I didn't know, or it didn't matter to me. But then they'd think *I* was gay or hiding something, because I couldn't give them a direct answer."

Ethan sighed. "Well, from now on, you can tell them that I am."

"I kind of knew you were," Craig said with an awkward shrug. "But you should have been honest with me and told me earlier."

Ethan let out an abrupt laugh. "Are you kidding me? You're always telling me not to *act like a fag,* or not to *fag out* on you. And the last time I spent the night at your house, you accused me of looking at your butt. If you were in my shoes, would you come out to *you*?"

"Hey, you know, you always tell me when I'm acting like a *dumb jock.* And I don't take it personally. And let's be honest, you *were* checking out my ass that night."

Ethan shrugged. "Yeah, I guess I was."

Craig stared at him for a moment, then chuckled. "It's a pretty fine ass too, isn't it? I'm sorry, man, but I'm saving it for Margarita McGovern."

Ethan cracked a smile. "Dumb jock."

"Fag."

Ethan nodded at the gift-wrapped CD in Craig's hand. "What's that?"

"It's a bicycle. What do you think it is, stupid?" He gave the CD to Ethan. "Happy Birthday."

"How did you know we were celebrating my birthday tonight?" Ethan asked.

"Your mom called on Wednesday and invited me over."

Ethan was dumbfounded. The last time his mother had spoken to Craig and Mrs. Merchant had been over a week ago in the school corridor. Ethan had only caught the last part of their conversation, but clearly, she'd been yelling at them.

"I don't think our mothers like each other much," Craig said. "But considering your mom just got made a widow and she's in the news and all, my mother could hardly throw any attitude at her when she called. You should know, a few weeks ago, your mom tried to put together a surprise party for you. But I screwed the whole thing up. I was an asshole. I'm sorry, man. I'm glad your mom gave me another chance. She's pretty cool." He shrugged. "So what's the deal? Are we okay?"

Ethan nodded. He wanted to hug Craig, but hesitated.

Craig, however, didn't hesitate. He put his arms around him. "Happy birthday, Ethan," he whispered in his ear.

Ethan felt himself blushing as they broke apart. "You want some dinner—and cake?" he asked.

"Hell, yeah," Craig said.

Things must have been back to normal that first Saturday in December, because Gillian felt lonely and depressed. She sat at the wheel of her Redi-Rental Chevy Aveo, heading to a Barnes and Noble signing in Tacoma. She had about a half hour to get perky. Ethan was spending the night at Craig's, and Ruth was having dinner at her daughter's house in Everett. So after this stint in Tacoma, what she had to look forward to was a Saturday night at home alone.

It had been over two weeks since she'd seen Jason, half-doped-up in his hospital bed. He'd never returned any of her calls.

The calls from her agent, however, kept coming every day. Gillian's book sales had tapered off a bit, but remained healthy. The flurry of film offers had died down as well, but there were some parties still genuinely interested and looking for backing. And her agent wanted to know how far along she was with her outline.

Maybe she would spend her Saturday night alone working on that.

Gillian found a parking space at the edge of the mini-mall's crowded lot. Emerging from the rental car, she felt a chill, and hiked up the collar of her trench coat. She noticed the lights and the garland trim around the store's windows. It reminded her that this would be her first Christmas as a widow. They wouldn't have those hoods hanging around the duplex, waiting for Barry to show up. He wasn't ever coming back. There was no more hoping for that.

She expected the place to be crowded with Christmas shoppers. Maybe she'd sell twenty books. *"A signed paperback is a great stocking stuffer!"* she imagined telling anyone who stopped by her table.

Walking into the bookstore, Gillian saw a line of people pressed against one wall, and winding around three aisles. "Who else is signing here?" she asked the store manager, Kris.

"Just you, Gillian. Some of them have been waiting three hours."

Kris was a thin, twentysomething redhead with glasses. She stood by Gillian's desk and kept the line moving. Gillian had never had a signing with this kind of turnout. Several customers wanted to have their pictures taken with her. There was barely enough time to talk to each one. Kris made sure nobody lingered for too long.

One person set a package on the desk in front of her instead of a book. Gillian stared at her name scribbled across a slightly bulky padded envelope. Then she glanced up at the handsome, golden-haired man in the aviator jacket. "Jason," she whispered.

"I'm sorry I didn't get a chance to return any of your calls," he explained under his breath. "They sprung me out of the hospital too early here. I got really sick my first night back in Missoula, some kind of infection. I ended up in the hospital there for over a week—and then at Rachel's house for another few days. It was a jolly setup there with my ex and her husband looking after me."

"But you're okay now, aren't you?" she asked.

He nodded. "How about you? How's Ethan?"

Gillian shrugged. "We're both—well, we're great. Thanks." She glanced at the line of people behind him. "Um, can you stick around?"

"I'm afraid not. I'm flying back to Missoula early tonight."

"Oh, I see," she murmured. She picked up the envelope. "What's this?"

"You might want to open that later," he said. He glanced at Kris, and then looked over his shoulder at all the people behind him. "In fact, better wait until you get home to do it."

Gillian nodded. "All right." She tucked the envelope in her purse—on the floor by her feet. "Well, thank you for coming. I—I hope you'll keep in touch. In fact, could you call Ethan? He'd love to hear from you. He misses you."

"You bet. Of course I'll call him."

"I've missed you too," Gillian whispered.

He leaned forward. "I'm sorry. What did you say?"

The woman behind Jason cleared her throat.

Gillian smiled up at him and shook her head. "Nothing. It was good to see you again, Jason."

He nodded. "Congratulations, Gill."

Then he turned and walked away. Gillian watched him from the desk.

"Could you make this one out to Tina? And the other book is for my friend Kim." The woman set two copies of *Black Ribbons* on the desk in front of Gillian.

Gillian worked up a smile. "Of course. Would you like me to say, 'Happy Holidays'?"

"Yeah, that would be great. I really love your books, Gillian. They're addictive."

"Well, thanks. And thanks for coming too." Reaching for one of the books, Gillian stole a glance at Jason as he left the store. He didn't look back.

Gillian wished she could run after him. But she couldn't. She told herself to keep smiling. All these people had come to see her, and she didn't want to disappoint them.

Gillian grabbed her pen, opened the book, and started writing.

It was 4:45 and dark out when Gillian walked back to her rental car. She'd signed 137 books. Her face hurt from smiling so much, and she was exhausted.

She got behind the wheel, and paused before slipping the key into the ignition. There was no way she could wait until she got home before opening the envelope from Jason. She switched on the dome light, took the envelope out of her purse, and tore it open. She pulled out the framed photo Jason had borrowed, the one of her and Barry in front of the Pike Street Market. There was also a smaller envelope. Gillian opened it, and found a cashier's check made out to her for $37,000.

She also found a note—handwritten on plain white paper:

Dear Gillian,

Barry put this money aside for you & Ethan. He wanted me to make sure you got it after I left. He thought if I gave it to you in person, you'd rip it up & throw it in my face. He was afraid you were that *angry at him. The last time I saw him, he came over to my house with this money . . . in cash (I got the cashier's check from your local bank when I was in Seattle). I told Barry that he*

*should write you & Ethan a note. He spent an hour
making several attempts. Finally, he just told me to pass
along this message. "Tell them to forgive me, forget me
& move on," he said.*

*You should know, Barry's gesture here isn't some
assigned step from a Gamblers Anonymous program. He
did this on his own, after he'd gone back to gambling.
Most gamblers spend money they don't have. It amazes
me that he managed to save up this nest egg for you &
not touch it. I understood Barry, and I know how incredibly difficult that must have been.*

*The one thing I'll never understand about him is how
he could leave someone as remarkable as you. Some
gamblers just don't realize when they're very, very lucky.*

*I'm glad I got to meet you & Ethan. I'll miss you,
Gillian.*

*Take care,
Jason*

Gillian put down the letter and the cashier's check, then
studied the photo of Barry and her in front of the Pike Street
Market.

"Hi, Gillian!" someone called to her. It was a woman's
voice.

She glanced up to see a young couple, passing in front of
the car. They had been at her signing. They were cute, and
friendly, and very much in love. They waved.

Gillian worked up a smile and waved back.

"She can't wait to get home to read this one!" the young
man called, pointing to the shopping bag his girlfriend carried. "Drive safely!"

Gillian kept smiling and nodded. From this distance—
and through the windshield—they must not have seen the
tears on her face. Gillian waved again, then switched off

the dome light. With a sigh, she put the picture and letter on the passenger seat. She wiped the tears from her eyes. Then she started up the car, and headed for home.

She couldn't find a parking place in front of the duplex, and had to settle for one two blocks away. Walking down her block, Gillian numbly gazed at the Christmas lights decorating her neighbors' houses. She thought about the $37,000, and figured Barry was going to be part of their Christmas after all.

Trees swayed in the frigid wind. She wondered if it would snow tonight. She'd have herself a glass of wine and a good cry in front of the fireplace.

She saw the duplex just ahead. The motion-activated light above the cellar door was on.

Gillian stopped dead.

She reached into her purse—past the big envelope Jason had given her, and through all the junk in there. She finally found her pepper spray near the bottom of the bag. When she looked at the house again, the cellar light was out.

With apprehension, she took a few steps toward the duplex. Her heart was racing. She stopped again when she caught a glimpse of a tall figure coming around from the side of the porch. For a moment, she couldn't move. As he emerged from the shadows, Gillian recognized the dark blond hair and the aviator jacket. Gillian put the pepper spray back in her purse, and stepped toward the house. "Jason?" she said.

He met her in front of the porch. "Hi. I'm sorry. Did I scare you again?"

"A little," she admitted. "But I'm all right. I don't scare quite so easily anymore. You missed your plane. I'm sorry." She let out a tiny laugh, and quickly shook her head. "No, I'm not. Actually, I'm *glad* you missed your plane. I was hoping you'd stick around."

"Really?"

Gillian nodded.

"Good, because I missed my plane on purpose," he said. "Did you get Barry's money?"

She nodded again. "And your note. Thank you, Jason."

"I meant what I said. I can't understand how anyone could leave you and stay away. I tried to leave tonight. But I couldn't." He took hold of her hand, and glanced at the front door. "Is it really okay if I stick around?"

Gillian smiled. "It's more than okay. It's great."

More Books From Your Favorite Thriller Authors

More Thrilling Suspense From Your Favorite Thriller Authors

HORRIFYING TRUE CRIME
FROM PINNACLE BOOKS

Body Count
by Burl Barer   0-7860-1405-9   **$6.50**US/**$8.50**CAN

The Babyface Killer
by Jon Bellini   0-7860-1202-1   **$6.50**US/**$8.50**CAN

Love Me to Death
by Steve Jackson   0-7860-1458-X   **$6.50**US/**$8.50**CAN

The Boston Stranglers
by Susan Kelly   0-7860-1466-0   **$6.50**US/**$8.50**CAN

Body Double
by Don Lasseter   0-7860-1474-1   **$6.50**US/**$8.50**CAN

The Killers Next Door
by Joel Norris   0-7860-1502-0   **$6.50**US/**$8.50**CAN

Available Wherever Books Are Sold!

Visit our website at **www.kensingtonbooks.com**.